Bloodline of Kings

Days of Our Past

Bloodline of Kings

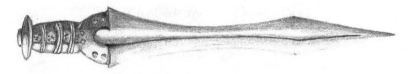

Days of Our Past

Volume One

G. R. Burns

Pacific Book Publishing
Washington

Works by G. R. Burns

Bloodline of Kings, Days of Our Past

Bloodline of Kings, An Ancient Prince

Forged Through Fire: Developing Preparedness for the Perilous Encounter

Pacific Book Publishing LLC

8911 Vernon RD #125, Lake Stevens, Washington

www.Pacific-Books.com

Copyright © 2021 G. R. Burns

Illustrations, Maps & Jacket Art © 2021 Melissa Burns

Cover Design, Steven Shepard

ISBN: 978-1-7373291-7-6

Printed in the United States of America

"After the kingship descended from heaven, the kingship was in Eridug. In Eridug, Alulim became king; he ruled for 28800 Sars... After the flood had swept over, the kingship again descended from heaven... In Agade, Sargon, whose father was a gardener, the cupbearer of Ur-Zababa, became king of Agade, under whom Agade was built.

Then the reign of man was abolished, and the kingship was taken by the viper of the hills, enemy of the gods, the one who carried the kingship away by the army of Gutium.
The Gutium, a people who acted violently against the gods, they were their own kings and ruled thus. He who had a wife, she was taken away. He who had a child, the child was taken away. Wickedness and violence reigned. ...It was this way, and on all highways the long grass grew."

-Sumerian Kings List & Utu-Hengal Victory Stele, Circa 2000 BC

(Above) Stone relief in the Temple of Ninurta

CONTENTS

Part II

Part III

Part IV

Part V

Prologue

<u>Valley of Dry Bones</u>

W hat is your name?"

The small boy did not reply. His gaze was transfixed upon the sword - the blade held resolute by the man's side. It took strong magic to make one. The elite warriors used flint arrows, and even more rarely, copper-tipped spears. A sword of bronze was a weapon which showed the favor of the Ancient Powers themselves.

The two figures stood alone in a low gully between rolling hills. The child, no more than eight seasons old, was bedraggled and thin. The man, in his prime, a tower of strength. A murmuring creek ran beside them, sifting its way through the grass.

"You are Ur-Kael, the eldest son of Ur-Zabab, king of Ur, are you not?" asked the man.

At the mention of his father, Ur-Kael's small fists clenched. The snarling, spittle-stained face of his sire beating his mother and sisters flashed across his mind. He surveyed the mighty man standing above him. Ur-Kael knew who the man was and why he had come.

He was Sargon the Great, and he had come to kill him.

Two belts of finely beaten gold held Sargon's red cloak in place, akin to the thick armbands glistening from his corded arms. Beyond the horizon, the mass of Sargon's encampment rested, making the final preparations to end their long siege of Ur. Its downfall was at hand and the vision that the enchanters received had been proclaimed: all the people of the land were to be slain.

"I know that you are he, from the inscription I received," Sargon continued, pacing back and forth. "Yet even as the son of my enemy, I see you are not the thorn which bites the dust of this land. You are just a child."

His eyes glinted with knowledge and pity as he studied the boy, a look Ur-Kael was unaccustomed to seeing. Surely the child knew that his own father sent him from the fortress as a desperate plea for the king's own miserable life. The coward! The fool! The sword in Sargon's hand faltered.

The sun sank lower until it was a glowing red slit on the horizon. Sargon clenched his jaw in determination, pointing with his sword toward a calm eddy in the stream.

"Look into the waters."

Ur-Kael's heart began beating faster and faster, throbbing in his ears. In a moment, he could see himself from high above. He was walking to the water. Now he was kneeling upon its edge. The stark chill of Sargon's sword, cold as it rested upon Ur-Kael's neck, brought him back to reality with a gasp. He was trembling, shaking with confusion and fear.

There was nothing he could do.

The current of the little stream was swift, its water brown with mud from early summer rains. Yet, like a gem in the shallows, there lay a crystalline pool. This mirrored surface lay at Ur-Kael's feet, the reflections within clear and sharp in the red dusk. Ur-Kael wondered if it could be another world. A world, perhaps, where he had a good father. A father who wouldn't send him into the hands of his enemies to be killed.

Sargon read the boy's thoughts like an unsealed tablet. Images of his own sons, about the same age, flashed across his mind filling him with despair. There was no turning back. The time was now!

Swiftly, Sargon raised his sword, ready to strike! But, the voice of the wind whispered through the reeds, unwillingly drawing his attention to their reflections in the water. They seemed more life-like than their counterparts, with every minute detail emblazoned upon their surface. Abruptly, Sargon felt something change. His arms grew heavy. He realized, suddenly, that he couldn't move. Everything around him slowed in suspenseful purpose, as though the great water wheel of time had lost its current and was coming to a stop. Frozen, his heart jolted with fear as he saw something happening in the water.

He watched the image of his face turn, beholding something in the distance. He had not moved, and yet the images in the water moved as if they possessed a life of their own. He saw fear cascade over his reflection, and the water light as if with a sudden fire in its depths.

Sargon fought to move his chained muscles. His struggle grew and then ceased, for he saw, from the corner of his eye, something that was appearing out of the center of the stream. The water stirred and frothed in agitation before parting into an abyss of an other-worldly nature, devoid of all light, consuming all that entered. From it grew a form that took the shape of an inverted tree, horrid and grotesque, planted so that its roots curled outwards against the sky and its branches were submerged, shriveled and cursed beneath the surface of the mud. Higher, and higher this tree invaded his world, reaching above his rigid form. Like a ravenous beast it grew, and the muddy waters vanished into the black abyss at its base. Dread rose from it like steam, reaching out toward him with its restless grasp.

The water receded, distorting the reflection he was witnessing. The sound of great wheels turning crashed and rumbled through the sky and Sargon was filled with terror. Still he could not move, nor could he tear his gaze from the vision before him. His reflection wavered and then disappeared completely within the chasm. Yet, the glow, which surrounded the boy, stood firm - resisting the depths of that unknown darkness.

The sound of the rumbling increased, jumping like thunder across the hills, striking Sargon's ears with such force they ran red with blood. Vapor rose from the bank of the creek, enveloping him with thick, sticky fog. Suddenly, Sargon fell back, released from his imprisonment. He scrambled backward, lost and afraid. Thick tendrils of moisture licked his face, adding to the beads of sweat that already pooled there. His heart was pounding. His eyes strained as the mist slowly cleared. The water of the little stream was gone. The reeds had died. The inverted power, black and gnarled as a tree, was all that remained.

Sargon was no longer looking at a reflection. He was in a waking dream and the images were as real as life itself.

He gripped his sword until his knuckles shone white, as the decaying tree, distorted with malevolent power and now monstrous in size, rose menacingly above Sargon's head. Faces and strange shapes, twisted and infernal, appeared within the canopy of enveloping roots. They reached hungrily at him with their gaze, bidding him to draw near, ordering him to crawl into their dark, twisting mass where they would bind him until there was no escape. But Sargon's legs moved like lead, a glance told him why. The hillsides around him were no longer grassy plains, they were dunes of sand; and the wind whipped the grains into his eyes and stung his face.

Sargon was thrown to the ground with the wind's gusting force, vainly his hand raised to shield his eyes. The wind stopped as suddenly as it had begun, and he found his hand pushing at nothing. He lowered it. He licked his cracking lips, struggling to stand as he sank into the soft sand. His mind lagged. How long had it been? An age of man, surely, yet not enough time for him to take a breath.

The distorted tree remained, standing alone in the dead valley, but its power over Sargon was gone. Everything was gone. All life and breath, wind and sea... all had been consumed. Yet, he felt something worse, a deep aching void, as if his *reason* for living had been devoured.

Hot tears blindly stung his eyes and he gasped, searching for breath. What was happening? The emotion assaulted him, yet he was bound by it. Were he a lyre, played on with a resounding note to the tune of a terrifying master, he might have felt the same.

He had no time to understand. The sand under his feet shifted. Slowly at first, then swelling, churning into a roaring torrent! The desolate land began convulsing, and the mighty turning of wheels started again in an uproar which shook the very foundations of the world. As far as Sargon could see, the sand stretching across the horizon trembled and then fell away like a curtain being pulled aside. A mountain of stone, gleaming white, carved with ancient symbols and shining with incandescent light, was rising out of the sand like a tidal wave.

Sargon swayed, his forgotten sword dropping from his hand as hundreds of thousands, thousands upon thousands of dried bones were revealed, climbing from the exposed earth. His knees shook, his chest palpitating with the quaking land and crashing peals, grating, grinding, and tromping as the tumult rose higher! The dead had risen! The veil had been torn and the heavens opened!

Sargon could see nothing else. The foreboding tree continued to rise in defiance. Countless ranks of dead bones closed in about it. The White Mountain reached into the sky, luminous as the moon. The shadow of mighty clouds darkened the land, promising a coming storm. Thunder and lightning broke apart the sky! The bones of the long-forgotten tore up the malevolent tree from the earth and cast it down. Fire was all around, the air crashed like a splitting drum! The dead cried out with such a noise that Sargon grew weak. He fell. His eyes fluttered, and then a soft rain touched him, quenching his pain as it pattered across the parched land.

Sargon opened his eyes and found himself on his back among damp reeds. His beard, customarily curled and waxed, was in disarray. His robe of red was torn and strewn upon the ground, revealing the bronze plates that covered his chest and shins. The stream continued murmuring along its fading course between the hills. The first stars twinkled in the east and a dim blue and purple was all that remained of the fading twilight. He quickly sat up and gathered his bearings. His hand found his sword by his side, he clasped it and slowed his breathing until he was calm. It had been nothing more than a dream, though the images were burned into his mind.

The boy was lying motionless nearby, his leg and arm partially in the stream. Sargon crawled over and gently picked him up. He laid Ur-Kael on the dry grass and brushed the mud from his face. He felt for a sign of breath. There was none.

That same desperate emotion he had felt in the vision, a strange and unusual fear, tightened Sargon's chest and rose in his throat.

A clamor of footfalls startled him. The sage Marqu stumbled into the small ravine, looking around swiftly until his gaze landed on Sargon and the boy.

Marqu was hardly able to speak as he tried to catch his breath.

"What... What happened? I felt... I felt like the Power of the Old World was among us. I was afraid when I came to your tent and the guards said you had left hours before and had not returned."

Marqu paused for a moment, taking in Sargon's disarray and the boy laying on the bed of grass.

"What did you do?!" Marqu managed to gasp.

Sargon did not answer the sage's question, but instead pointed to Ur-Kael.

"He is not breathing."

Marqu raised an eyebrow at Sargon's concern and bent over the boy's still form.

"Is this not why you came here?"

Sargon looked at Marqu blankly and some of the intensity of the vision crossed his face. "There... there was... there has been, a sign." Sargon trailed off as he failed to put what he had seen into words.

Marqu's eyes flickered with understanding as he watched Sargon struggle to regain his bearing. He waited.

"I do not know what has happened," Sargon finally stammered. "The boy must live. He must, or I must turn from this course and find another way."

Marqu knelt by the boy's still form.

"Are you sure? Sparing the king's son...others will see it as weakness!"

Sargon's face was barely visible in the gloaming, but even in shadow, Marqu saw that it was drawn and Sargon's hands trembling. Another man would have discounted Sargon as little more than a timid leader hiding behind a façade of power. But, Marqu knew the terrors of the Old World and the Power that came with it. He knew them all too well.

The sage drew from his robe a short necklace, its small, clay tiles clattered as he held them aloft. He sifted through them, each one containing an arcane rune until he found the one he sought. Marqu studied it, then closing the tablet in his hand, he placed it on the boy's head. He glanced once more at Sargon and then spoke a Word of Power from the Old World.

Sargon had never seen a sage recite a Word of Power. He had heard stories of cities crumbling and days halting, the blind receiving their sight and the lame walking - the raw substance of the world orchestrating to man's will with the mere utterance of a syllable. Even so, nothing, outside of the vision he had just received, would have better prepared him. In the darkness, Sargon was unsure if Marqu's mouth was open or shut, as the sound he heard seemed to come from the earth itself.

The terrifying whirr of the great heavenly wheels seemed to be present again, though more distant and remote. A sudden white light flooded the area in which they sat. A metallic rawness filled his mouth. As soon as it had begun, the moment passed: the spoken word was left fading like a dream. Darkness was once again all around them. Sargon and Marqu turned their eyes toward Ur-Kael and saw his chest rise and fall. They did not notice the flowers that had suddenly bloomed, or how tall and green the grass had become in the circle around them.

After a time, the boy awoke. He sat up wordlessly and stumbled back in the direction of Sargon's encampment as one in a trance.

"The rest of his family was slain at dusk," reported Marqu as they strode, glancing sidelong at the boy, "and now await the King, who hides still in Ur, until he joins them in Sheol."

Ur-Kael panicked and tried to flee down the hillside. But his cold, exhausted limbs betrayed him. The boy fell, tumbling down the hill until he struck a rock and came to a senseless halt. Sargon covered the space in a few large strides and picked up the crumpled form, carrying him back up the hill and into the silent tents of his army.

"Then it is nearly done," said Sargon. "Yet the fate of his family will not be shared by all." He addressed the unconscious figure in his arms with a hoarse whisper.

"From this day forth, Ur-Kael will be your name no longer. You will be known as Areoch, and will live under the protection of my hand. For you have proven to be set apart from those who have cursed this land."

Sargon lay awake. He had exchanged his armor for a silken robe, yet his cares still burdened him. He arose, his restless feet drawing him past the tents of his sleeping soldiers. They stopped before a hastily made awning slightly removed from the others. Two guards stood at its fore and rear.

The boy started when Sargon lifted aside the woven-haired flap. As the monarch's eyes adjusted to the dimness he saw a worn, tattered sleeping rug near the entrance. A basket full of bread, fresh celery and papyrus stalks lay uneaten beside an empty clay cup. Areoch's eyes were red from weeping, and his lip quivered.

"Will I see my father now?" Areoch's high voice broke the stillness.

"Is that what you desire?" Sargon asked.

Areoch's eyes fell. He shook his head silently.

Sargon knelt beside the child. "Do you wish to be alone?"

Areoch quickly glanced at Sargon and then into the darkness, as if it held unseen tormentors. He shook his head again.

The image of Areoch, scared and alone, was almost too much for Sargon. How much Areoch was like his own sons! Still boys, grappling with their fear of the dark and unknown, yearning for companionship.

Yearning for their father! His heart broke for Areoch's suffering.

"Do you remember me at all?" Sargon offered. "I was once a cup-bearer in your father's house. Many times, I saw you, hiding in the kitchen fig-basket from his wrath!" Sargon paused, stemming a smile at the youthful memory. "It was your best spot. Often, I rustled those figs to cover your hair...and then looked for a hideout of my own! You were many years younger, but *I* still remember."

Areoch did not answer, his eyes searching out the dirt at his feet.

Sargon waited.

"I cannot sleep tonight," Sargon softly mentioned, "will you walk with me? There is nothing to fear."

Areoch fixed his gaze on Sargon, like one who was accustomed to being deceived. Hesitant, he rose, and together they left the tent.

They stayed to the edge of the camp. The warm winds of early summer made the night pleasant, and Sargon led Areoch in silence up toward a lonely knoll. The guards trailing them stayed at its base with a motion from Sargon's hand. Man and boy graced its crest alone. Clusters of lavender, thick in bloom, surrounded Sargon as he cast himself upon the purple bed and looked up at the stars. Their fragrance rose around him, like an offering in a temple grate. Areoch was silent, almost unnoticed in the moonless night.

Sargon's thoughts turned within as he wafted the thick, rich fragrance. It brought no peace. Flashes jarred his mind. The blood coursed through him. He was no stranger to the feeling. The trauma came upon him before each battle where he knew he would take life. With the rawness of the day's events still upon him, it was worse than usual. The feelings of the vision were still near at hand, amplified and acute. He looked around and saw only Areoch, disconnected and looking away. Sargon brought his knees up to his chest and held them like a child. Clenching shut his eyes, he allowed himself to face that tide of emotion and power.

Sargon felt a small hand upon his face, touching the silent tears that spilled from his eyes and into his thick beard. The mighty leader looked into the face of Areoch - whose expression was a mix of shock and relief.

"Did you never see your father cry?" Sargon whispered.

Areoch managed to shake his head. Without further word Sargon drew the child into an embrace and the two wept together.

In time, the night grew still. A far-off sand lark trilled a light, clear song.

"I tell my sons," Sargon whispered to Areoch, who rested on his broad chest, "not run from those pains you carry in your heart. By Enlil, we must find the strength to face them, or they will consume us and..." Sargon stopped short of saying, *turn us into men like your father*.

Sargon swallowed and looked down at the boy. He was asleep.

Sargon rose and carried Areoch once again as they returned to his encampment. As he let fall the flap of Areoch's tent, a form stood from where it had waited in shadow.

"The Power lingers still," Marqu said in the darkness. "You, and the boy, will never forget what has happened this day."

"What does it all mean?" Sargon asked.

Marqu did not immediately answer. When he did, his voice was a whisper.

"The Sages of the Old World have long been sought after by the wise; but very rarely are we understood. Some believe we are diviners or magicians, others say we are priests. In truth, we do little more than remember. We recall the Power our fathers before us knew, in the days of the Old World when life was fresh. Sometimes we find that power and can even call it to our lips.

'Ever does it fade quickly, like a forgotten dream. As does all memory of the Old World, where those words belonged. Even as they fade, we remain haunted by what we cannot understand or put into words. It is a reckoning of the soul. Is it not so?"

Sargon did not need to answer.

The encampment was awake and on the move as the colors of morning promised a clear day. Countless copper spear-tips glinted in the sun, stretching across the horizon. At their head a chariot rolled, pulled by horses richly haltered in silver and gold and surrounded by men of importance. General Rahmaah and a few others raised questioning glances at Areoch, who walked among the members of Sargon's household. A sharp look from Marqu informed them a decision had been made, and they set their faces without further question toward the city of Ur and the battle which lay ahead.

Sargon mounted his chariot and stood upon its platform at the head of his army. General Rahmaah took his place on Sargon's right. Row upon row of spearmen fell into rank behind him. General Beckma rode on Sargon's left. Archers behind Beckma strung small bows of yew as slingers fit rocks into leather slings. Hundreds of axe-men shouldered their weapons and great leather shields.

The air was sweet with the crispness of morning and the sky golden in anticipation for the sun as the army set out at a brisk march across the rolling foothills separating them from the city of Ur. The sun had risen less than a reed's length when they halted again, gazing down on the city from the western ridge of the valley. The city still lay in shadow, but the wall which faced them stood nearly twenty-five feet high and six feet thick. Layers of cleverly stacked basalt rocks could be seen leaning noticeably inwards, top-heavy and uneven.

At one time, the city of Ur had been a great and mighty place, perhaps even the greatest city in the Early World. It was not so now. From their height, they could see that the buildings behind the wall stood in ruins. Belongings littered the roadway from the people's hasty flight. Discarded baggage and items too heavy to carry lay across stone thresholds. Wild dogs tore at dead men. The invading force was largely unchallenged.

Sargon raised his hand to signal. Two-hundred men with thick black beards over bare chests came rushing to the front, balancing rough cut logs of massive proportion upon their corded shoulders. They formed a straight line, two men deep and staggered. Three-hundred men, bearing wide shields held with both hands, came before them in a V-like shape. Axes and bronze daggers gleamed from their belts. Another two thousand men stood ready behind the initial breaching force, waiting.

The warmth of the sun chased the shadows into the valley of Ur. Sargon nodded his head, and with a mighty yell the group charged, into the shadow as the rest of the army advanced slowly behind.

Two-hundred paces from the city the shield bearers wheeled sharply to the wall's outer corners, stacking against them and pushing in unison. They were not enough to defeat the might of the crippled wall. The mighty men barreled forward, angling their logs high above their heads. They cried out, deep voices rising in a fierce chorus as they slammed against the wall in unison. A shudder flexed throughout the length of the structure. It swayed this way and that... and then fell. Great stone blocks collapsed inward with a mighty crash, pulling down several of the buildings that stood near. A great rumbling echoed through the city.

The sunlight reflected off the rising particles of dust as the first shafts of light chased away the valley shadows and fell on the breached wall. Sargon dismounted his chariot and strode forward, drawn sword and bronze spear bright in the sunlight as he walked calmly across the stone perimeter unchallenged. As Sargon crossed the boundary, all marveled, for in the cloud of dust above the city a crown seemed to take shape, drifting down as Sargon stood among the rubble.

"Ancient of Days," whispered Marqu, as all the wise men and diviners stood to their feet in wonder and amazement. "So, the Kingship falls once again upon a city of man. Such has not been seen since the days of Atrahasis upon the slopes of Eridor, at the end of the Old World."

The rest of the army charged into the city with victory in their hearts. Small pockets of resistance met them as they advanced. There were periods of intense fighting as the citizens realized they would not be shown mercy. The cobblestones ran red with blood. Every home, ziggurat, and temple were emptied into the street. Bodies of the dead, along with gold, silver, precious lazules and bronze, idols and weapons; everything was piled in a large mound at the center of the city.

Rahmaah and Beckma stopped Sargon's march on the steps of Ur's palace and before the ancient temple which stood there. In days past, the center court of Ur was renowned for its wide expanse, and flowing pool.

9

Now the court's stones were blackened. The open pool, designed originally for the rainbow carp of Enki, lay festering, its exit from the city blocked by stone and the fish left rotting upon its green and slimy surface.

In the center of the pool an enormous tree stood inverted; its twisted roots reached heavenward and its branches lay drowned and lifeless beneath the poisoned water. The sight sickened even the Strong Men. They wretched and their bowels turned. It was not just the smell of death. Every man could feel, deep in his heart, something else: a living, growing fear, a shadow in their minds. They knew that their weapons of bronze had no power against it.

Sargon's Strong Men broke down the doors of the barricaded palace and rushed inside. The sound of a brief struggle echoed into the court. Finally, the King of Ur was dragged out and tossed down in front of Sargon the Great. Areoch's blood-father bared his teeth. His purple robe was stained and torn. A fresh cut bled over his eye and into his mouth, giving him a chilling appearance. The wise men joined Sargon and gazed in horror at the tree and ancient temple. Marqu's face drained, as though some long-lost torment had come to life from the fantasy of his mind.

"Ur-Zabab," spat Shazier, chief of Sargon's Diviners, gesturing toward the wretched form, "you have been stripped of your kingdom. You have removed the good from this land. You have delivered your household into the hands of your enemies in an attempt to save your own miserable life." All gripped their weapons tighter in their hands, "You are a beast who leads none but dogs, who return to their own vomit." Shazier wiped his mouth with disgust.

The Strong Men held Zabab down while Shazier and the other diviners stripped him of his clothing, adding it to the high pile of treasures which lay in the square. Men poured into the palace, emptying its valuables while Ur-Zabab lay prostrate. Gold and bronze clattered across the earth around him.

"You have slain your people," Shazier continued, "though they have remained among the living. It has been decreed: *You shall lead them into Sheol*" which has been prepared for you. Such is the reckoning of all who go after ill-gotten gain."

Ur-Zabab remained resigned as his judgment was pronounced, thinking perhaps he might be spared if he did not resist. He was picked up and tossed mercilessly upon the pile of precious items and dead bodies heaped before the palace.

Marqu pulled Sargon aside and whispered earnestly in his ear. Sargon looked on him with concern, Marqu trembled with fear. Sargon listened, nodding.

"Cast down the tree!" Sargon commanded loudly. "Quickly! Throw it into the palace. Then burn it all."

Flames soon licked up the fortress. A large net was thrown over Ur-Zabab, the dead of the city, and the treasure, and tied to a train of oxen. The fallen king began to struggle violently, but it was too late. The oxen, along with a hundred men, pulled the massive pile of treasure and death into the festering water. Ur-Zabab fought his way to the top of the sinking net and floated there, cursing those who watched as he gagged on the decaying waters of bile and blood.

Marqu paid no heed, his attention fixed on the burning fire which licked up Ur-Zabab's palace. The tree, still black and visible through the doorway, wavered in the heat, unscathed. A blackness, deep and other-worldly, seemed to shimmer in the air around the trunk. Marqu took a step back. Memories he had long buried flashed before his eyes. With a mighty crack, the stone of the palace shattered, and the building collapsed upon itself. The trepidation Marqu felt within his heart lifted.

"Break down the stones of the waterway!" ordered Sargon. "Let it run free from the city!" The stagnant water began to flow through the city dike. Sargon picked up a round mace as the net passed him and struck Ur-Zabab on the head. The former king of Ur was swept, along with the remains of his city, toward the sea. He was never seen again.

Fires spread, leaping from building to building.

"Let it burn," Sargon commanded as they departed. "Rahmaah, send messengers back to the city Lugal: send for the chief mason, wagons of grain, supplies, and all the men who can be spared or those who wish to settle in the protection of the new Ur. There is land to cultivate and a city to build, once the fires have completed their purge."

Rahmaah gathered himself, making sure he was still well-dressed for victory. Orders spewed from his lips for the fastest runners to be brought to him at once.

"General Beckma," commanded Sargon. "Take a thousand men and proceed to Elam of Kish by the sea. If he does not open the city gate to you, send word, and the rest of us will march upon him. I think he will see the smoke of Ur and think better of denying you entrance. Once there, you will take command of the city. Bind Elam and his household, all their chief advisors and warriors, along with their households. Send them north to the basalt and limestone quarries to begin our work. Tear down all the temples, regardless of their powers, and burn any such atrocities as we have found here. Send their gold, silver, and bronze vessels to the chief smith to be melted and purified. Send me word when all this has been accomplished."

Beckma strongly clasped Sargon on the shoulder before departing, taking five-hundred axe-men and four-hundred bowmen in his wake.

The city of Ur was destroyed. As the fires burned, Sargon stood alone on the western hill watching the flames and his men diligent to their tasks. Presently, Shazier and Marqu joined him.

"Of all the horrors I imagined, none so offended my soul as the one we destroyed today," commented Shazier. "Ur-Zabab was clearly counting on some dark enchantment to protect him, but what it was none of my diviners can say."

"It is a sign that has not been seen since long before your time," Marqu murmured, gazing up at the sun. "A sign of great darkness and power that was present during the Old World. Many, many generations of men has it been since I have last seen it." Marqu paused. "I hope to forget it again."

He shook his head as if ridding himself of the memory. Sargon said nothing.

"The Kingship has once again descended," Marqu finally said, triumphantly changing the subject. "We shall raise the new White Temples! Three cities in one, and one king to represent the people." He looked sidelong at Sargon.

"I did not think I would live to see this," Shazier commented. "Perhaps we do have some chance at reclaiming the strength and honor our fathers lost long ago on the Plains of Eridor."

"Do not mention that forsaken place," said Sargon in a low murmur, as Marqu grew quiet and his face fell. "Some would say those days were even worse than the Dark of the Old World before them. They too began with high ideals."

"And after much death and destruction," added Marqu in a whisper.

"If there is an ancient evil rooted here," reflected Sargon, "how much more so will that evil be present in the north and in the far-off west, where the stories of old say it was first born?"

Marqu did not answer.

"More, I would guess," concluded Shazier. "Much more."

They all paused in thought, gazing down on the city.

"Then we should turn our attention to what we have gained," Sargon exclaimed. "There is much to protect, it must not be allowed to be tainted again. Towers! Walls! And warriors! Strong Men, ready for battle at a moment's call."

"What will become of the boy?" asked Shazier, looking down at Areoch in the distance, working alongside the rest of Sargon's household.

"Did you see him, watching as his father died?" murmured Marqu. "Yes, he saw from afar. I have never seen such a steely gaze... except, perhaps, from you," he noted, nodding at Sargon.

"He hated that man," growled Sargon. "As much as a youth of his age can. I remember what it was like, to be in the presence of Ur-Zabab every day. Though I was only his cupbearer, it was worse for his family. The stifling, suffocating greed, strange magic, haunting sacrifices of those closest to him... you never knew who was going to die next."

"Let us not speak of that either," suggested Marqu. "Kez-Dedan would have been the boy's tutor and that is something. He was one of my kin: a sage who had been with Ur since its foundations were set."

"Kez-Dedan was nothing more than a fool slain by his master at the end," spat Sargon. "It has been fifteen generations of men since Ur was built. Yet, he sat among the rubble and watched the city fall, doing nothing. He deserved death."

Marqu looked at the ground. "He also planted the seeds of goodness and justice in the boy. How else could Ur-Zabab's son hate the evil of his father if he did not know something other than that evil?"

The fire of the city rumbled in the distance as hot stones burst and fell.

"He should be slain and sent down to Sheol like the rest," Shazier insisted. "That was your decree. The bloodline must be purified."

"He has been set apart," Sargon replied, "though I do not know why. And I have slain his father. By ancient law, that makes him mine to do with as I will."

"It would be foolish to make him a servant in your house" said Marqu. "Look how the others respect him and are fond of him, as young as he is."

Sargon paused in thought. "He will be my son," he said finally, "and will dwell with the rest of my family. Marqu, I entrust you to continue whatever learning of the world he may possess with the rest of my sons. Make it known his name is Areoch."

"So be it," said Marqu.

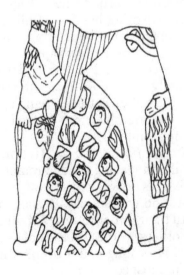 

Sargon the Great's Victory Stele of Ishtar, circa 2400BC

Chapter One

Darkness Within the *Taradium*

Bahira seemed to float upon an unseen breeze, while soft hands carried her over valleys of shadow and into the quiet night. From far away, the lapping of the sea lulled her to a feigned peace as she remembered her home. Suddenly, like a serpent rearing its ugly head, reality broke through the veil of her consciousness, seizing her in its forceful bite and dragging her back down to the pain of the present.

The sound of the sea remained, frothing against the wooden bulwarks of the *Taradium* as it glided swiftly northward through the Tanti Sea. It was night, but exactly when and where she might be, Bahira could not fathom. She lay still on the ship's deck, afraid to move. Afraid to breathe. Shouting voices and running feet scrambled around her. Bright lights flared up, dim through the thick cloth covering her face. Dull screams echoed out, along with hoarse cries. She mustered her courage and tried to stand, but failed and fell back. Her breathing grew rapid, while her heart beat increased. Her hands throbbed, bound so tightly before her that they bled. Bahira clawed desperately at her coverings and cried out in pain. She could not remove them! She shut her eyes, wincing every time the flickering lights drew near. Fading blackness pushed inward against her mind, calling her to its empty embrace.

"No. No!" she thought. "Berran! I must find Berran..." Her brother's face appeared in her mind; first joyful and teasing (as she remembered him best), then pitted with pain and fear, as he was ripped away from her grasp. He was a child, no more than nine winters old. Berran was her responsibility, hers to watch over until their father returned. Berran, her only brother. Bahira had lost many others to the diseases of the early world, she was not going to lose him! How long had it been? Minutes? Hours? Blindly, she reached for him and lost consciousness.

All was still when awareness returned. It was dark. She could feel the rough scratch of wool on her nose and ears as she turned her head back

14

and forth. Her head was in a bag.

Throb. Throb. Throb. Her hands were still bound, pulsating with each beat of her heart. A dull dripping and splashing sound surrounded her.

"Berran... Berran!" she whispered, daring not to shout too loudly.

As if in reply, she was seized and dragged harshly forward. Still blinded, she struggled - kicking, biting and clawing, until a sharp yell rang out and she was dropped to the deck. A chorus of gruff chuckling echoed around her. Something struck her hard several times and she lay stunned, blood trickling from her lip.

"Got more than you can handle there, Sapu?" Laughed a deep, dark voice. Someone cursed and spat above her before she was seized and dragged once more. They came to a stop a few moments later.

"What is it, Sapu?" The words were hissed more than they were spoken. She could feel the hands holding her tremble slightly before they dropped her. She cried out, striking her shoulder as she fell.

"What is this?" asked the thin voice again.

"You may recall, Captain," whined Sapu, "of what you instructed me to accomplish in Cartegin. Your faithful servant has done that and more."

"Yes, much more" hissed the Captain's voice. "You nearly destroyed all of us. The entire city was raised against us, as though they knew we were coming! I don't recall that being in my orders, my love."

A quick whimper was followed by the sound of something else being quickly drug across the floor and coming to a stop near her. There was another thud, followed by the coarse sound of a cloth being pulled away.

The Captain inhaled sharply. "Oh, Sapu. You have done well. All may be forgiven. What else do you have for me?"

Bahira was suddenly rolled over and the sack removed from her face. Through the strands of her long, dark hair she could see several candles lighting up a sparse cabin. Rough-hewn, well-worn boards made up the deck she lay on. Sacks of food and tied herbs swayed with the ship from where they hung on the ceiling, casting restless shadows across the room. She pushed herself up, finally catching sight of her captors.

Behind Bahira stood Sapu. He was squat, with broad shoulders and thick forearms. Coarse, black, bristling hair gave him a stubby and ragged appearance. His face was angled and mis-shaped, and his behavior reminded Bahira of a stray dog begging for a scrap. Closer at hand, a strong, young man lay slumped against a barrel which contained some foul-smelling liquid. Occasionally, he dipped in a small gourd and drank from it. His eyes grew wide as he gaped at Bahira's revealed features. In the middle of the room, another thinner, wasted form was kneeling. The Captain's features were as gaunt and stretched as a dead fir tree. His narrow head was embellished with a wide black hat, frayed and faded. Bahira recoiled as the Captain's face drew near, for it was painted white, like a dead-man's bones, and his eyes were sunken back in a ghastly appearance.

She wasn't sure who repulsed her more: Sapu, the rat standing behind her, wringing his hands like a sullen weasel; or the man in a stupor, red eyed and lingering with the smell of deceit and self-worth; or the sheer terror of the white-faced Captain, lean like a hollow skeleton without soul or flesh. She wondered what kind of terrible desire could draw all three of these very different kinds of men to itself.

Bahira found her feet and stood resolute as these thoughts passed across her mind. Her jerkin of light green was stained and torn revealing a graceful figure, fit from frequenting the hills of the Durgu Mountains. A necklace of jet stones marked her as wealthy, part of an affluent household in Cartegin; and her proud head reflected a strong defiance against her captors. She opened her mouth to speak... then all was forgotten as she saw a small, fair skinned boy laying still at the Captain's feet. The boy's face was almost unrecognizable, its entire left side bruised and swollen. Bahira's eyes flicked quickly to his hand: there, shining dully in the candlelight, was the bracelet of jet Birsha their father had given him.

"Berran!" she cried, leaping forward. She cradled him, touching his face gingerly in horror, oblivious to those around her.

"Berran, Berran! What have they done to you?" The boy did not respond. His breathing was jagged, his chest rising and falling in pitiful spurts. Bahira was grabbed abruptly from behind and dragged away.

"No!" Turning in blind fury, she struck Sapu across the face with her bound hands. Sapu howled in pain and his nose bled red, down his misshapen face.

"You'll pay for that!" Sapu ruefully spat. Grabbing her in an iron grip he threw her to the floor. She tried to rise again. Sapu grabbed her by the hair and held her down, pinning her cheek into the cracks of the deck.

The Captain chuckled softly as he watched.

"You have some *hyruiti* in you, for being so young. And so lovely." he hissed.

"Where have you taken us? Who are you?" Bahira cried, struggling uselessly against Sapu's weight. Anger and fear blazed in her eyes.

Sapu kicked her, she gasped as the air was driven from her. She ceased her struggling, eyes watering.

"Be silent cur!" Sapu cried, sputtering through a bleeding nose. "What is to be done with her, Captain?" he whined.

"Take her to Re'Amu's cabin," the Captain said after a short pause, looking in the direction of the slumped man near the barrel. "A reward for his... faithfulness."

Bahira looked in disgust and fear at the intoxicated Re-Amu. He struggled to his feet, swaying from side to side, trying to stay balanced;

but toppled against the barrel of grog, sending his dipping gourd spinning across the room.

"You should not drink as much of that, my trusted lieutenant," suggested the Captain. "It was not made for you."

Sapu seized Bahira's hair, dragged her forcefully down a short corridor, and flung her into a small room sided with thick leather and planks of wood. Her bound hands and sore limbs vainly clutched at a swaying hammock, then a small table, as she fell, hitting the planks hard. She groaned and saw Sapu standing in the entrance, ready to throw her down again if she rose. Bahira remained still. Sapu chuckled, some festering part of him rejoicing in his limited power over her, then departed. A leather flap fell from above, blocking the dim candle-light of the room beyond.

After a few moments, Bahira pushed herself up until she sat, hugging her knees as close to herself as bound hands would allow. The adrenaline firing through her veins had slowed, and her mind reached out in a panic, looking for a safe harbor of thought that would help quench her fears. All she could see in her mind was the image of Berran: the vulture-like Captain leaning over him, a skeleton of bone and skin, his claws extended out softly toward her brother's cheek.

The light in the adjoining rooms went out, leaving total darkness. The tears finally came, her sobs stifled by the sounds of the sea and her own fear of being heard. How could this be happening? Perhaps this was all a terrible dream; soon she would awake, and find herself back at home. She closed her eyes and imagined herself waking that morning: soft, green vines crept in from her window, dotted with sweet white flowers; the sound of the sea floated up the hill, mixed with the bustling shouts of Cartegin as the city murmured into life; Mattur pushed open the door of her room, bearing in a sweet platter of honey and bread.

The sound of the leather door-flap being pushed aside broke through her mental escapade. She looked up quickly, brushing away tears. She was still on the *Taradium*. A shadow entered. Fears of what would happen next filled her mind and she cowered farther into the small room's corner.

A few sharp scraping sounds - a *pop* - and then the sudden, rich smell of burning fat filled the room, along with a sputtering light. A thin bowl of tallow sat affixed to the table, giving a dim glow to her surroundings.

Re'Amu towered over her. His features were darkened by the flickering gloom, but enough light showed that he was much taller and stronger than her. The swaying hammock partially concealed her and she tried to disappear by pushing herself into the boards at her back. Re'Amu fumbled with the flap at the door until it was closed and then sank heavily against the wall, sliding down until he was seated on the floor. His feet, covered with salt-crusted leather and smelling of sea-water almost touched her. He did not move.

Bahira's heart pounded. Nothing continued to happen. Could he be asleep? Her eyes darted from Re'Amu to the surrounding cabin and settled on the leather flap of the door. Her stomach knotted as she gathered her legs under her, preparing to make a quick dash, then she froze. Re'Amu was looking directly at her.

"I can see your mind," Re'Amu said with thick, slurred words. "There is no escape for you there. You are in the middle of the sea and those upon this ship will do far worse to you than me. Whatever hope you have is misplaced. There is no escape from here." Standing, with much effort, he swayed and then collapsed heavily into his hammock.

Bahira breathed in sharply and then darted underneath the sack. Re'Amu did not attempt to stop her. Bahira burst through the leather flap, pushing it behind her with some difficulty. She looked rapidly to the right and to the left, the fighting blood of her ancient fathers rising once more within her. All was dark, but for a dim light to her left. She ran for it, thinking Berran might be there. A hasty image formed in her mind of floating in the sea, Berran's head resting on her arms as the dark ship sailed slowly away. Yes! She would find Berran and they would throw themselves into the sea! She clutched at the thought desperately, blind to its folly. Abruptly, she stepped out on the main deck of the *Taradium.*

It was a dark night, broken by tendrils of circling star formations high above. A brisk breeze struck Bahira's hair, pulling the dark strands away from her high russet cheeks and over her ears. Bahira's eyes were alight, reflecting the high and distant prow-fire of the *Taradium,* a resolute flame as she thought of escape. Unseen waves were felt rather than seen, rising high upon either side of the bulwarks as the swells passed. Had terror not surrounded her, the scene would have been altogether beautiful.

Bahira's eyes were drawn down, past the stars and shapeless waves. Torches lined the deck's railing, revealing the hopeless faces of many, bound to their oars. They stared at her with sudden interest. Blood caked their hands and backs, and dried bile filled the seams of their tattered garments.

Shadowy figures leapt up in surprise as Bahira appeared and, after a shocked moment, the largest of them boldly approached her from the fore of the ship. He was dark and tall, standing head and shoulders above the rest of the crew. Tattooed within his skin were blue, swirling lines of an ancient design that glowed sharply, catching and reflecting light like the eyes of an animal. His smile grew and his teeth seemed extraordinarily white. Bahira stood riveted, unable to force her limbs to move. He carried a whip in his left hand, bloodied and studded with small pieces of bronze. It dragged upon the deck, carelessly marring the boards as it passed.

18

"Come here, little honeycomb," He growled, his smile growing wider as he neared. "Let me see you closer."

At his words, Bahira turned and fled back into the darkness of the low cabin from which she had come, striking the wall and a table as she stumbled blindly. She screamed as she imagined the ghostly face of the Captain rising out of the darkness in front of her.

Bahira tripped into empty space, smashed her arms against an edge with a cry of pain, and landed on her back. Stunned, she looked up at the deck she had just fallen from. Puddles of liquid pooled into fibrous joints and an unbearable stench filled the air. A flickering torch appeared in the hole, four feet above her head. A harsh laugh echoed down.

"Fine!" the dark man cried, as several others gathered eagerly behind him. "Ruin our fun." He bent down so that she could see the intricate blue lines of his face clearly.

"...And sleep well," he whispered.

The hatch above slammed shut and darkness reigned. The gurgling sound of passing water and the loud creaking of timbers drowned out the laughter from above. Bahira groaned, rolling onto her side. Once again, she could see nothing. Fear rose like phantoms from the edges of her mind.

This time that fear was horribly different. It was not from having her life being torn away, of being captured unexpectedly and forced onto a strange ship, or even of being hurt and molested. Here in the depths of the *Taradium,* her fear took on a life of its own. A wheezing, moaning came from deep within the oppressive darkness.

"...Hello?" whispered Bahira. She stood, shaking and trembling, and struck her head on a low, heavy plank. She fell, unable to catch herself. She touched something slimy and wet. She recoiled, falling back to the floor in her haste. A rotting, putrid smell took her breath away, penetrating her pores with a sense of death and decay. Bahira scooted herself backward until she felt a wall of wood and curled against it, afraid to move and struggling to breathe. She closed her eyes, then opened them. She did it again. Was there a change? No. Wait... maybe there was. She tried again, harder this time, ignoring the rancid smells and grating sounds. Bahira's breathing grew rapid as she imagined that heavy, oozing air growing within her - like a thing alive, a parasite squirming its way inside.

Bahira woke to a sharp light. Or had she been awake when the light appeared? She didn't know. She gagged then sprang to the side as heavy boots landed where she had just been. A torch was passed down to a cursed looking man. Bahira sobbed and retched, her stomach rolling, as she saw for the first time where she was. Near her lay some small wooden barrels and supplies. The remainder of that dark pit below the *Taradium* was stacked, floor to ceiling, with bodies. The weight of those slaves at the top of the pile mercilessly crushed those below. Even as she watched, her captors walked among them, poking the ones who seemed to have some life left. Buckets of seawater doused the liveliest, bringing forth new cries of mercy and pain as they were hauled through the hatch into the light above.

Another captive, stumbling with sheer exhaustion and hunger, was flung down the hatch, stacked and bound hand, foot, and head to the shivering form on top of the pile. Bile, feces, and blood sloshed back and forth with the seawater on the floor. Toward the back, the bodies were dead. Bones gleamed white out of sacks even further fore. Bahira had no time to grasp the nonsense of shipping the dead, instead of burying them in the sea, and what reasoning could have possessed these men to do so.

Just as quickly as the light had come, it vanished. Darkness again pressed against Bahira and the presence of the dead filled the room with more fear than that of the living. Bahira wept, first from the demons that rose against her at every turn of her imagination, then for herself, and finally, for her brother and for the dying. Surely, she would soon be among them. Her sobs mixed with the faint cracking of whips and cries of pain from above. Steady and disregarding waves passed. Bahira tried to remember something of hope, something that held a whisper of life. No memories came.

The rotation of slaves happened every few hours, though Bahira had no concept of time. Sometime in the night, Bahira found herself panicking. She scraped against the side of the ship and struggled to free her bound hands, pressing her face against any crack to find a breath of air that was free of that foul chamber. She cried out, begging to be taken away. She was either ignored or unheard. No one came.

When they entered next to alternate the slaves, she grasped blindly at the man, who threw her aside with a cruel laugh. She lay stunned on the ground, shaking.

"Do not give in to fear," a feeble voice whispered in her ear. "Do not let it control you."

Had it been her own voice, a trick of her mind? Bahira's vision focused. An old man lay beside her, a shriveled form half-exposed near the base of a pile of bodies. The torch light flickered and moved back and forth. Shouts and groans, cries and voices of begging men rose as the light passed.

"Who are you?" Bahira whispered, hoping he could answer, hoping she hadn't imagined the sound.

He spoke, his voice hoarse and weak.

"My name is Huando." His hair would have been long and white, were it not tangled and matted from the grime below. "And I am a dead man. In life, I was a carpenter upon *The Anchton*, a merchant vessel." He stopped to gather himself, managing to wipe the filth from his mouth with an even dirtier arm. "They betrayed us. Lied to us! They killed Cenrill and then they murdered Kassu, the master of my house." Huando choked back a sob. "They took us in the night - and now keep us here, in this place where none know if they are truly living or dead."

"Who are *they*?" Bahira whispered. "What have *they* come for?"

Huando did not answer, as though gathering all of his strength.

"They are the Urudu," he finally whispered back. "And they have come for our souls."

Bahira recoiled, her eyes growing wide. The Urudu. She knew that name. The stories of their kind were told in the markets lining the golden-red streets of Cartegin.

"Marauders. Raiders! Men cursed by the ancient powers, cast out from their cities," Bahira whispered.

Suddenly, the pieces fit together in her mind. It had been evening, the sun had just set. She had seen a dark ship floating near the bustling city dock. She hadn't thought anything of it, so immersed was she with the narrative she was preparing for her father... Her plan was broken by screams and shouts. Flames rose high from the docks! They tried to run, tried to escape... but they were taken. The *Urudu* had taken them!

Despair filled her mind. She imagined her father, looking among the rubble, unable to find them. Unable to find Berran.

"Even in death, you must not let them have you," Huando whispered. "You must not let them have what they seek! By Enlil, find the truth, deep inside of you, that will outlast the darkness."

Bahira looked upon this elderly man with fear and amazement; as she was about to speak, strong hands grabbed and pulled him forth, dousing him with cold water before dragging him to the hatch.

"No!!" Bahira screamed, struggling after him. But, she was struck on the head and fell again into darkness.

Chapter Two

Prisoners and Slaves

The taste of blood in Bahira's mouth was strong as she awoke. Huando was gone. Small slits of natural light snuck into the hull from the floorboards above. Though they were thin, they pierced the darkness. Bahira realized the night must be over and some measure of hope filled her mind. Surely Cartegin would come for her. Her father would stir up the city! The chief would summon the Strong Men to his banner and help her father! Her face fell. Would they even know she was alive? Would the chief allow the men to abandon the damaged city to pursue them?

An image of a man, young and strong, bearing armbands of a deep, rose-colored wood and a spear of bronze caused her heart to beat faster. Surely, he would come for her. Of all people, couldn't he save her? Wouldn't he cross any distance to come for her?

The hatch opened and an Urudu lowered himself down, pinching his nose and carrying a wooden bucket full of thick mush. He ladled the mixture into the faces of the slaves. Like a tight cord of leather wetted, so the vicious desire to live had slowly choked humanity from the desperate. They bit and gagged on the slop, those on top of the pile devouring as much as they could before it dripped beyond their reach to those further below. Bahira had never been hungrier. For the first time in her life, she didn't care what her food was. Her mouth watered and she was tempted to dive in among them. Her legs did not respond to her impulse and she remained helplessly aloof.

As the rays of light grew dimmer and darkness enveloped her for a second time, any glimmer of hope Bahira had felt with the morning dissipated. When the hatch opened again, the Urudu came for her. She was too weak to resist, and they pulled her out of the lower deck. The air above that dark hole seemed the sweetest breath of air that had ever been. She smiled as she drank this sweet draught, oblivious to the captors that carried her. Suddenly she was doused with seawater. It hit her like a cart of bricks, washing away her euphoria, sinking her like a stone to the bottom of the river called reality.

Her vision was veiled by hunger and thirst. The floor was rougher and harder than she remembered. She brushed her sopping hair from her face and looked around. The same small table and hammock filled the familiar room of Re'Amu's cabin. The pleasant gold of evening light sifted through the leather exterior. The flap entry was pulled aside and Re'Amu once again appeared. This time, his feet were firmly planted. His gray eyes were clear and they studied her with renewed interest. His hair was black and long, hanging down to his shoulders. She was surprised to see his dress was fine, the expensive red dye of his soft tunic distinguishing him as one of the upper-classes and wealthy. He held a bronze knife loosely in one hand and Bahira's eyes grew wide.

"No... Please..." she said, weakly scooting away from him. There was nowhere to run and little strength remained, had she tried.

He approached swiftly, letting fall the leather flap behind him. He pinned her to the floor, flipping her on her side. She cried out in fear and pain, but with a quick flick of his knife Re'Amu cut her bonds and let her roll free.

Bahira pushed herself into a sitting position. Her throbbing hands gave way, unable to support her weight. She wept and lay curled on the floor, unable to move. Re'Amu stirred something near the little flame on the table before turning back to her. He knelt and she shied away.

"Come here," Re'Amu commanded sternly. His voice was sharp and clear, unlike the night before. His gaze was intense and unapologetic. Although Bahira was afraid, she did not push him away.

"Your hands," Re-Amu ordered, gesturing. She held them out. The bonds had cut deeply into her wrists, leaving a bloody indent that was now inflamed. The dirt and grime of the hull had found its way into the wounds. Re'Amu grasped them firmly. Taking a soaking rag from the table he scrubbed them hard. Bahira cried out in pain and tried to pull away, but Re'Amu held her mercilessly, scraping away the decay and infection that had started there.

Finally, Re'Amu released her. He withdrew to the leather wall and sat with his legs outstretched and ankles crossed, watching Bahira whimper. He couldn't tell that her dress had been a light green, hemmed with silver. Her necklace was gone. Her face and hair were matted with filth and blood, smelling of seaweed.

"There is bread and water there, upon the table. Take and eat." Re'Amu's voice seemed unconcerned, as though he had seen much worse than her pitiful state.

His words revived Bahira even faster than the seawater. Grabbing the bread and gourd, she retreated into the opposite corner, as far from

Re'Amu as possible, drinking and eating as quickly as she could swallow. Eventually she slowed. The dim veil around her mind began to clear. She studied Re'Amu. He gazed at the floorboards between his feet, his face cast into shadow as the golden light of outside faded and the flickering of the tallow-wick grew.

"Who are you people?" Bahira asked finally. "Where are we going? Where is my brother?" Bahira tried to calm the panic that rose in her voice as she thought of Berran. She paused, steadying herself. She didn't want to be thrown down below again. Bahira cowered, whimpering at the thought that Re'Amu could do so at any time.

Her defiance would not easily die. Before she knew it, she was speaking again.

"You are the Urudu, aren't you?" she continued in a low whisper, laced with anger. "I have heard of you, among the gossip of Cartegin. They say you steal people from their homes, feeding upon them until you are filled with the power of their very souls."

Re'Amu said nothing. Bahira cringed, waiting for the command for her to be removed, or for the heavy strike of his hand. She gave a sudden start as a sound burst from him, shattering the stillness of the room. It was a sob, a desperate, broken cry that escaped through the tight net of his eroding facade. Bahira's mouth fell open in shock.

"We are not powerful," Re'Amu whispered, struggling to speak. He had covered his face with his hands so she couldn't see his expression. "We are dead men, floating on a ship of death and surrounded by the souls of the departed. We seek the rich splendor of joy; like a man grasping at another's woman, or a thirsty man drinking deep of our own potent grog. And what happens to those men? Like oil slipping through the hand they are deceived, all of them, and when they finally awake from their stupor they find they are enslaved to the very thing they thought would bring them life. We are all already dead."

When Re'Amu finally removed his hands, she could see his face was wet with tears.

Bahira was silent, overcome at his stark reply.

"What have you done?" Bahira finally asked.

The question hung in the air unanswered. It needed no reply.

"No more questions," Re'Amu said, regaining his stern tone. "If you do nothing useful, you may return to your confinement. Talk! Tell me about your life and from where you come."

Involuntarily, Bahira reached out with her mind to happier days. Now, above the darkness of the hull, with her belly full of bread, she could remember. So, she told Re'Amu about her life. It was some comfort to her, to remember her home, recalling the safety and routine of Cartegin. Bahira closed her eyes and saw the sun rising, its rays broken by the fishermen laying nets in the river; the green slopes of the Durgu

Mountains standing tall, dotted with the wildflowers of spring and giving way to the rolling hills of Cartegin; shepherds herding wandering flocks here and there; the din and gossip of the early markets floating on the warming air. The red-stone walls of her home caught the warmth of the day, calling her hand to graze across them, an imitation of her father's habit. Creeping vines snuck in through her windows, bearing the faces of white flowers that filled the household with a sweet smell. It paired nicely with the thick scent of unleavened bread rising from the ovens. She laughed mercilessly at herself as she thought of how much she hated that routine. She wept as she remembered the days she sat in the tall grass of the Arron-Ken, looking at the distant sea and rising ziggurats, dreaming of grand adventures. She could feel the entire land, city, and household bustling with life and energy - the carving, the baking, the teaching, the mending. Life. Life that she was not satisfied with. A life that she wanted to leave.

She paused as the sharp stab of remorse hit her. Re'Amu was looking deeply at her, a feeling of longing hovering about him.

"Go on," He said in a gruff whisper. Bahira wondered if it was more of a pleading request, than a command.

She closed her eyes again and saw Areoch. His fine armbands were smooth. They made him look strong and tall, although he needed no more of either. His hands were thick and tough, though gentle, as he moved her hair away from her eyes as they walked through the fields. That feeling which made her heart beat with excitement didn't last. Instead, she saw Berran running before her in boyish joy as she walked toward the port of Cartegin to see her father, her face drawn and apprehensive. She knew her life was about to change.

She hadn't imagined it would change like this. The ugly face of Sapu standing over her brother, the whizzing of arrows, and the shrill cry of horns raising the city to arms, chased away the thought of what could have been. The memory of Berran's face brought Bahira into silence. She tried again to speak, to remember those happy days, but was grounded back on the hard floor of Re'Amu's cabin. She wept.

Re'Amu, slumped and downcast, was silent as he listened. The night drew on. Soon all was dark, except the remains of the flickering tallow bowl. Even in the darkness, in the midst of her pain and filth, Bahira's features were fair.

"I could not protect my brother," Bahira sobbed, "though it was my duty to do so."

"It was not your duty. It was your fathers!" Re'Amu interjected, his voice harsh and rising. He leaned forward, as if desperate to convince her: "They are all the same! You were abandoned! Alone! You should curse the man who gave you breath and be glad he is far from you."

Bahira recoiled at the outburst, drawing away from Re'Amu as though he had become a snake. She shook her head as he grew quiet, the tears still streaming down her face.

"How can you say that?" Bahira whispered. "My father never abandoned me. He was not there. I have looked after my brother since he was a baby, being as old as I am. He was under my care. I failed my father. I failed everyone. I will not blame another."

Re'Amu looked aside, hiding his tears. In flashing images, Re'Amu saw his own father lying by a crackling fire. Dark forms crept through the trees, encircling the light. Greedy eyes and hungry knives gleamed from around the circle of shadow. Re'Amu blinked, forcing the images from his mind. He looked at his hands, they shook uncontrollably. In the low candlelight they caught a strange sheen. It was a red color, dark and dull, that looked like blood. He hastily wiped them on his jerkin.

"Why did I have you come here?" Re'Amu whispered, avoiding Bahira's questioning gaze. "You pierce me sharper than any spear. Be silent! You have said enough. You may stay here, if you wish, and not return to the hull below. But say no more."

"And what of the others who remain trapped down there?" Bahira ventured

"I said be silent!!" cried Re'Amu with sudden anger, standing to his feet. "Unless you wish to join them, hold your tongue!"

Bahira winced at his sudden change, but he did not move in her direction. He merely collapsed again in the hammock and was still. As the light flickered and went out, Bahira allowed herself to fall into an uneasy sleep.

When she awoke the next day, Re'Amu was not there. She did not dare to venture out into the rest of the *Taradium*. The ship seemed to be moving slower than usual and she peered through the cracks of the cabin's covering. The day outside was bright and clear. Morning was long past and midday drew near. The water was blue and glistening. Tall gray cliffs were visible in the distance. A thought came of trying to force herself through the leather covering and out into the sea. Just then, Re'Amu reappeared.

"You look better today," Re'Amu remarked, setting another loaf of bread and some sliced apples on the table. "I have made it known that you are in my keeping. You may stay in my cabin in safety. Venture out from it and the Urudu will not look upon it kindly."

"Why are you helping me?" Bahira asked.

"I am not helping you," Re'Amu said quickly. He paused as Bahira sucked gingerly on one of the sweet apples. "It will not matter anyway," he said finally. "To where we go, there is no escape. Not for the living or the dead."

"Where is Berran?"

"He is aboard and alive," Re'Amu muttered. He looked away as he spoke, and his face was downcast.

"He is ill, isn't he?" Bahira ascertained. Re'Amu did not answer.

"You might see him again, soon enough. For now, you will remain here."

The day passed with increasing despair and soon night began to fall. Re'Amu checked her, on occasion, leaving an irregular bit of food and water. There was coming and going about the ship, though Bahira could not see much nor hear more than running footfalls, the cries of those captives that had the strength, and the shouting of commands. At one point her view through the cabin-crack was blocked. Another ship, dark and blackened like the *Taradium,* pulled up along its side. It stayed there momentarily before vanishing out of her sight. Whether the two ships sailed together or separate, she did not know.

Just after nightfall the *Taradium* came to a noticeable halt and Re'Amu came into the cabin.

"Have we arrived to wherever we now sail?" inquired Bahira.

"No," answered Re'Amu. "But you may come out for a little while, if you wish. Only a few of the Urudu are here under my command."

Re'Amu turned and left. Bahira tentatively followed him, glad to stretch her sore limbs. The main deck appeared abruptly before her. The oars sat empty. Stars lit up the sky and the breeze blew past with the sharp refreshing smell of pine trees. The dark shadow of land stood to the right of the ship, close at hand. The other black ship was some distance away, closer to the rocky shore. Beyond it the dim glow of firelight could be seen. Figures moved to and fro on the stone-covered beach.

Two other Urudu sat on the main deck, carelessly using sharpening stones on their long bronze daggers. They looked up as Bahira appeared and shot questioning glances at Re'Amu. He ignored them, standing alone at the prow. They soon went back to their task, whispering together. Bahira shuffled by them and joined Re'Amu.

"Do they not care that you help me?"

"They know that you are mine and care little about how I treat you, as long as you keep quiet," Re'Amu muttered. Bahira fell silent. The men on the distant beach moved back and forth. There seemed to be many.

"What are they doing?" she asked.

Re'Amu nodded toward the other ship. "The *Bermiis* has been here many days attempting to... do Urudu work. Our Captain is helping," he said.

"You stay behind," Bahira remarked.

"I watch the *Taradium* as his second in command."

"And you stay behind."

Re'Amu tightened his lips and seemed about to turn away, but he did not.

27

"Why do you stay here?" Bahira asked softly. "You are out of place among these men. Surely you must see it."

Calm waves lapped against the *Taradium's* sides and the methodical scraping of knives echoed in the background.

Re'Amu opened his mouth as if to answer and then shut it again.

"You do not know who I am or what I have done. This is where I belong," Re'Amu answered finally.

Bahira looked at him closely.

"You have nowhere else to go. That is what you mean, isn't it?"

Re'Amu did not answer.

"How did you end up here?" Bahira asked again.

"I think it's time you return to the cabin," Re'Amu said shortly, gesturing toward land. A group of torches separated themselves and were quickly moving their direction over the water.

"Now!" he commanded sternly. Bahira turned and fled from him. One of the Urudu whistled as she passed and the other laughed.

It was late before Re'Amu entered his chambers. Bahira seemed to be asleep, propped up in the corner. He looked over her features: they were fair, even after her long ordeal, and his face blushed. For a brief moment, he looked as if some distant hope of living a different life had entered him. Then his face fell with shame. When Re'Amu looked upon Bahira again, despair shone there like a well-known companion.

"There is no escape from what I have done," he muttered to himself. "There is no escape from who I am."

Bahira awoke the next morning. Re'Amu was not there, though the customary morsels of food were left on the table. He did not appear that morning. Bahira couldn't see anything through the small slits in her confinement, a heavy gray fog concealed all.

When he finally entered, Re'Amu was ashen-faced. He held a leather cord in his hand.

"We are here," he said. "Turn around."

She stood, letting him fasten the cord around her wrists. His hands trembled as he touched her.

"Will I see my brother now?" she asked.

Re'Amu sighed. "Perhaps you shall."

"What will happen to us?"

"We will turn you over to the Laḥmu."

"The Laḥmu?" Bahira repeated.

"The guardians of Angfar. You will see them and many other things you will wish to never see again. I can do nothing more."

Bahira found herself crying softly as she thought of Berran. Re'Amu set his face. Grasping her resolutely he turned her toward the door.

"Thank you, Re'Amu, for what you have done for me," she whispered.

28

"I hope someday you find freedom."

"I am no slave," he answered firmly.

"Yes, you are." Whether or not Re'Amu heard her words, she never knew.

As they exited the cabin everything was gray and shapeless. The sun shone from high above into the mist making it seem both light and dark. There were not any slaves on the main deck. The Urudu pulled upon the oars, while the Captain stood at the prow, hunched over like a vulture, keenly looking ahead.

Suddenly, like the opening jaws of a beast appearing out of the mist, two great pillars of black rock towered out of the ocean's depths. They joined nearly sixty feet up in the air, forming a wide, arching entrance. A cliff-face of jagged rocks ran away on either side, not unlike sharp teeth encircling a maw. There wasn't any sound: no birds called nor seals barked. Only the grunts of the Urudu and the small lapping of waves against the ship could be heard. The air was heavy and thick. It was difficult to breathe.

The *Taradium* passed through the opening and the fog dissipated, retreating back to the ocean shores. Bahira gasped at the sight. They sailed through a narrow channel and into a land-locked bay. Though it must have been well past noon, the surface of the water was dark, flat, and its depths unfathomable. On its far shore a low hill rose. Beyond it, tall black mountains jarred the sky with staggered shelves and dangerous precipices, like knives thrust through the land's crusty surface.

The Urudu laid aside their oars, yet the *Taradium* continued forward at an increasing rate of speed. Bahira blinked her eyes, thinking that the fog must be playing a trick on her, but when she opened them again she saw a baffling sight: in the center of the great water, where the darkness was the deepest, there was a mighty swirling chasm. It was at least ten times as wide as the *Taradium* was long. The water swirled about, churning and frothing into a dull roar before vanishing into an abyss at its center.

"Mind your course now Sapu!" shouted the Captain from the fore.

Sapu stood atop the cabin at the aft of the ship. He held a long steering oar with both hands, digging the blade deep within the water. As he pulled, the ship turned farther north. Their pace became slower. The low hill of the oncoming shore grew larger. As they approached, Bahira could see roads leading around the water to the north and west, busy with carts and small figures. The hill itself was potted with black holes, as if the earth had turned molten, bubbled, and then popped during some long-forgotten history.

Between these small caverns the tracks converged. Dark turrets of stone rose from the base of the hill and the ridge above. In the center of it all stood a tall tower, blending in with the living rock around it. Many structures and awnings were placed in a circular pattern around the tower, stretching out into a vast city network. Figures moved back and forth, up and down. Steam shot out of holes and caves. The sound of chisels and hammers, barking and shouting scarred the blackened land. Past the fortifications, farther south and west, the cliffs seemed to form a natural wall. What was beyond, she could not tell.

The *Taradium* was now more than halfway around the great bay. Layers of sharp rock made any landing impossible, except for a wide flat expanse on its northernmost reaches. Small docks and mooring posts were quickly growing larger. Bahira could see three other ships floating there, all different in design and all blackened like the *Taradium*.

"Mooring ready!" called out Re'Amu. Six of the Urudu heaved long poles of wood, sticking them over the sides to fend off the shallows. Sapu turned the steering oar sharply and the *Taradium* rotated, slowing quickly. Bahira lost her balance and when she looked up again the ship was already moored to a wooden post.

It was clear they had been expected. A group of about ten figures stood on the shore waiting for them. They seemed tall and hunched over, but she could not make out any other details.

"Get them out!" cried the Captain, turning from the prow with a wide smile. "Drag them up! Throw them over! Give them a warm welcome to Angfar!"

A familiar face stood close by, blue tattoos standing out sharply against his skin. He threw back his head and howled with joy. He turned and seized Bahira, dragging her away from Re'Amu. The Urudu cheered and clapped.

"Ah, Re'Amu's little pet," he chuckled, drawing her near. "I've been wanting to do *this* for a long time." Without warning he threw her overboard.

The water was colder than ice, chilling her bones to their core. She came up gasping, struggling for the shore. Her hands were still bound. She floundered and sank, choking on the water. Suddenly a hand with a grip of bronze grabbed her by the hair and pulled her through the shallows. She kicked, gasping for air, but the hand upon her head held her down. She was soon being dragged over hard, porous rock and then she lay choking and gagging on the shores of Angfar.

A hideous form was standing over her. Whether it was man or beast she could not tell - its face was more snout-like than a man's, though it stood upright and carried a heavy cudgel in one clawed hand. Hair grew from it in dark clusters and its skin was black, heavily scarred, and pitted, similar to the earth on which she now lay. It gave a hoarse guttural sound and Bahira realized it was laughing.

The sounds of screaming echoed out from the *Taradium* and the Laḥmu above her turned away. Bodies of both the living and the dead were being thrown overboard. Those that were alive shouted out with renewed vigor as they were submersed in the icy cold. Six of the Laḥmu and two or three wild-looking men seized them as they fell, dragging them through the water and onto shore. Soon, many gasping and choking slaves were mercilessly piled around Bahira. The dead floated in the water where they had been tossed.

While this was happening, several of the Urudu disembarked on a thin dock stretched between the mooring posts. They struck, with long poles, any of the slaves who did not immediately swim inland. The Captain stood among them. The Laḥmu who had pulled Bahira from the water approached him.

"You bring a good catch, Behram-Rais, as is your custom. The Dominant is pleased with you." The Laḥmu's voice was hoarse, rasping like a wheat sheaf dragged over gravel. It was barely speech at all. Rais looked upon the creature with disdain, though the Laḥmu towered above him a full head and shoulders

"I do as the Dominant commands. I also bring word from Captain Felixis of the *Bermiis*. He should be here in two days' time with a full load, healthy and alive from the Isles of Brak." Rais reported.

"That is good. Save your details for Commander Z'gelsh. He is eager to speak with you in person." The beast turned and spoke something that sounded between a yelled word and a yapping growl to the Laḥmu behind him.

"We will make the official count for you, so you and your crew may go and receive your reward, and we may return to our watch."

Bahira was made to stand. The surviving captives were forced to do the same. Those that did not have the strength were thrown into the water with the dead. The Laḥmu walked between them, sniffing the slaves individually as they moved down the line.

Even as they did so an old man, who stood at the far end, made a dash into the water - throwing aside the broken leather thongs that had bound his wrists.

"Huando!" Bahira exclaimed, recognizing his face. The skin hung loose on Huando's boney arms and his face was hollow from lack of food; but an unquenchable vigor burned in his eyes and with the experience of a natural swimmer, he dove into the water.

"*Guaff OUZZ!* Grab him!" the Laḥmu howled. Those in the water were slow, they scooped at the water like lizards and Huando was soon past them. Several Urudu ran to the edge of the dock, but Huando cut wide, out of reach of their long poles.

"Go!! Go Huando!" Several of the slaves called. "For *The Anchton*! For Kassu!!" they cheered.

The Laḥmu leader chuckled deeply, revealing several rows of fangs.

"Quiet them down," he ordered. "And make them watch."

The cheering died away. Huando's emaciated body was visible a few hundred feet offshore. His form seemed to waver in the water as he fought against the current. Suddenly, he turned back and his thin voice floated across the water.

"No, no, no! It is cold. Cold. My heart is like ice! No! Don't let it take me! Please!"

He cried out, flailing in sudden panic against the swirling waters while all on the shore watched. The Laḥmu howled at him.

"Come, old man! Come back to us and we'll eat you," they taunted. "That will be more pleasant than your current fate!!"

Huando's strength soon failed and with a terrifying scream he was swept away toward the swirling blackness and into the abyss. Bahira imagined that as he disappeared over its edge an inhuman shriek echoed over the waters.

The beast chuckled again.

"Anyone else want to take a little swim, hmm?" the Laḥmu challenged, scanning the faces of the captives. "You may feel free. But know that you go to an even worse fate than where we take you. There is no escape from the Dominant! That one will still count toward you, Rais, though I shall put him with the dead. It was your Urudu's fault he was not properly bound. Your final count is eight alive and twenty-four dead."

Rais nodded and turned back to the group of Urudu gathered behind him. Bahira saw Re'Amu standing among them. He looked at her with sadness, though she looked on him with even more pity.

Bahira was tied to the slave before and behind as the dead were pushed into the current and swept toward the black pit. With a sickening jolt of despair, Bahira recognized a familiar face in the water.

"Berran! Berran!" she screamed. She pulled the entire line to their knees as she scrambled into the shallows. A cudgel slammed into her elbow. With a shriek of pain, she fell into the water before being pulled backward.

"This one should count for two alive!" hissed one of the Laḥmu as he threw Bahira back into the line. She stumbled forward again, not paying the creature any heed. It dropped to all fours and blocked her way, pushing her over with its snout and trapping her onto the hard rock as she tried to crawl by.

It licked her with a long, black tongue and began to salivate. She tried again to push by and with a quick snap the Laḥmu grabbed her limp arm in its mouth and dragged her away from the water. She cried out as its teeth sunk into her flesh. It released her, licking its chops eagerly.

"Next time I will take the whole thing," it threatened.

Bahira was trapped in a fog of grief as they walked up a small track, nearing a city nestled in the low hillside. Those that were not strong enough to walk were dragged by the others as they were driven up the hill. Similar beast-like Laḥmu came, yapping at them from all sides as they walked, swelling in numbers as they approached the hill. They passed rock fortifications and entered among short towers. Bahira wept. As she looked about her, the pain in her arm dulled into a throb and her tears dried. Hundreds of slaves, bound as she was, were being driven into the fortress from the south and west. The Laḥmu of Angfar seemed countless, going here and there on ceaseless patrol. Wild men worked among the towers, going in and out of cave entrances. They resembled the Laḥmu, but with less hair and longer arms that drug near the ground.

"Sorting!" the lead Laḥmu yapped. They came to a halt under a wide awning. Something like a man sat under it. He was large and fat, standing nearly as tall as the Laḥmu and wider than two of them together. His face was bulbous and covered in cancerous sores. He approached, looking at each of the *Taradium's* slaves in turn.

"Pits!" he cried as he stood in front of one who could barely stand.

"Camp!" he yelled, looking upon a slave who stood firmly on his feet.

On down the line he moved. 'Pits' echoed out again and again.

He stood in front of Bahira.

"Camp!" he cried.

Instantly Bahira was grabbed and taken aside. Two others were taken with her. They were thin and bedraggled, but they could walk. Most of the others were not so fortunate. Like cattle the three were driven up the hillside, cresting its peak so they looked down on the city and the water's edge.

A thick gray fog was a blanketing wall, hiding the sea. Into the north, the scarred points of the Black Mountains were closer than before. Directly below, the whirlpool churned, its center a bottomless void from which no light came. The bay could be seen stretching away farther inland to the west. Beyond it to the south, countless reddish-brown hills and steep ravines dotted the landscape.

Wherever Bahira was, she was far from Cartegin.

They were herded by the Laḥmu, snapping and biting at their legs, away from the hill's edge and into a low sunken grade. Other slaves were huddled in the declivity as Bahira and her two companions were pushed in among them. In time, more were driven in, until almost thirty slaves were pressed together.

A squat, wild man, shriveled and marred, watched Bahira enter the group from the lip of the ridge. He stood only three or four feet tall, gripping a spear with arms that hung as long as his entire body.

"Well, looook at this, looook at this. A pretty thing? Yes, a very pretty thing," he muttered in a raspy voice. He approached her, hopping like a frog over the distance; his eyes glinted as he peered closely at Bahira.

"How did you end up here, my sweeeet? Yes, myyy sweet." He looked her up and down, reaching out a shrunken hand to graze against her as he hopped in a circle. "You are much better suited to our towers below. Yes, much indeed. You don't belong here. No, you don't belong here at all."

Bahira recoiled, and as he reached out to grab her, a yapping growl suddenly interrupted.

"Yeowmon, what is your business here? You belong in the refineries, this is our watch." A large Laḥmu hunched over the little creature, its teeth bared.

"I come and go as I please, *Laḥmu*," Yeowmon jeered, spitting out the word. "What is this woman doing here? There must have been a mistake, she belongs below. I will take her there." He turned and tried to grab Bahira's arm again. A heavy, clawed hand pushed him aside. He fell into the dirt.

"She is from the Urudu and has been sorted. Those from the Urudu do not go into the towers."

Yeowmon struggled to his feet, gripping his spear tighter. He spat at the creature.

"You are a blind mutt! What do you know? The Urudu bring back the dead or those about to be there. She is not one of those! I say she belongs below, where we can get some real use from her. Stand aside dog! She comes with me."

The Laḥmu did not move at Yeoman's order and even more Laḥmu flocked around them, curious as to the commotion.

"She has been sorted, as is the will of the Dominant," the Laḥmu growled again, baring its teeth, "and has been chosen to serve at the high camps. That is where we go, unless you would like to take this up with the commander, Yeowmon? I don't think he cares as much about your personal pleasure as you would like to think."

The pack of Laḥmu yapped hysterically at Yeowmon's crestfallen face.

"Such a waste," he muttered as he returned to the lip of the hillside, backing slowly away from the circle of teeth.

The Laḥmu snorted with satisfaction and turned, addressing the slaves huddled together.

"Pick yourselves up! We are moving," it snarled. "If you flee, you will be eaten. If you cannot keep up, you will be eaten. Move! Move your pathetic pads!"

Bahira found herself running over hard, black stones and surrounded by terrified faces. Upon either side the Laḥmu ran, nipping at their legs. They trotted on all fours, herding the group up and away from Angfar into the charred mountains.

Chapter Three

<u>Pack of Fear</u>

Weariness and sadness weighed down Bahira. Whenever she stumbled, the sharp snap of a Laḥmu's teeth made her blood pound and her legs move. Other than the two strange faces from the *Taradium*, she did not recognize anyone around her. The majority seemed in better shape than her two companions. Some were young, some old, some were men, and some were women.

They were pushed deep into the mountains, sometimes walking, mostly running as the Laḥmu drove them. The day faded and the moon rose, but with the coming of its pale light the Laḥmu's speed increased. Finally, one of the slaves from the *Taradium* could run no longer. The Laḥmu yapped, nipping him as he straggled behind, stumbling. Soon he fell to the earth, his bare back rising and falling as the man gasped for breath.

The largest Laḥmu let out a ghostly howl that ricocheted off the black crags above. The pack took up the call.

"Tired, are you?" it growled. "We have no time for resting." Leaping forward the beast seized the man with his sharp jowls and pulled him along the rocky road. The man kicked and screamed, then lay still.

"Does anyone else want a break?" snapped the Laḥmu, turning on the rest of the huddled group. "No? Forward then! Move your paws!"

Bahira wanted to cry, but no tears came to her eyes as they stumbled along in the darkness. Her tongue stuck to the roof of her mouth and her feet slapped against the hard stones. They did not go much farther before a beautiful sound filled her ears, rising ever so slightly above the scuffing of the captives' feet. It was the sound of water. A rocky turn revealed the source: a stream, shimmering with moonlight, poured out of a rock wall to their right. It ran down and away from the black hills. The group collapsed at its edge, burying their faces in its refreshing cold, while the Laḥmu prowled around them.

"We will break here," the Laḥmu rasped. "Do not get comfortable."

The cool water cleared Bahira's mind. She searched for a place to rest, but there was no bank or soft place to lay. Sharp, black rock was everywhere, cutting through fabric and flesh. Around her the group arranged themselves among the stones as best they could. The beasts disappeared within the jagged outcroppings. Every time she looked up, green eyes stared out menacingly in the moonlight, stealing away any peace in the night.

Bahira felt a light touch on her shoulder and turned sharply, expecting some new predator. Instead she was met with the face of a girl, not more than a season younger than herself.

"Oh," the girl whispered, edging over the stones a bit closer, "I'm sorry. May I sit next to you?"

Bahira gawked. Her mind felt submerged from the suffocating darkness of the past few days. It had been such a long time since she had heard a friendly voice, it startled her.

"Yes, of course," Bahira finally answered. She slid over, making room and looking closer at the girl who settled in beside her. The girl was lean and strong for her age, with a face deeply tanned from long hours in the fields. She wore a coarsely woven tunic that seemed to have fared better than Bahira's garments. She would have been pretty, were it not for deep scars, that seemed to melt the skin in layers down one side of her face. They started upon her brow, travelling in light furrows down the right side of her neck, half-concealed by rich brown hair roughly cut at shoulder length.

She leaned in close to Bahira.

"I know you," whispered the girl with a shy smile. "You are Bahira of Cartegin!" She giggled at Bahira's look of shock.

"How do you know me?" Bahira whispered back.

"Em, I too am from Cartegin!" she said with a mischievous look. "I know of Birsha, your father. My friends and I would see you in the streets and the markets, going here and there. We would talk about what it would be like...to be like you!" She giggled again and Bahira found herself unexpectedly smiling.

"How is that? Does your family dwell within our quadrant?"

The girl's face fell. "Well, em, no," she stammered. "My family lived outside of the city, near the banks of the Dan-Jor."

"Outside of the city walls? I always thought it was just the beggars and the lame that dwelt there," Bahira said wearily. "My father used to warn us of tarrying among them."

The girl answered meekly, "Oh. It is the only home I have ever known. I never knew my father, my mother fished for us." She said no more and stood to leave.

"No, please," Bahira whimpered, reaching desperately for her. "I am sorry, I do not know why I said that. I did not think... it doesn't matter now. Please. Please stay. What is your name?"

The girl's face brightened. "Oh, my name is Eli'ssa."

"How did you end up here?" Bahira asked.

The Laḥmu yipped and snapped some distance away causing the girls to huddle closer together.

Eli'ssa leaned close, answering. "My mum heard rumor that there were riches and promise in the Jezrial lands. We took all we had and joined with a caravan heading north. The journey took several weeks, and we passed through many dangers. On the last night before reaching the city, I woke up from my sleep. Oh, my hands were bound and my mouth was gagged! I could not call out to my sisters. I was loaded into a cart with several others until I arrived here."

Bahira shook her head. "It sounds not unlike my own tale. Though I was taken upon a ship with my brother and he.... he..." Bahira stopped, fighting back sobs.

Eli'ssa watched her struggle.

"I've been such a fool, Eli'ssa. My whole life, I've been such a fool! I feel so... so..."

"Powerless."

Bahira nodded. Eli'ssa gently grasped her hand. An understanding of Bahira's pain shone in her eyes.

"After we left Cartegin, we came to a land that looked beautiful, dotted with rich pastures and springs," Elissa said quietly. "Mum said that surely everything she had heard was true. She said we would finally be able to live well. That very day my sister went running through the fields and fell into a foul pit of black tar. We could not get her out and the caravan would not wait for us."

Bahira held her hand tighter as the clicking claws of a Laḥmu passed behind them. The sound of snarling filled the night.

"I am glad to be with you, Eli'ssa" Bahira whispered. "Please don't leave."

Eli'ssa smiled, and it seemed to fill Bahira with strength she never could have summoned on her own.

"Do you think he'll come for you?" Eli'ssa asked with a sly smile.

"Who?" Bahira asked.

"Oh, that young wanderer your father took into his house. I saw you both, walking through the fields in spring. He looked like he would come for you. He looked like he could save us."

Bahira gave a small smile, but her face fell.

"If anyone could, it would be him," she whispered. "But..." Bahira hesitated, looking around. "I think we're on our own, Eli'ssa. I'm glad you're here."

The night's chill pierced the torn and stained clothing of the two girls.

They huddled together, shivering, until weariness overcame them.

It seemed they had just fallen into an uneasy sleep when they were awakened again. An Angfar Laḥmu stood over them, its muzzle bloodied and flecked with saliva. The rest of the group was already standing, being driven across the stream. It was still night, though the stars were in different places and a dull eastern glow hinted at morning.

"Get a move on, hairless ones," the Laḥmu growled. Eli'ssa grabbed Bahira and they both stumbled on groggily, grateful for the cold of the stream as it poured over their sore feet. They were wide awake when they saw the fallen slave from earlier in the night. He had been dragged into the stream and now lay face-down, his flesh torn and half eaten.

Bahira turned and threw-up her empty stomach. They continued, tripping and helping one another as they scrambled over loose rock. Slowly the light changed to gray and the stars faded away. The sun rose behind them, revealing their road for the first time.

It was little more than a path cut into the mountainous side. Sharp, black peaks rose high on their right. The land sloped down to the left, opening into rocky ravines and gullies. Far, far down Bahira could see the black mountains give way to low hills and sunlight reflecting off water. Beyond, flat plains stretched into a brown horizon.

The pace of the Laḥmu lessened as the sun rose, though their loping strides still pushed the group at a breathless pace. Near mid-morning a shallow cave opened out of the hillside and the Laḥmu halted.

"Rest!" the leader growled. "We continue at nightfall."

The captives were herded into a loose circle. The sun was hot upon the dark rock and there was no shade from its glare, except for the shadow of the cave where the Laḥmu lay. Nonetheless, hungry and parched from thirst, the two girls passed into an uneasy sleep.

When they awoke, the shadows of evening were long.

"Water... I can hardly speak" Bahira gasped, struggling to swallow. Eli'ssa looked about them and shook her head, fighting to keep her swollen tongue from sticking to the roof of her mouth. She picked up a small pebble and sucked it.

"Hunger and thirst are no strangers to me," she whispered. There was no self-pity in her voice, only a rigid determination to survive. Bahira marveled. In all of Bahira's childhood, and even through the famines of the latter years, Bahira's father had been one of the wealthiest in Cartegin. Eli'ssa knew she had never felt hunger until now.

"Em, there is none to be had," Eli'ssa said louder, looking at her feet as she beheld the fear in Bahira's.

The Laḥmu drove them into the night. There were no breaks. Two and then three people fell upon the sharp stones and could not get up. They did not stop. The sound of beasts devouring the fallen, faded as they continued forward. Bahira's vision was blurry. Her feet were raw and bleeding. All feeling in her legs had long since vanished. Each time she stumbled, Eli'ssa was there, pulling her back to her feet and helping her on.

The second dawn came. As the sun burst through the low clouds the Laḥmu allowed for a brief rest. Everyone immediately fell to the ground, limbs swollen and shaking from lack of nutrition and rest. Eli'ssa gazed at the still forms and then up at the blue sky of morning with a hint of expectancy.

"Oh, what would I do for a bit of rain?" she murmured with a small grin.

Bahira offered a weak smile in return, amazed at Eli'ssa's strength.

"Where are they taking us? There is nothing out here," Eli'ssa muttered to herself.

"Eli'ssa," Bahira hoarsely whispered, "I cannot... I will not make it much farther. You must leave me this time." Eli'ssa moved Bahira's head into her lap and stroked her long, black hair.

"I don't have many friends. I am not going to leave the only one I have left," she reassured. The Laḥmu rested in a circle around the remaining captives and the sun rose higher.

Suddenly, its bright rays were dimmed. Eli'ssa turned her head, looking back down the road from which they came.

"Oh, did you feel that?" Eli'ssa whispered breathlessly. Bahira's eyes fluttered open, and she saw Eli'ssa staring intently down the road toward the sea. The sunlight shimmered across her scars and then vanished behind towering black clouds, leaving the face of Eli'ssa in shadow. Bahira summoned the strength to reach up and touch the scars. The furrows were soft as Bahira moved her fingers across the sunken depressions.

Eli'ssa caught Bahira's weak hand as it fell back, holding it gently. She turned her eyes away from the road.

"What is it?" Bahira managed to mumble.

Eli'ssa shook her head, watching the towering, black clouds gather as they blotted out the sun, advancing with a great force from the sea.

"I thought I heard a voice," Eli'ssa murmured. "Though it felt like, em, it felt like a memory."

"A memory of what?"

Bahira's voice was so weak, it could barely be made out. Eli'ssa adjusted Bahira's head on her lap.

"When I was young, mum would often go to the temples in Cartegin. Sometimes I would come with my sisters. Every time, I remember she would ask the priests if Enlil would heal my scars. They would say yes, and mother would ask them why Enlil hadn't done so."

"What...would they say?"

Eli'ssa smiled and shrugged.

"Oh, different things over the years. One time, as mother asked and the priest gave the usual answer, I had, em, a feeling. It was like a voice, but it seemed to be all around me. It promised me, '*Eli'ssa, I have a way for you.*'

'I don't know why, I thought I heard it again."

Bahira's eyes fluttered again with exhaustion, and she fell into slumber.

By late morning the sky was dark and gusts of wind howled through the sharp peaks. All of the captives were in fitful slumber. Splash! A large raindrop fell on Eli'ssa's forehead. It ran down her nose as she sat up. Another pattered against a nearby rock, followed by another.

"It's raining. OH, It's RAINING!" Eli'ssa cried, shaking Bahira until she gave a low moan. The Laḥmu jumped to their feet and a few other captives managed to sit up, looking around with bleary eyes. The largest Laḥmu flattened his ears and emitted a low reverberating growl.

He advanced toward Eli'ssa, the hair on his back bristling, but stopped as a large raindrop splashed on his nose. In an instant, water was pouring from the sky. The captives lifted their mouths and hands, crying out in joy. Water cascaded off the rocks. Sudden streams filled the rocky crags.

Eli'ssa helped Bahira to the nearest pool where she drank, choking in her haste as the life-giving water filled her. The girls found themselves laughing and smiling as they splashed water back and forth. Hope rose within them. Even the fear of the Laḥmu lessened as their hair grew matted, making them look thin and bedraggled. The Laḥmu were not pleased, and after a few brief moments, they herded the captives and continued on.

Though they were still dizzy from exhaustion and hunger, the rest of the day passed quickly. The rain faded in the early afternoon and the landscape leveled. The sharp rocks and mountains drew back to their right. Shrubs and trees grew intermittently. One resembled sage and had a sweet fragrance. Eli'ssa grabbed its leaves as she passed, sucking on them. She motioned for Bahira to do the same.

The group cleared a low rise and Eli'ssa pointed ahead.

"Look, Bahira! Do you see that?"

Bahira shaded her eyes. "I am so weak I can hardly see the ground before my feet."

"There is some sort of wall rising up, not a mile before us! I think we are almost to the end."

As they drew near, the object came into focus: two large plateaus of immense stone blocked the countryside. One was jagged and black, the other was sheer and red. Between them was a small space, as though the opposing colors of rock were loath to meet. Across this gap was built a tall palisade of interlocking sharp logs. On it gray men patrolled, and one of them blew two sharp blasts from a bull's horn. The Laḥmu yapped and quickened their pace, driving the captives toward the structure.

A tall gate opened as they approached, leading them into a dirt courtyard which stretched between the red and black stone cliffs. Another fence of less intimidating size stood some distance behind the first, and the weary group came to a panting halt before it. Twenty men stood there, wielding short spears fastened with bronze points. They all looked similar, with long, stern faces. Gray cloaks shrouded them and they parted, revealing a man of tall stature. He surveyed the group with hard eyes as the largest Laḥmu approached him.

"You are early, Swiftpad! We did not expect you until tomorrow morning," the Gray Watcher cried.

"Our pace was quick, Tizqar" the Laḥmu growled. "Much quicker than a *human* group could manage."

"Perhaps this is why there stands here only twenty and three that you bring me from Angfar," Tizqar snapped, swiftly counting the group. He turned his steely gaze upon the towering Laḥmu. "Are you not instructed to bring them here alive and in good condition? Yet you cannot even manage to carry out half of your orders."

"Do not think, Tizqar, that your status or sweet human words will keep you safe here. Angfar is a long way away. This is our country. Rumor is *they* are not pleased with your work here. They say that you are soft." The Laḥmu's lips curled back and his teeth glistened as he licked his chops.

Without warning, Tizqar raised his spear and quickly thrust its point into the fur of the Laḥmu's throat. It took a step back. The rest of the Laḥmu flattened their ears as they were quickly hedged in with spears and gray cloaks.

"Do not think to threaten me in my encampment, Swiftpad," menaced Tizqar with an ominous tone. "You have been here only a brief while and have already outworn your welcome. Go! Take your pack and return to your caves and rotting meat. Tell Angfar to send me usable captives if they desire more from me."

The beasts retreated slowly and fled out of the main gate. It was slammed and barred behind them. Bahira and Eli'ssa looked about. The outer palisade of logs was built along both the red and black plateau faces, running between the cleft to form a natural fortress. The main wall was paralleled some distance within by another fence of similar design, only shorter and thinner. Between the two walls stood several houses and buildings made of wood. Gray-faced men looked down from ramparts at every juncture.

"Stand!" Tizqar commanded the group. They looked at their new captors with a sense of relief and with a sense of fear. Bahira and Eli'ssa swayed as they clambered to their feet.

Tizqar walked among the prisoners, shaking his head as he did so. One of them could not remain on his feet and fell as Tizqar walked by. Tizqar was swift. Reaching out he caught the thin form and laid the man gently down to the dirt.

"Take them in," Tizqar ordered the gray figures around him. "Inform Guzzier that many are worse than expected. Tell him that if any need special attention to request for my aide. And, add a watch to the walls, I want no Laḥmu within a league of this place!!" With that he stormed away, up the stairs of the high wall, where he stood looking out over the captives and the countryside.

Chapter Four

<u>Slave Camp</u>

Bahira and Eli'ssa were ushered through a small gate. Behind it was a flat, open space. Shacks and lean-tos made of sticks, mud, and straw covered much of the area; a sharp contrast to the well-built structures that covered the courtyard they had left. Many curious faces looked at them from among the hovels. A tall outer wall could be seen on every side, hemming in the expanse, overshadowed by the contrasting bluffs of red and black.

Two of the gray-cloaked men disappeared through the huts and then returned leading a tall, black man. He wore little more than a lower covering of tattered cloth. His hair was short and his face was potted with black scars. Behind him, over a hundred people of various origins and ages, gathered. He nodded solemnly as the stern men in gray exchanged brief words with him, gesturing with their spears at the newcomers. Then, the Gray Watchers departed, leaving the huddled and weak captives in their new surroundings. The gate was closed, and the firm thud of a wooden beam being set over the door, resounded in their ears.

Its echoes had not died before the newcomers were met with helping hands. Kind words of reassurance and hope were murmured in their ears as they received sweet mush and water, carefully distributed out of clay jars. Litters were brought for those too weak to walk themselves.

Bahira and Eli'ssa scooped the sweet slop into their hands, eagerly shoveling it into their mouths. It filled them with strength. Slowly their minds sharpened and they looked up to see who served them. She was a thin, black woman of middle age. She laughed as they perceived her, revealing white teeth. The sound was as welcoming and friendly as if they had just arrived at home.

"Ah, there you are! And look! So beautiful, the both of you, even after your long journey. My friends, you should enjoy the splendor of your youth!" She chuckled and slowly drew the bowl away from their desperate hands with a playful smile. Eli'ssa raised a curious eyebrow at the woman, while Bahira quickly reached out for the bowl.

"Ah, Ah," the woman clucked, looking gently at Bahira. "Look about you, young one. Raise your mind off yourself! My Guzzier will teach you to be mindful of your body so it does not control your mind. Look up! Do you see these others in need? Almost all are worse off than you. You are fortunate. We are here to help. Quick, come with me so that you may eat away from this gate! The Gray Watchers observe us closely when we are near it. Come!"

She led them off to the side where a large lean-to was set up. It cast a delightful shade from the late evening sun. Some of the weakest were already there, and others were being carried in by strong hands. All were being tended and treated for their wounds.

"Em, what is this place?" Eli'ssa asked in amazement as the bowl of food was placed back in front of them.

"This is your home, for now, and we do our best to try and make it such," said a loud, deep voice behind her. The black man with the potted face approached and gestured for the girls to sit. Flakes of gray marked his stubble, but it was the only sign of age he possessed. His hands bore the marks of many seasons of toil.

"Rest, please," he insisted. "It has been many weeks since you have last done so." He smiled at the woman who tended them, lightly touching her shoulder before moving on.

"My name is Shukiera," the woman said softly. "Eat! Grow strong again! Find rest from your burdens for a moment." Shukiera had them both sit on woven mats as she poured clean water from a jar into a shallow basin. From a coarse sack she produced a dried herb which she crushed and mixed into the water. A poignant, yet, delicate fragrance wafted about them as Shukiera tilted back Bahira's head, and began washing the blood and grime from her matted hair.

"I think this is nothing more than oats soaked in water, but it is the best thing I have ever tasted," Bahira said around a mouthful. Eli'ssa nodded.

Many of those who had arrived with them were hardly able to open their mouths. Several choked as they tried to swallow food and water.

"The groups that come in from Angfar are always in the worst condition," Shukiera explained as the clean basin turned red under her hands. "Many do not make it the first night."

"Groups?" Bahira murmured, hardly able to speak from the pleasurable euphoria of a full belly and fragrant water cleaning her hair. "What do you mean?"

Shukiera grimaced, and then smiled a sad smile, as if the reminder of her true circumstances was a tightening throttle around some natural joy of life hiding deep within. With experienced fingers, she cleaned Bahira's arm, examining the closing wounds of the Laḥmu teeth for signs of infection; and Bahira's feet, checking for broken bones. Shukiera washed with the sweet-smelling sage, regularly needing to refresh the basin.

"You are the sixteenth group to come to us this season alone," Shukiera said as she worked. "For six years we have been here, me and my Guzzier. We are the oldest survivors of the climbs. You will learn more after you have rested and we will learn more about you. Close your eyes now and rest. You are safe."

It was dusk when Bahira and Eli'ssa were gently awakened. For the first time in many days they had clean faces and hair. They could see streaks of red and gold filling the western sky from under the awning where they lay; though the dark shadow of the outer wall, the men upon it, and the plateau beyond, blocked their view of the sun's setting. Shukiera stood over them.

"Please come with me," Shukiera beckoned. "Guzzier is ready to speak with all of you." She led them and several others out of the awning. A short distance away a large fire burned, sending sparks high into the darkening sky. Bahira's muscles ached, but she felt rested and curious. About twenty of their group from Angfar sat gathered around the flames. She noticed that several were missing. The black man with the potted face stood before the firelight.

"My friends, my name is Guzzier," he began in a deep, rolling voice. "It is likely that most of you do not know each other, where you are, or why you have been brought here. We now share the same fire and the same fate. I will answer as many of your questions as I can. You are, to the best of my knowledge, at the western and southern most edge of the S'adu Mountains and the eastern-most corner of the Mountains of Oodan. Here these two ranges meet." Guzzier gestured at the red and black plateaus shadowing either side of their camp.

"You are likely far from your homes. All of us were once where you now sit: confused, afraid, and alone. For me, it has been six, long years. I have survived. I still have hope. And I will help you to do the same.

'Captain Tizqar is commander over this encampment and he will come soon to give you the greeting he gives all newcomers. Do not ask him any questions! Do not speak to him or any of the Gray Watchers! They are a friendly respite from the fangs of the Laḥmu, but they are not your allies."

It looked as though Guzzier was about to say more, when suddenly a host of gray cloaks appeared out of the twilight. Tizqar himself stepped into the firelight, revealing his presence. Guzzier quickly bowed and backed away until he sat among the circle of captives.

Tizqar threw back his cloak. He carried a sharpened spear in one hand and in his leather belt was a keen, bronze dagger.

45

He slowly paced between the captives, studying their drawn, ragged forms in silence. The shadows lengthened and darkness crept in about them. Lastly, he paused at Bahira. His steely gaze bored into her and she cowered before he turned away.

"You have lost much," Tizqar finally whispered. His voice was barely loud enough to be heard, drawing those far away to lean closer. "You have lost your homes. Your livelihood. Your loved ones. Hear this: do not mourn over them!! For you will soon forget them!" His voice rose, harsh and savage as he finished - those nearest to him recoiled with surprise and fear. His eyes narrowed and his spear leveled at their faces.

"You are now in the encampment of the Gray Watchers!" Tizqar cried in a booming voice. "I promise you that if you stir up discord, attempt to flee, or attack my men, I will crush the lives from your very bones. If you do as I command, you may live. Cling to that hope. Guzzier will instruct you as to your tasks tomorrow. Be grateful I put you under his care."

He turned for the gate, but a hollow voice rose from a thin and balding man who reached out for his cloak as he passed.

"Um... Um, master, there must be some mistake. I am from Zoar, a follower of Tiamat. I set out to see three hundred head of Ibex that I purchased upon the northern fields and..." his voice wavered as Tizqar turned back into the firelight. Tizqar's eyes grew narrow and his grip tightened on his spear.

"Come here," ordered Tizqar, motioning with the butt of his ashen shaft. "I did not realize there was a misunderstanding."

The thin man swiftly rose from the circle of captives and scurried into the firelight.

"Thank you," he said, licking his lips. His eyes darted about him. "I am close partners in business with King Amri, he will be most... AHHGG!!" He screamed in pain as Tizqar's spear-shaft slammed into his left knee, shattering bone and tearing sinew. The man careened forward onto all fours. Bahira and Eli'ssa drew back in shock, while several others turned to run; but all were pushed back as gray cloaks appeared from the shadows like menacing ghouls.

Tizqar waited until the captives grew silent. Their eyes were wide in fear. The man at Tizqar's feet rocked, whimpering in pain.

"When you speak to me," Tizqar explained calmly, "you will do so from your knees. It is becoming of your position."

"Make no mistake!" Tizqar cried, turning to address the rest of the captives. "I care little about your circumstances. You are slaves of Angfar now. You will do what we say without question." He pushed over the man, so he fell on his side.

"No, please," the man begged, "I have a family. Little ones at home. Please..." Tizqar looked at him coldly.

"It would be best for you to listen more attentively when I speak. Do you not remember what I just commanded? Do not mourn. You will soon forget them." He struck the man sharply on the head with a jeweled fist before turning away. The Gray Watchers closed in about their leader. One kicked the man backward with a heavy boot so that he rolled half in the blazing fire. The troop streamed through the gate and secured it soundly behind them.

Guzzier bit his tongue. As soon as the last gray cloak had turned away, he leapt forward, pulling the man from the flames while calling out behind him in an urgent voice.

"Kah-Mel! Bandages, if we have any, and water, quickly. Bring some of the *fela* leaves, if any remain! If not, the bark will do. Someone douse this fire!"

Shukiera ushered Bahira and Eli'ssa away, leading them and the remaining new captives toward the far end of the encampment as others ran to do Guzzier's bidding.

The moon was still bright and fell among many rows of thatched huts. In each hovel, mats of dried thatch were rolled out upon the ground and a jar of fresh water sat prepped for bathing.

"Everything will be ok now. Just rest," Shukiera assured them as she left. "Don't be afraid. A new day is coming."

Bahira collapsed on her mat and felt as though she was living in a waking nightmare. Assailants surrounded her on every side. When she shut her eyes the horrors she had witnessed flashed before them, worse than the reality of the present. Suddenly she found herself sobbing uncontrollably. Eli'ssa came beside her, and together they wept until the night enveloped them with its quiet embrace.

They awoke late the next morning. They might have stayed in the safety of the thatched hut had not Shukiera come. She gently led them out and took them back toward the center of the camp.

"Guzzier and I will take you about the camp today, and show you your tasks. Tizqar will not allow you to sleep as long again, you will awake early with the rest of us."

"I do not understand him," Eli'ssa said confused, glancing quickly at the Gray Watchers patrolling the high border of the palisade. "Why does he seem kind one moment and so horrible the next?"

Shukiera scooped the sweet-smelling porridge onto clay platters and handed it to them.

"The Gray Watchers are not from Angfar. They are bought as mercenaries to do another's will. Tizqar knows we will complete what he needs quicker if we do it of our own resolve. But he is not afraid to show the boundaries of our freedom, with our blood if need be."

"What is it that we are used for?" Bahira asked, her voice slightly trembling.

"Nothing worth being afraid of, my dear," Shukiera assured kindly.

"At least, not at the moment." She gestured to a far corner of the camp. "Come with me and I'll show you." She turned and led them back into the vicinity of the gate they had entered the previous day. Underneath two large awnings over thirty women sat, working with nimble toes and fingers.

"Here the weavers work, and it is where you will be the most. We peel and dry the bark of the *fela* sage, weaving them into these." She held up a piece of thick rope in one hand and a large, brown sack in another. Each smelled faintly of the same herb that covered the hills. They followed Shukiera as she proceeded around the camp's edge. Ever the outer wall loomed, shadowed by the mighty cliffs of black and red. Gray-cloaked figures looked down on them. A rumbling sound became louder and louder as they moved west.

"Over here are the grinding mills." Shukiera gestured to six, tall structures that stood at the far end of the camp. Each building was two stories of roughly planked wood, which stood connected to the interior fence. The bottom levels were barred off from them, but a flight of stairs ran up the outer side of each to a second-floor entrance.

"Forty-eight man these at a time, eight to a mill," Shukiera explained, pointing to each structure in turn. "Everyone takes a shift here during the day, though Guzzier will keep the men here the longest. He rotates them every hour, for it is hard labor."

Bahira had to shout to be heard above the rumbling din, "What are they doing?"

Shukiera beckoned for them to draw nearer until they were underneath the closest structure. The fence blocked them from going any further, and they peered through its cracks. It was dark under the mill and the rumbling echoed down to their toes. Directly ahead and out of reach through the fence, a round stone was mounted upon a wide, circular table of granite. The table was easily the size of the hut they had slept in the night before, and the stone upon it was twice the girls' height. A deep groove ran about the edge of the table. In this groove, the stone rumbled around, powered by a large shaft of wood driven through the floor above their heads.

Bahira and Eli'ssa blinked, staring in amazement, for the groove of the table was filled with a mystic light. Glowing blues, greens, and purples rippled like water and danced across the walls as the stone passed through. Eli'ssa jumped backward as she noticed a Gray Watcher staring at them from the shadows.

They backed away and Shukiera laughed at their dazzled faces.

"It is beautiful, is it not? Above us eight men push a turnstile which moves the rock. Each of these here are the same," she said, pointing at each grinding mill.

"Oh, what is it?" Eli'ssa asked in awe, looking back where the sticks of the wall now blocked their vision. "The light, I mean - what was that?"

"It was not long enough to see!" Bahira insisted, turning her head to try and get another view. "It was the most beautiful thing I have ever beheld. I wish to see it again." She stepped forward but was stopped by Shukiera's outstretched arm.

"The Gray Watchers will beat you if you idle here or if you are seen looking upon the light too long." She sighed, looking out over the high walls toward the Red Mountains. Her hands guided their unwilling forms back into the camp, where the noise of the mill was less.

"Near the center of our camp is the water well. Four of us take shifts, raising water and taking them to the grinding mills. The stones must be kept wet and the shacks get hot quickly, the men also need to drink."

"Why?" Bahira asked, stopping sharply. "I was taken from my home. My brother was killed. Why are we here? What is all this?" She felt tears rising to her face and her cheeks flushed.

Shukiera's face fell, "I am sorry," she whispered. "You must understand, Bahira, so were we all. We have all lost our homes. None of us have all the answers. What you saw are what we call the crystals of Oodan. Our purpose here revolves around them. Every three months we are taken and marched west and north, deep into the Red Mountains. The journey takes many weeks. There we are forced to climb the crags to the nests of the flying S'acar. We take their eggs. Everyone must bring back ten. If you do not, you are left there to die."

She spoke as though in great pain. She shook her head, offering them a small smile.

"My Guzzier grew up close to the borders of the Oodan Mountains and he knows something of the S'acar. They are fierce and their stabbing beaks are deadly; but he is a mighty man. For six years, we have been captives here and for six years he has brought back twenty eggs every journey: ten to ensure my freedom and ten for him. It is for this reason that I am still alive. Kah-Mel is the second longest survivor, he has made it almost a full year now. No one else has survived this camp more than a cycle of the seasons."

"You have seen many people come and die here," Eli'ssa surmised, looking at Shukiera hard. "Each new friend you make, you expect to lose shortly thereafter."

Shukiera did not answer at first, her head bowed in silence.

"Yes," she finally murmured. "Almost all die on every journey. They are replaced in the following months by groups from Angfar. You wish to know your purpose here? That is what it is."

"And when you return from the high crags, you take these eggs and crush them? Is that where the light comes from?" Bahira asked.

"They are more beautiful whole, upon the high crags," Shukiera whispered. "Yes, there is something magnificent about them. We are not allowed to touch them from the moment we descend. They grow harder with time, until only the stone mill has the strength to break them. Once they are crushed, they form crystals and are put into the satchels we weave. Tizqar and his men take them and send them to Angfar. We do not see them again except briefly through the wall, as we did today.

'In the land where I am from, the egg of S'acar could heal the sick and give sight to the blind. Even one was more precious than any item one possessed. I never saw one until I first met Guzzier." She looked as though she would say more, but trailed off into silence.

"For years before I was captured, people would go missing if they ventured too far from the borders. It seemed our village grew smaller and smaller, and then Angfar came for all of us."

"What is happening in Angfar?" Eli'ssa asked grimly. "Who could do this?"

Shukiera shook her head. "I have never been to Angfar. For six years Angfar has taken everything from us. That is all I know," she finished.

"When is the camp to be sent out again?" Eli'ssa inquired.

"In two weeks' time," Shukiera answered, but she beckoned for them to draw their heads near. "Do not be filled with despair," she whispered urgently. Hope and determination sparkled from her eyes. "We have been planning something for a long time now. Guzzier says we are almost ready. We will act soon! Say nothing. Guzzier will tell you more when he is prepared."

Chapter Five

A Hidden Trainer

The girls spent the remainder of the day among the weavers near the gate. Eli'ssa quickly learned to make the braid of the ropes tight and strong, while Bahira pulled green bark from the limbs of the sweet sage. Shukiera hummed a melody in a language they did not recognize as she went here and there, switching out weavers and water-fetchers.

By the time the day came to an end, their hands were sore and the space between Eli'ssa foot and big-toe were raw from gripping the fibrous strands. The evening deepened, and the sun fell. Nearly two hundred slaves gathered together in the open space before the main gate. Ten large fires were lit and jars of steaming porridge were passed around to every hand. Bahira and Eli'ssa sat next to the most central fire. Shukiera and Guzzier came and ate with them. Guzzier asked each of them their tale of woe and he listened, nodding as Eli'ssa told him of their journey.

"Your story, Eli'ssa, is all too common," Guzzier exclaimed. "Many have been deceived and are now enslaved from the cities on the plains. Curse their treachery!"

Guzzier turned his gaze on Bahira. "It is rare that one from the Urudu makes it all this way. I can remember only one or two in my time."

Bahira offered no more of her journey and was silent. Guzzier paused thoughtfully. "I can see the pain of your journey is deep, Bahira. Will you not tell us of it? Tell us of your loves and losses, your home and your history. Share your burden here with us around the fire. Such is the way of my people."

Bahira stared into the fire, un-answering.

"What of you?" Bahira finally asked. "You speak the common tongue well, though I have only once seen a face as dark as yours and Shukiera's, and it was upon the Urudu ship I was taken upon."

Guzzier laughed a little. "Ah, my Shukiera and I have known each other long. We are from El-Loz, near the great salt flats not far from here. Never did I think I could win her over to me! For she was the most precious gem of our land and captured the eye of everyone. Little did I know we would find ourselves here, perhaps the only place I could win her heart." Shukiera smiled and laid her head on his shoulder.

"I would have chosen you in any land," Shukiera promised.

"In your land are not the women paired to a man, chosen by the household leaders?" Bahira asked in amazement.

Guzzier threw back his head and roared with laughter.

"As if Shukiera could be given to any man without her leave! No, our women choose a man as they please. They hunt with our warriors and many are renowned for their speed and agility. Is it not so where you are from, far south where you say the land is covered with green mountains and the people are pale? Many are the strange things I hear from those far-off places, but this one is by far the most interesting!"

At this Bahira fell quiet once more, and fresh tears came to her eyes. Guzzier looked at her thoughtfully. Eli'ssa gently stroked her hair, while Guzzier opened his mouth as if to speak. Shukiera's light touch restrained him, and he let Bahira rest in silence.

Soon the embers of the fires glowed brightly and the stars grew in glory overhead. Guzzier's deep voice rolled out over the encampment and a small hand-drum was produced that carried a pounding rhythm.

"Upon the shores of Par'adam, there the ancient water rose in fathoms

Cutting caves and caverns deep, burying those for whom none weep.

The citadel of stone, red with blood, washed clean in the mighty flood.

But high above the fortress' reach, above the mountains and the keep

There the altar of El'Perran, risen high of stone and crystal sand.

Egal-Mah, the Lord of Old, touched the floor of red and gold

S'acar came forth, bound no more, to the dust which was his home.

Oodan! He cried, and bespoke the name, which freed of old the earth's

deep chain.

The land rose, quaked and fell. He took to flight while men befell

The ancient hills and forts of sand: the home of S'acar, the Par'adam."

Suddenly, Guzzier was up on his feet and dancing, around one fire and then onto the next. As one, the people joined him! Jumping, clapping and moving until all but the newcomers twirled between the flames!

Bahira and Eli'ssa watched them in amazement, smiles playing on their faces.

At times it seemed Guzzier moved as fast as lightning, ducking and rolling, weaving and shaking his hands. He spun his body as he rose and fell, swinging his elbows and fists in swirling patterns. His legs kicked out in time with the drum. The others followed his motions, creating a chorus of shaking feet and clapping hands. The rocky earth trembled in unison. Shukiera rose and joined, but Bahira and Eli'ssa stayed near the fires, lost in the winding rhythm of drums and limbs.

The looming shadow of the outer wall rose above the firelight and Bahira could see the outlines of the Gray Watchers, surveying all. Shukiera eventually collapsed beside them, panting, and she followed their gaze to the forms beyond the firelight.

"You needn't worry," she whispered. "Tizqar seldom comes in here. His point yesterday was to make an impression. Guzzier has us do our work well. Tizqar gives him much freedom for it and we do not disappoint him."

Bahira slept easier that night. She felt that she had hardly laid down when Shukiera was shaking her gently.

"It is the start of the day," she announced softly. "Awake! Today will be your first full day with us. Come, eat, and then we must begin." Eli'ssa and Bahira stumbled out into the cool morning, wiping the sleep from their eyes. The sky was light pink, the sun had not yet risen.

They started the day much as before, peeling and weaving the thick fibrous ropes. By midday they were faster, but their hands and feet were raw with labor. While they eased the pain of their sores in jars of cooling mud, Shukiera came to them.

"It is time for you to learn the crushing mill," she said. "It will give your blisters a brief respite, though it is hard elsewhere on the body. You will be with Guzzier and he will show you what to do."

She gave them each a bladder of freshwater and led them to the mill where they had been the previous day. Again, Bahira turned her neck, trying to see between the thick, wooden pillars of the lower chamber; but she could not see any light from the Oodan crystals. The rumbling of the great stone filled their ears, vibrating through their legs as they walked up the steep wooden steps and into the upper room.

The heat of the chamber was stifling. A dim light filtered in through cracks in the structure revealing eight men, bare-chested in the heat. Four thick beams formed the turnstile. Two men pushed against each, pouring sweat as they strained against it in a great circle. Bahira and Eli'ssa recognized Guzzier among them. He and two others stepped aside as they entered. He drank long from the bladder Shukiera offered him before placing it near the door. She departed with a smile and the two men left with her.

53

Guzzier shouted to be heard above the rumbling din. "You will not be here long, it is good to give us some respite! Here the task is simpler and, well, more circular than you will be used to!"

He beckoned for the girls to come closer until they were right next to the great turnstile. It did not turn with much speed; but the men who pushed it grunted, their muscles fighting the great weight of the stone below. Guzzier positioned the girls on an empty beam as it rumbled by and slipped into the open spot ahead of them. He turned to face them, pushing with his back braced against the beam. Guzzier flashed them a wide smile and the girls chuckled at his antics.

"Push!" he cried. "Push! But keep your ears and eyes open. Here alone can we talk without fear of being overheard. You must listen well, for you do not have much time."

The girls leaned forward, as they pushed, eager to hear what Guzzier had to say.

"In two weeks, the camp will break and make for the Mountains of Oodan. There we will harvest the eggs of S'acar and more than half of you will die. I do not intend to let that happen! Long have I planned, though always the time was not ripe. Never did we have enough people and never did we have enough survivors who knew. Now, I think, we finally do. It is time we make our move."

"Move? What is that?" shouted Eli'ssa. "Are we to escape?"

Guzzier nodded his head. The man pushing beside Guzzier turned, facing the girls as well.

"My name is Kah-Mel. I have been with Guzzier the longest. Six trips I have made with him into the Mountains and on each I feared I would never return. No more! I will not go again. It is time we go home."

"How? How are we to do that?" Bahira asked.

"We are going to fight," Guzzier answered. "We outnumber the Gray Watchers three-fold! Is the man who is outnumbered three times in charge of his own fate? No, it is the other way around."

"How can we fight?" Eli'ssa wondered. "We do not have your strength, nor do many of the people here. How are we to overcome the Gray Watchers unarmed and unskilled?"

"There must be another way," Bahira's face was crestfallen. "Could we not flee into the mountains, or take some other path by night on the trek? Shukiera said it was a long journey."

Round and round they walked, sweat soaking their clothes as the great rumbling continued.

Guzzier shook his head. "I have been trapped here for six years my friends, I know the ways and the routes we take well. There is no way out of the Red Mountain gorge once you enter! There is no better way, though I wish there was. We must make our stand here."

"Guzzier is not as he appears," Kah-Mel interjected. "He tells many that when he was free, he was a carpenter, a worker and shaper of wood. That was not all. I too lived in the lands around El-Loz. Guzzier was a renowned hunter, a warrior, and a trainer. Many sought him out to learn his ways. He teaches us now."

"You have much to learn and you do not have much time," pointed out Guzzier quickly. "If we are to succeed, we must do so together. Together we have strength. You must watch me closely and follow my ways. Here, at the stone wheel, and each night around the fires we train! You must join us."

"Around the fires?" Bahira asked quizzically. "As you all did last night? I was there! You were all dancing."

Guzzier flashed her another smile. He and Kah-Mel turned around, pushing with their arms.

"That may be what it seemed," he cried. "Watch us again tonight. Tomorrow you and the rest of the new ones will join us here for two hours a day until you know the most basic of motions and are strong. Leave us now! Go back to your weaving and rest. Remember, do not speak of this outside these rooms, or you will kill us all."

Bahira and Eli'ssa worked in silence throughout the day, thinking about Guzzier's words. Doubt filled Bahira's mind every time she saw the Gray Watchers, stern and vigilant upon the wall. Their spears looked sharper and shields thicker than before. Night fell, and like the previous day, the entire camp gathered together in the open space. The cool of the dark was refreshing after the day's heat. Bahira and Eli'ssa were glad to stretch out their sore limbs. Soon the fires were lit and it was not long before Guzzier was up and dancing about them. Almost all the encampment danced with him, sometimes in lines and other times in a mad array around the fires. Only a few of the newest group stayed behind.

Bahira watched them closely as the hand-drums throbbed. Guzzier seemed a blur of motion: turning, twisting, moving sideways and forward. Doubt again filled her mind. She could not see how this would help defeat their captors. But, as Guzzier danced she saw one of the distant Gray Watchers silhouetted against the fading sky. He was far removed from where Guzzier danced, but from where she lay it looked as if they stood head-to-head: the spear-carrying watcher and Guzzier. Suddenly, Guzzier stepped sideways and advanced. His fist cut through the air where the neck of the Gray Watcher stood. In the same moment his hands rose, clasping the air exactly where the haft of the spear would have been. His hands spun as his body lowered and turned, and Bahira saw in her mind's eye the spear come free even as it ran through the Gray Watcher in the blink of an eye.

She sat up sharply, blinking as Guzzier and the crowd about her continued their lively dance. She did not notice Shukiera looking at her intently from across the fire. Shukiera rose and came near to her.

"Come!" Shukiera invited, reaching down and taking Bahira's hand in her own. "You see clearly. Do not be afraid! Come and dance with me!"

Eli'ssa jumped up as well and the three spun around the fires. They found themselves right next to Guzzier and they laughed, for it seemed impossible to follow his movements. The tune was merry, and as their feet moved in time with the rest, their hearts were free to feel joy - something neither of them had felt in a long time.

Bahira collapsed by the warm fire long before the camp had finished their dance. Eli'ssa came to be with her. The stars wheeled overhead, shadowy flames shifted across the distant red crags, and Bahira and Eli'ssa drifted off into slumber.

When they awoke, the fires were low embers. They were alone, and both hastily stood, uneasy in the silent, open expanse. They shook their stiff limbs and hurriedly walked back among the thatched huts, toward the safety of their own.

Whispered voices caused them to slow as they passed through the shadows.

"Eli'ssa is strong. She'll join us without fear, I have no doubt." The low rumble of Guzzier's voice could be discerned.

"You worry for Bahira," a female voice spoke.

There was a pause.

"I see in both of them something the others lack. A ray of hope that has yet been quenched. Yet, Bahira... it is plain she comes from a wealthy family. This trial is hard for any, but I fear Bahira would have perished long ago were it not for Eli'ssa."

"Yet to make it here, from the ships of the Urudu, unscathed as she is?" Shukiera's voice whispered in reply. "You and I know that no such thing happens of its own!"

"Has she told you more of who she is or where she comes? She is not an agent of Angfar," Guzzier said fervently. "I would feel such a thing about her! Instead I feel only loss and sadness."

"It is not what I meant," Shukiera added hastily. "Eli'ssa clearly knows more of her. They have talked much in secret."

"Why is it that all the lands in the south seem to be the same? They strive after bronze and weapons, they build walls and alliances... and they forget what is actually worth fighting to protect. For Bahira to share her heart is a *struggle*! She has hidden herself away and succumbed to another's will for her life for so many years she has forgotten what it means to be free, except in those secret recesses of her mind."

"I see strength in Bahira," Shukiera whispered. "Though she is proud. She sees her loss as great. Though too many around her now, like Eli'ssa, those losses are no strange thing. Eli'ssa has been fighting to survive her whole life! Bahira is learning this, and re-learning the world, and it is hard for her to bear."

"We all must relearn what we think we know, especially in the hard times. Perhaps now, here at the end of the world, with Eli'ssa, she will understand."

"We will give them all we have, and perhaps when the gray men are overthrown, we'll fill the water jars and return home."

Guzzier was silent.

"El-loz lays close to Angfar. You know this," he whispered sadly.

Shukiera sighed.

"What is in those black mountains? And why does Angfar seek the Eggs of Oodan and our lives to purchase them?"

"If only we knew! If we could solve this riddle! I seek answers from all who come here, I have found none that are complete. Just loss and pain and death, from every corner of the world, it seems. Whatever is growing in Angfar, it is strong. Its influence, vast! Oh, the peril of our escape weighs upon me. I fear that no matter what happens many will not have a home to return to."

Their voices dropped, and Bahira unwillingly let Eli'ssa pull her away into the quiet of their own hovel.

The next day, they were sent to the crushing mill early in the day. It was still cool and they were not surprised to find Guzzier in the loud room, waiting for them as he pushed the great stone wheel. Five others pushed with him.

"Today we begin," he said. "You have less than two weeks to become strong and fast, I will show you how." Turning back to the great wheel he chirped loudly. All six men stepped out and forward in unison, switching places in a weaving pattern. They moved quicker than the eye could follow, smoothly pushing the turn-style with the edge of their forearms as they transitioned.

"You will have little time with the Gray Watchers," Guzzier explained. "You must move first and quickly: step outside of his spear thrust! To his weak side! Then *he* will be trying to catch up to *you*. His mind will change to that of a defender, you will become the attacker. That is the first and most powerful skill! Control their mind, and then overpower their senses."

And so they moved. Slowly at first, then quicker as their feet learned to slide around the steadily rotating beams of wood. Guzzier and Kah-Mel coached them, raising their hands and positioning their bodies, telling them where to look and when to breathe. They pushed the great stone wheel continuously, and after an hour Bahira and Eli'ssa were exhausted.

Guzzier sent them back to Shukiera and others came to take their place.

"I have never felt this many sore muscles on my whole body!" Bahira exclaimed to Eli'ssa, as they sat in the weaver's awning. Eli'ssa nodded, stretching out her neck with a grimace.

"Oh, I did not know these many muscles existed," she groaned.

That night, they danced with Guzzier. They felt slow and uncoordinated. Yet, as the encampment twisted and turned, stamping their feet and raising their hands, they recognized and understood some of the patterns that the people wove.

Time seemed to pass swiftly. Every morning they rose before the sun and long after dark, they collapsed on their thin mats. It was amazing to Bahira how much they learned and how quickly their motions became smooth and in-time with the other captives. She rubbed the calluses forming on her palms. They learned that many of the captives had been there just a few weeks longer than her group, while the majority had been there only a few months.

It seemed that every waking moment of thought was bent on escape. Even at night, Bahira's dreams were filled with captives storming over the wall, against the unseeing watchers. Within a week, almost all of the new-comers blended into the dance seamlessly. There was much they did not know, and Bahira still shuddered at the thought of having a real Gray Watcher before her.

"You must be confident," Guzzier encouraged the next day at the grinding mill. "You must trust your body. When you get ahead of the Gray Watchers, you must stay there. Remember what you have learned! Step off your foe's center-line! Strike his eyes and ears! Overwhelm his mind, *then* defeat his body. In two days, we make our move or travel again to the mountains. That must not happen! All must fight, when the fighting begins. None must hang back! Though I desire your safety, even more do I desire freedom from this place. One person could change the tide of the battle when it begins. Trust me! Follow my lead. I will start, we all must follow."

That night there was no dancing. Tizqar entered the camp unexpectedly at dusk, surrounded by his Gray Watchers. He marched to Guzzier's hut. Bahira and Eli'ssa watched them pass nervously. He was not with Guzzier long before the Gray Watchers returned to the outer wall.

Guzzier appeared and the captives crowded around him.

"Tizqar has spoken: tomorrow we leave for the Red Mountains of Oodan. That means tonight we must get ready. Pile the rope so they may be easily carried, fill the water jars, bladders, and grain sacks for the journey."

He paused and looked across the many faces. He took a deep breath.

"And be ready. Follow my lead," he whispered.

Chapter Six

<u>The Uprising</u>

Dusk deepened as the women worked near the main gate, stacking the completed ropes into bundles. Shukiera looked about nervously, always searching for Guzzier; but he was going back and forth with the men - filling jars of water and placing them near the wall.

"What are we waiting for? What is the signal?" Eli'ssa whispered as she passed.

"Just follow my lead," Shukiera whispered back. "Guzzier will give us an advantage, then we must be swift. Keep the ropes close at hand!"

The darkness of night enveloped the camp. Bahira's hands trembled as she stacked rope. Eli'ssa seemed calm beside her, gazing at the stars above.

"Oh, summer is almost over," she remarked. "The ship and the bull of heaven rise lower and lower, time has passed so very quickly. It feels like just yesterday we made ready to depart from Cartegin. How I miss the refreshing waters of the Dan-Jor and my sisters' laughter as they play beside its shore!" She closed her eyes, remembering.

"Are you not afraid?" Bahira asked.

Eli'ssa chuckled and turned back to coiling her pile of long rope.

"Oh, I am terrified. But I would much rather die here among my friends than far away, alone upon a mountain-side. And if we win, then perhaps I can go and find my family." Her eyes blazed with hope. Bahira set her jaw and her hands grew still.

Just then, a shout echoed from the outer wall and a dull horn rang out in alarm. Abruptly, the sky grew brighter. Tall flames leapt up from the far side of the camp, barely visible over the small huts, but quickly growing.

"This is it!" Shukiera cried, grasping a rope firmly. "Wait! Wait for my Guzzier! Do nothing yet! Stand still!"

Time seemed to trickle by as the thudding of the Gray Watchers' heavy boots dissipated around the outer wall. Suddenly, from the shadow of the licking flames, ran the bold form of Guzzier. Over a hundred and fifty men were at his back, grasping tall sticks of wood tipped with shards of clay jars. In their other hand they carried thickly matted shields of thatch, speedily lashed together from the roofs of huts and bedding mats.

"My friends!" he cried, running forward, "Now! With me! For those you have lost! For the life you will yet live!! FORWARD!! *O'GLA SATAR!!!*" The men behind him cried out and the sound of their battle cry shook the walls as every person of the camp fell in behind him.

"Now!" Shukiera yelled! The women picked up the heavy ropes and ran toward the main gate.

"Throw! Throw the ends over the wall!" Ten, twenty, almost thirty of the ropes cleared the short wall and fell into the empty courtyard beyond! Their fibrous cords twisted and snagged on the jagged wooden tops as Guzzier and his force joined them.

Horns of the Gray Watchers called out in the darkness. Somewhere behind them a mighty explosion shattered the night, shaking the timbers with its force. Flames soared even higher, the bright light flickered on the small, wooden picket ahead and the mighty outer wall in the yard beyond. Spears now fell among them and one or two cried out, but Guzzier was not dismayed.

"Every hand to a rope!!" he commanded in a loud voice. "Heave! Heave! HEAVE!"

The ropes strained and stretched, the picket fence wobbled, and then at once the gateposts snapped and the whole of the wooden section fell into the camp.

"Now! Fight for your freedom!" Guzzier cried. Like a thundering bull, he charged through the dark opening and into the courtyard between the two walls. A Gray Watcher suddenly appeared out of the shadows. The Watcher opened his mouth to issue a command, but none came forth. Guzzier spun about his enemy's spear and landed a mighty blow to the side of the Watcher's throat before he could speak. He crumpled where he stood and Guzzier picked up his fallen spear. Other gray faces appeared, hemming him in. There was the sound of many running feet and the slapping of spear-haft against spear-half.

Guzzier was not alone. The entire encampment surged forward with a great cry and there was battle in the yard! Kah-Mel tackled into a group of foes as they tried to make formation and knocked them about, smacking heads and limbs with a thick shaft of wood. Guzzier stabbed this way and that with his spear and other captives bent to pick up the weapons of their fallen enemies.

Bahira followed with the surge of bodies into the courtyard. The clashing of wood and the hoarse cries of battle rose around her. Without warning, a stern face appeared through the chaos. His gray cloak was thrown back and a sharp spear, bloodied and stained, was clasped firmly in his hands. He charged her with a shout! Bahira froze, unable to move as he closed the gap. She tried to think of what Guzzier had said, but all that filled her mind was the bloodied tip of the bronze spear, flickering in the distant firelight.

"AHHYYAA!!" A shrill cry broke Bahira's stillness. Eli'ssa appeared from the smoke and dust, smashing a piece of timber over the Gray Watchers shoulder and knocking him from his course, even as his spear passed within inches of Bahira's face. Shukiera appeared behind her, wielding a thick piece of knotted rope. She swung it about her head and fell upon the dazed man, beating his face and head with such a furry he collapsed upon his backside. His spear fell from his shaking hands. As Bahira swiftly picked up the weapon, he scooted away and vanished into the darkness.

There seemed to be five or six slaves who attacked every Gray Watcher. Quickly their captors were pushed back. A second explosion resonated from the far side of the camp and new, bright flames licked into the night.

"Kah-Mel! Around the perimeter! Forward to the stone mills! The rest of you, up the wall! With me!" cried Guzzier. Thirty men followed behind him, some armed with spears and others still with bloodied logs and flaming brands. Guzzier mounted the steps to the outer wall's ramparts. He ducked under a spear thrust from a Gray Watcher and tossed its owner off the side of the high wall as fluidly as if he were dancing. There was a sickening thump below.

"Follow me!" Kah-Mel called to those that remained. He raised his smoking brand and charged into the shadow of the wall. Shukiera and the rest followed him, still several hundred strong. They passed well-built log and stone buildings that had been raised between the two palisades. Some were held against them, and these they lit on fire until their occupants fell out, coughing and choking. Others were barricaded inside as the flames consumed them.

At one point a group of Gray Watchers hid until the majority of the captives passed by - then they sprung out from the darkness, falling upon the captives' rear where the most timid walked. Many fell. The ground was thick with blood by the time Guzzier saw their peril and threw spears from above to end the Watchers' rampage.

They moved forward slower after that, making sure to check every building and dark corner. Bahira and Eli'ssa stayed close to Shukiera. Often Gray Watchers would appear from the darkness. While the men struggled to overcome them, Bahira, Eli'ssa, and Shukiera would dart behind, overwhelming them until they fell to the earth.

The great stone mills suddenly rose above, the farthest two still smoldering in flames. Bahira looked about her in shock: they had made it almost completely around the perimeter to the far side. The stars above were growing dim and the horizon behind was growing brighter.

Kah-Mel came to a halt, raising his hand for those following him to grow quiet. Before them, the outer-wall made its final curve, pulling away from the red plateau. Ahead stood the rear gate. It was held against them. Tizqar stood among all that remained of his men. They were in tight formation directly within the exterior gate. Their spears bristled above their shields in the low light, creating a deadly hedge that could not be passed.

Guzzier walked half-way down the final flight of steps of the outer wall and stopped.

"Tizqar!" he challenged, brandishing his spear. "Order your men to lay down their weapons. The fight is over, no more of you remain."

Tizqar stepped boldly forward. His face was smeared with dust, but his eyes were firm.

"Nay, Guzzier! You have not thought this through. You have played my trust, Guzzier, and risen against me! What wrong have I done you, in the years that you have been among us? Look! Look at the blood you have spilled this night. We are not the Laḥmu! These men and women will never rise again. And for what? There is no escape to be had. You can still come out of this victorious, Guzzier. I cannot let you pass, but turn around! Go back through the main gate! Then you will be free to go where you will."

"I am no fool, Tizqar" growled Guzzier. "There is no escape that way, except to go back to Angfar. Do not play your words on me! Does the master who orders his servants to kill and skin the boar for his table do no hurt to the pig? Does the son who bears the knife at the request of his father keep his hands clean? You are guilty both ways, Tizqar!" Guzzier shouted. "Thousands have I seen go to the depths of Sheol, hounded by your men's spears. You try to lay claim to be better than dogs who eat the flesh of men! Look how low you have fallen, to even try and compare yourself to such things."

Tizqar's face fell as Guzzier talked. He let his words settle on Tizqar as the sky grew lighter.

"Throw down your weapons, gray men!" Guzzier commanded. "You are outnumbered twenty to one. Throw down your weapons or face your fate."

Tizqar shook his head. "The Gray Watchers are men of pride, Guzzier. We will not let you pass before we run each and every one of you through with our spears! Such is the oath we gave."

"So be it!" Kah-Mel cried out from below. "Such is the judgement you have brought upon yourself. Death! For the death you have wrought among our people."

Tizqar bowed to his adversaries before stepping back into his line, which closed in about him until he was but one more gray cloak in the link of spears and shields.

"Wait!" cried Guzzier as Kah-Mel and his forces encircled the gate. "Wait!" he commanded again. "Shukiera! Go, take some with you and fetch the long ropes. Bring them here. Kah-Mel, hold the Gray Watchers fast! If they try and advance from the gate, let them. Then encircle them and deal out your justice."

Shukiera came back quickly and Guzzier had the ropes tied and let down over the outer-wall from the high walkway.

"What is this, Guzzier!" shouted Tizqar. "Are you to run away instead of face us in battle? You are a coward! There is no honor to be gained from that!"

"Come and give us battle!!" the Gray Watchers taunted, clashing their spears and shields together.

Shukiera halted, holding the rope in her hand, about to scale the wall. Guzzier looked at the faces of the remaining captives and held up his hands.

"You may still hold some illusion of honor, Tizqar," Guzzier said slowly. "But we, my people, we have nothing except the desire to see the homes and families you have taken from us. If you wish for honor, then I have some for you."

Turning, Guzzier threw his spear down among the Gray Watchers with such force and accuracy that it struck the shaft in Tizqar's hand, shearing it in half before pinning his shield down into the dust.

Tizqar fell back, struggling to pull his arm from the pierced shield. He looked at the broken spear in his hand with amazement. Guzzier jumped down the steps from above, landing directly in front of the Gray Watchers.

Guzzier held open his empty hands. "Is honor what you seek, Tizqar? Long has it been since you have had any. You assume I am a slave, dull and weak, and that you are strong. So are the battles that you have long chosen. Come and show me what honor means to you now, man to man."

Tizqar rose shakily to his feet and stood unmoving. The sky faded from gray into the pink of morning. Guzzier's eyes were hard, but sadness filled his voice. Tizqar hesitated and he opened his mouth to reply: no answer came. Instead a howl echoed forth, rising on the wind from behind them. High it pierced and sharp it fell. Nobody moved. Suddenly, it was joined by many others and it seemed that hundreds of howling voices closed in upon them. A sharp crying filled the air, accompanied by dark swooping forms - birds of carrion, hungry, following the pack.

It was hard to tell who looked more afraid: Guzzier or Tizqar.

"Everyone! Quickly up and over the wall!" Guzzier cried out.

But it was too late.

From around the corner came the Laḥmu. They were numerous, as though several packs had come together. Behind them ran countless savage men dressed in black, bearing clubs and maces of stone. There was no escape.

Shukiera grabbed Bahira and Eli'ssa, dragging them with her near the outer-wall. There they huddled together as the Laḥmu charged into the ranks of captives, plowing them over with their great girth before tearing into the fallen with bared fangs. Screams rose, chilling the hearts of those farther ahead.

Many of the Laḥmu fell, pierced by spears, but still they came on. The smell of blood filled their nostrils and several charged into what remained of the Gray Watchers as they slay in a frenzy. Suddenly, a piercing whistle rang out and everything ceased. From around the corner of the inner yard appeared a wide palanquin carried by six slaves. Laying upon it was the largest man Bahira had ever seen. His face was swollen in many places and his fingers were fat and thick. A wooden whistle was in his mouth and the Laḥmu drew back at his call. Swiftpad, chief of the Laḥmu, sat at the foot of his litter as it came to a halt.

Wild men, armed with clubs of stone and teeth (sharpened like fangs), pushed back the survivors. They wrenched the weapons from the hand of captive and Gray Watcher alike, throwing them to the ground. When Guzzier saw Shukiera surrounded he cast down his weapons. The sun dawned, spilling rays of sun over the horrors of the night.

There was silence. Then, with a booming voice, the man upon the litter spoke.

"Where is Tizqar, the servant of Angfar who is ordered to hold command over this encampment?"

None answered him. Tizqar slowly rose from where he knelt, turning away from the still body of a Gray Watcher. It was mangled and torn by fangs.

"I am the commander here," Tizqar answered. His voice was tired, as if their sudden saviors were more unlooked for than their past predicament.

"You are in command of nothing!" the man scoffed, but then his tone grew more soothing. "I am Z'gelsh, the acting hand of the Mighty Ninĝinĝar, Dominant over this world. I have been sent here, in the middle of this forsaken desert, to teach you something of order. It seems I come none too late. Assemble your men and rest in the shade outside of the western gate. There you will wait for my next instruction."

"Gather also the slaves there, who are able to work," he ordered a bony wild-man who stood near him. The wild-man held a high standard. Mounted upon it was a banner of deep black that serpentined in the wind in several long strips. On each strip there was a line of red. "Bring two thick pillars of wood and stake them deeply into the ground. Then have your men gather all the remaining supplies of the camp. Bring them here in this yard where we stand. Inform me when this is all completed."

The wild-man bowed and Bahira and Eli'ssa were pushed through the western gate. For the first time, they could see the landscape beyond. The black mountains faded away and steep plateaus of red stone, stacked back to back and side to side, took their place in the west. A thin track wove away from the camp into the shelves of red rock, disappearing between the high tables.

The captives were pushed down into the dust at the foot of the outer wall and the wild-men set up a perimeter about them. Bahira recognized these men from Angfar - they were twisted and mangled, with long matted hair that hung down past their shoulders. Their teeth were blackened and filed to sharp points. They did not speak, but grunted and snarled at each other like beasts, though their eyes foretold that they could understand the language of men.

Tizqar and his Gray Watchers sheltered on the other side of the gate, similarly surrounded. Bahira could see Tizqar from between the legs of the wild-men. He paced back and forth among the remaining Gray Watchers.

"Where is Shukiera?"

"I think she went to look for Guzzier," Eli'ssa answered.

"There are so few of us left," Bahira whispered as she looked about her.

Only a hundred of the captives remained. Many of them were bloodied with cuts and fresh wounds.

"I would cry," Eli'ssa admitted, despondent, "Oh, but I do not have the strength. Why has this happened to us? We were so close, I thought we were free."

No time was given for an answer. Z'gelsh appeared from under the arch of the western gate, still within the confines of his litter. The wild-men grew quiet.

He gestured for Tizqar to join him and the wild-men parted, allowing Tizqar through. Z'gelsh leaned down and exchanged brief words with him before shifting his great bulk so he could see the circle of captives. The knees of the slaves that carried his litter quivered.

"Who is the daring man who organized this rebellion?" Z'gelsh cried out. No one answered him.

"I have no time for games," Z'gelsh insisted with a menacing tone.

"It was I!" The deep voice of Guzzier rolled out from behind them. Guzzier walked forward until he was at the captives' fore and Z'gelsh could see him.

"There is no need for games, it was I and I alone."

"Ah-ha," Z'gelsh chuckled. "Bold instigator! Upraiser! Captain Tizqar, go and bring this man forward. Bind him to that stake of wood there!"

A short piece of rope was placed in Tizqar's hand. He slowly drew near until he stood before Guzzier. Guzzier's hands and arms were still covered in the blood of his enemies, forming a lusty sheen upon his dark skin. Muscle quivered throughout his body and Tizqar's hand trembled as he grasped Guzzier by the elbow. Tizqar swallowed, and led him forward.

Guzzier made no resistance and allowed Tizqar to bind his hands around the shaft in the middle of the yard. Guzzier's steady gaze did not turn from Tizqar as the Captain's fingers fumbled. Finally, Tizqar stepped back, his task complete. His head drooped low and his eyes searched the dust about his feet.

"Good!" Z'gelsh laughed, applauding him with a slow, mocking clap. "Now it is your turn!!" Strong hands suddenly gripped Tizqar as well, dragging him alongside Guzzier to where the second stake lay ready.

"Fool! You are worse than your own slaves! Bind him! Tie him tight!" Tizqar briefly struggled but he was no match for the horde of clawed hands. Soon he was bent around a stake of his own, tied so tightly that the cords bit into his skin.

"I am a servant of Angfar!" Tizqar cried helplessly. "I have done nothing except the will of the Dominant."

For the first time, Z'gelsh dismounted his litter. Bahira was surprised his legs could hold his great weight. He wobbled forward until he stood before the two bound men.

"Do you know what the will of the Dominant is?" he whispered, leaning forward next to Tizqar. Tizqar opened his mouth, but no words came forth.

"Of course you do not," Z'gelsh muttered. "You are a slave to weakness. Angfar is strong."

He held out his hand and in it was placed a long whip. Knotted cords of leather ran from it and curled about Z'gelsh's feet. Bits of bone shone here and there, tied in among the knots.

"Lieutenant Galbad informs me two of your grinding mills have been destroyed. They will need to be rebuilt."

"Strip the Gray Watchers, Swiftpad," Z'gelsh called to where the Laḥmu sat. "When we are finished here, you will take command of them. Rebuild this place and put it in order. Then put them to work upon the grinding wheels."

"No!" Tizqar shrieked, but his bonds held him fast. The beasts encircled his men, licking their chops.

"What is even worse," Z'gelsh continued, stroking the leather whip, "is that your entire store of S'acar crystals was also lost. Nearly four months of labor, lost in one night. You put Angfar behind our schedule!! Do you know what the Dominant desires?? Let me show you!!"

Spittle flew from his mouth in rage as he raised the whip and let it fall

66

upon the backs of Tizqar and Guzzier alike. The skin was torn from them as the leather brand struck again and again. Shukiera cried out in horror, pushing forward as Guzzier groaned with pain. The wild-men threw her back among the captives with cruel laughs, barking like the Laḥmu.

Z'gelsh finally paused, heaving for breath as the bloodied whip fell from his hands. He climbed back into the litter, kicking viciously at the servants who tried to help his massive bulk fit within its confines. Finally, he was settled. Drawing forth a small bronze knife, he threw it down between the two posts.

"Cut them loose," he said to his lieutenant. "Swiftpad will remain here and take charge of the camp. Disperse the rope, the water, and the grain jars! Drive forth the slaves! We make for the citadel of Par'adam without delay."

The wild leader gave a long, shrill cry before marching forward on the winding path into the Red Mountains, his black banner held high. Bahira and the slaves were pulled up and they stumbled ahead in a long line, closely guarded.

Tizqar and Guzzier's bonds were cut. Both rolled free from the posts they clenched, collapsing into the dust.

"One of you shall die here," Z'gelsh announced. "The other will die upon the high crags, you may decide which of you will meet the sooner fate."

Z'gelsh's voice was a distant sound to Guzzier. Tears and sweat filled his eyes. The sharp, high screams of Shukiera called him slowly out of the walls he had built around his pain-filled mind. His eyes cleared. There, standing weakly and covered in blood, was Tizqar. In his hand the bronze knife gleamed. Guzzier pushed himself slowly to his feet and faced him. His limbs shook from weariness and exhaustion. Tizqar's hands lowered.

"Perhaps I have regained some honor now," Tizqar mused, his voice cracking as tears rolled down his cheeks. "I have paid for some of what I have wrought. Go and lead your people, Guzzier. I have failed to lead mine."

Tizqar turned the knife so its tip was at the base of his own ribs. With a sudden push, he sunk it deep within his own flesh and crumpled onto his knees. He gasped and fell silent.

Z'gelsh snorted in amusement.

"So be it," he laughed, as he was carried to the rear of the long procession.

Shukiera ran to Guzzier.

"Guzzier! Guzzier!" she wept.

Blood dripped from him, soaking into the dirt. Kah-Mel was close behind and he supported Guzzier as he began to fall. Guzzier's grip on Kah-Mel loosened and his feet drug behind him. His eye's glazed. Kah-

Mel seized Guzzier firmly and fear shone in his face.

"We must walk brother. We walk to the high crags and to our death, but you must not leave us yet! Stay in my company for a while. The journey would be lonely without you."

Chapter Seven

Red Mountains

The procession wound into the Red Mountains. Rope was swiftly tied together to form a loose litter, and Guzzier's unconscious form was laid upon it. On either side the table-top mesas rose high and the path grew narrower. Prickly plants grew from the cliffs, covered in bright flowers of yellow and orange. Pieces of cloth were passed down the line of weary captives, soaked in water from those who carried the jars, back to where Guzzier lay. Shukiera pressed them lightly about his wounds.

The slave camp disappeared behind, shimmering in the heat, swallowed by the red land.

Before the evening was high, Z'gelsh brought the captives to a stop. They cast themselves into the shadow of the rocks, exhaustion overtaking them. The wild-men settled at the rear of the column, blocking escape out of the gorge. Bahira and Eli'ssa waved the air above Guzzier, deterring some of the flies from settling on him. Their hands were limp. No energy remained. Shukiera sought out a yellow-blooming cactus from the rocky slope and broke it apart, spreading it as a cool salve on Guzzier's wounds.

"Rest," Shukiera said to Bahira and Eli'ssa, seeing their nodding heads. "We will likely continue when the heat of the day has passed."

"There is no watch to the forward, can we not escape?" whispered Elissa to Shukiera.

"All paths now lead to the same place," Shukiera murmured, shaking her head. "Guzzier was right, once you enter this gorge there is no way out."

"How far is the road?" Elissa asked, craning her neck to look farther up the path. Nothing could be seen above the plateaus hemming them in.

"We are making for Par'adam, the ancient fortress of Oodan. This road winds deep within the mountains and will take us there. It will likely take two full weeks. Always the trail is covered in places by some new slide of rock. The Mountains of Oodan are perilous. They are not like any others you have ever seen."

They slept fitfully in the heat. When the sun was low they continued again, marching until the half-moon was high. As they walked, the red stone cast ghostly shadows. The air rapidly grew cold and soon Bahira and Eli'ssa were shivering despite their exertions.

Shukiera applied the cacti salve daily, and Guzzier healed remarkably fast. Within a few days, he could walk on his own. Thick scabs formed on his back and sides that would leave dark scars when they finally diminished. The mountains changed as they progressed deeper. The plateaus faded and perilous fingers of stone took their place. Stacked as tightly as trees they rose, with intermittent boulders and arches of natural rock. Each was as tall as a mountain, but rife with balanced stones and wind-chiseled corners. Clear shades of red and yellow wavered through the sides of the stone in layers, jumping from one rock to the next.

"It is as if the wind and rain swept through these mountains like a stone-mason's chisel," Bahira remarked in awe, gazing up at the majestic columns, archways, and narrow valleys.

"It would take a long time for the wind and rain to do such a thing," Guzzier commented, shouldering a thick strand of rope. Since awakening, he had refused to let anyone carry any measure of his daily burden.

Eli'ssa let her hand run along the smooth, hard stone nearest to her.

"At my home, along the banks of the Dan-Jor, I would see the waters rise in spring. Oh, they would rush, a churning torrent, eager for their rest in the sea. Often, the bank of the Dan would change in a single season, its entire side eaten away in a moment."

"These mountains have been here since I was a boy," Guzzier said again, laughing. "They have not changed stone for stone! Look there, up ahead. Those four stones have always been perched as they are, though it seems they would topple with the first gust of wind."

Bahira and Eli'ssa inadvertently held their breath as they walked by the stones, four atop each other, each as large as a house, balanced off the path they traveled. The wild-men threw stones at it, laughing. Z'gelsh did not find it amusing.

"Tie them to it! Hand and foot! We'll come get you on our return," he snarled, ignoring their begging cries as they were seized. "Angfar does not have time for your petty amusements. I will not be crushed from some great stone that you fools have upset! That goes for the rest of you as well. Stay on the path or I will make sure you do not return from it."

Twelve days into their journey they met their first serious obstacle. For many hours they had been following the path as it wound alongside a squat plateau. High above their heads, perilous rock-mountains stood on the plateau's top. To their left was a thin lake, trapped against a red-layered wall on the farther side. The path ran down to the water's edge and turned, following the ravine into the mountains.

"The water is not as it seems," Guzzier warned as it came into view. "It is very deep and its edge is sheer. Do not stray into it! One step and you will find the bottom disappears."

Half-way around the lake, the path was blocked by enormous stones which had fallen from above. Z'gelsh looked up timidly and his entourage moved as close to the plateau wall as possible.

"This is no break!" he bellowed. Several of the wild-men jumped up, cracking their whips importantly about their head.

"Move those stones! Make a path through!" they barked.

Kah-Mel led a group forward. Only six of the captives could fit between the lake and wall at a time. They heaved on the stones, attempting to roll them aside. Even the smallest stone they could not lift or budge.

"Did you not hear Z'gelsh! Get those stones rolled aside! Clear the path, or we will knock your head against them until they move," Lieutenant Galbad spat.

"It is as if they have roots that grow deep into the ground!" Kah-Mel panted, straining against a stone. "We cannot move them."

"You will move them," Galbad insisted venomously. "Stalling for time will help you little!" He struck a small stone upon the ground with his standard, expecting to see the rock tumble off into the water. Instead his shaft splintered and cracked. He dropped it from his stinging hands.

Z'gelsh came and inspected the blockade himself, surveying the boulders with narrow eyes.

"Send them back," he ordered Galbad. "An hour behind us. A slide of loose rock covered the hill, have them bring it here and make a ramp."

It took the captives a full day and night, under the watchful eye of Z'gelsh, to pile enough stones for his litter to mount the rise. Fortunately, the rear of the stone slide was not a sheer slope, and with some mounted ropes they were able to move his bulking litter down until it reached the other side of the path.

"We are almost there," Guzzier said as they descended. "By tomorrow we will have reached Par'adam." His face was drawn and his words tight.

By mid-morning the next day their goal came in sight.

They entered a thin valley with towering, wind-worn walls when the first signs of the ancient fortress appeared. Crossing the valley was a man-made wall. Its design was ancient, with red stones stacked upon a cracked foundation. Its ramparts were broken. A gaping hole destroyed the wall and through it the captives were driven. Beyond the wall, a pathway, once well cobbled, but now chipped and cracked, stretched on down the valley as it twisted and turned. Suddenly, the valley widened and the cobbles opened into a large space. Above rose the fortress of Par'adam. Dark windows appeared from a tall, natural formation of rock, jutting out from the cliff side. Chiseled directly into the stone were old towers and ramparts overlooking the valley floor. No door or entrance into the fortress could be seen - only the high, inaccessible windows and ramparts looked ominously down upon them.

The wild-men cracked their whips as the newcomers craned their necks to see the ancient fortress. All the slaves were ushered through the wall and wild-men closed in behind them, blocking escape. Guzzier sighed as he walked through, holding Shukiera close to him.

"We will make it," he whispered to her.

"What happens now?" Bahira asked them.

"This valley continues," Guzzier explained, gesturing past the fortress to a large cleft in the rock, "and ends at the crags of Oodan. I will not describe it to you. It is a beautiful place, the highest in these mountains. It is not a journey for the faint of heart, but you will have no choice."

They were driven on with haste. The valley narrowed. Every step and hushed whisper echoed back and all around them. The ancient fortress had not passed from sight, before the cobbled path ended sharply at the tallest rock wall. Cracked, broken statues of unrecognizable beasts bordered the paths ending. Bahira and Eli'ssa stared at them, wondering what shapes they had taken in older days.

The cliff face was covered by woven ropes, some old and some newer, that led to unknown heights above. Under the ropes were ancient hand-holds, worn smooth and shallow. All the slaves gathered together, pinned against the wall by the wild-men. Z'gelsh came forward, born on his litter, and surveyed the heights.

"Rabble rousers!! Today you will pay for your insubordination!" Z'gelsh yelled, his voice harsh and amplified. "Tizqar gave you too much leave, you will find I am not as forgiving. Go up to the crags! You must pay your due to return to the land of safety: twenty eggs of Oodan will earn your way! If you return empty handed, you will be ripped limb from limb."

The few among them who had made the climb before cried out in dismay at the command.

"Z'gelsh," Guzzier said aghast, "ten was asked of us in the past and such a quota killed almost all."

Z'gelsh chuckled and raised the flat of his hand. The wild-men lowered their weapons, driving him and the others back against the wall.

"That is too bad," Z'gelsh sympathized. "Had you not destroyed our store of crystals, perhaps I would have been more lenient. Go! Or you will be slain, one at a time, and the quota of eggs from those slain will be distributed among the survivors."

Guzzier turned away, his face drawn. He gave a reluctant gesture for all to tie the woven sacks, with the meager supplies that remained, around their waists. Bahira and Eli'ssa followed his example, as did the others. He pushed his way to the wall and reached up, grabbing the mesh of rope. Many hundreds of strands disappeared above, some of them ancient from generations past; and others new, only a few seasons frayed. He tugged on it and then began ascending.

"He means to kill us all," Eli'ssa whispered.

"Guzzier will save us," Bahira assured confidently.

"Stay behind us!" Shukiera instructed, just loud enough for the captives to hear. "Some of the ropes are not safe, Guzzier knows the best way."

The more experienced ones were given extra stores of food and water, rope and other provisions for their journey. None could take much. From what they had heard from Guzzier, the return back down that first wall was the most perilous due to starvation and dehydration. Eli'ssa and Bahira could see why. They climbed, their forearms burning from continually gripping the knotted ropes. Their feet slipped from the worn rock-face, leaving them hanging with trembling hands. Ever did their eyes search back and forth as they ascended, looking for the best strand of rope to bear their weight among the web and tangle. They rose higher, leaving the shadow of the valley. Over the red hills, the scorching sun beat down upon their backs. Still, they climbed, into the sky, until Z'gelsh could not be distinguished beneath them and the turrets of Par'adam were far, far below.

There was no talking. Just hand over hand, foot after foot.

"We are almost to the first ledge!" Guzzier cried, high above them.

"The first ledge?" Bahira muttered, hugging a knotted rope as large as her arm.

"Oh, I hope that doesn't mean there is a second and then a third!" Eli'ssa gasped. Their arms and legs shook with exhaustion. They passed others wrapped hand and foot in the rope, unable to grip any longer and unable to continue.

Soon they were being pulled up and over the edge of a flat, rocky shelf. It was hardly wide enough to hold twenty people. Above it the incline of rock continued; but instead of a single precipitous face, the rocks split into many ledges and peaks. Some areas were less steep and the mesh of ropes stopped. The jutted landscape was marred with holes and wind-caves large enough to be used as shelter. Grasses grew among the rocks, and small, blue flowers hung from many of the ledges in marvelous clusters.

A warm breeze blew up the rock-face. They were high enough to see over the red plateaus. On every side, the mountains stretched on, far into the distance. The view to the north and east, where the crags still climbed skyward, was blocked. Guzzier's hand softly touched the flowering clusters, bursting with beauty and life from the dry, rock face. He sat heavily within a thick patch of waving grass, closed his eyes and sighed deeply. Then he turned to them and smiled.

"Do not be dismayed!" he encouraged. "I cannot think of a better place to make my final rest. These mountains are in my bones."

"We head for the highest point of the ridge," Shukiera said, gesturing above them. "From here up, the passage is safer. Beware the loose stone from above or the one you send below!"

She ushered the two women into a nearby alcove of rock, leaving a small satchel of supplies and a length of rope with them.

"It will be safer for you to stay here tonight," she whispered. "Your arms need to rest before scaling the final length. Some of us will continue, nearer to the nests of the S'acar. Join us tomorrow when you have the strength."

"How will we know where to find you?" Bahira worried.

"Just keep going up," Shukiera smiled. She, Guzzier, and a score of others arose and continued ascending.

As the day passed, Bahira and Elissa pulled stragglers up to the first ledge as they appeared. Many could hardly move. Many fell, just out of reach. Their hearts ached.

Night came swiftly to the high crags. The wind swept across the peaks of the mountains, howling with a biting cold.

Finally, the girls could not wait any longer and they both stood, shaking and rubbing their chilled limbs. The moon was bright, and the stones threw shadows around them. Captives had not appeared over the treacherous ledge for many hours.

"Oh, I cannot sit here in the cold any more," Eli'ssa whispered, rubbing her shivering arms. Bahira nodded in agreement and shouldered the rope.

"Let us see where the others went, the slope above is nowhere near as steep as the last!"

They found the small, blue flowers glowed translucent in the moonlight, lighting up the crags with a striking beauty. They were able to scramble up the stone, using both hands and feet in many places. The exertion of the climb kept them warm and time passed swiftly. Soon, only one more ledge of rock stood before them. Eli'ssa helped push Bahira up and then grabbed her hand, scrambling up the final shelf. For the first time, they could see what lay to the north.

Before them was a gigantic, alpine boulder field. Flames from a single, small fire flickered on the nearest boulders, marking where the main camp was set. Beyond it was a thick fog; like a wall, it crossed the boulder field from east to west in an impenetrable line. Nothing could be seen through it. Bahira looked at Eli'ssa with wide eyes.

"That must be where we are headed."

Shukiera sat up, awakened by a rolling stone. Her face betrayed surprise as the girls walked into the firelight.

"That was foolish," she chided, standing. "Others have died scaling that face, as easy as it seems after the first."

"Where are the others?" Eli'ssa asked, looking around. Only Shukiera could be seen.

"They are within the fog. It is warmer there," she said, gesturing behind her. "I will take you. I only remain here to lead others the right way when they arrive." She didn't ask how many had made it after their departure.

She turned and led them deeper into the boulder field. The house-sized rocks cast shadows of deep night between the rays of moonlight. They lost all sense of direction before Shukiera brought them to a stop. The wall of fog appeared suddenly across their path. A continual hissing sound echoed through the rocks nearby and they looked at Shukiera in fear.

"Come," she said simply. She disappeared into the mist.

Immediately the air was warmer. It stuck to their skin and smelled of sulfur. Just within the fog they came upon the score of captives. Kah-Mel lay across the path and he sprang up as their shadows appeared.

"It is me," Shukiera whispered, calming him. "I bring Eli'ssa and Bahira, they are early."

He nodded and sat back down.

"The mist is frightening to most," he admitted to the girls as Shukiera left them, disappearing back the way she had come. "It dissipates somewhat during the day."

"What is it from?" Bahira asked. "It is so warm. I feel as though I could finally sleep."

"It is a blessing," Kah-Mel replied. He pointed over his shoulder. Behind the stone that he rested against, was a black fissure. From it, heat blasted and the smell of molten earth was strong.

"Without it we would surely not survive the frigid nights," he continued, settling back down into a comfortable position. "We do not know what they are from. The ancient tales of El-Loz say these mountains were once alive with giant creatures that breathed and moved. Some think they still do. If so, this is their breath and we are but unnoticed ants upon them." He chuckled. "Do not stray too near, for they will burn you severely. Sleep now! Early in the morning you will meet the S'acar... and perhaps earn your first eggs of Oodan."

They could not tell if he was excited or petrified, but he rolled over and went back to sleep. They did the same.

In the morning, the girls awoke simultaneously. They sat up quickly and covered their eyes, for in an instant the darkness seemed to vanish and blinding light shone all about them.

Guzzier laughed as he walked over to them, the mist swirling about as it dissipated. For each of them he held in his hand one of the blue mountain flowers.

"Good morning my friends!" he cried. His voice was cheerful, but his face was drawn. "Morning comes abruptly in the high crags. Take these flowers, they are found nowhere else in the world. Do they not smell sweeter than anything you can remember? The people of my land learned to crush them and place their glowing color within the skin of thieves. It would serve as a warning in the darkness that they were coming. Soon the mist will burn away, we must move while we can!"

They found that eighty captives had made the climb and were already with them. Apparently, the sun had risen much earlier on the lower faces of the mountain. All held rope in their hands and stood behind Guzzier expectantly.

"Follow me quietly. Do not disturb a single stone! Today we have the best chance of acquiring our freedom. Walk with soft footfalls."

He stalked through the swirling tendrils of mist and, like a silent army, they followed behind.

Chapter Eight

Eggs of Oodan

Time was difficult to determine among the steam. Huge, red rocks appeared to the right and left, before being swallowed again in the fog. Blue sky peeked at them from above, as the haze thinned. Guzzier came to a halt. He waited, and Bahira and Elissa peered over his shoulder. A wind blew from the east and like a sheet being pulled aside, they saw what was ahead.

A spear-throw away from them, the high plateau on which they stood ended abruptly, falling steeply to the valley floor. Beyond the edge was another bulbous mountain top. Next to it was another, and so they continued, like islands in the sky, stretching on atop perilous fingers of rock and mountain boulders with an unfathomable drop of space in between.

This was not the only wonder. Guzzier stood on the edge of a mountainous pool, which stretched all the way to the drop-off. Crystal clear, the red rock of its bottom could be seen, yet sharp hues of purple and green swirled mystically in its depths. The water steamed, heated by the underground fissures, and was bordered with blue flowers in thick clusters. Each plateau, stretching into the distance, showed signs of a similar marvel.

Guzzier, Shukiera, and Kah-Mel looked at the sky. Eli'ssa and Bahira looked as well, imagining sharp beaks and high nests. There were none.

Kah-Mel made a quick motion for all to watch. Guzzier removed the rope which wound about his shoulders and cast it aside. Kah-Mel tied a shorter length around his waist. Guzzier's empty, woven satchel hung loosely at his hip. With a deep breath, Guzzier dove into the water, hardly making a splash.

The ripples faded into utter silence. The marvelous colors under the water stirred and the steam swirled. Bahira and Eli'ssa looked at each other and then back to the water.

Suddenly the rope grew taut, snapping so tightly that water droplets showered from its singing vibration! Kah-Mel heaved upon the rope and Guzzier burst forth from the depths with a piercing yell! Something had a hold of him, dragging him back into the water! Others came, grabbing and pulling as Kah-Mel staggered toward the edge, overwhelmed. They pulled in unison and Guzzier broke free. He sprung from the water to the edge of rock and pulled himself up, hand over hand.

Kah-Mel reached out to help him - and then leapt upon him! Striking something lodged in his back with all his might! Stones, fists, and elbows rained down in a fury! Eli'ssa and Bahira ran forward to aide against the unseen attacker, but froze in shock as they saw what had him. There, with a beak deeply lodged into Guzzier's back, was a strange creature. It had a long tail, thick and slimy, batting violently between Guzzier's thighs. Its four splayed legs (with many claws), scrabbled frantically, further marring Guzzier's back. To each leg was attached a thick webbing that ran to its body like wide paddles. Its head was narrow like a bird and its mouth was sharp and pointed, hinting at what would soon be a razor-sharp beak. It covered the whole of Guzzier's back, looking like a clawed tadpole of massive proportion. With one final blow, Kah-Mel broke it free, and it flopped back into the water with a guttural squawk.

Guzzier rolled over, panting and spitting out water. Blood ran down his back and legs. His hair steamed. From his satchel rose a magnificent light! A cluster of objects were within, at least eight of them, each the size of a fist. Over their surface ran many colors, vivid and crisp, as if they contained a poignant radiance deep within.

"Was... was that the S'acar?" Bahira gasped.

Kah-Mel did not answer. Instead he quickly reached into the sack and withdrew one of the eggs, separating it from a slimy film which clung to the others. It was leathery in his hand, though it quickly began to harden in the air. Kah-Mel didn't hesitate: he smashed it into Guzzier's back, pressing it deeply into his gaping wound! Bahira nearly cried out when he broke it, so painful was it to see something so beautiful destroyed. When Kah-Mel removed his hand, Guzzier's back was whole. No wounds remained, nor any trace of them. All his former scars and blemishes had disappeared.

"That is not the S'acar," Guzzier explained, rising slowly to his feet. "They are the larval form, its offspring. For many years they stay in the warm waters until they mature."

"What do they become?" Eli'ssa gasped.

Guzzier and Kah-Mel again looked at the sky about them.

"Pray to Enlil that you do not find out today," Shukiera whispered to her.

"Quickly!" Guzzier said urgently. Follow our lead! They communicate swiftly, today is our best chance. Tomorrow they will be ready. Dive! Dive for the Eggs of Oodan! Use them sparingly, only if you have a need!"

Without hesitation Guzzier and Kah-Mel ran to the edge of the mountain and leapt over the precipice. Clearing the sheer, unfathomable drop they landed on the other side. Guzzier now tied the rope to Kah-Mel and he leapt into the water of a pool.

A few followed while most spread out, surrounding the large pool nearest to them.

"Oh, I'll go first," Eli'ssa volunteered breathlessly. She handed Bahira a length of rope. Bahira tied it around her with shaking hands. Then Eli'ssa leapt into the water.

The rope was slack in Bahira's hand. Suddenly it went taunt! Bahira was ready, her feet set. She gave it a mighty jerk and Eli'ssa came shooting out from the depths. She clambered out of the pool, dripping and limping, but her smile was wide. She showed Bahira her sack: a cluster of three, precious eggs were within.

"Bahira," she whispered, "it is beautiful. The water, it is as if you can see clearer underneath its surface than up here."

Bahira inspected Eli'ssa's leg where a deep gash was evident. It bled freely, though the blood gave no sign of clouding the water's edge. Bahira began reaching for one of the eggs.

"No!" Eli'ssa cried, stopping her. "They are precious. Each one spent is one more we must obtain. I will be fine until the next dive."

So they continued. It seemed the deeper they dove, the greater the clusters of eggs became. How Guzzier found a cluster of eight they never knew, for they saw none greater than four. The S'acar spawn were vicious and fast, but there did not seem to be many. At least two of the slaves dove under and did not return. One man was pulled free with a larva firmly attached to his throat. Shukiera examined him closely.

"No," she said, as one of the slaves reached for an egg to break upon him. "He is dead. The eggs of the S'acar do not bring the dead back to life. Go back! Continue! Much of the day is left and with each moment we run out of time." She gently closed the man's eyes.

It was almost noon. Bahira was forced to use one of their precious eggs when Eli'ssa had a near miss, suffering a long and deep laceration upon her cheek and neck that sputtered blood with Eli'ssa's pulsing heartbeat. As the S'acar egg melted into her skin, the wound closed. The scars on Eli'ssa's face waned and then vanished. Eli'ssa looked into the water, staring at her reflection and softly touching her unmarred face. She sat silently for a while and when Bahira gently touched her shoulder, Eli'ssa turned. Her eyes were full of tears.

"You are...beautiful," Bahira whispered, unable to conceal her shock. Eli'ssa brushed the wet hair from her face.

"Thank you, Bahira," she whispered back. In her satchel at her feet, the eggs seemed to glisten with wonder, but Eli'ssa paid them little heed.

She knelt reverently, looking across the towering stones and haunting pools on the far horizon. "Do you think, Bahira, that all those times my mum went to the house of Enlil and prayed for me... Did Enlil hear her? Did he hear *me*?"

Bahira unwillingly thought of all she had lost. The face of her brother, the comfort of her home, the life in Cartegin. She would have given anything to be able to return. But, as she looked upon Eli'ssa, Bahira saw a resolved contentment - as though this girl possessed all the treasures of the world without regret, shame or fear of tomorrow. Bahira did not understand.

Elissa turned, looking upon Bahira's drawn face, and smiled a kindly smile. Eli'ssa gently embraced her.

"I am happy to be here with you, Bahira," Eli'ssa whispered. "No matter what happens, there is a way for us."

The mist of the boulder field still hung about the ground in tendrils. The eggs in the pool lessened and they were forced to spread out as the day passed, even traveling to taller islands of rock. Many of the slaves had ten or more glistening eggs in their satchels. It felt like victory was near! Then a sudden cry rang out over the mountains.

They all stopped and looked around. It was Guzzier and Kah-Mel. The light of adventure was gone from their eyes. Terror had taken its place. They were running toward them, three or four sky-islands away, waving their arms. No one else who had gone with them could be seen.

Shukiera stood up slowly from the water's edge and looked at the men with wide eyes. She immediately began running to them.

"Flee!!" she cried back over her shoulder. "Return to the boulder fields! Haste! *Run!*" Fear laced her voice. The captives stood riveted, not knowing what to expect. She reached the edge of the mountain and seemed ready to jump toward Guzzier. But, up from the mountainous crack at her feet, there was a flash of light and she fell back! A bright form exploded from the gap: red, blue, and black, twisting and tumbling in the air faster than the eye could follow! Then the form hovered over their heads upon a draft of air and Bahira saw, for a moment, the S'acar.

It was not a bird, yet like one. Two great wings stretched out from each side, the span longer than two men. The colors of their feathers were striking, bright to the eye like the eggs of their kind. Two muscular hind legs stretched behind it (also covered in feathers), some over a foot long, that gave the appearance of four wings instead of two. Similar to a bat, long claws protruded from its forward appendages; while a single, thick, curling claw, like an oversized eagle's talon, sprouted from its hind legs. Its tail was long, longer than its wingspan, thick at its base but thinning and fanning out into a wide spread of many-colored plumage at its tip. Where the feathers faded, its cold-blooded body was covered with a soft black fuzz. Its head was narrow and sharp, mounted with a high, red crest. Beady eyes sat above a deadly, red beak, surveying them.

Even as Shukiera fell to the ground, bright plumage permeated the gap and innumerable S'acar soared into the air around them. Their harsh cries filled the sky. They dove among the fleeing captives - some ripping free the sacks of eggs while others attacked, grabbing those near the edge and forcing them over the precipice. Their massive wings stirred the air and their beaks were quick to find any exposed head or neck. When the S'acar landed on the ground, they stood as tall as Bahira. They ran forward on their feathery back legs with frightening speed; their long claws clicking upon the stone, while they batted their wings violently.

Bahira and Eli'ssa scrambled away, into the boulder field as fast as they could run. The other captives did the same, screaming and diving to the earth as the S'acar dove on them, only to find the creatures deadlier upon the ground than in the air.

That night, only half of the captives were accounted for. The steam from the mountains of Oodan rose above them, providing a cover that the S'acar did not dare penetrate. Guzzier came into the camp last, carrying Shukiera. He knelt beside her and pulled forth several eggs from his satchel, straining to break open their hardening husks over her many, grievous wounds.

Bahira and Eli'ssa helped him.

"Kah-Mel?" Bahira asked.

Guzzier lowered his eyes.

"He fell," he whispered.

Shukiera stirred beneath them and sat up slowly. Her eyes filled with tears as she looked around.

"How many of us remain?" she asked.

"Forty-one," Bahira whispered.

Guzzier stood and left them, walking away until he was partially concealed in a boulder's shadow. Shukiera followed him. "We have never been struck so early," Guzzier whispered. Shukiera silenced him and they both wept together, shrouded by the mist

"We must count how many eggs we came away with," Guzzier decided, wiping his eyes and turning back to the group. "All of you, bring them forward! Lay them here."

They brought what satchels remained. The glowing light of the eggs now seemed haunting, filling the mist with their strange colors. Guzzier counted them.

"Three hundred," he whispered

"The S'acar took many of them," Eli'ssa said, drawing her hand over them. They were hard now, and could roll across the stone like glass. "More were used to heal those hurt."

"There are only enough for fifteen of us. And you," Guzzier said, turning to Shukiera. He pulled twenty more eggs out of his satchel and pushed them into her hands.

"You will lead these people,"

Shukiera shook her head, more tears falling.

"I am tired of coming to this place," she cried. "I am tired of being haunted by its beauty. I will not come back here again. I will stay with you."

Guzzier drew her close and buried her face in his thick arms, running his hands through her hair.

"I do not mind dying here," he whispered to her. "I can think of no better place, as long as you are with me. I am not afraid of death!"

He turned, facing the others gathered.

"Sixteen of you will go and live" he said loudly. "Who shall it be?"

Silence drew over them as thick as the fog. The light of the eggs danced within their midst.

Then one survivor came forward and placed twenty eggs into his satchel. Guzzier nodded to him.

"There is no shame in this," Guzzier reassured him.

Another, and another came until the eggs were gone. Bahira and Eli'ssa had not moved.

"Go," Guzzier said firmly. "Return the way you came. Go slowly, do not waste your lives! And bring hope to those who will come this way after you. I will not be among them."

He turned away. Those with the claimed eggs departed, vanishing like a shadow into the swirling darkness.

Just over twenty survivors remained. They sat in silence. Suddenly Guzzier's voice rose, heavy and damp in the mist:

"Upon the shores of Par'adam, there the ancient water rose in fathoms

Cutting caves and caverns deep, burying those for whom none weep.

The citadel of stone, red with blood, washed clean in the mighty flood.

But high above the fortress' reach, above the mountains and the keep

There the altar of El'Perran, risen high of stone and crystal sand.

Egal-Mah, the Lord of Old, touched the floor of red and gold

S'acar came forth, bound no more, to the dust which was his home.

Oodan! He cried, and bespoke the name, which freed of old the earth's

deep chain.

The land rose, quaked and fell. He took to flight while men befell

The ancient hills and forts of sand: the home of S'acar, in Par'adam."

A silence followed. Finally, Guzzier broke it.

"In my land," he whispered hoarsely, "when the land fails, when the water runs dry, and when our people mourn, we look back to where our feet have been, to give us hope for the days ahead."

He wiped the tears from his eyes and sat among them, bidding all to draw closer.

"Now is the time to fill our hearts, for they are empty. No matter our strength, no matter our goal, we cannot go on until they are full again."

Shukiera took a determined breath and seemed to look up at the stars for encouragement. There were none, only the restless mist and the shifting darkness of the high crags.

"Who here has a story to tell?" Guzzier asked solemnly. "Who here has a hope they hold onto in the secret place, when all seems dark?"

Bahira looked at Eli'ssa, expecting her to answer. Instead, all eyes seemed to turn toward her.

"You have never shared with us your story," Guzzier said to Bahira softly, his gaze kind but penetrating. "Perhaps it is time."

Bahira's face was veiled and her eyes cast down. A sob escaped from her before she could catch it.

"I cannot bear the weight of the present," Bahira whispered. "How can I also bear the weight of the past?"

"By sharing, the joys and the sorrows, with us," Shukiera answered. "So my people have done in times like these for as long as we can remember. Trust in their wisdom."

Bahira drew a shaking breath and held it long before letting it go free.

"I have a story," she said. "I don't know what hope it has, or where it leads." The finality and quietness of her voice drew all of the survivors nearer to her, their ears sharp, their hearts beating.

"You have a secret one," Eli'ssa said alluringly. "One you hoped would come after you. One you hoped would save you."

Guzzier unwillingly smiled.

"None of us know the end of our story, Bahira, until we stand upon the brink and have that last moment to look back. We only know the beginning," Guzzier encouraged. "What was this man's name?"

"Areoch," Bahira answered. "His name is Areoch."

Chapter Nine

Plotting of Assassins

Areoch wiped the sweat from his eyes as he tried to focus. Rimuš and Manish were with him, their feet sinking into the cool sand of the training arena as they circled. Pillars of wood occasionally rose up, obscuring Areoch's view as he stalked silently through them. Their adversary could barely be seen through the wooden beams. He did not move, nor did he give any sign of recognition that he was about to be attacked. His eyes were closed. His arms were thick and corded. A dark tattoo emblazoned the man's chest and the same symbol was deeply etched in his bronze armbands. It was the mark of the dragon, the symbol of the E-Kur elite, warriors of Agade.

This was no ordinary lesson in the art of combat: Zakkaria, commander of the E-Kur and leader of Sargon's Legions was their tactical opponent. Though the three boys had been training all morning, they had not come close to getting the best of this man.

Zakkaria breathed. A smile hovered at the corner of his mouth and his eyes remained closed. He could feel his muscles quivering, tense, ready to engage and spring into action. His sweaty, left hand was covered in sand as it supported his upper body, his legs angled behind him to allow quick movement in any direction. Sweat trickled down his back. Zakkaria had been training in combat his entire life and was the commander over thousands. The boy's grating footfalls drug through the sand, telling him both their current location and destination.

Ten years had passed since the boys' father, Sargon the Great, had washed his weapons in the great Tanti Sea, a symbol of his complete victory, uniting the three greatest city-states of the ancient world into the Kingdom of Agade. Ten long years, filled first with famine and then wealth. Zakkaria knew that the boyhood of the three before him were drawing to an end, he wished for it to pass with fine style.

The boys didn't stand a chance, but winning was not the lesson

Zakkaria was trying to teach them. He looked up under his dark, thick eyebrows. The boys circled out of reach, bare-chested and bearing the thin beards of youth. Rimuš and Areoch crept toward his weaker left-hand side while Manish remained crouched like a tiger, unmoving behind the nearest pillar.

Zakkaria let his eyes close again, the image of the boys' movements inscribed in his mind's eye, painted there by the noise of labored breathing. They searched for a weakness. They would never get a chance to find one.

Zakkaria exhaled. His green eyes opened and narrowed. Without warning, his right foot (which had been burying itself deeply in the soft ground), snapped forward and around, spraying a wide arch of sand high in the air. The sand seemed to hover as his body quickly moved, sliding left and sweeping the legs out from Manish. Without stopping he shot ahead, muscles springing. Grasping Rimuš's throat he tossed him like a sack of wheat down onto the arena floor.

The sand settled. Areoch hesitated, while Manish leaped back to his feet. Then the two, seeing their loss of ground, charged recklessly at Zakkaria.

"AHHHHH!!!" they cried. It was exactly what Zakkaria was expecting. He was already waiting for them. This time he side-stepped the incoming fist of Manish and brought his heel cleverly around behind his knee, the pressure on the tendon causing a gasp of pain and the resounding thud of a face-plant. Areoch leaped through the air, legs extended for a powerful kick to Zakkaria's head and shoulders.

Zakkaria hooted with laughter, it would have seemed ridiculous to a passerby. As he flew into the commander's waiting arms, Areoch realized his critical mistake. He was spun by his feet up and over Zakkaria's broad shoulders before his face slammed hard into the dust.

The sage Marqu stood at the edge of the sandy arena, apparently under a fit of coughing as he tried to quench his laughter. He called the boys over. They picked themselves up with groans of pain and knelt around him. They spit grains of sand from their mouths, rubbing their battered limbs and developing bruises.

"How did he beat you... again?" Marqu asked the three. He stifled his amusement and put on a lecturer's face.

Rimuš shook his head and gasped for air. "He's too strong. Too fast."

Areoch and Manish nodded their heads in agreement.

Marqu raised an eyebrow. "Is that so? There are three of you and one of him! Are not three men - I'll take the liberty of calling you men - stronger than one? No, you were soundly beaten, not because of your speed or strength, but because your minds are an unsealed tablet, open for all to read! What use is it to devise a plan if you unfold it to your enemy before you attack? You must learn to conceal your actions in

85

battle until the action itself has passed."

With a loud thump, Zakkaria sat down next to the group calmly brushing the sand from his legs.

"You must also learn how to gauge and foresee your enemy's actions," he added. "A good enemy might know your first three steps, but if you know his first four, the fight will end in your favor. Most importantly, boys, learn this: when fighting a stronger opponent on even ground, you will surely suffer defeat. You must recognize this and change the field! Take a piece of wood in your hand or sand in your fist! Use what is available to you and gain the advantage."

A servant ran into the arena and approached the sage, whispering quick words in his ear before departing.

"That is enough of a lesson for today and one you'll feel tomorrow, I am sure," said Marqu. "Your father requests your presence in the White Court. Clean yourselves up and go. Do not keep him waiting!"

The three boys scrambled up and departed. Marqu and Zakkaria watched the trio exit the arena before openly laughing together.

"When I asked you to teach them a lesson, Zakkaria, I did not necessarily mean for one with such a hard landing!" Marqu chuckled.

"It will be well remembered," the commander said with a smile, reaching for his tunic and weapons piled at the edge of the sandy pit. "It may well be the last chance I have with them. Tomorrow I must return to Kish. I escort a supply of bronze for the chief smith there and Sargon has ordered that I personally oversee the finishing of the watchtowers by the sea."

"No doubt until these rumors of pirates pillaging the coast have died down. What do they call them... the *Urudu*?" Marqu asked.

Zakkaria shook his head, slipping his tunic over his broad shoulders. "People are easily made afraid, Marqu. Perhaps north of Agade pirates lay waste, pillage, and burn, but we are safe here. I make sure it is so. More is Sargon's concern bent against smugglers passing through our borders, if I had to guess."

Marqu nodded. "So, the rest of the watchtowers have been completed?"

"Nearly," said Zakkaria. "Once the five along the coast are finished, they will number twelve in all. With a surplus of grain filling our stores again this spring, the E-Kur will number nearly twelve thousands of Strong Men getting fat and lazy, building dikes as needed and waiting for an excuse for battle!"

"The history of men has never seen the like," remarked Marqu in amazement. "That makes..."

"Twenty thousand Strong Men whose sole occupation is the art of war," finished Zakkaria as they departed the training grounds. "It will change the perspective of battle between men forever."

"It already has, friend," said Marqu, shaking his head. "No longer will the household blacksmith and the carpenter wield spear and shield in battle. War has become a trade, as hunting is the living of the *Aett* and stonework the art of the mason."

They paused and walked some distance together in silence.

"Will you be returning from Kish for the Festival?" asked Marqu.

"I do not know," answered Zakkaria. "Ensi Rahmaah will be making the journey from Kish to Ur, if he has not yet arrived already. I imagine I will help govern the city in his absence, though I am sore to miss the festival of Akitu and the first days of spring!"

"And you'll miss what happens beyond. I'm sure you've heard?" asked Marqu.

"Yes, I have," said Zakkaria, looking with a furrowed brow to where the boys had vanished. "And I have a mind to speak to Sargon about it. The lots have been thrown, and their Giĝal has come." Zakkaria grew silent and his face was grim. "Doesn't it seem strange to you, Marqu, that *all three* have been chosen? All three of Sargon's heirs to be sent out at one time?"

Marqu shrugged. "As you say, the lots have been thrown, as is customary. You think too much Zakkaria! The time comes for all."

Zakkaria's face was uneasy, but he let out a sigh.

"I will be sad to miss their departure. They will hardly be able to keep their composure when Sargon tells them. Are they ready?"

"None ever are," reflected Marqu. "That is the point of the Giĝal: to depart a boy and return a man."

Even as Marqu and Zakkaria left the training arena, another conversation was happening in a secluded garden deep within the heart of the city of Ur. A white ziggurat rose high above curling spring vines, though the dense hedging made little visible. Two men sat studying a wide, stone board, engraved with a crisscross pattern of squares. They spoke in low voices as they moved pieces upon it.

The taller of the two men picked up a piece and jumped several squares before setting it down again.

"Tell me, Ensi Beckma, how is it in Lugal?"

The smaller man pondered the move before answering. "The people of the city are again growing fat; the harvest last year was more plentiful than we have seen in the past five combined. The air is ripe for change... and for a new order."

"Good, good, Beckma," the tall man cooed, nodding with understanding at the other's meaning. "Then you remember the last conversation we had here. Have you heard the news?" The tall man gazed around, making sure they were still alone.

"There is much news these days," answered Beckma. "Rumors of strange disappearances in the north echo through the passes in the mountains, even past Sargon's watch-towers. Fears once again come alive after the sun sets. The great walls Sargon has built are not as prominent in the minds of the people as they were five years ago. Like sheep in a pen, the wolves are circling outside of its gate."

"*Such ideas and people have no business contaminating the whole of the world,*" Beckma mocked in a mimicry of Sargon's voice. The tall man scoffed.

"More and more think twice of Sargon's decree: that no man, woman or child may pass through Agadian lands into the north. Why are those that are hungry and careworn turned aside in the northern passes? The people are ready, Rahmaah. They are ready for change."

"So I have heard also. More and more people are turned back at the passes, who claim to seek refuge from the death and famine that still lingers in the north."

Beckma leaned closer. "I have heard whispers of worse. My city is closer to the borders than Kish and travelers still sometimes pass through there in secret. They say in the north entire cities have disappeared. They say strange beasts have been seen, far within the black mountains of the high regions. Some have even said..." he looked around nervously, "that *Uttuki* walk again, as in the days of the Old World."

Rahmaah raised his eyebrow. "Is that so? Fairytales and gossip! I have not heard tales that ignorant, though I have heard of other foul creatures wandering. It is for this reason we have shared our thoughts in secret." Rahmaah considered a move on the board before executing it. "But, it is not this news I have spoken of - Sargon's sons, Manish, Rimuš, and Areoch, have been chosen for the Giĝāl."

Beckma paused over the board. "All three? Are they to be sent out at the same time? That is a strange turn of events that speaks of more than chance. You've been busy, Rahmaah."

"Fate, it seems, is with us," Rahmaah replied with a sly chuckle, straightening his robe. He studied the board, cracking his neck as he paused. "There is little more we need. The pieces are set, it is time we make our move."

"What is to be the plan?" asked Beckma.

"You have men, ready and willing to do what is necessary?"

Beckma nodded.

"Then we have little to do but wait. I will arrange for the boys to be sent out on paths less traveled and more dangerous. It will not be overlooked, then, when they never return from their journey. When they are gone, we can strike here and finish the course we have envisioned. There will be none left in Sargon's royal line! Once he falls, the Kingdom will turn over into the hands of the *Ensi*."

The fire of greed lit in the eyes of Ensi Beckma as he nodded. The two men paused from their game and walked together in the direction of a large, columned building sitting in low shadows beneath the massive Ziggurat. The finely graded white gravel of the garden pathway crunched under their sandals.

"Beckma," Rahmaah reminded, "no one here in Ur must know of this. Our cities may be ready for change, but Ur is still under Sargon's order. We must be careful. Prepare the men you have in mind and tell them to meet us at the Eastern sheep gate in two weeks' time, when the youths are to depart. Change begins then."

The fresh air of early spring was cool and clear as the two Ensi walked along the garden paths in their heavy robes; but Areoch, Manish, and Rimuš were hot and covered with grime from their training. They bathed in a cool fountain outside of the training arena and donned flowing tartans of woven fabric, held together with tanned belts of leather and silver. None of the boys wore armbands, which distinguished boys from men, the men from the warriors, and the warriors from the heroes of men.

The three swiftly made their way through the city to the center of Ur - paying little attention to its grandeur and magnificence, to which they were accustomed. Ur's mighty walls stretched across the southern foothills of the Durgu Mountains, obscuring the view in the distance. Four E-Kur warriors could walk abreast on the wall's thick top and several were doing that, their long, bright spears reflected in the pale evening. Red and white banners bearing Sargon's ensign flew in the wind above their heads. The walls gave way to Ur's sprawling centers of living and markets. Here traders and wealthy craftsmen lived in safety, working their wares. Goods were hauled in on overloaded carts from the rich, surrounding villages where crops were sown, herds were grazed, and the center of Agade's economic success was mined and turned into the most precious metal, bronze.

The bustle of trade diminished as the three drew closer to the heart of Ur. They passed through wide-open courts adorned with the steles of Sargon's victories, statues of bronze and stone, and many grand fountains.

Above it all rose the White Temple of Ur. A mountainous ziggurat, stacked with intricately carved white basalt rocks, loomed in the center of the city. The brothers followed the lily covered stream of Enki as it wound around finely cobbled pathways and into the magnificent White Courtyard, where the shadow of the White Temple fell. The courtyard was several hundred yards long in length and width. Gardens spilled from behind important structures along their sides. The Ziggurat's peak sparkled in the sunlight as the three entered a long and low-lying stone building.

The boys walked in silence, anticipation growing in their minds. Soon a set of large, double doors appeared - well-guarded by two E-Kur who stood stiffly on either side, bearing spear and dagger drawn and ready. As they approached, the din of dispute grew louder in their ears.

"Please, Lord Sargon! Listen to our wisdom! What is a little brass and tin, that you have so much of? We have a great deal we could offer: artisans, gold, silver, precious gems by the cartful! And for bronze we would trade men you could *own*. Beasts, who would do whatever you will - at your whim and command! Would that not advance your Kingdom into a new age of prowess and strength? Could you not accomplish great things? We only ask that you share a small token of gratitude for this wisdom..." a whining voice faded from behind the door.

"We have no need for such things!" boomed the unmistakable voice of Sargon. "Does an ox need anything from the dry grass across from his pasture, which he has long since turned aside from? You sell your worthless items like fratles at the public market. When that fails you try and sell even yourselves! Get out! Or you will be beaten and then thrown out."

The doors suddenly opened and several armed men appeared, escorting and somewhat dragging a group of disgruntled foreigners. They were dressed in strange, rich garments. Areoch and his brothers paid them little heed. It was not an unusual occurrence for other tribes and cities to send delegates to Agade, especially from the north, to plead for trading rites to Agade's bronze. They were always turned away.

"Perhaps it is time we turn an open ear to those who come to us, seeking only to increase the wealth of their people," a level voice echoed in the chamber, as the protests of the foreign men died away down the hall. "Do we not have a greater supply of bronze than we can use? Are we to horde this wealth behind our walls while the rest of the world advances?" The noise of scattered approval and sharp words of objection increased from behind the door.

"An open ear?" cried several voices. "What has entered your mind, Rahmaah? Do you want the diseases of the north spewing into Agade? Did you not hear what these *Jazieriens* were saying? What has Zoar to offer us?"

The boys entered the chamber. Several men stood in groups around the circular hall's wide expanse, debating the issue at hand. Many stood around a raised dais where Sargon leaned casually against a tall, white throne of marble.

"That is enough!" thundered Sargon, standing up straighter and bringing an end to the debate. "We will not discuss this matter further. My word is final. We will stand upon the principles with which Ur was founded: the world advances at the pace of this kingdom! We are the example, the exception, the chosen. Speak no more of these ill thoughts and waylaid schemes of other nations!"

Sargon stood tall, his beard was curled and interlaced with bronze and gold. On his arms, bronze armbands glinted in the light. The debate was ended, no one would dare to speak against him. A servant stood near the throne bearing Sargon's standard: the horns of a bull mounted at the base of a white triangle.

The boys approached Sargon's throne as the men of the hall departed in twos and threes, some still covertly discussing what had taken place. Whatever concern was on Sargon's mind, left in an instant as he saw Manish, Rimuš, and Areoch appear out of the crowd. His face broke into a beaming smile.

"My sons!" he cried, walking down to them, "Come, embrace your father. How are you, Rimuš? How is your training? And you Manish, have you learned to use your legs for strength in battle along with your arms? Areoch, draw for me here the runes Marqu has taught you this week."

He knelt on the small step before the foot of his throne like a boy himself, listening and asking questions about their learning and training. They talked at length, fully answering Sargon's questions, excited to share their adventures with him. Sargon was their father, yet he was also the King. There was little time to spend with his family. Like most men of prominence, he left the training and tending of his children in the hands of others. It was not for lack of care or concern he did so, but out of necessity. The three boys could see the love in their father's eyes. He nodded and smiled with them as they told tales of their past week.

Manish, Rimuš, and Areoch re-enacted their scene with Zakkaria in the training arena.

"I would have given much to see that!" Sargon said, chuckling as he heard the tale.

"Nay, my lord, it would have brought you despair to see three princes from your house so easily defeated!" cried a familiar voice. Marqu strode across the wide hall and joined them.

"I see you have been keeping them busy, as is in keeping with your duty," exclaimed Sargon. "And for good reason," he continued, looking back at his sons with excitement in his eyes. "Defeat, my sons, is not a bad thing. It is what cultivates you for victory in the future. You have long prepared to move into the next season of your life and it is for this reason I have called you here today." The boys crowded together, straining their ears, their hearts racing in their chests.

"The Festival of Akitu is upon us," Sargon reminded, standing up and pacing in front of his throne as though practicing a well-rehearsed speech. "People from every corner of Agade have been summoned. In two days' time, we will stand in the shadow of the White Temple to remember the old cold of winter and welcome in the new days of spring, as our fathers long before us made a custom."

'But it is not on account of the festival that I wish to speak with you," he said, observing them closely. "The Festival of Akitu will come and go, as it always has since the time of Eridor... This year, it is what comes *after,* that excites me most. Since you were young, you have trained to be sent out into the world. You have watched your elders return with glory and honor, to take a wife and wear the bands of manhood. Now, it is your turn! The Giġāl awaits you." Sargon turned suddenly, regarding them.

The boys looked at each other, wondering which of them their father had spoken to. Sargon laughed aloud at their expressions. "You need not wonder which of you is chosen. It is all three of you! You are *all* qualified and ready.

'I have spoken with Shazier and the wise men," Sargon continued. "You will be sent forth after the festival of Akitu has drawn to its end. Since our fathers in the ancient days, stretching all the way back before the Great Destruction unmade the world, our household has sent our sons out into the world to become men. So now it will be with you. For a years' time you will wander, seeking adventure and honor among distant lands before returning home."

"We have long prepared you for this day," added Marqu solemnly. "The lots have not yet been thrown to determine which direction you will be sent. If the lots dictate you are all to travel the same road, you may well decide to travel together. That will be your decision when the time comes."

The three boys were speechless and felt as if they were in a waking dream. Each of them had longed for this moment for the last five years. All the older boys before them, one by one, had gone out and returned changed. Proudly they wore the armbands which distinguished them as men among their household and their kingdom. Only men could choose a craft based on their gifts and their hearts desire: hunters in the Aett, warriors of the E-Kur (under Zakkaria's command), workers of wood, rawhide or bronze, men of the soil, or diviners and wise men.

Areoch looked at Manish and Rimuš with wide eyes, stifling the shout of excitement which rose in his throat. There was much honor and glory to be gained. It was here, finally before him! He had but to walk into it.

"Go now," said Sargon, "and rest for the festival. Your questions will be answered later, when the casting of the lots determines your fate. You and I will meet again and I shall give you gifts and advice for your journey. Until then, prepare and rest. Do not stray far from the city! Be with our household and family until you depart, for you will be gone long and will not return the same."

Without another word the three boys were dismissed. Their cries of excitement echoed back into the chamber as the doors closed behind them. Marqu smiled and shook his head.

"Like their father at their age, I imagine," he said, casting a twinkling eye upon Sargon.

"Yet, I fear Rimuš is too young. They are all too young." Sargon commented.

"Are not all too young before they are sent on the Giĝāl? And they return older. Such is the way of things, and it has much honor to it."

A tall man, who had stood nearby in the shadow, walked over and looked toward the entrance where the three boys had departed.

"Ah, Ensi Rahmaah. What say you regarding this matter? Are they too young?" asked Marqu, facing him.

"I think not," concluded Rahmaah after a pause. "The gods would not have determined it, if it was not so. Change is in the air."

Chapter Ten

Throwing of the Lots

The Durgu Mountains were north of Ur, their peaks occasionally dusted with snow as they ran west from the sea. During most of the year, Ur's tan walls blended well with the brown grasslands of the foothills; but as the onset of spring brought warmer days and the clouds deposited their stores of early spring rain, the hills turned into a luscious green landscape, dotted with sparse clusters of evergreen trees.

It was in these high hills that Areoch found himself on the eve of the Akitu festival. Fields of wild lavender had sprung up from the rolling knolls and little gorges ran between them, filling the air with sounds of gurgling water and swaying rushes. The lavender would not flower for several months, but it still gave a sweet and crisp fragrance. Areoch breathed in deeply. He lay nestled in a ring of flattened stalks. The city of Ur seemed small and hidden through the growing plants which stood tall around him. The day was bright and slowly warming. Areoch sighed with happiness as he let his eyes drift closed.

"Your father is going to stone you alive if he finds you up here, especially today!" interrupted a cheerful voice, startling Areoch out of his reprieve. Areoch sat upright as the recognizable face of a middle-aged man, stained with a dark scar that stretched from ear to brow, appeared over the edge of his make-shift nest. Areoch grinned and then settled back down into a more comfortable position.

"You must not scare me like that Rafael!" huffed Areoch. He allowed his eyes to drift closed once more.

"Warden to you, youngster," chided Rafael as he stepped over the shrubbery and sat with Areoch in the little circle of crushed grass. Areoch opened one eye as the warden pulled a short bow from his back and busied himself with its cord and a block of wax. Rafael was much older than Areoch (though not an old man by any means), dressed in well-used leather breaches. A forest-green cloak covered his shoulders, despite the sun's relief from the morning chill.

"Out for a few days?" asked Areoch. He noticed a leather satchel at the warden's hip, brimming with necessary supplies. "Need some company?"

"Nay, I would be glad to be rid of you for once!" the warden replied with a chuckle. "I am still surprised that I remained breathing after your father found out about our occasional outings last time. I am journeying quickly today - the priests require more wild fare to supplement the festival and by the looks of things I do not doubt we'll need it." He peered down the hill where long lines of people and wagons could be seen streaming along the road into Ur, like ants entering a hill.

"Ten hunting Aett's have been sent out already, but feeding the whole of Agade for two weeks takes every helping hand. There won't be an ibex left in these foothills for the next week! I'll be back in a few days, before things are well under-way. You should return and rest. The first night of the festival will be long as it is!"

The warden strung his bow and stood, stepping out of the ring. He started to make his way farther into the hills. Areoch scrambled to his feet and looked at the warden with pleading eyes.

"Just as far as the pass! Please? I may not have another chance to come with you."

The warden stopped and pursed his lips.

"So I hear on the streets of Ur," he said. "The rumors say the Gigāl awaits you and your brothers - a man's first great adventure." He was silent for a time and looked into the distance of the mountains, as if recalling some great and life-changing time.

"No, you cannot come," he answered shortly over his shoulder. He walked off at a brisk pace leaving Areoch crestfallen behind him. After about ten paces he paused.

"Fine! Fine!" he shouted back. "But no farther than the old fir. It is Umu Lion country past that, and your father really would kill me if I took you into the mountains a week before your Gigāl."

Areoch cried out with joy and caught up with the warden in a few leaps and bounds.

"You are too easy, Rafael!" Areoch cried. Areoch ran ahead, down into an adjoining gully and up the opposing hillside. The warden shook his head and smiled as a rabbit shot out from the brush and away from Areoch's escapade.

Drawing back his bow, he loosed an arrow with a twang.

"Better than a good hunting falcon," he laughed silently to himself.

Truth be told, the warden was going to miss the boy dearly. Rafael had few friends, and that by choice, for he was well respected at the city gate and the best hunter in Ur. They had spent many long days roving the hill country together (not in secret from Sargon, as Areoch supposed, for Sargon knew the warden well) and Rafael had grown quite fond of

Areoch. Areoch had much to learn, but his spirit was sharp and his heart fully alive - which is as much as one could ask for.

"Tell me, Rafael" asked Areoch, as the Warden plucked his arrow from the hare and placed the animal into his satchel, "how long were you away on your Giḡāl?"

"A year, as is customary," the warden replied. He cleaned his arrow before returning it to his quiver. "Though many stay out for longer, if they wish, and some don't return at all! I spoke with a man last summer who, for three years, never knew what became of his son. Then on a trip to Magen for grain, he came across him! Fat, happy, and married into another household! The power a woman holds over a young man! Can you believe it?" Rafael slapped his knee with a chuckle and then realized he was getting far off-topic. He absentmindedly unstrung his bow.

"There is much to be seen of the world, Areoch, to the east and south and even as far west as the great Shinar River. Great kingdoms of men, oceans and deserts, riches and temples, beasts and adventures, and unknown lands... It is an amazing time, one you will never forget."

"Did the lots send you to the north? Have you seen the Red Mountains of Oodan? Did you walk among ruins that have lain empty and bare since the time of Eridor?" Excitement shone from Areoch's eyes as he spoke from the lore Marqu sometimes referenced, but the look in the warden's eye humbled him and he grew silent.

"North? The lots have not sent one toward the dynasties of the north for many, many years. Hope that you will not be the first." He looked at Areoch strangely. "What is it that makes you ask?"

Areoch shrugged his shoulders. "My father does not tolerate their ways," Areoch said bluntly. "I wonder if all that is said about the northern cities can be true. It seems strange that a people could be so hated without reason, other than they dwell on the other side of the mountains."

"Sargon's decision regarding Agade and the northern cities has nothing to do with likes or dislikes," the warden stated curtly.

"So, you *have* been to a northern city?"

"No," answered the warden irritably. "But I have heard much about what goes on in those lands. It is not for lack of reason that your father has no commerce there! Few of us may set foot beyond the borders. Agade is a safety net, a dam that stems the tide from poisoning the rest of the sea. You know the old stories."

"I do not understand why we do not try and seek a cure, if they are poisoned," said Areoch.

"You sound like some of the wise men who now speak into the ear of Sargon!" cried the Warden with surprise, looking keenly at the boy. "Some sickness is rooted too deep, Areoch. Has Marqu not instructed you in lore and legend? There are older and more ancient tales that are long forgotten in other places of the world. Clearly they are spoken of less frequently these days."

Areoch had heard these tales, but rarely outside of the priest's gibberish. Rafael was his best source, and he enjoyed them, so he waited for the Warden to continue.

"They say that before the Great Destruction came upon the Old world, ancient beings of Power - many think they were gods themselves - watched over the lands. It was the Lord Núnimar," the warden reflected, "that was said to have watched over this region, where Agade is now. The stories say he was a great Being of light, full of strength and goodness. Others watched elsewhere: The Lords Egal-Mah, Ud-Sahara, and Gibil, all stewards of the land, giving it power to grow and change."

"I have heard Marqu say as much on occasion, when he speaks of olden times," said Areoch. "Though he never says more."

Rafael laughed aloud. "That is no surprise to me. Few talk of the Old World anymore, and though I think Marqu knows its history better than most, he is slow to speak of it. It is a lost time, though it should never have become so."

"I do not understand, Rafael" persisted Areoch, whacking the surrounding foliage with a stout stick he had found. "Why is the north so evil if such Beings governed the lands? If it is as you say, I would think that power of goodness would stay. Why is Agade the only region that is good?"

The warden paused and took a long drink from his water skin. The sun was high in the sky, and they had walked far.

"It is just a story, Areoch. Even the legends say many of these powerful Beings were evil, torturing the land and dishonoring all they could. The north was where they dwelt. That darkness still lingers there in the marrow of the earth, and the people that dwell there show it. Some evil simply does not die.

'But we have far surpassed my knowledge of history and stray into myth," Rafael said with a smile. "I am no sage or wise man, I see only what my eyes tell me. I venture farther north than most, into the Valley of Dry Bones even, to hunt gazelle and ibex for your father's table. I go no farther, for that journey is fraught with peril. The roads are not safe, men beyond the Durgu Mountains kill without thought or cause. They take much and waste more. They make their own laws to justify their own evil deeds! Such is a sight you do not want to see, Areoch. Stay away from those places! They are perilous. There is a sickness that lies upon that land which no eye can see... but when you cross the borders, you can feel it. Trust me when I say: the north and its peoples should be far separated from Agade!"

Ur fell away behind them among rolling hills. They drew nearer to the shadow of the Durgu mountains, which seemed to Areoch like great walls holding back floodwaters that he could not see.

"Are none on the Giğāl sent north then?" Areoch ventured.

"I cannot recall any in my time," the warden answered. "East and South the lots fall, by whatever fate commands them. And sometimes I have seen the lots fall to the west, though that is little different than south, since one must turn that way at the banks of the rushing Shinar. North is never chosen. Agadians do not pass that way."

It felt like little time had passed before a tall pine tree loomed up. Smaller trees dotted the mountain slopes here and there. The pass through the Durgu Mountains was visible, looking to be little more than a gap between the high peaks. Areoch could make out two thin shadows, which he knew to be the E-Kur towers that stood watch there.

The Warden turned and gazed at Areoch.

"It is likely I will not see you again until you return as a man," Rafael said resolutely. "I will clasp your arm now as one whom will return with honor and might! Remember: walk this road with low expectations and a high sense of adventure." He held forth his muscular forearm and Areoch clasped it with his own. Areoch marveled at how small his arm seemed in comparison.

"May Enlil watch over your path and lead you on the high road!" the warden shouted as Areoch turned and ran down the foothills toward Ur.

Over 100,000 people had packed into the white square and its surroundings by the time Areoch returned. The White Temple gleamed in the brilliance of evening. Slowly the shadow of the setting sun climbed up its base, giving the strange impression that the temple was sinking down into the blackness where they all stood.

The Chariot, the constellation of summer, was rising on the purple horizon. It was not seen during the cold months of the year. Slowly, the bright red star which hung at its base rose, attempting to show its face for the first time since winter laid an icy grip on the land. The people held their breath, waiting, waiting. Then, it cleared the horizon!

Fires flared up bright across the white square as Ub drums, massive in size and girth, were beaten by the swinging of great mallets. They throbbed, deep and vibrant from each side of the temple. Altogether over a hundred thousand Agadians leaped to their feet, stomping and clapping with the rhythm of the drums as they sang in one voice:

In those days, those far-remote days

In those nights, those far-away nights

In those years, those long-forgotten years.

Before the time of memory

98

Before the time of thought:
Morning and Evening.

You closed up the days, made the months enter their houses.
You brought light in the darkness, Life in the chaos.
Morning and Evening.

O Foremost, greatest in all the lands;
the Strength of battle, a terrifying storm
The Enveloper of all men,
You gave Strength to the Shedu:
Lord Ninĝinĝar, The Lord Núnimar, The Lord Egal-Mah
And set them on their thrones.
Whatever enters You is unequaled, whatever leaves endures.
Morning and Evening.

The Terrifying Mystery, the House of Radiance
Your white temple and reaching judgment
Which Lord Núnimar has filled with awesomeness and dread.
You're sovereign, a terrifying wild ox, a lion, a flash in the sky
The mighty one's, the Lords without Rival, the Sons of Enlil

They have taken their seat upon your Dias
The Word, The Kingdom, The Sword restored.
The holy mound where Destiny is determined, beautiful as the hills
As peaceful as the sea.

Long was the song of the Akitu festival and Areoch did not recall all of it, for it was sung for many days. It was a song of oral tradition: resonant, with echoes of primordial memories, reaching as far back as history could be preserved by their forefathers. The tribal lore of barbaric herders, it may have seemed to some, but tribes still roamed much of the world. Even in the Kingdom of Agade, such blood coursed deep through their veins.

So, the festival of Akitu ran its course. Some days after, the people began to disperse back to their homes. Sargon, Marqu, and the priest Shazier gathered together in the White Temple to determine the course of the boys' Giĝāl. They stood within the Temple's main chamber, high above the city where only the diviners were permitted to go. The Ensi Rahmaah of Lugal and the Ensi Beckma of Kish, Sargon's right and left hand, were also present to witness the throwing of the lots.

Inlaid lines of gold and silver ran throughout the floor, walls, and ceiling of the chamber; weaving around statues of winged beasts and thick columns. Near the center of the room they came together like veins of a great leaf, flowing upward like an inverted drop of water entering a still pool. From this, a pedestal of gold rose from the floor in the shape of a shallow bowl, and around this the leaders gathered.

"We are all present," spoke Shazier, addressing the small group in a hushed whisper, "and we will now witness which path the sons of this city will be sent down. It is customary that Sargon has the honor of throwing the lots. As this matter concerns him closely, a substitute must be chosen. Who will be determined?"

Without hesitation Rahmaah stepped forward. "It would be my great honor," he said, bowing low.

Shazier nodded and beckoned for Rahmaah to step up to the platform. He handed him three bronze triangles, similarly fashioned in the manner of dice. Each side was marked to indicate a point on the compass: north, south, east, and west.

"You will cast these into the bowl," instructed Shazier. "One for each of Sargon's sons. First: Manish."

Rahmaah nodded and clenched the dice firmly, his hand hovering above the surface of the bowl. He let one drop. It hit the bottom, ringing through the entire room like a connected wind-chime. They peered over the bowl's edge.

"West," said Shazier with finality. "Now, Rimuš."

Another triangle fell from Rahmaah's hand with a soft echo.

"Again, west," said Shazier. "Lastly, Areoch."

Rahmaah stretched forth his hand and let drop the final dice. It bounced from side to side before spinning to a halt. Shazier looked at it for a moment without saying anything. Sargon glanced anxiously at Marqu and then back toward the bowl as his eyes read the inscription.

"It says ...north," said Shazier in a baffled voice.

"That cannot be," Marqu interjected. "One has not been sent north from here since the kingdom has been established."

"It is what the lot says," insisted Shazier.

"Curse your dice!" cried Marqu in a moment of frustration. "*I* know Power and there is no Power in these! This is the work of man and of fools."

Shazier's face grew red and he opened his mouth in retort, but Sargon's voice cut through the tension.

"Throw it again."

Objection was written over Shazier's face and Beckma ventured his opinion.

"My King," he said, "We have always let the Powers of the city decide! If Enlil wishes him to go a new way, then he should go forth upon it with courage!"

"It would be a death mission," interjected Marqu. "Can a man scoop hot coals into his lap without being burned? The peoples of the north hate us. They would kill him at best and he would be captured and bartered with at worse."

"Throw them again," ordered Sargon, and his tone informed everyone present that his decision was final. "If it is as you say, Shazier," said Sargon in a lighter tone, "nothing will change. Throw them again."

Rahmaah slowly picked up the dice and let it fall from his hand. It bounced from side to side of the bowl before finally rolling to a stop.

"I cannot believe it," said Marqu as he read the inscription, running a hand through his white hair. "North! That is not possible. Sargon, stop this madness! Making Areoch travel north would be little better than making Manish and Rimuš cross the Shinar River and then continue, journeying into the Plains of Eridor and the cursed city of Asurla beyond!"

"Do not speak of that place here!" yelled Shazier in a shrill voice. "This is holy ground!"

"It is the truth!" retorted Marqu. "The same evil that once filled the heart of all men, lives north of the Durgu Mountains. There is no insight, no understanding there. They are barbarians. They do not remember the old ways. If you send him that way, you send him to his grave. You were here, all those years ago, when we found what Ur-Zabab erected on this very spot! Do you not remember the screams and the decay?? Yet now you turn a blind eye because your dice say otherwise? You are a fool. You condemn Areoch to death."

"Who are you to speak of power and death? I know who you are, *Kez-Marqu*, and what you have done. You defile this place!" yelled Shazier as his face turned a deeper shade of red. "You may bring worse calamity upon this city at the very mention of such things. I was wrong to let you in here. Out, all of you! OUT!"

Marqu would not be moved until Sargon laid a hand on his shoulder and led him from the temple. As they entered into the open air, Rahmaah approached Sargon and bowed low before him.

"My king, I feel as if this were somehow my fault..." he trailed off, unable to find the words to finish his sentence.

"No, Rahmaah," Sargon consoled, "This is no fault of yours. Perhaps Beckma is right: Areoch was long ago set apart. Maybe now we will finally see what fate awaits him ...and the rest of this Kingdom."

Sargon met privately with each of his sons that night. First, was Manish, then Rimuš, and lastly Areoch was called. Areoch entered the hearing hall and saw his father sitting alone, looking more care-worn than he had ever seen.

As a rule, no one spoke of Areoch's younger years or the history of his bloodline. But, on this night, the images of Areoch's beginnings were engraved upon Sargon's mind.

"Come in, my son, come in," Sargon said, his voice heavy. He stood from his throne and sat down upon the low step, patting the ground beside him. He resisted the urge to put his arm around his son, and was then struck by the thought that Areoch was as tall as he was. He sighed deeply.

"This is an exciting time, Areoch. It is also hard, hard for those of us that will wait for your return. Take these small treasures upon your way. Here, stretch out your hand. A ring of bronze, cast with the image of my household, so you will remember your family. And here, a bronze dagger and stout spear, bear them well to earn glory and honor!" Sargon trailed off as if he had more to say but could hardly bring himself to speak.

Finally, he continued in a low voice and Areoch leaned forward, knowing this part of his father's speech was for him and him alone.

"Areoch, listen to me. You and I have seen many things and you have endured much. Nearly ten years ago I adopted you as my son. I did this, and you are my son just as much as Manish and Rimuš. I knew from the first moment I saw you, that you were different. I was shown that you were set apart from those who dwelt in this land. The Powers have chosen you, Areoch, to travel north."

"What will I find there?" Areoch asked breathlessly.

"I do not know," answered Sargon. "When I first came to this city, I did not know what I would find, though I knew it would be evil. I fear it will be worse for you. While I do not know what that means or what lies ahead, you must take courage. You are my son. What skills have you learned to take with you on your journey?"

"Marqu has taught us many things: I can read the stars in the sky and I know the manner of growing things in their time and season. I can use the carpenter's saw and chisel for carving and know something of the magic of the smiths. Also, we have been taught in the arena to think with our minds in combat. Tracking and hunting have long been a virtue for us."

"You can tan a hide?"

"Yes father," answered Areoch.

"Can you hold a shield in the line of Strong Men, and move as one unit?"

"Yes father, though I never felt we mastered that discipline as we ought."

"It takes years and years to become one of the E-Kur elite, even upon the return from the Gigāl," assured Sargon, his eyes shining with pride. "Marqu has informed me you can read and write runes exceptionally well?"

Areoch's face flushed. "I enjoy them and the story of history. It makes the task of learning them easier than it is to most," he answered humbly.

"That is well," commended Sargon. "Scribes and wise men have long been sought after by kings and leaders among men. Such a skill may serve you better than any talent or precious item you could take with you! Guard that knowledge well, for it will set you apart as the son of a king among barbaric men!" Sargon trailed off, knowing that this moment with his son would be the last he would ever have with the boyish nativity he treasured so much. From this day forward, if he ever met his son again, he would be a man.

"I am not afraid father," said Areoch resolutely, but he saw the fear in his father's eyes and his own heart fell. Sargon reached forward and stoutly gripped his son's shoulder.

"Treasure the wealth of knowledge you have been given here, Areoch. Guard it closely. Remember that you have been chosen for this journey for a purpose. Keep your eyes set forward on the straight path, as is Enlil's way, for crooked are the roads that wind through the northern lands! Stand firm, my son!"

Areoch left his father's hall, pondering in his heart the choices that had been laid before him. Part of him was excited, for he had often wished to see those far-off lands that held so many rumors and hidden tales. He imagined what the ancient northern deserts looked like, and the towering majesty of the mountains beyond the Shinar. But another part of him was now afraid. It was one thing to have everyone around him speak of danger (long off and far away), and another thing to find that same danger before him. He knew that his first task, as a man, would be to accept that danger and choose to face it.

Areoch's head was bowed in contemplation as he walked, and he nearly collided into another man who strolled the dark halls of his father's house.

"Ah, my pardon, young one!" cried a voice. "Ah, Areoch it is you. You must be excited for tomorrow."

"Do I know you, master?" asked Areoch. "It is late, and I can hardly see in this light."

"Of course! I am the Ensi Beckma, your father's servant. He speaks of you often and I feel as though we have long known each other, though we have rarely met."

Areoch nodded, still deep in thought.

"You seem heavy laden, Areoch," remarked Beckma in a kindly tone. "I cannot imagine what you feel. Know this! You may not be able to enter back into Ur for a year, but as the Ensi of Lugal, I extend you welcome. I know I can speak for Ensi Rahmaah of Kish as well. Many who go upon their Gigāl do not have to go far to find a wealth of new adventure. Our cities are open to you."

"Thank you for your kind words, Ensi Beckma. I do not know exactly what lies ahead, but should fate take me upon a road close to Lugal or Kish, I will be grateful to share your house."

Beckma smiled as Areoch walked away, disappearing down the dark corridor. They never met again.

Chapter Eleven

<u>A Northern Road</u>

The three brothers walked together the next morning toward the great northern gateway of Ur, each fingering their weapons and thinking of the words Sargon had spoken to them the previous night. Fine jewelry was hung about their necks and each of them bore the signet ring of their father's house. A bow of yew was on the back of Manish, while Rimuš carried a corded sling with smooth stones and a broad leather shield. Areoch held his long, bronze-tipped spear. They all received a bronze dagger and bore them proudly in belts of silver. Bronze plates (woven to light jerkins of leather), rested over their tunics and sparkled in the sunlight. More bronze armor was strapped securely to their shins. Each had a small satchel of necessities at their side.

Sargon, and some of his household, stood upon the gatehouse wall looking down on them as they approached; while others of the city lined either side of the roadway. Some of the women of Sargon's household were weeping. Areoch noticed several boys watching them from the roadway in awe.

Shazier addressed them before they passed through the gate.

"Sons of Sargon! The lots have chosen which direction you are to travel. Go that way, until your course is steered elsewhere. You are not to return to the city of Ur until a season of the world has passed. When you do return, you will do so as men and will receive the armbands of manhood. May Enlil watch over you!"

The men touched their armbands and muttered low words of strength as the boys walked down the line. Areoch took a deep breath before walking through the towering northern gate with his brothers. It closed ominously behind them. The dusty road divided. One way ran east toward Kish and the sea, one west along the foothills, and the last ran north, overshadowed by the peaks of the Durgu Mountains. The three brothers grasped each other's forearms tightly and then departed, heading in their respective directions: Manish and Rimuš west, along the foothills; and Areoch north, toward the Durgu pass.

Rahmaah and Beckma stood under the eaves of the eastern sheep-gate of Ur, hidden in shadow. Four other men stood with them.

"Are we clear, Jagu?" asked Beckma, addressing the largest of the four.

Jagu scraped his hairy back with a curved knife and spat on the wall beside him.

"Clear? That's a fact, it is. My boys and I won't have any trouble, if that's what you mean."

"What about our payment?" whined one of the ugly thugs, scratching his head with a clawed hand. "I thought we would get paid before we had to leave."

"Shut your shriveling mouth, Dumbar," said Jagu. "That's not how it works, see? We bring back the bodies and the signet rings, and *then* we get paid. Right?" He turned a questioning glance to Rahmaah, who rubbed his brow irritably.

"Yes. They have nearly an hour start on you, and I grow impatient. Go and complete your task, trust you will be well rewarded upon your return."

Dumbar opened his mouth again, but before he could speak Jagu cuffed him about his ears.

"I said shut your mouth, Dumbar. Ensi Rahmaah grows impatient! *And* they have a head start on us. We will be rewarded upon our return."

"Which way did they go?" growled a large character with a murderous gleam in his eye. He hefted a large ax upon his shoulder.

"They went west," sneered Jagu, pointing a finger south.

"No," said Rahmaah, the frustration clear in his voice. "One went north, two went west. Which is *that* way," he said, pointing toward the foothills. "Get on after them!"

"Yeah. They went *that* way, you fool!" cried Jagu, addressing the ax man. "And one went north. You and Bel-Siles go after those two. Dumbar and myself will go north."

The four men departed from the gate, two heading west and two heading north into the mountains at a brisk pace, leaving Rahmaah trembling with rage.

"I thought you said you had good men at your disposal," hissed Rahmaah as Beckma closed the sheep-gate with a slam, sliding its bolt back into place.

"What's wrong with those four?" asked Beckma coolly. "They'll do their job well enough and it will be easy for us to bury them... and their stories... upon their return."

The anger disappeared from Rahmaah's face.

"Ah, I see. Well done Beckma. It is not without reason Sargon made you the Ensi of Lugal!" They laughed together before departing into the flowing streets of Ur.

Areoch's spirits swelled and his stride lengthened as the shapes of his brothers grew small. He waded through the rolling fields of lavender, their crushed stems filling the air with sweetness, as he contemplated what lay ahead.

The sun rose high as Areoch traversed the low foothills. The lavender faded and he pushed onward, past the tall pine tree. By early evening, he had entered the Durgu pass. Dark clouds had begun to cover the sky and Areoch smelled the sweetness of rain on the wind. The last two watchtowers of Agade rose before him, tall and lonely sentinels among the pillars of rock. Areoch strode between them, and even though he did not see any movement within their high, dark windows - he could feel eyes watching him. As he passed under the fortified columns, Areoch thought of Commander Zakkaria and his great task of leading the E-Kur.

Areoch looked ahead and surveyed ground that was new to him. The road disappeared into the mountains and toward the Valley of Dry Bones, fading in the direction of strange city states and dynasties of the north. He stopped, as the darkness of the sky increased, and looked back. The two towers stood still in the sunlight and welcoming green hills shone far off behind them. He thought he could see Ur, small and square somewhere among them. He looked ahead again, down the unknown road with its sharp mountain peaks upon either side, and some measure of fear filled his heart.

At that moment a call, like the shrill cry of a bird, rang out. Turning back once more, Areoch could see a small figure standing on the mountainous hillside near the E-Kur towers. It was the warden, his hand raised high in farewell. The two towers seemed to answer in reply: red and white banners suddenly unfurled from their battlements and brazen blasts echoed from their archways, the sound reverberating down the mountain road like a thousand warriors paving the way before him.

"Stand tall my friend!" floated the voice of Rafael on the wind. "Many great things lay ahead! Take them in stride, have courage, and remember your home awaits your return. Stand firm! And now: forward!"

Areoch raised his spear and would have shouted in answer, but at that moment a cloud swept across the last rays of sunlight and a wind raced down the pass, chasing away his words and making the scene fade into shadow. Areoch once again faced the onward journey and he strode with renewed confidence down its winding path. Neither he nor the Agadian watchtowers saw the shadowy figures scurry from rock to rock through the pass, unseen, a fair distance behind him.

The evening drew to a close as Areoch wound on. The road had become more treacherous: a sharp, steep ravine ran off the eastern side of the path; while the mountains formed a sheer, impenetrable wall to the west. Through this the northerly road ran and the wind howled. Areoch had long looked for shelter among the rising cliffs, for night was fast approaching, but he had found none. Storm clouds were thick, and drops of rain began to fall from the sky as the darkness of night seemed to come upon the mountains without warning. The pass was bare, a few gnarled trees clutched to rocky surfaces and jagged stones stood out from the cliffs like razors, providing no relief from the wind and rain. Areoch struggled onward as the night fell deeper, hoping to come across a cave or clove in the rock which would provide shelter from the storm.

Thunder rumbled across the sky as the downpour above broke loose in fury. Lighting struck the rocks in the high ridge above his head, causing them to tumble downward, whistling across the narrow road and into the deep ravine. One boulder, nearly the size of Areoch himself, came out of the darkness above so suddenly, Areoch instinctively ducked to avoid it. It flew over him with inches to spare, striking the spear in his hand and snapping off its point in the darkness. Areoch cursed and threw the shaft aside, searching the wet ground for the bronze head. He could not find it, and there was still nothing for shelter. Areoch drew his jerkin tighter about his dripping shoulders, wondering why he didn't have the foresight to bring a cloak. He gritted his teeth and plunged forward blindly.

Dark rocks, glistening wet, loomed up from the darkness as he passed, and more crashed around him as he slid and stumbled. One of these dark shadows seemed to rise up from its resting place. Areoch choked back a scream of terror and surprise as it brushed against his leg. He shied back against the cliff, his wet hand groping for the dagger at his belt. Then he saw that it was only a small, black cat - skinny, bedraggled, and wet from the downpour.

"Hey there, little guy," Areoch coaxed, wiping water from his eyes as he released his dagger hilt. He bent down and picked up the thin form, hiding it away in the dryness of his arm.

"What are you doing way up here? Looking for shelter like me, I imagine." The little cat shivered, looked at Areoch with knowing eyes, and then back out into the darkness of the pass. Its ears perked forward as if hearing something Areoch could not. Areoch stared into the darkness until his eyes hurt, hardly daring to breathe. Slowly, another dim shadow separated itself from the inky blackness. It was the shape of a man, just out of sight, where Areoch could not distinguish between reality and imagination. The form seemed to be watching them. Areoch drew back again, dropping the cat as it landed with a hiss in a puddle.

"Who goes there?" cried Areoch.

There was no reply. Areoch managed to draw his dagger from its clasp. Its color was a dull fire and the rain bounced off its smooth edge.

"You could do little more to make yourself a clearer target, should one be wishing to find you," said a low voice from the darkness. "Better a cloak at night than a bronze exhibition." The shady form bent down and the little black cat ran into its arms. The figure came nearer, revealing the wizened face of an old man beneath a dark hood and cloak, dripping with the downpour. His eyes were piercing, as if they had seen many ages of man.

"Not as tall as I thought he'd be," said the man quietly to the cat who stuck its head out of his cloak. It said nothing in reply. "Still, we better get him into some shelter before a rock turns him into a barley cake. Come along with me," the elder said, addressing Areoch, before turning and walking with a head bent into the storm.

Chapter Twelve

Riddles of History

Areoch hesitated and the dagger loosened in his hand. It was the cat, however, that finally convinced him. He had always assumed animals had a good sense of things; if the cat was so trustworthy of this man, he would risk following him in a storm. He ran to catch up with the odd couple.

The old man led them farther along the pass until he suddenly veered off, close to the cliff face. A small fissure opened, impossible to see in the darkness, which revealed a sheltered path twisting its way up into the mountains beyond. They took this track, and for the next few miles Areoch struggled to follow his guide, who seemed unusually spry for his apparent age. The man pressed ahead, never hesitating, as the path forked and twisted - always going steeply upward, until Areoch lost all sense of direction.

When Areoch felt he could not go any further, they slowed. They were high; Areoch could feel rather than see the broad, open expanse of alpine tops surrounding them, lonely sentinels in the night. The rain was lighter, but colder, as it fell in thin sheets. In front of them stood a single pillared mountain top, a shadow in the darkness, and their path made straight for it without any deviation.

They continued, gusts of wind and rain bit at their faces, until it abruptly ceased. The air became dry, and the man paused in the darkness, muttering something under his breath. A light was revealed. They stood in a passageway, nearly a perfect tunnel carved into the rock. The old man carried a torch in his hand. He looked back at Areoch with a wry eye. The cat walked alongside him. As they made their way deeper into the cave, Areoch wondered where he was and who this strange man could be.

Soon Areoch felt the ceiling expand above his head. As his guide thrust his torch into the middle of a stack of firewood, Areoch saw why.

A cavern rose high around them. An exit led out the opposite side of the mountain, about a stone's throw from where they stood. The path they had entered looked as if it had been tunneled by hand, until meeting the natural chamber. The fire crackled merrily and the old man busied himself with a large, clay pot from which some pleasant aroma was already drifting.

Areoch's attention, however, was fixed upward and his mouth gaped open in awe. The light from the fire danced across the walls revealing a mural, grand and eloquent, stretching from floor to ceiling around the entirety of the cave, blanketing Areoch in an unexpected brilliance. The man chuckled when he saw Areoch's expression and the cat twitched its ears as it curled up next to the fire.

"Come, sit and eat. Warm yourself by the fire. You're drenched!" he welcomed.

Areoch became aware of his aching limbs and cast himself down, his armor steaming by the fire. He gratefully accepted a bowl of soup and warmed himself. Even though spring had arrived, the nights were still cold, especially as high in the pass as they were.

"Who are you?" asked Areoch finally.

The old man seemed to be lost in thought, oblivious to the fact that Areoch was present. He started at Areoch's question.

"Eh, what was that? Who am I? That *is* a bold question" he said, looking at the cat instead of Areoch. "He might as well ask who *you* are." He looked again into the distance and a long silence followed.

"I am a clam in a large ocean, if I have learned anything about the world. But some call me Melkezadek. You may do likewise."

Areoch raised a quizzical eyebrow at the mysterious reply.

"What is that?" Areoch asked, hoping to garner a better answer from this strange character. He pointed upward, toward the fine brush strokes and figures that filled the cavern ceiling, with emphasis.

Melkezadek stretched out his legs by the fire and turned his head upward.

"That is the story of the world, both Old and New... or at least the parts that will be remembered," Melkezadek added, glancing sidelong at the cat. The cat walked over to the entrance of the cavern as if it did not much care about their conversation.

"What does it say?" Areoch's eyes lit in wonder at the mention of the Old World.

Melkezadek shook his head. "You do not know what you ask, youngling. If I retold this story, your bones would be white and clean in this cave by the time you were finished listening. And, by that time, you might even rise up to let me know I did an excellent job telling it." He chuckled to himself quietly as if pleased with his wit.

Areoch studied the pictures, craning his neck. Depicted were great battles and people, fire and water, giant cities with banners flying, beasts with many faces, and many other incomprehensible things. Several sections were empty, or at least he could not decipher the things hidden among the shadows.

"What happened?" he wondered in amazement. "It seems like a great story, though I cannot make it out."

Melkezadek sighed. "Less than twelve generations of men have passed and already they do not remember their own story; yet even the wise of lore do not have a care to. How should I expect a young one to do so?" The cat returned from the cave entrance and curled up near Areoch, who stroked it absentmindedly.

Melkezadek continued, and as he spoke Areoch saw the pictures on the ceiling come together in a way, so that he could comprehend some sense of their tangle:

"There was a time, long before your forefathers, in which the Crown of heaven was worn by man and Lords of the Old World - the servants of Enlil - walked among us. We called them the Shedu, the Lords of Light. I can see you have heard of them, at least. That is good, for many have forgotten them entirely."

He paused and the cat purred under Areoch's hand.

"It was in this time, nearer to the beginning of the Old World, that a dark power rose up and ruled the earth. The history of this power I cannot say, none but the Shedu ever knew the full story. But there is such a thing as malice in the world, my lad. This power slowly, ever so slowly, corrupted the hearts of many Shedu... and then of men. It took the Kingship from men and turned the world into darkness. The source of this power, the great Enemy, began to be called by name: Ningîngar. The dark Shedu that followed it were called the *Uttuki*. The earth, then, became a battlefield between the remaining Shedu and the Uttuki. Of this battle I cannot tell any tale, for it began long before my memory of the Old World begins."

Melkezadek paused and the cat looked up at him, kneading its claws into Areoch's garments. "The result was the Great Destruction."

"I have heard some of these things mentioned in the Akitu festival," Areoch murmured idly. "We sing of the Great Destruction. A torrent of water. And death, always death."

"Yes, parts of this story your generation has not completely forgotten," said Melkezadek. "Such things are not easily lost from memory, even by a blinded race. The Great Destruction was the single most definite event in the course of the world."

"But what was it?" Areoch asked.

Melkezadek looked shocked.

"The Great Destruction? By Enlil's mercy, do not even you know?"

Areoch's face was blank and Melkezadek shook his head in wonder.

"We wonder why our youth have no direction," he murmured, looking at the cat. "What are we teaching them? Nothing of their fathers' ancient mistakes. We leave it to them to make their own path, and we suffer for it."

Melkezadek ran a hand through his hair and turned back to Areoch.

"The world was destroyed, boy, unmade as it had been made, and nearly all that was within it, that we had been given power to govern, was taken. The words of your ancient fathers had the power to change the very fabric of nature. But we drew away from the *See'rs*, our wives, and could no longer see the effects our words had. We drew away from the Shedu. The Uttuki played their hand well. In the end, both the heavens and the earth were fought over and a great rift was placed between man and the role we once held in creation. Ninĝinĝar and its Uttuki were cast down, the catastrophic results of our abused words were abolished, and mankind was given a second chance to rule the earth, albeit different than it was in the beginning."

"So... you're saying the Great Destruction, the Shedu and the Uttuki... that is all real?" Areoch whispered.

Melkezadek no longer concealed his shock at Areoch's questions.

"Areoch," Melkezadek said solemnly. "Open your eyes." Before Areoch could ask how this man knew his name, Melkezadek's hand reached out toward Areoch's face. Like a strike of lightning, the man's fingers touched his eyes.

Areoch froze, for in an instant he stood aboard a mighty ship. Three-hundred cubits long, it must have been, and half that wide. The timbers shook and trembled beneath him, straining to hold against the mountains of undulating water that stretched as far as the eye could see. The air ripped and crackled with thunder. Rain and hail pelted him from every direction. All around was a shifting, shapeless torrent of darkness, and a fear filled Areoch that passed beyond that of death. Something else was out there: something else was moving over the surface of the water. Without warning, the ship tilted, cavorting up a wave a hundred times the size of the ship itself. Areoch fell, sliding with a sickening jolt across the rough timbers and toward the edge of the ship. He reached out, flailing, and grabbed a rail. He held there, straining, dangling over the water. With a flash of lighting, Areoch wretched, for the water was filled with floating corpses. His hold slipped. He tumbled toward the silent faces.

Areoch fell back, spilling his soup across the floor of the cave. His trembling hands caught himself upon the stone and he scrambled to his feet. His eyes were wide as he recognized the fire and Melkezadek - who looked at him calmly. Above him, the mural seemed to surge and Areoch could make out one section clearly. Torrents of water rose like mountains, and a ship (small it seemed upon the wall), scaled their great heights.

"I was there, Areoch," Melkezadek whispered. "This I saw."

The rain continued to fall outside the entrance of the cave in a steady patter as Areoch gathered his bearings.

"You are a sage," Areoch determined slowly. "You speak like one." Areoch was shaking. "I can see your words in my mind. Do not touch me again!" he demanded. "I have heard Marqu speak like this, though I can get no more out of him regarding the history from which he comes or how this power works. Why is that? Why do I feel..." Areoch gasped, struggling to suppress the thoughts and emotions which rose within him.

Areoch grew quiet and found himself remembering his real father, the father who had sent him to his death. His emotions seemed amplified, as did his voice, under this mysterious ceiling of stone.

Melkezadek sat back, pondering Areoch's question.

"Kez-Marqu," he finally muttered, "Yes, I have heard he lives still behind Sargon's walls. We are the *Kez*, Areoch. Survivors of a time you cannot remember, of a world that will never come again.

'What is a sage nowadays?" he asked himself. "Any man may claim to be a diviner or priest. They mimic power, using common practices to imagine something extraordinary. Man is not what he was before the Great Destruction."

Areoch stood still until his breathing leveled. A long silence followed.

Melkezadek stroked his beard as his eyes traveled across the cave's mural. Eventually, he spoke again.

"Even more time passed. Men multiplied and once again grew strong on the earth. A leader rose among them who called himself King Asurla. He hated the Old World: its memory, its pain, and its Beings. Asurla promised the people that he would never again allow for such a destruction. He promised they would be in control of their own fate, and they flocked to his banner. He united all of mankind under his Kingship. *All* of them, you understand? Then he convinced them to destroy the Ancient Powers that remained from the Old World. Asurla was called 'Hunter' by some, and 'Slayer' by others, and so he was. He hunted the remaining Uttuki and Shedu alike (both now cast aside by men), along with the remaining Kez (the firstborn of the ancient times). Of these there were only nine families: The Seven, who joined him in his cause; and the Two, who saw the shadow of what was happening and fled from him. Oh, how Asurla feared and hated all that was from the Old World!"

Areoch gazed at the faces of the men and beasts high upon the ceiling. His heart had calmed. Keeping a wide berth from Melkezadek, he returned to the fire.

"You must understand, this was a momentous period," Melkezadek continued. "Weapons of metal were first crafted, the art of smelting and casting discovered, cities were built so large and tall they looked down upon the mountains. Bright were the banners of King Asurla's Strong Men and high were the calls of their horns upon the plains of Eridor."

Melkezadek's gray eyes shone as he spoke and Areoch seemed to hear the sounds of shouting and horns blasting in the distance. Areoch gripped the rock upon which he sat, as if clinging to present time and space, unwilling to depart again. Melkezadek pretended not to notice, and continued.

"Change was in the air. And when change is paired with fear and united under one leader, many great ...and evil... things may happen. They were all wrong. All foolish."

The cat had stopped purring and now looked at Melkezadek intensely.

Areoch looked up at the ceiling of the cave and thought he could pick out legions of men and bright banners flying.

"Why did the plains of Eridor become such a place of fear? Why was the city of Eridor left abandoned?"

Melkezadek shook his head. "I was not there, Areoch. I fled east. I do not know what happened. Men have never since been unified together and it may be that is for the best. Perhaps it was just as bad for man to try and make no Power exist at all than it was to follow a Dark one."

"Ever since I was young," Areoch whispered, "I have heard only whispers of where I come from and even less regarding where ...and who... the people of these lands used to be - other than they were evil. I was one of those people. My father was their king. They were my family. My people."

He paused and shook himself, as though ridding himself of a spell Melkezadek had woven. "Who am I, in this great story that no one cares to remember? I feel in my heart that things can change, that the hate of Agade toward the north is misplaced, if one was unafraid of what he might find there. My father wishes to attain some of the glory of the older days, but what that glory is, who can tell? For none speak of it openly. None remember it, and those that do sing only of death and despair."

Melkezadek looked at Areoch closely, stroking his beard as the sparks drifted upward toward the ceiling.

"Answers, it seems, are a rare commodity from those who are not themselves willing to go out and open their eyes," he said knowingly. The cat flicked its ears in agreement.

"Answers, it seems, are the one thing no one is telling me plainly! You claim that you have walked in the generations of my ancient forefathers and seen the very destruction of the world," Areoch surmised doubtfully.

"I am a clam!" said Melkezadek with a comical face. "Though I could be called a historian, or a prophet, perhaps."

The cat blinked lazily.

"You ask who I am, Areoch, and you seek to understand the reason behind what you feel, but I cannot give you any proof that would satisfy you. Some things you must learn for yourself. Truly, I am a remnant." He finished meekly, looking away into the darkness.

"I *don't* understand," agreed Areoch, letting his eyes wander across the ceiling. "Why are you telling me this at all?"

"You asked, didn't you?" cried Melkezadek. "Don't ask an old man to tell a story if you don't want a response! But even so, I do not believe in happenstance. This story you need to know, for in it you may play a key role, Areoch, son of Ur-Zabab and adopted heir to Sargon the Great! Yes, I know who you are and that you travel north on your Giġāl."

"You are from Agade? How did you pass by the E-Kur towers? None are allowed to venture past them and into the north."

"I did not say I was from Agade. I said I know who you are," answered Melkezadek with a mischievous glint in his eye. "There are many paths less traveled if one is willing to look hard enough."

Areoch did not reply and looked upon Melkezadek with growing suspicion.

"You are quick to trust, Areoch, and that could prove dangerous in the coming days. The Darkness is again awakening. The cities in the north bear strange rumors of an unknown power. Ancient tales are told anew from the mouths of wanderers, claiming to have seen amazing things. And your father, hiding behind his walls, has done little."

Areoch shook his head, and turned his eyes away from the cavern's ceiling.

"What is there in the world besides the flesh of man and the dirt of the earth?" Areoch challenged. "You speak of strange things, Melkezadek. You talk as if these Shedu and Uttuki are here among us, if they ever were at all. You speak of Asurla and Eridor, the forgotten kings and the forbidden cities, in the same breath. You have shared with me your food and your fire, and for this I am grateful. Yet, what you say is hard to swallow. Ancient Powers, long ago battles... It affects us here and now, little. Whatever darkness there is has been destroyed. All that is left is what mankind now creates for itself. If we simply lived at peace with each other, it would be cured."

"Darkness is not something which sits defeated, Areoch! And it is not something *you* can cure. A candle in a dark room drives away the shadows, it does not destroy them. They remain, hidden in possibility, behind every bowl and table until the candle grows dim - then they come forth again. This evil is the same. It festers and multiplies, like a small infection which then consumes the whole body. And, it has been allowed to sleep far too long."

While Melkezadek spoke, his face grew thin and drawn as if he was remembering a terrible time, or something he had long tried to avoid and now saw coming. The look passed from his face and he continued in a lower tone.

"Areoch, you may doubt what I tell you. Your father has tried to shut it out, with walls and legions of men, and in part, he has succeeded. But no region of the world can stay immune if the world itself is sick. Heed the advice of an old man: when you face the chance to turn back on the adventure that lies ahead of you, don't flee or take the safer road. Trust that you are *there* for a purpose. You and I may meet again, after a time, and you may understand more. For now, your journey lies ahead. Much of what you think you know, will be undone; and much of which you don't know, will be revealed. Rest here, Areoch, son of Sargon. I fear you will need it."

That was all Areoch remembered of the strange man and his strange cat, for when he awoke late in the morning they were gone. Sunlight streamed in through the caves entrance, blurring the shadows of the cavern. The embers of the fire were still warm and the paintings about the cavern walls (while seemingly less grand), remained. If it had not been so, he would have written off the night as a delusion of his mind. He looked at the mural for a long time before he departed into the sunlight, trying to make sense of it, he could not. He could only remember imagining, sometime before he fell asleep, that he saw a haunting image of himself standing in the shadow of a mighty tree.

Chapter Thirteen

Mauling

Areoch stumbled out of the cave and found himself high above a land bathed in morning sunlight. A rocky ravine gashed into a steep slope, opening into a dry valley far in the distance. A road stretched horizontal across the distant floor, little more than a thin line running into the east from the west between rolling foothills. It arched gradually north, continuing until it vanished beneath a carpet of green boughs that Areoch assumed was a distant forest. He imagined he could smell the fresh pine needles and budding branches sweeping toward him in the wind.

Another road could be seen on Areoch's left, winding through the sheer passes of the Durgu Mountains, until reaching the valley floor. Not a single traveler was visible, moving in any direction, on either road. Had Areoch been looking at a map, he would have realized that by following Melkezadek through the mountains, it had cut off nearly a half-day from his journey. As it was, he only knew that he stood on the northern slope of the Durgu Mountains.

The valley road, which seemed close at hand from the mountain top, was soon lost to view as Areoch descended. The foothills loomed up as he struggled in the direction he thought would take him toward the road and the forest. Dust and shale kicked up small avalanches as he scrambled down. He paused at midday, drinking some of his water skin and having a small respite of dried fruits and meat. With a clatter of stones, the shale slid behind where he rested, and Areoch thought he saw the lithe form of a marmot or squirrel dart between the rocks. He paid it little heed before pressing on.

He did not have to struggle for much longer, over the next rise the road came into view. He found himself much farther west than he had hoped. Dark caves opened within the hill on the opposing side of the valley. As he crossed the final expanse, Areoch wondered to himself why it was called the Valley of Dry Bones.

As Areoch approached the road, two dots detached themselves from a group of nearby boulders. Soon Areoch could make out the forms of two men. They were covered in dirt and grime from quick travel. Their garments were tattered, dry at the fringes but still wet elsewhere, as if they had been drug across the stones of a shallow river. The men looked as if they had been plagued for lack of sleep. Areoch found the idea of another traveler welcoming and he was curious to see what the people north of the Durgu Mountains would be like.

"Greetings, fellow traveler!" cried the larger of the two men in common Agadian. Areoch trotted over the last bit of sparse turf up to the road. The men stood at some distance, watching Areoch descend, then approached him with renewed energy and a casual stride - the leader grinning broadly with a lopsided and toothy smile.

"Fine bit of weather we have now, after those rough few days. Quite a relief says me traveling companion Dumbar here. We was forced to travel all the night through and only just arrived here! What a bit of luck! Jagu's the name, how do you do, what's yours?"

"They call me Areoch," he replied, somewhat surprised at their friendliness. "From where do you come? I am stunned to hear the Agadian speech across the mountains."

"Areoch! Now that's a name, ain't it Dumbar?" said Jagu, grinning broadly. "You must'a come through the pass over yonder," said Jagu, nodding his head toward the mountains. "Agadian land, those parts. We're from 'round here, and it makes sense to speak the tongue, being so close to such a Kingdom! You won't find anything like Agade north of here. Cities govern themselves, so to speak, from here on out."

"I suppose so," answered Areoch. "I travel forth on my Gigāl, so I will undoubtedly learn more."

"Ah, the Gigāl! Now that's a journey. Where might you be headed, if a traveler can ask another?"

"I go north," said Areoch, surveying the road as it curved away. "I imagine I'll head along this track northeast and see where I come to."

"This track here?" asked Jagu pointing off to the distant trees. "Why, that'll take you to the city of Cartegin within a week's time, I'd imagine, and farther if you had a mind for it. Say, Dumbar and myself here, we're heading that same way if you wouldn't mind a few weary companions?"

Areoch did not dislike the friendly strangers' company, and they soon found themselves walking along the road. It was less used than it first appeared from the mountain heights. It was, in fact, little more than a large deer track. It was easy to follow.

"You both seem quite knowledgeable of these parts," asked Areoch as they walked, "Where is your city?"

"We's from Lugal," answered Dumbar.

"Ah-ha. Yes, we're from those parts alright," said Jagu quickly, shooting a look at Dumbar that promised a good cuff about the ears.

"You are from Agade!" cried Areoch. "It is against custom to travel north through the pass, though you are the second group I have met within the past two days that appears to have done so!"

"Well, strictly speaking no one is allowed, of course," agreed Jagu scratching his head. "We're not the strictly speaking types, see? We're wanderers of sorts, on a special mission."

Dumbar fingered the large bronze-tipped club at his belt nervously.

"I see," said Areoch cautiously. "And what mission brings you two wandering into this part of the world?"

Jagu looked baffled for a moment as if trying to think. "Ah, the Valley of Dry Bones, you mean? Why, this is lion country. Dumbar and I fancy ourselves as genuine Umu lion hunters, ain't that right Dumbar?"

Dumbar nodded his head and looked around as if expecting to suddenly see a lion pop up out of the shrubs.

"Yes," said Jagu, taking the axe from his belt. He flipped it in the air, catching it easily in his hand. "We're hunters, we are. Takes a rare type, it does, to be a good one and catch the prey you're after."

Areoch didn't like the change in Jagu's tone as he spoke and the hair on the nape of his neck rose. The road took a sudden bend, widening out and heading straight for the line of trees in the distance. All three came to a sudden and unspoken halt. Jagu flipped his axe in the air again and caught it, flashing Areoch a toothy grin.

"Say, Areoch me boy, you know why this here Valley is called 'the Dry Bones'?"

Areoch suddenly realized that Jagu and Dumbar were standing on either side of him. Jagu didn't give him a chance to answer.

"It's cause they say this here valley has claimed so many people. The Umu's roam this here territory... and they are always hungry."

Jagu nodded to Dumbar and before Areoch could draw his dagger Dumbar had wrapped his long, hairy arms around him in a vicious grip. Jagu lunged forward, plucking the knife out of Areoch's waist. Areoch delivered him a hard kick to the face as he flailed, but it was of little use.

"Eh, you got some fight in you," spat Jagu, wiping a trickle of blood from his mouth. "We were told you might." Jagu delivered a hard blow to Areoch's ribs, admiring the dagger before placing it securely in his satchel. "That's an offly petty toy for one so young, don't you think Dumbar?" He struck Areoch again, knocking the wind from him. Dumbar let him fall to the dust and pulled out his bronze club.

"Er's a few other pretty things I think he could do without," suggested Dumbar casually, and both men fell upon Areoch with the ferocity of fighting dogs. Areoch struggled, but he could do little as they beat him with foot, club, and fist until he was nearly senseless. They stripped him of his bronze-armored jerkin and tore the signet ring off his finger.

"Ah, now here's a special item!" crowed Jagu, holding up the inlayed band to the sun where Sargon's insignia sparkled with the light. "Ten times worth your weight in bronze, to the right people," he said to Areoch. Areoch lay crumpled in the dust, struggling to breath. "Makes a poor man quiver with delight when he thinks about what one might pay for all *three* of Agade's heirs to vanish."

Areoch tried to sit up, thoughts of Rimuš and Manish racing through his mind, but Dumbar kicked him back down on the road.

"Let's finish this mess up Dumbar," said Jagu, placing the ring in his satchel. "You remember how he wants it: clean cut. No untied ends."

Areoch's mind whirled. He? Who could that be? He didn't have time to contemplate. He lay in a haze, the shrubs off the road swirling in his vision as Dumbar stood above him, preparing his club for the final blow.

Areoch's face was caked with blood and swollen. He looked up through the dust of the road, his eyes tearing from pain as Dumbar pressed his cheek into the ground with a dirty foot. He thought he saw the face of a small black cat peer through the thicket before him, its head crooked to the side, looking at him with big eyes. Areoch blinked. When they opened again there was nothing there.

Dumbar raised his club high, fingers tight around the wooden handle. His arms quivered and the club began to fall. Suddenly, a splitting roar burst from the thick foliage! It came from so near the road that Dumbar's hair was blown aside from the warm breath of the mighty beast. Dumbar froze, his eyes wide with fear. Jagu groped blindly for his axe.

A huge form leapt gracefully over the dry shrubs and landed lightly on the edge of the road. It stood over six feet tall at the shoulder, black as the night with muscles quivering. Its teeth curved out of its mouth and downward toward its powerful neck. Its huge paws were inches away from Areoch's head as he lay motionless, unable to flee. Claws the size of daggers unsheathed from the beast's pads. This was an Umu: the man-hunter of legend that stalked its way through stories and elders' tales.

With a snarl the huge cat sprung over Areoch without a second glance, hungry for the prey that was willing to give some sport. As the screams rang out from behind, Areoch's head dropped to the dirt and he heard no more.

Chapter Fourteen

The House of Birsha

The day was well past noon when a caravan of carts, herders, men, and women paused at the crest of a rolling hill. The Valley of Dry Bones lay almost five days behind them. A gentle breeze whispered through the eastern eaves of the Asur Forest. There, still several miles in front of them, stood the towering walls of Cartegin, bright and shining in the late afternoon light. Stillness stretched down the line as each cart, donkey, and wagon stopped to gaze upon their long-desired destination. The mudbrick walls of Cartegin towered fifteen feet above the surrounding moor, stretching from the banks of the Dan-Jor river to the great Tanti Sea, encompassing an entire peninsula. In the center of the peninsula a small hill rose. Even from their distance, a few of the sharpest eyes in the entourage could make out buildings, squares, and rough-cobbled roads.

Birsha of Cartegin paused at the head of his household. He stood on the knoll in silence, taking in the glorious view. The sun flickered on the waves of the sea beyond. He knew every twist and turn, every pillar and dock of that far-off city, though he had not set eyes on it for nearly two years.

"Nin-Kasi!" exclaimed a man beside him. The man looked at Birsha's weather-worn face with fondness. "Great is it for a man to return to his home. You have been gone long, Birsha. Now you have returned. May you enter once again into your city with glory and honor."

Birsha smiled.

"Meshêk, I am glad you are here with me. Let us walk down this final road together, as we always have!"

"It is far from the final road," replied Meshêk with a wink. "But it is one that we have long journeyed. I will be happy to walk to the end of *this* journey with you, at long last!"

Birsha laughed at Meshêk's jibe as only a long-time friend would.

Meshêk was older than he, though Birsha himself was considered later in years. As Birsha looked at his friend, he thought about how time seemed to have little effect on his servant. Meshêk stood taller than most, wrapped in the same care-worn cloak he always travelled in. His long hair made a thick braid that hung down his back, flecked with the slightest gray. He had a prominent chin and a short, gray beard.

"You change little, Meshêk. It seems you have always been beside me giving me counsel, long even before I had wealth or power. Twenty years ago, you fled Shardana with me and have served me faithfully ever since. You helped me establish myself in Cartegin and now you have helped me prosper once again. May your reward for your faithfulness be great, as it is written in the law of Cartegin!"

"Cartegin's law has little to do with the course of power, friend Birsha."

Ignoring his comment, Birsha clasped Meshêk fondly on the shoulder before turning and examining the long, trailing caravan behind him. His two children, Bahira and Berran, were nearly of age and stood close to the fore. Lines of cattle and sheep came next, accompanied by several herders. They were followed by scores of Birsha's household, who tended small groups of animals, carried tents, and towed baggage. Then came the staggering sight that all eyes were instantly drawn too: carts of gigantic proportion, swaying as they were pulled by the weary flanks of sweat-stained oxen. Their wooden wheels were taller than a man, and they were stacked high with the red trunks of immense cedars. Somewhere out of view was the strange wayfarer whom they had picked up on the road through the Valley of the Dry Bones, who lay unconscious and heavily bandaged on a servant's litter.

Those in the caravan were of one household and looked to Birsha as their patron. They had been passing through the outer fields and dikes of Cartegin for most of the day. The edge of the Asur Forest crept down the far hillside of the Durgu Mountains to their right. Birsha's normally stoic face could not suppress a wide smile, he raised his fist high as he faced his household.

"Cartegin!!" he cried out. Cheers and hollers broke out in a joyful din as he turned and the train made its way down the hillside and for the city.

Word had spread like wildfire: Birsha and his kin were not dead! They had returned! The gate was more packed than usual as the people of Cartegin craned their necks and the important men of the city shouldered for room.

Cheers and greetings rang out from the throng as Birsha led his household in victory down the stone-cobbled road, into the heart of the city.

"Faithful architect of Ishshak, your praise be good!" shouted voices from a group of fishermen.

"Hail, Hail the faithful servant of Cartegin! You are blessed by Enlil and Tiamat alike!" rang out cries from brightly dressed men and women.

"Birsha you will come clean your sandals under my roof, yes?"

"Birsha of Cartegin, Ishshak wishes you to stand before him as soon as you have put your home in order!"

"Birsha, you have many requests from the chief brick-layer to be handled at once!" cried an official voice.

This and more was shouted to Birsha from the crowds, as the train of his household wound through the city and neared the sea. The carts creaked under the massive weight they carried and many wide eyes stared in disbelief at the size and length of the cedars as they rolled past.

"You have saved us Birsha! You have delivered us!" voices shouted up at him.

The people of the city made way and most faded back to the markets, the fields, and their homes as evening began to fall. They passed mud and wood huts near the western quadrant of the city - where the river ran sparkling between sandbanks and people squabbled with upraised voices from markets. They passed white limestone columns, which covered the city's central quadrant at the base of the hill, where the larger buildings, temples, and courts ran up to Ishshak's palace. As they neared the sea, the buildings changed to that of a dull, red stone, radiating warmth from the receding sun.

Birsha let his hand graze across the many surfaces as he walked, feeling the small bumps and minute grooves under his hand as a painter gazes at the minor imperfections of his masterpiece. For he was Birsha the architect, the designer of the city. He let the thought fill him like a pleasant smell. Finally, he had made it: he had secured his place in the analogues of Cartegin.

The group travelled deep into the city, until the sea was visible and the height of the hill stood behind them. The hillside sloped away to meet the ocean and the red-clay houses stretched on, evenly spaced until the land fell sharply downward to Cartegin's port. From where they stood, the port looked like a small circle with an oblique island within, standing at the mouth of the ocean.

The group turned aside on a bluff above the water and came to a halt within a broad courtyard. Orders were given for the carts to continue onward until reaching the port, where the great trunks were to be unloaded and stored until further orders from Birsha.

Maturr, the chief servant of the house, met Birsha on the front steps of the main entry and bowed low, raising up a golden chalice for her master to sup from.

It had been two years since Maturr had seen her master. She had been with Birsha since settling in Cartegin, and even before either of the children had been born. Nearly seventeen years had passed and Bahira,

Birsha's oldest, was now more beautiful than any spring blossom. Berran was many years away from his coming of age, but it seemed all too near.

"Children!" Maturr cried. "My, you are so big! As big as those cedars your father has brought home! Something must be in the earth over there that makes things grow tall!"

Birsha looked over his children and home with another smile before turning from his doorstep, back into the city. He felt that these times would not last, unless he worked hard to preserve them. There was still business for him to attend to.

Chapter Fifteen

The Plans of Chief Ishshak

Ishshak's pillared palace formed the heart of Cartegin, resting high on the crest of the city's central hill. Birsha walked, climbing steadily toward the hilltop as he traversed along the main road. More and more of the city sprawled out below him. The temples became fewer and Ishshak's own household buildings took their place. The basalt rock, of which they were built, gave the evening a darker look, though the sun had only just set.

Birsha paused for a short breath at the top of the hill before coming at last to Ishshak's palace. Ilishu, the Champion, greeted Birsha as he entered the wide expanse at the palace gate. Ilishu was dressed casually, but his quick eye and strong hand (along with a belt of woven gold around his waist), betrayed his status as elite among the men of the city. Long, braided, brown hair fell down his back, and gold armbands showed his position as a City Champion, ready to rouse the men of Cartegin in times of need.

"Birsha. Welcome home from your long travels! Chief Ishshak and I hope, and hear from the streets, that you bring good tidings." Ilishu clasped Birsha's forearm with his own before turning and leading him into the palace.

Chief Ishshak's palace was hardly a worthy comparison for even the smallest delegation hall in the Kingdom of Agade, but it was well adorned among the city-states of the north. A wide hall, mounted with the heads of many animals, opened before them. Bright, smooth grains of wood stood out from the pillars which lined the hall. Gold and silver vessels decorated shelves and sat on mighty tables where feasts were often held.

Ishshak stood at the eastern end of the hall, his large hand resting on the city jewel: a round, black jet-stone, as large as a man's head, mounted at the topmost point of his carved, oaken throne. The gleam of the evening sky shone in from two open windows, basking Ishshak's broad shoulders and rich fur cape in brilliance. Incense smoldered in bowls, filling the air with a sweet aroma that blended nicely with that of the sea. Birsha noticed Cärmi the diviner, cowering in the shadows like a cur waiting for a treat.

Ilishu mounted the low step before the throne and bowed briefly.

"My lord Ishshak, Birsha has returned from the lands of Magen and brings you his report."

Ishshak sighed deeply, gazing out the window and across the sprawling port. Dark hair grew thick about the Chieftain and at first glance, it was difficult to determine where his fur mantle stopped and his own hair began. Birsha's laden carts could be seen below, their shadows long in the twilight.

"Birsha, Birsha, my friend, you bring upon yourself much favor in this hour!" Ishshak turned and the resemblance between the Chief and Champion made it clear, they were brothers. Both were of a powerful build and swarthy stature, standing a full head and shoulders over Birsha.

Birsha inclined his head. Ishshak had been his friend for many years, and he humbly accepted the gifts of jet and gold Ishshak's servants laid at his feet in honor.

"Come, Birsha! Sit at my table! It was my forefathers who first settled this hill, building these walls by the strength of their hands. It was my grandfather who set the laws of Cartegin into place. And it was I that appointed you over the building of Cartegin's quadrants, nearly twenty years past.

'Now, like the bones in my beard, this is your hour! Your drive and dedication have prevailed and advanced our people. Over two years ago we planned this mission, though every road seemed as black as jet. Our people were starving, wealth unable to be found. Curse Agade and their senselessness!"

Ishshak pounded his fist into his open hand with each sentence, releasing some of the frustration he and all Cartegin felt. Birsha knew it only too well.

"I am glad Cartegin has recovered some, my lord," said Birsha. "The rains have returned to the land and the famine has ceased."

"Ceased? Ceased?" Ishshak asked quizzically. "It may have in the western and southern lands, Birsha. Here the land still yields little. We are surviving. Some even say we are prospering. But, in the shadow of Agade we can do little. They have abandoned us, turning aside our people when death is at our door, refusing to give us grain when none can be sowed and none can be harvested. They have rejected us - slaughtering us like sheep should any of my people desire to leave these lands. Sargon hates the very earth we walk. Curse him! May the earth suck the marrow from his bones!"

Ishshak ignored the chiding hiss which came from Cärmi in the shadows, followed by an inaudible murmur about 'kingship' and 'power'. The Chieftain shook his head as he sat at the wide table, beckoning for Birsha to do the same.

"I will not stand by any longer. *We* will not stand by. It is time to do as we have always done: cut a path for ourselves through the wilderness. Don't you see, Birsha? You have given us more than a new road. You have given us power to take back what should be ours. This is our hour."

Birsha sat down slowly, giving Ishshak's wild eyes a quizzical look.

"My lord Ishshak, you speak of power and strength against Agade as though to assault them. When we devised this mission all those years ago, it was on the hope and might of *trade* that we would make Cartegin strong. I despise Agade as much as anyone..."

"Times have changed, Birsha," Ishshak explained slowly, leaning back in his seat to look down on the port. "For years, we have tried to work around the thorn in our side - it is time we pull it out."

"Even if we had the might, forcing ourselves upon the bronze of Agade would bring us nothing but downfall, as we have discussed many times," chimed in Ilishu as he reclined at the table, popping thin wafers in his mouth one at a time. "We know nothing of their strength, other than they are impossibly strong. If we are to force a road, we must have more information. Perhaps Cärmi can gather the wise men and foretell us what to expect."

"Kingships. Foretelling. Diviners." Ishshak shot a distasteful look in the direction of Cärmi. "Useless, the lot of them! Why everyone babbles on about *diviners* and *fate* is beyond me. Nothing is free in this world. It must be earned or taken."

Birsha nodded his head in agreement. "How so many people believe such trivial things I will never know, my lord."

Cärmi began to open his mouth, but Ishshak raised his hand. "You have your place, Cärmi, you need not worry. Be it from greater Powers or nay, we cannot stand by our walls defenseless in these times. Battle is coming, I feel it in my blood. We must have bronze at any cost. We must be strong."

Ishshak turned and looked at Birsha expectantly. "Friend Birsha, you have travelled far, and you know my thoughts without my ceaseless mutterings. Tell me about your travels. First, let me refresh you from your journey."

Ishshak beckoned and servants entered with silver goblets brimming with sweet juices and trays with fine meats. Birsha refreshed himself while Ishshak looked down the table, eagerly waiting for him to begin his tale. Birsha took his time, measuring in his mind what level of the Chief's patience he could levy, to gain the most from the conversation.

"My lord," Birsha began finally, "two years may change many things.

128

My servant, Meshêk, told us plainly at the beginning of this journey that it would take longer than we should expect. Yet, the famine has passed and here, still, we all stand. Desperation is now far from us. Our people thrive, our lands increase, our trade and wealth grows."

"Yes," said Ishshak, "It is not from Agade that this growth comes. The Jezrial Dynasty has become our close partners in trade. A new item they seem to seek with vigor, and will pay for it - not with bronze, of course. Of that there is still none to be found," he added.

"What is this new thing that we have in such plenty?" asked Birsha.

Ilishu leaned across the table. "The weak, the poor, and the lawbreakers," he said with a small grin.

Birsha raised a questioning eyebrow.

"It has been over a year since a head or hand has fallen in the fountain court," continued Ilishu. "The King of Zoar and his Queen pay for them, the people that is, and richly too! Some of the poor even, on their own accord, now leave and sell themselves into his service instead of finding a household to serve here."

"As servants to his household and courts?" asked Birsha.

Ishshak shrugged. "I do not know, nor do I care. We send them north in return for precious items by the cartload. It seems absurd, but it matters little. The diseased leave and wealth runs through the streets in their place! We look to our own advantage and all is in our favor, but for the lack of bronze. Not for any price can we make quality weapons, armor, or tools that belong to our current age. We must begin to look for ways to take such things by force."

Ishshak and Ilishu looked at Birsha expectantly.

"So, we still face the same obstacle," Birsha said evenly, "with less haste or need. Ishshak, battle with Agade would only cost Cartegin more lives. They are not our open enemies. I have passed Agade, from east to west, travelling its border north of the Durgu mountains. The walls of its cities are high and thick, and watchtowers have been built upon the mountain sides and in the open places, whom the people say are manned by a standing fighting force called the E-Kur."

Ilishu leaned over the side of his seat curiously. "A standing fighting force? No king could pay a man to sit and wait for battle!" He laughed. "Those who would accept would sit and grow fat from grain wages, and those who had any spirit of fight would decline for a nobler course of action, an *Aett*, perhaps! What kind of numbers does this 'fighting force' claim to its cause?"

Birsha held Ilishu's gaze solemnly. "By my own estimate, I would guess ten thousand men patrol the borders, waiting for battle, and I have heard it said that triple that number stand by within the cities. I have seen them Ilishu! Strong do they seem, training on the southern slopes near the land of Magen! Bright is the bronze of their spears and broad their shields! Agade is prepped and primed for battle."

Ilishu nearly fell out of his chair. "Ten or twenty thousand? Of battle-hardened warriors? It cannot be. Such a thing is not possible."

"With my own eyes, I say it is so Ilishu. They seem to outnumber the grains of sand on the shores. The few travelers who seemed to have blessings from Agade to travel north of its borders claimed it was so as well. When we questioned them, they inferred their numbers were so great commanders of commanders were needed in appointment." Birsha turned back to Ishshak, whose crestfallen face sunk in despair into his cupped hands.

"Few from Cartegin, or anywhere in the north for that matter, have been able to bring us tidings in these past years. I do not doubt you, Birsha. This news is indeed devastating. It is for this reason we have called you here and it seems our need is greater than we first imagined. You, Birsha, must build Cartegin a fleet. With an armed fleet, we could control the waters of Agade - we could take bronze from their ships! We could grow strong and answer to no other master."

Birsha shook his head slowly. The conversation was proceeding far from what he had hoped. He stood and walked near the open windows, where the red glow of the sky could be seen mirrored on the waves below.

"Our freedom comes from the sea, you are right. We discussed and laid plans, my lord Ishshak, of a journey to the land of Magen - where the great cedar trees have been told to grow, in legend and tale. We planned to take carts of silver and gold, jet and cypress, and trade in this far-away land for the mighty girth of such trees if they indeed existed. And upon the return of a successful journey, to build a fleet of ships like the world has never seen: ships of trade, to sail by Agade to the southern kingdoms! To turn these ships into vessels of war... it would be suicide. Agade would need but march twenty days' time until they reached our city gates with enough force to crush our people! Cartegin is not ready for war, Ishshak. We must focus on trade. Let us grow strong first and strike back when ready."

Birsha paced back and forth on the balcony overlooking the port, sipping occasionally from his goblet as he drew in Ishshak.

Ishshak sighed.

"I had hoped, Birsha, that your eyes would have been opened more from your travels. I see now that you are afraid of Agade's might. Perhaps you are right. Cärmi, go and divine from the smoke and the stars that which you will. And inform the holy men of Tiamat to skewer the animals and bring me the word laying hidden in their entrails."

Cärmi left with a bow. Ilishu stood and joined them at the end of the hall. The three men gazed down at the port in silence. They might have heard the occasional crack of rope, the bellowing of a far-off oxen, the dull throbbing of a holy ub drum from a Tiamat temple, or the laughing of children in the city streets. Yet Birsha, Ishshak, and Ilishu were of one focus. Even from their great height the mountainous shadows, cast by the bulks of the red cedars, stood out clear in the sinking twilight. Ishshak raised his golden goblet.

"Whatever you may need, Birsha, it is yours. Let the building begin, as speedily as it may. I want you to turn your full attention to this matter, my faithful servant. The future of Cartegin rests in your hands - remember our need!"

Chapter Sixteen

The Fate of Areoch

Areoch awoke to darkness. He strained his eyes, but the intense pain made him cease immediately. He struggled to maintain consciousness. He tried bringing his hands up to his face, and found his arms heavy and hot, unable to do more than twitch at his side. Then the pain struck him. As if all the nerve centers of his body woke up at once, floodwaters of agony began to overwhelm him.

He struggled to suppress it. The pain and panic in that unknown darkness was too much. He opened his mouth and cried out. Almost instantly he smelled a thick, sweetly scented aroma which calmed his mind. He felt himself sinking back into unconsciousness. He fought it, struggling to remember who he was, where he was. He had flashes of memory: the worried face of his father, the forms of Rimuš and Manish disappearing west, the ugly face of Jagu and Dumbar standing over him - holding the signet ring of Sargon so that it glinted in the sunlight.

"No! No! It cannot be! Rimuš! Manish!" he cried. He must warn them. He must save them! The roar of an Umu swept across his memory and he passed back into blackness.

Meshêk closed the door quietly and walked down the stairs, weaving through corridors until he came to Birsha's private room. Birsha sat near a well stoked fire, lit to keep off the night's chill. He looked up as Meshêk entered and then turned back to the small model of a boat he held in front of him.

"Meshêk, it is good you are here. I need your hand to write down some things that are about to pass from my memory."

"You know it is unwise to work within these walls," chided Meshêk as he poked at the fire. "It dishonors the strength of your home."

Birsha waved his hand above his head. "I'm sure the foundations of my house aren't cracking any quicker than usual this evening, despite your meddlesome comments," replied Birsha. He laid aside the little boat with a sigh. "Work orders of straw and brick, axes and chisels, wood and resin, grain and twine... I will be grateful to hand over these matters to the mistress of the port in the morning."

"I highly doubt you will let the port handle anything without your supervision. Let them rest for now," advised Meshêk gently. "Your conversation with Ishshak went well, I assume?"

"He is still the same," answered Birsha. "Singular of mind. What he does not see is that what he wants, will come with time and patience. We can accomplish all Ishshak dreams and more. But... in short... yes," said Birsha with a small smile. "He has given us what I hoped."

Meshêk nodded absentmindedly, stirring a large clay bowl which lay steaming near the coals.

"How is our guest?" asked Birsha, changing the subject.

Meshêk dipped in a ladle, pouring himself a large mug of hot water. He sprinkled in a crushed mixture of dry herbs from a leather pouch at his hip before sitting across from Birsha. He heaved a sigh of contentment as the tea's aroma drifted through the room.

"He lives," reported Meshêk, sipping on his drink, "though I would have thought otherwise. His face will be badly scarred, but he is showing some spirit."

"Yes, I heard," said Birsha. "I would be sore if he were to die, after the trouble we have spared on him. It was foolish for Bahira to insist us to his care. There is no law that states it is necessary and I distrust his origins."

Meshêk looked over the edge of his cup. "Many things are necessary that are not written in the law of Cartegin," he pointed out. "Bahira's care was from her heart. That speaks well of the deed and better of her."

"She is too head-strong. No man will wish to be paired with a woman who won't submit to his call."

"She takes after her mother, then," remarked Meshêk and they both trailed off into silence, thinking of the dangerous escape they had faced from the far away Shardana Islands, long before they settled in Cartegin. Birsha once had many wives and children. Now, Bahira and Berran were all that remained of his kin.

The fire crackled, flickering light on the stacks of papyrus and models of ships piled on several of the tables. The warmth of spring, while promising, had not yet entered the night's cold and they were grateful for the fire.

"From where does he come? The Tar-Lands of the twin cities? The lands of Magen?" asked Birsha.

Meshêk shook his head. "It is hard to tell, there is little of him unmarred. Perhaps he is a servant who forsook his master upon the road after some quarrel. Though he speaks in his sleep of names that are of southern rhyme and he shows no markings a servant would bear of his household. It causes me to think that maybe he is of the western lands - at least, those still inhabitable east of the Shinar - and travels forth on his Giġāl. Maybe he came upon misfortune on the road."

"It cannot be," thought Birsha, shaking his head. "Few lands follow the customs of the Giġāl. And he is too old."

"There is little of him to see beneath his bandages to make a strong claim. He has no arm bands, nor marks of them. He has been mangled and may be younger than you guess."

"Even so," retorted Birsha, "we both just spent more time in the western lands than I would wish. How many of their young men did you see sent out upon the Giġāl? It is a discontinued custom in that part of the world. Herders, rovers, and outcasts are all who remain upon the western plains. They do not follow the old ways."

Meshêk looked up at Birsha from under his thick eyebrows.

"Then... if he is as young as I guess... he must come from farther south, where the customs are still followed in the Old Way."

The fire settled and sparks flew upward.

"Nay, your guess is wrong," decided Birsha. "From where would he have come? Marasi? Arali? They are too far of a journey to be made on foot - and he would never have been allowed to pass through Agade. You saw the watch they keep!"

"What if he is from Agade itself?" reflected Meshêk slowly.

Birsha chuckled, shaking his head. "They may be fools, but they do not slaughter their own. They know it would be a death mission, to send a boy north alone on his Giġāl. He could have only come from the west. ...Or perhaps he comes from Cartegin herself."

Birsha swiftly told Meshêk of what Ishshak and Ilishu had told him of the Jezrial Dynasty and the new trade of outcasts to the north. A concerned look passed over Meshêk's brow and his face darkened.

"I do not like the sound of this at all," he muttered. "King Amri has little say over the Northern Dynasty. It is Izével, his Queen, who holds power, and they say she is ruthless. What cause has she to pay so richly for the presence of the poor and diseased?"

"I do not know and it concerns us little," said Birsha. "Let the fools pay for them. They are useless anyway."

"Useless?" Meshêk raised an eyebrow. "Useless is a dark term to describe anyone, even the lowest servant who has come to feed the dogs in your house. How can man pay for another man as if he was no more than livestock? Have you ever heard of such a thing before?"

"It is not against any of our laws, so if a man wishes to sell himself to another, who can stop him?" Birsha passed off the cloud on Meshêk's face with a wave of his hand. "Our visitor could easily be one of these, who fell into some hardship upon the road, or thought better of his decision."

Meshêk looked down, puzzled, and a long silence followed.

"I should inquire of the Diviners on the purpose of our guest," said Birsha finally.

"No!" cried Meshêk, spraying a mouthful of tea across the room in his haste. "That is no better than walking up and telling Ishshak yourself about this matter, and you were right not to do so when we first arrived. We would have little say in his fate then, regardless of where he comes. *Better to make one indebted to you, then to give quick counsel to others* says the wisdom of Šuruppag, and we would do best to follow it. We will find out soon enough where he comes from and on what journey he travels."

"Far be it from us to not aid him, should he be on the Giĝāl!" exclaimed Birsha. "Berran is near to his coming of age. Too near, I say. I would not curse his journey by refusing to give a good hand to another's. Such is the way of things: good comes from good and ill from ill. We will provide this man safety. It will bring us fortune."

"Safety is not the purpose of the Giĝāl, therefore it will bring you no more fortune than your wisdom can discern," replied Meshêk dryly.

"You are not a father!" Birsha snapped angrily. "You are my servant until Berran is of age, and you would do well to remember why!" Birsha's sharp retort hung in the air and he wished he hadn't spoken so hastily. He rubbed his temples and threw aside the small boat in his hand. "Meshêk, I did not mean to bring up... If it hadn't been for you, we all would have perished..."

"No, no," said Meshêk, interrupting. "There is no ill between us friend, nor will there ever be. The oath I swore to you on the far shores of Shardana has not faded, though the years certainly have. Your decision in letting this man stay is right, no matter how you arrive there in your mind."

Birsha sighed. "The heart is deep waters, is it not? The surface may give a reflection, but who can see beneath the surface? We shall watch over him until he heals and then allow him to choose his own way."

More days passed. When Areoch awoke again he found the swelling in his face had lessened and he could see. He was in a well-furnished room. Warm light and a refreshing breeze streamed in from an open balcony, bordered with white cloth that fluttered in the breeze. Through it he saw blue sky, bright and revitalizing. The walls around him were of a soft, smooth, red rock, from which the ends of cleverly placed beams jutted out. Plants, curling with vines and full of spring buds (promising white flowers), crept along many of the walls where they snuck in from the balcony.

His mind was clear. The pain in his side was sharp as he breathed, and his arms and legs were stiff, sore, and weak. Furthering his discomfort, his head was encompassed by a tight rope, making his temples throb and his skin feel like it would tear from the pressure. Though he did not know where he was, he felt in his heart it was a place of peace.

The door to his small room opened and a turbaned woman, with colorful garments, bustled in. Areoch could tell by the large tray she carried that she was a well-respected servant of the house. From the corner of his eye, Areoch could see that behind her came a young woman and two children, all carrying white linens and bowls of clean water. The steaming smell, wafting from the first tray, caught Areoch's attention and he realized that he had never been hungrier.

The servants raised him on soft pillows and then began to change his bandages. Meanwhile, the young woman poured a sweet-smelling mush into a bowl near his head. She untied the painful ropes encircling his jaw, rubbing the tender flesh with a smooth salve that helped ease the throbbing.

Areoch opened his mouth to speak, but cried out with pain as he tried. The young woman placed her hand gently over his mouth. She said nothing. The look in her eyes and the swelling under her hand told him enough: his jaw was broken. Judging by the feel in the rest of his body, it was not the only bone on the mend.

The others were now carefully sponging his hurts and he clenched his teeth, causing tears of pain to stream down his cheeks. He endured, while the young woman grimaced with him and wiped away his silent tears. She carefully spooned the mush into his mouth, which he found as sweet as honey and easy to swallow.

Areoch could do little more than focus on eating and breathing in a way that didn't cause him excruciating pain, but the woman in front of him could not be ignored. She looked to be about his age, much older than the small ones who helped change his bandages. Her hair was black as the night, tied in a bun to give room for her mending hands. Her garment was a soft red and her skin a fine olive, as if she had been formed from the very earth of this wonderful land. She was without any doubt the fairest woman Areoch had ever seen. In Agade, he and his brothers would have wrestled or thrown logs end-over-end to try and catch her eye. Here he was helpless. He could not help but chuckle at the ironic thought.

The woman smiled a kind smile, imagining for herself what he might be thinking. While she said no word to him, her presence was more soothing than any salve that could be applied. Finished with their task, the group departed without a second glance, leaving Areoch to ponder his fate and the strange circumstances.

For the next several weeks, this routine continued, until Areoch was desperate to stretch his limbs. Sores had developed on his back from lying down. Often the young woman would be part of the small entourage which faithfully tended him, and though they still did not speak to him, he began to look for her coming every day. Soon he could stand of his own accord and make small laps around his confinement. He did not dare try the door and the stairs beyond without invitation. He found the balcony a most refreshing place to rest, when the spring rains did not keep him away. From there, he was able to gather something of his bearings.

The balcony overlooked a rich and thick household garden, which sprawled along for some distance before meeting a short wall. Beyond that, a gentle hill strewn with household buildings (similar to the one in which he stayed), sloped away so that he could see above their roof-tops. Gulls circled and cawed. The dark blue of the sea stretched across the horizon in an unbroken line, except for a large port which lay at the center of his view.

Areoch, though somewhat knowledgeable of the surrounding world, only knew of one port city which could hum with as much energy and activity as this one, so in his mind he pieced together the following story: after being attacked on the road, the diviners of Agade must have sensed his peril, or perhaps been warned by a wayward traveler. Even the strange man Melkezadek might have played some role. Regardless, help was sent to him immediately from Agade. And, as he was not allowed to return to Ur, he had been taken to the nearest city, Kish, which rested on the edge of the great Eastern Sea. No doubt, he was now in the household and care of Rahmaah, Sargon's ambassador and Ensi over the city.

Because of this, little worry entered his mind - and perhaps it was for the better. He healed quickly, and his heart was at ease during the passing days. Every so often, early in the morning or late in the evening, he would catch a glimpse of the young woman strolling along the well-manicured paths of the garden below. He imagined that she looked up toward his balcony once, when the light was fading. He withdrew hastily and shrunk back against the leafy wall until she had passed.

Had Areoch travelled to Kish, or even spoken to Commander Zakkaria in more detail, he would have known the houses built from the quarries of Kish were of pale limestone and the port was not only larger, but overshadowed by the great watchtowers of the E-Kur standing along the coast. As it was, Areoch did not know better.

It was in this mindset that Birsha first visited Areoch in the upper room and (to Birsha's great surprise), found Areoch standing nearly upright enjoying the fresh air of the balcony. So immersed was Areoch in the comings and goings of the port city that he did not realize Birsha's presence for some time, and he gave a painful start when Birsha spoke next to him.

"Peaceful, is it not? To watch laborers toil in their work from a high place?" Birsha laughed softly, but not heartlessly, at Areoch's wince of pain. Birsha leaned at ease against the railing beside him.

"Do not be afraid. I am the owner of this home and the maker of much of what you see. I remember when I first built this place! I too would come and get lost here, looking out across the sea, imagining the comings and goings of other men. I did not mean to startle you. You seem to be healing quickly."

'Indeed,' thought Birsha to himself as he looked over Areoch, '*he seems to be just a youth. But stronger than most, and accustomed to those who listen to his words... the scars upon his face are pale, even more pale than the kingdoms south of Agade.*' Questions of the boy's origin flashed through his mind, though Birsha did not betray any of his thoughts.

"Only due to your kindness, it seems," said Areoch in reply, bowing as low as he was able.

"Don't strain yourself on my account!" cried Birsha, noticing how Areoch leaned heavily upon the rail. "You have healed with favor and better than we thought possible. Still you are far from full health. You must have many questions! You have been bed-ridden longer than you think: nearly four weeks have passed since you were found upon the western road and brought to my house."

Areoch bowed low again, as Birsha's words lulled him into believing his own guesses were true regarding his circumstances.

"I am indebted to you further. My father Sargon will be just as grateful. Truly he appoints his Ensi well! Had I known Kish was so beautiful or sat so close to the sea, I would have made a point to visit it long before. Nonetheless, I am grateful my Giĝāl has brought me here. I do not doubt Enlil had a purpose in doing so!"

It was a mixture of Areoch's naivety and his lulled sense of peace that betrayed him. As soon as the words left his mouth, Areoch knew that something was deeply amiss.

Birsha did not say anything in reply for some time, and he looked as if he had been assaulted. Some great mixture of fear and shock shone clearly through Birsha's expression. His mouth fell and his eyes grew wide.

"I hope I did not offend you, my lord. Are you not Rahmaah, appointed by my father to this city?" Areoch quickly stammered. He found himself taking a small step back and clutching harder at the rail.

Birsha said nothing. Turning on his heel he swiftly left the room.

Chapter Seventeen

The Wisdom of Meshêk

P lace a bar over that door!" Birsha ordered as he slammed Areoch's door shut and took the stairs down to the main floor two at a time. Meshêk was waiting there and Birsha pulled him by the arm toward his study. Several members of the household stood still with surprise. Questioning eyes eagerly following them.

"Maturr, you will direct my house to their appropriate tasks for the day!" Birsha commanded. "Now!"

Maturr jumped as if stung and quickly gathered everyone in that portion of the house, escorting them outside.

"Lots of chores to be done... Outside and not here!" she clucked, waving a dirty broom violently over her head.

Birsha plowed into his study, dragging Meshêk in before closing the door with a slam. He paced back and forth as Meshêk stood patiently, calm and with a slightly arched eyebrow.

"THAT," exclaimed Birsha, gesturing at the room above them, "is no servant's son. Nor a man from Cartegin. That is the son of Sargon. Sargon *The Great*, King over all this city's loss and pain," he said with emphasis.

The birds outside of the study window chirped and ruffled their wings among the shrubbery. Meshêk nodded, his face remaining expressionless. He tucked his hands away in the folds of his robe.

"That is quite interesting."

"Interesting?! Interesting, you say?!" Birsha cried. "Are you mad? The son of Sargon the Great, who thinks he has been dwelling in Kish, of all places, for the past four weeks, is in *my* house! And you say *interesting*?!" Birsha wiped a hand over his sweaty brow and steadied himself. "What should I do?"

Meshêk stroked his beard. "Naïve," he said in thought. "He must be on the Giĝāl. Why send the boy north unless they wished him death?

Sending him across the Shinar River would have been little better." Meshêk trailed off.

"He looks as if he comes from there, what's more!" exclaimed Birsha exasperated. He sat in a chair before standing again. "He is as white as a *Monlua* shell."

"He is Sargon's son?" asked Meshêk quizzically. "You have no doubt in this?"

"The boy spoke to me as if I was... was... what is his name, Sargon's Ensi of Kish..."

"Rahmaah."

"Yes, *him*. There can be little doubt. He is one of Sargon's sons."

"This is a most interesting turn of fate," commented Meshêk. He paused briefly before saying more. "I do not think our previous course of action is now illogical."

"But this could be the answer, Meshêk," argued Birsha. "We could hold him at ransom! Negotiate a deal with Sargon! Force him to open his borders..."

"And to what end will that lead?" asked Meshêk carefully. "We have in our hands a pawn, a pawn which conceivably sits very close to a king who has ruled an empire without compromise and with strong idealism. What will change, if his hatred of the northern world and its ways are allowed to have a focal point on a single city? Are the stories of Asurla the Slayer so far from your mind as to not remember history? All of man knows the pain and death that comes from such a combination! And what will happen if this boy is turned over to Ishshak? He would be tortured and then ransomed, at best killed, for his own regard, and we would be found in exactly the same place, or worse. Much hatred has grown against Agade during the hard years and our recovery after has made that resentment grow, as you well know."

Birsha did not answer.

"You must use wisdom and look down the long road, for if Ishshak discovers this, he most certainly will not stop to think. It would be our end. It would mean open war. Listen to my counsel."

Neither of them said anything, and the birds outside of the window were strangely quiet.

"We cannot let that happen," said Birsha finally, though it took him significant effort.

"It seems our options are to force him away, immediately, or allow him to stay here as he wishes," concluded Meshêk. "He would not be foolish enough to reveal himself again."

"The first is the easiest," admitted Birsha, almost hopefully. "If he stayed it would not be long before he caught word of our plans, and the fleet. It could ruin everything."

"Easier paths are not always the wisest to take," quoted Meshêk.

140

"Curse your lore and crusted tablets!" cried Birsha. "They are gibberish, the words that weak men hold on to in times of trouble. I will not let the past six years of toil, hardship, and death be wasted! You are wrong, I won't allow it! He will be sent away at once. Take some Strong Men of my household and drop him off north of the Dan-Jor. Or sell him there, if it is true they pay for such things."

"Birsha," said Meshêk softly, "You know who I am. I have counseled kings of men and seen the world shaken and formed under the consequences of an individual's actions. You know this, and you know *me* better than most."

"Perhaps you should divine on the matter then," Birsha retorted, tautly, "and we can trust the reading of your magical insight. Such is the oath you owe me until Berran is grown!"

"I am not a sorcerer!" cried Meshêk with annoyance. "I can no more control that power than you. That is the risk. Do not try to corner me Birsha, it will do little for you."

"The last time you spoke a rune on one of those blasted magical tablets, the entire city of Bulha-Mit collapsed upon you," Birsha protested. "Yet, you don't consider this to be important enough of a decision?"

"Have you forgotten how much pain and loss that moment caused us both?" Meshêk softened. "You do not understand, Birsha, the influence and change that Power reveals. Please, Birsha, listen to my counsel in this matter."

Birsha hesitated and then drooped his shoulders in defeat.

"So be it," he finally managed, nodding his consent. "You have not led our family astray over all the long years we have been friends. Indeed, I would not now sit in the position I hold if it weren't for you. If the boy is to stay, it must be under the strictest conditions... if you deem it worth the risk."

Meshêk nodded and a small smile appeared on his features.

"I wish we had left him on the road," muttered Birsha. "But we did not. And we cannot return him there now. We will need some explanation for our visitor, should Ishshak or his household start asking questions."

"There is no reason for him to," said Meshêk. "He will be busy enough watching over your work at the port. I have a few ideas anyway."

"I leave it to you then," sighed Birsha. "I want as little to do with this matter as possible. I don't like it. Not one bit."

Areoch found the door barred after Birsha's departure and there was no answer to his cries of pardon or help. He stayed up most of the night, trying to fit together Birsha's reaction to his imagined chain of events, until finally drifting off into a fitful sleep in the early morning hours.

He awoke sharply, late in the morning, to find a man at the foot of his bed. The man had long, braided, black hair, noticeably flecked with white and gray. He looked tall, even as he sat. His eyes were deep, and he would have been intimidating if it were not for the small cup of tea which he occasionally stirred with a small stick. He sipped upon it and nodded, as if appreciating his own work.

Areoch pushed himself back against his cushions until he was as far away from the man as he could get.

"Who are you?" Areoch asked.

Meshêk sat back in his chair and gazed thoughtfully at Areoch. New scars, deep and noticeable, ran down one side of the youth's face from his encounter in the Valley of Dry Bones.

"The problem, it seems, is who *you* are. I am here to fix that problem."

Meshêk stood up briskly, causing Areoch to jump, and maneuvered his chair closer to Areoch's bedside. Areoch recoiled, but there was little he could do.

"Jumpy, are we?" chuckled Meshêk. "Maybe that means you are now a little wiser. Do you know why being the son of Sargon the Great is such a problem?"

Areoch did not answer, thinking of the harsh words the thugs had spoken on the road, and then Birsha's reaction to him the day before. Areoch had a difficult time swallowing.

Meshêk continued without waiting for an answer.

"It is because everyone needs someone to blame for the problems of the world. When a powerful man, a long distance away, denies your people food and shelter in a time of need and then stipends your wealth and power for years on end... it is easy to hold spite. That spite festers over years, and grows into hate. This is how nearly all the lands north of Agade feel when they hear a southern rhyme or story, and čertainly on the wayward chance they meet an actual person from the south. And even more certainly when that person is from Agade. And a hundred times more so when that person has any direct affiliation with Sargon. Whether this is a justified way of thinking or not is a different matter. You are in grave danger regardless." He sipped his tea and sat back resolutely.

"To answer your question, I am called Meshêk, and you are now in the household of Birsha the Cartegin, the Chief Architect and shipbuilder of this city. He found you near death along the western road, south of the northern turn where the road enters the Asur forest. The valley of *Imagual*, or Dry Bones, that area was called in the elder days. He has since brought you into his home, allowed me to heal you, and - to your great benefit - kept your existence a relative secret until finding more about you."

Areoch nodded, putting the pieces together in his mind.

"What happens now?"

Meshêk poured another cup of tea and handed it to Areoch, sprinkling in some herbs from a leather pouch on his hip before giving it a good stir.

"That depends on you. I give you two choices. The first: you trust me. This should not be difficult, as I am Birsha's servant and you are already indebted to me ...and him... with your life.

'The second: we escort you to the door and send you about your own way. There, an inquiring eye will undoubtedly spot you (you do look a fair bit paler than regular people in these parts), and you will find yourself standing, or most likely kneeling, before Ishshak, the Chief of Cartegin. From there it will not take him long to find out at least where you are from and you will be tortured, ransomed, and bartered, a process that will undoubtedly take several years."

Meshêk sipped on his tea while Areoch looked at his own and wondered what might be in it.

"You make my decision sound rather difficult," Areoch tried not to sound too sarcastic.

Meshêk watched the lad from under his bushy eyebrows in silence. Then Areoch raised his glass and drowned its contents. Its bitter taste made him sputter, and Meshêk smiled.

"Good, isn't it? Ground *felou* herbs, found in the shade on the gentle slopes of the Asur Forest. Wakes you right up in the morning."

Areoch coughed, his eyes watering.

"What is your name?" asked Meshêk.

"Areoch of Ur, son of..."

Meshêk raised his hand, stopping him. "No, no, not anymore. Areoch will be fine. No one would recognize the name if they heard it. But, from now on, you are Areoch, an artisan and wise man from the land of Magen, staying within our household by the request of Birsha, to better educate his children in the ways of the wide world. You'd better not mention Sargon, Agade, or Ur again for some time."

Areoch nodded slowly.

"You will find our languages hardly differ, for the founders of Cartegin came from the same ancestry as those of Ur. It is good for you, in this regard, that you made it no farther north. You will wear these, as the men of Magen commonly do."

Meshêk handed Areoch two beautifully carved and well-oiled armbands, made of dark wood inlaid with deep red veins.

"That is all for now," Meshêk said. "We will speak more regarding this matter after you have supped. You must be hungry."

Meshêk stood and left, leaving the door open behind him and Areoch alone to ponder this most recent change of events.

"Wise man? Educator?" questioned Birsha skeptically at the foot of the stairs.

"I would have gone with carpenter, regarding the great building we are undertaking, but I felt you might grow tired of his professional assistance in the port as he upheld his disguise."

Birsha did not smile at Meshêk's jest.

"Clever, as always," he said. "Who knows? Maybe the young ones will actually get something useful out of him. Have him teach something boring from the west. Or have him tutor Bahira. She would be able to drive away any teacher."

When Areoch finally ventured down the stairs, the bright, turbaned caretaker (who had helped change his bandages), greeted him.

"Good afternoon!" cried Maturr with a beaming smile. She ushered him into a wide circular room, across which lay a large table, the slab of a single great tree. On it there was a gourd, full of a steaming, savory substance and a loaf of brown bread, still warm from the kitchen fires. Areoch was hungry and needed no second bidding.

"Meshêk will see you once you have supped, master Areoch of Magen."

Areoch tried not to look startled upon being addressed as a man.

As he fell upon the meal with enthusiasm, he drew his gaze away from the beautifully patterned veins of the smooth table and looked over the household of Birsha. All the walls seemed to be made of the same material: red rock and earth pressed together and dried around a structure of dark, wooden beams. This gave the walls a rather rounded look, and it appeared several of the circular rooms were adjoined and even stacked on top of each other, producing many living spaces.

Every so often a figure would appear, bustling about whatever business motivated them, and then vanish through one of the doorways. Animals seems to wander in and out of the household at will. Plant life, similar to his room above, seemed to commonly crawl across the walls. They were well-tended and guided, arching above and around doors and windows, giving the place an enchanting look. The sunlight filtered through the vines and the sound of sea-waves floated in from the port.

When he had finished his meal, Maturr came and cleaned away his gourd and platter.

"Meshêk will see you now!" she exclaimed enthusiastically, with the thick accent of northern speech and a welcoming smile. Maturr bustled through several, arched doorways and circular chambers; while Areoch limped behind, trying to keep up. Countless people moved back and forth throughout the rooms.

Finally, Maturr ushered Areoch into a room that was different, and she departed without a further word. Diverse sizes of clay tablets and papyrus sheets lay neatly along shelves and stacked against the walls. Old maps, jars filled with fragments of wood and bone, and other assorted herbs and items, covered the remaining shelves in a meticulous order. Areoch noted that each shelf looked like it had just been cleaned, and the red rock even looked worn in some places from a pattern of wiping. Meshêk sat at the far end of the room, behind the only disheveled table. Several other empty tables lay bare around the chamber. Two eastern facing windows, high in the walls, were thrown open behind Meshêk, filling the space with a warm, glowing light.

"Welcome! I'm sure you must have many questions, and most of them will be answered in time. For now, I will inform you of that which is most necessary. Please," Meshêk pulled out a chair and gestured for Areoch to sit.

"First," continued Meshêk as Areoch looked about, "You will not be permitted to leave these walls and enter into the city until some time has passed. You are not a prisoner," he said as Areoch's expression darkened. "No one will try and stop you from doing as you will. But the oath my master has taken to shelter you during this time will be void if you do not heed my advice. If you leave these walls before I think you are ready, you will venture out at your own peril. You must understand: this is for your protection. Until you learn some of our ways and customs, any watchful eye will know you are a foreigner. Which brings us to our second point: you will need a suitable disguise during your stay here.

'Being one of Agadian upbringing - not to mention the son of a King - I am sure you have been well taught. Are you knowledgeable in scribal work? The movements of the stars? The order of growing things? The history and traditions of the world?"

Areoch nodded at each inquiry and listed off a few others he had studied under the watchful eye of Marqu, though he did not make the mistake of openly stating his master's name.

Meshêk nodded, pleased. "Very good! It is as I anticipated. I am, among other things, the teacher of Birsha's household. His children, Bahira and Berran, and several others, both young and nearly of age in this house, are under my guidance to learn the ways of the world. Birsha is a wise man of high renown in this city, it would not be altogether uncommon for him to hire an artisan or teacher from far-off lands to come and expand the knowledge and honor of his kin.

We will use this to explain your stay with us, and it may also be a way for you to repay my master's kindness. I am a busy man, with many tasks to complete. I will soon be spending incrementally more time with Birsha at his work. When I am not with him, Birsha wishes for me to personally focus on Berran, Birsha's eldest son, to prepare him for his own coming of age, which is fast approaching. Having a stand-in teacher, who can instruct without my counsel, would be more than helpful. Well?" Meshêk raised an eyebrow expectantly, "Are you willing to share your knowledge as repayment for our kindness?"

Areoch half suspected he could be grabbed by the Strong Men of the household at any time and taken by ropes to the city's center. *What choice do I have?* thought Areoch to himself. *I am indebted to these men and must do as they ask.*

"I am willing" he said aloud. "How long will my service be, if I am to repay this debt I now owe?"

Meshêk thought for a moment, "You have spent a month, dependent upon our care, and you will not be fully healed for at least another. I should think that time over again would be a fair repayment."

Areoch nodded his head. "That does, indeed, seem fair. While I have learned many things, I fear I have not learned enough of any to teach them. You may find me unable to do what you have asked."

"Then it is settled!" Meshêk pounded the table, ignoring the comment. "You will be Areoch of the far-away eastern lands of Magen, where the great cedars grow. And do not fear, young master. This is not Agade; few households take the time to broaden the knowledge of their youth, and these here have only this old man to teach them. Your learning is broad enough for my purpose. You will learn how to teach as you go and you will find that it is a teacher's way to learn lessons better as they are taught.

'Come, Master Educator! Let me show you your new home, for so it will be while you stay with us."

Areoch wondered how many titles he would have by the end of the day.

Meshêk briskly left the room. For the next hour Areoch saw nearly all of Birsha's extensive household. They were not half-way through the grand tour when Areoch stumbled and caught himself on the wall. Meshêk looked him over.

"That is enough for today," he decided. "There is much to take in, and you are not fully healed. Go and rest. Maturr will take care of all your needs, if you ask. Most of all, do not forget who you are - and that means no mention of *who* you are! Should you be asked any questions you cannot answer, send them to me!"

As evening fell, Areoch found himself sitting in the wide garden (which lay below his balcony), on a secluded ledge. The large shrubs provided some respite from questioning glances. He found himself breathing easier as he watched the sun's rays dissipate over the water.

A small sputter of repressed laughter, as bright as a flock of warblers springing forth from the bushes, startled Areoch out of his reprieve. He sat up stiffly, glancing around, though he could see nothing but the surrounding hedge. The stillness and peacefulness of the garden resumed and he allowed himself to relax again.

Suddenly, the leaves of the nearest shrubbery rustled. Areoch jumped to his feet with a start, peering questioningly into the greenery. A pair of deep, brown eyes, full of mirth, appeared, staring back at him. He fell back with surprise into the sitting position from which he started. A lithe form, clad in pale green, jumped gracefully from around the hedge and stood smiling beside it.

Areoch realized with a combination of horror and delight that it was none other than the young servant he had so often seen from his balcony. She wore a lightly colored tunic of fine cloth and her rich, black hair was allowed to flow freely behind her slight figure. Her features were precise and smooth, speaking of gentleness. Her smile conveyed a sharp wit and restrained mischief. She flashed a smile, causing Areoch's mouth to gape and he found no words to speak. She was even fairer than he remembered. Finding himself now face-to-face with her, left his heart stuttering.

His expression must have been ridiculous for she laughed merrily. It made his heart jump over the garden wall and race away down the hillside toward the sea.

"You start and fall away," she said with the same look of mischief. "Surely you must not mind being watched in the garden while you seek solitude?"

A smile played at the corners of her mouth.

She came and stood a little nearer, speaking with more humility as she looked him over, her eyes traveling over his scars before resting on his deeply colored armbands.

"I hear you are from Magen, a wise man, come to teach us. This is good, for I do not see how Meshêk is suitable for such work. He seems to make everything dusty and dull, and that only when he is not meddling about in others affairs." She spoke as if in remembrance of some personal argument, but then the cloud left her brow and the light returned to her eyes.

"You seem young to be a teacher of all things and a wise man of many. Tell me, what is it exactly that you teach?"

Her probing question left Areoch still speechless and he wondered who this woman was, for she seemed to be as quick of wit and speech as she was beautiful. Clearly, she was one of those whom Meshêk taught often. She gazed at him as he searched for an answer, the same smile playing at the corners of her lips.

"I know of no one who can teach all things, and it seems you will be one of those who may judge whether I be but a poor teacher of just a few," he said finally. The sound of his own voice grounded him, and he continued with confidence. "Stories and the written runes, which do not fade with time, are what I teach best." He wondered if that was a good answer and partially winced, thinking it sounded rather dull.

She shrugged her shoulders and sat down on the bench next to him.

"It would be just like Meshêk to bring someone else into this house

147

that is over-fond of lore-books and wet, clay tablets." She seemed satisfied with his response. Areoch suppressed a sigh of relief and wondered how long his cover would last, facing such interrogations.

"What is it," he asked, "that makes you turn aside from knowledge of runes and stories?"

She scoffed and stood up, facing the red and golden sunset which shone in brilliance over the low stone wall.

"Who has time for them, when the entire world waits for those having a heart to seek it? I cannot bear to be trapped in that cell with only a hole of light for hours of the day."

"What would you be doing, then?" Areoch ventured to ask, hardly daring to risk disturbing the scene.

"Living stories of my own," she expressed with sweeping arms. "Walking among the wild-flower fields of the Arron-Ken, or deep into the trees of the Asur Forest where the Bulls butt their heads like the crashing of waves. Or farther, even, beyond the Durgu Mountains to the south, or across the Great Tanti Sea... who knows what lies there? What would one see to walk there?" she trailed off in thought.

"Perhaps, could you read the runes in Meshêk's classes, you would glimpse a part of those things, though you will never go there yourself," Areoch suggested.

She spun around and faced him. "Who said I will never go there?!" she cried, with sudden anger in her eyes. "Am I not free to choose where I go and who I am as I will?"

Areoch was startled by the sudden change.

"I did not mean that," he stammered. "I only assumed you would honor your household and remain..."

"Because that is what a good maid would do? Work the loom, marry the wealthiest man my household chooses, have many children, and increase my domestic honor? Is that what I am to do, as all others have done before me?"

Areoch was speechless. Many women he knew and loved in Agade, especially within his father's household, worked hard to bring honor to their home, and would fiercely defend it. But none had ever spoken like this, or talked of leaving their home and honor, to seek the glory that was customary of men.

"It is common and highly respected, where I come from, for that to be the case," tried Areoch with a wince, for he anticipated another outburst. He wondered if this was common among the lands north of Agade. Instead, the woman before him drew up her head proudly.

"Very well. Good evening to you, then." With a curt nod she disappeared around the shrubbery, leaving Areoch staring dumbly at the wall. He leaned back against the bench and sighed, cursing himself for being such a fool. Who was he, to correct her? He wished he had not spoken, to enjoy her presence longer. Just as soon as she had vanished, her beautiful form once again appeared. Where the proud head had been held high before, it now drooped low.

"I beg your pardon, master educator," she said. "I am a most wretched daughter among my kin and I should be grateful. Where else would I be, if Birsha did not have authority over the daily grain for a hundred men and entrust the women of his household to uphold his name? I should be glad he does so much for us."

Areoch was so glad to see her he jumped out of his seat with a wince of pain. She smiled at the gesture.

"Nay, you need not ask for any pardon!" he cried. "What you say would seem uncouth, perhaps, to an older man. The customs outside of my homeland are little known to me and I come to be taught as much as I teach. The lesson of the day should be that: *one can never know the end of a story until he has read it through completely*. For things may change in an instant, and small things turn the tide of the future. Certain skills may be valuable to some, and others less so. Your path may lead you to many places ...but my heart is glad to have met you...here." Areoch felt the blood rush to his face as he finished.

She smiled and gave a small bow before turning away, fading with light footfalls into the bustling household and leaving Areoch marveling at what had taken place.

Chapter Eighteen

For the Heart of Bahira

The next day, Areoch arose somewhat late and to an empty hall. He broke his fast and then wandered among the massive complex that was Birsha's household, exploring his new berth. He soon grew tired of the questioning looks and found himself resting back in the garden.

It was there, around midday, that Meshêk found him and brought him into his study.

"Today, you will help me with our first lesson," Meshêk informed, as he picked up several clay tablets and laid them across the tables. "It is Birsha's wish that the youth of his household be taught better than anyone in the land. Laborers are easily taught by sending them to study and work with the master smiths, carpenters, herders, weavers, and potters. But, scribal work is rare in these parts of the word, and the skills are highly sought after. Hence, that is what we focus on most and your long apprenticeship in Agade will be of much use."

Finished with the tablets, Meshêk began laying out several dried reeds, each tip cut with a different pattern. Areoch was familiar with the routine: the clay tablets, covered by a thin piece of wood to hold in the moisture, were easily stenciled by pushing the reeds into the soft clay. A combination of these runes would form a word or a sentence that could be dried, preserving the thought of the scribe. It was a powerful concept.

"We spend a short amount of time each day with a variety of students, as you will see," continued Meshêk, "including several of the youngsters that show promise in the household. Of special concern to Birsha, however, is his son Berran and eldest daughter, Bahira. Berran is preparing for his coming of age, as I mentioned. Soon, I will be spending more time with him directly. Bahira is not fond of scribal work or learning. Nonetheless, she is of the age to entertain suitors, and they will expect her to be able to manage their estates and bring them honor.

Birsha intends to see her well-equipped and to have none but a high-standing man enter his household when the day comes. I hope you will be of use in mending her ways."

At the prospect of teaching Birsha's eldest daughter and son, Areoch's heart fell. He had hoped he would be able to spend time evenly among the pupils, and thereby spend more time with the young woman he had met in the garden.

"Don't worry," consoled Meshêk, mistaking his downcast look for doubt in his ability to teach, "Your best in this matter will be all that is needed."

Areoch could tell that taming this daughter was no easy task, but he set his mind upon fulfilling the duty, no matter how dull and wearisome it might be. He nodded.

"Ah, here they come now," said Meshêk gazing at the door.

Even as he finished speaking, a motley group of young people began to enter. A group of three younger children, none older than eight winters, came and sat near the front of the room. Behind them came two older girls, who were a few seasons younger than Areoch. A boy followed. Areoch did not recognize any of them. The boy was small of stature and somewhat wider in girth, with relatively soft features. He had sharp green eyes that Meshêk knew came from his mother, but the remainder of his characteristics spoke of his father, Birsha.

"That is Berran," explained Meshêk in a low voice to Areoch, "Birsha's only remaining son. And *that* is Bahira."

Areoch looked to see which of the two girls he was gesturing to, but Meshêk was looking toward the door, where the last student of the class had finally entered with a somewhat late and unconcerned demeanor. Areoch caught his breath and turned red in the face. Bahira was the same girl he had met in the garden!

She sat between the other two girls and Meshêk started the session leaving Areoch somewhat winded.

"Good afternoon class," welcomed Meshêk. "Today we will be continuing with our transliteration of *The Instructions of Šuruppag*. Most of you are nearing section forty. Please reference your written copies only if necessary. Try and reconstruct the runes by your memory alone!"

As the class busied themselves, Meshêk walked about, monitoring their work. The clay tablets in front of the students were broken into two halves. On one half, the scribal hand of Meshêk had drawn the correct verses. The other half lay empty, waiting for the student to fill it in by transcribing or by memorization.

Bahira paid Areoch little notice as he watched her inscribe several lines with ease. He was surprised that she did not reference the written text, but inscribed the verses by memory. He read aloud over her shoulder what she had written:

"*You should not inscribe properly: it will lay a trap for you.* Daughter of Birsha," he continued, "I believe you have mis-recalled your section. It should say, *You should not speak improperly: it will lay a trap for you.*"

Bahira continued stenciling without paying Areoch much heed.

"I am aware, Areoch of Magen, of what the wisdom of Šuruppag states. I have decided to modify it in order to reveal loftier wisdom. Are you not pleased?" She turned and gazed up at him with the same mischievous glint in her eye and small smile at the corners of her mouth that made Areoch's heart flutter, waiting for an approving word.

The girls on either side of Areoch burst into a fit of giggling at her wit, and Areoch gazed over the tablet again. Her lines were straight and formed and her translation all but perfect (albeit her modified rendition of the text in several places). The girls entered into a hushed silence as Meshêk suddenly loomed over them.

"Well," said he, looking over Bahira's tablet, "It seems Šuruppag had a little left to learn, if only you could have been present during his lifetime. Please continue," Meshêk gave a scolding look, pulling Areoch aside to help other students.

"I'm sure you won't forget," he instructed Bahira, over his shoulder, "to include lines 56-58 in your vigor: *Don't pick a quarrel with a wise man. You will disgrace yourself.*"

The class went on and Areoch did not find a chance to return to Bahira's work. Meshêk finally clapped his hands and the group departed. Bahira hurried out the door without looking at Areoch. Meshêk sat down with a sigh.

"Now you understand why I may find your help useful," said Meshêk, nodding in Bahira's direction.

"I don't think I have ever seen a student so apt with the stencil. How long has she studied?" asked Areoch as he watched Bahira's form disappear, wondering to himself if he had again upset her.

"She has studied with me since she was little. You are right, she is very bright, but has little focus. This concerns her father."

"Lucciene and Morica seem to help little," Areoch ventured, indicating the two girls that sat on Bahira's either side.

Meshêk nodded. "They follow her lead. Do you think you can teach such a class, facing such odds? I hope so! Tomorrow I will be absent, and I will leave it to you to continue this lesson!"

As the days passed, Areoch regained his strength and the confinement of Birsha's house became increasingly stifling. Always he taught the mid-day class of studying scribes. In his spare time, he busied himself, helping the masters in the house work wood and clay. Meshêk rarely returned to help him after his first absence. Perhaps he thought Areoch taught remarkably well, or he had other matters to attend to. The remainder of the household, from the craftsmen to the keepers of the house, marveled at Areoch's usefulness, finding him a treasure to have on-hand to help with their work.

Bahira was as consistent as a whirlwind. She seemed to fly between seeking his approval in class to mocking him openly. Areoch was patient. By the end of his lessons, Bahira was typically subdued to a modest demeanor. He found her a remarkable student. When Areoch had the class inscribe the epic of Gal-Banda and the Anzu Dragon, she was focused and adept, even passionate about learning the lore and rhyme of the hero's tale. With works of oration, wisdom, or rites, she seemed to fade and lose interest - as if she was far off in the distant fields and mountains of her mind - or she would seek to busy herself with creating fun at Areoch's methods.

One day, Lucciene openly joined in with Bahira's fun, testing the limits of Areoch's patience.

"Do they have wise men at all in Magen, or just blocks of wood?" She mocked, glancing for approval in Bahira's direction. "I fear a tree swaying in the wind would be more interesting than your teaching!"

"What is it about him that you despise so?!" cried Bahira, in a sudden rage. Areoch stood with his mouth halfway open, in shock at her quick rebuttal. Lucciene drew back in surprise at her mistress' change. "Is it his patience or kindness that makes you throw him down to the dirt? How dare you stand against his words when he has paid you nothing but wisdom! Brat! Urchin!"

Areoch quickly called the class from session as Lucciene flew from the room with tears streaming down her cheeks.

"She had no right to speak to you like that," insisted Bahira, trying to hold her composure. "As father would say, *A sharp word for a sharp word.*"

"Do you really think you have a right to speak to her in turn?"

"I am a horrible friend, aren't I?" she sobbed, as tears ran down her cheeks.

"What is it that drives you so?" asked Areoch gently as he sat across from her. He resisted the desire to reach forward and brush aside her tears.

"I do not know," and she wept even more bitterly. "I do not know anything other than this lore, and these reeds - this household will soon have the best of me."

Areoch nodded, swallowing the lump in his throat. "I know, I must bore you here. You wish to finish your learning and find a husband - to be far away from this daily routine. I am just a part of what you must hate."

"Do you know me at all?" objected Bahira. "You are perhaps the one thing I can look forward to in a day! I am occasionally sent away with the older women who trade in the city - that is something, at least. I do not long for the loom. I hate its gossip and the way of the women there. And my father and Meshêk rest daily upon me the burden of being desirable for a suitor, locking me up here all the more. I want to be free, Areoch. I just want to be free! And, it is the one thing I am not allowed."

Areoch couldn't bring himself to speak, as he found was often the case around Bahira. She fled the class leaving him alone with his thoughts.

Meshêk returned from the port the next day. Though Areoch had it on his mind to speak with him about Bahira's outburst, he had no need.

"Areoch, there you are!" Meshêk cried as he saw him. "You must forgive me, the work at the port grows, and Birsha has need for my hands. You look well," he added, eyeing Areoch up and down. "How do you feel?"

"Cramped," admitted Areoch. "Birsha's house may be large, but it grows smaller by the day."

"Ah, it is as I imagined and also why I wished to speak with you. You have been teaching for nearly four weeks and you have grown more accustomed to our ways. I think it is time you were shown around Cartegin, for your own benefit."

"That would be a refreshing change!" agreed Areoch with delight. "I feel as if I would go mad if I had to stay in-doors much longer. When will we leave?"

"We?" cried Meshêk, laughing at his excitement. "I have no time, Areoch, to show you about this city as an honored guest from Magen, as I should. We will need to have someone of relative importance guide you, to introduce you and explain away your presence with us as you meet others. Traditionally, an educator would have Birsha himself make the introductions. Tor'i would do, though he is busier these days, as we all are..." Meshêk trailed off in thought.

"What of Bahira?" Areoch ventured tentatively.

Meshêk stroked his beard and raised an eyebrow. "Bahira? Hmm, yes, I can see your point. It would be good for her and good for Birsha's purposes as well. Yes, for her to be seen with an educator from distant lands! It would increase the honor of Birsha's household and increase her status in the minds of those families that may seek to join with her in the future."

Meshêk paused and looked closely at Areoch, studying him until he felt his feet squirm. Meshêk finally nodded as if approving.

"Very well! You are a smart one, Areoch of Magen. I will have Bahira informed. She will meet you in the garden courtyard tomorrow morning and will introduce you to the life of Cartegin. Study well! Cartegin is unlike your home, but it is not a wholly bad place."

They met the next morning in the garden, shortly after dawn. Bahira had been informed of her new task. On seeing Areoch she threw her arms around him in a tight embrace before stepping back, her eye's twinkling.

"I do not know how you did it nor even why you would. Know that I am thankful, Areoch of Magen," she said.

"Please, daughter of Birsha, I had little to do with anything..." Areoch stammered, his heart racing after her embrace.

She smiled and raised a hand to his mouth, stopping him mid-sentence. Her finger on his lips was like lightning that sent tingles down to his toes.

"Bahira, Areoch of Magen. Call me Bahira."

"...Bahira," he said slowly.

She smiled broadly. "Well, it looks like it is your turn to follow me for a while!" she cried, and the best of Areoch's time in Cartegin began.

They spent the entire day in the city. Bahira took him through the bustling markets, where fish, oil, and wood, along with all manner of day-to-day needs were to be found. She led him around the city's four quadrants, each built from a different style of material: the red clay of the eastern district, the black basalt rock of the central district, the wood shacks of the northern, and the tanned tents of the southern.

"Cartegin may not be an old city," she explained as they went, "but its peoples are very old, stemming from when only herders and rovers wandered this land. Each quadrant has a primary household, master of their appropriate task: crafting, growing, fishing, or hunting. Long ago the families gathered here and found that together they could supply each other's needs. The city of Cartegin was born."

"What lays down that way?" inquired Areoch, nodding toward the eastern district and the sea, where the port was barely visible.

"My father's work," she replied simply, before introducing Areoch to one family, and then to another and another.

"Areoch, wise man of Magen, to teach within the household of Birsha," she would say, and then move on. Areoch clasped many forearms and the smell of wood and crushed grain enveloped him. The shouts of trade and of city life rang in his ears. Always the smiling face of Bahira was before him, occasionally glancing back with her mischievous smile to make sure he was still following. Looking back, it was all that he remembered of the day, other than the eyes of the young men that watched her pass. He remembered those too.

The day finally came to an end. Nearing dusk they arrived back at Birsha's household. They stopped briefly outside the gate and watched the light waver on the water's surface as the sun sank. Areoch observed Bahira sidelong, as she closed her eyes and breathed deeply. The rays of sun reflected around her hair, creating a warm glow that Areoch felt he could almost touch. She opened them again and seeing Areoch's gaze upon her, gave him a quick smile before running inside and disappearing from sight.

The next day at class, Bahira seemed happier and more agreeable than Areoch had ever seen. Their subject was only mildly boring: inscribing the names of the stars and charting their course in runes across pieces of Papyrus. Bahira was the model student, asking questions and giving insightful responses.

"I have never seen the like," remarked Meshêk thoughtfully after class, wondering at Bahira's behavior as he stirred two cups of potent tea. Areoch had grown rather fond of the strong mixture. "Birsha will be pleased with your work, Areoch. You have done well."

"I have done little," insisted Areoch, "except introduce the same thing in a new way."

"It is all that was needed," replied Meshêk, "along with a bit of air," he added thoughtfully.

"You have repaid us nearly half of your time, and I think it would be good, perhaps for everyone, for a change of pace," Meshêk suggested with a twinkle in his eye. "Starting tomorrow, for your last month with us, I would like you to be exposed to a little more of life inside and outside of Cartegin. You will continue teaching classes here, on occasion, but mostly your focus will be on Cartegin itself. Remember the Cartegin you learn, Areoch! It is not for without reason I want you to know this place: its beauty, its strength, and my hope in its people. Bahira will continue to be your guide. As she shows you our ways, you will invest in teaching her, for she has shown much improvement."

By his tone there was some underlying meaning to his words, but often the full meaning of what Meshêk meant was left unsaid.

Through the following days, Areoch and Bahira strayed outside the city walls, and Bahira led Areoch through places which she had long been absent. On the third day, Bahira showed Areoch the way of the fishermen on the banks of the Dan-Jor. They swung nets from rough-hewn piers in the middle of the waters, far from the river's banks. An occasional small coracle of tightly woven reeds floated gently by. On the way back they passed through many harvest fields along the outer edge of Cartegin. Some were sprinkled with shoots of plants, while others were black and lifeless.

"It has been fewer than two seasons since the master farmers started this practice," Bahira said, gesturing at the burnt land, "and I still do not understand why they set fire to their crops at the turn of the year. It causes the soil to be black and lifeless, where nothing grows. Why would they do such a thing?"

Areoch kicked at the soft chaff.

"They have done the same, where I come from, as long as I can remember," said Areoch, "and my father made sure I was well taught in the ancient lore of the master farmers, for it is deeply rooted in the survival of a city." Then he sang in a low voice:

The goddess Anu, one of three

Came down as a seed, to nurture the ground.

When winter's chill hit, she paid no heed

She died like a son of earth, and was placed in the mound.

So Enki of the Sea, one of three

Came down as the sun and saw the winter's bite.

He made the winter flee

But in his love there was still no life.

So Enlil the King, Lord of the three

Heard the cries of God Enki

He lit fire to the ground, to burn up the chaff

And from it rose Anu, from piles of Ash.

Bahira raised a quizzical eyebrow, lost to Areoch's meaning.

"The farmers sing that song to our children," explained Areoch. "It tells them about the mystery of growing things. If one planted in the land, year after year, plowing the same soil again and again, the earth would soon grow old and fail to produce plants that yield grain. But, if a farmer sets fire to it and destroys it, the earth remembers that after death comes life... and it is reborn." Areoch reached down under the layer of ash and soot and pushed up thick, rich soil. "It is again ready to yield a harvest of plenty."

"It looks and smells horrid," said Bahira, shrugging her shoulders. "Better the fields of wildflowers that grow with each season and have no master!"

Areoch smiled. They walked for a while in silence, enjoying the fresh air of spring.

"You have learned much from your home, Areoch of Magen," she said finally with a mischievous grin. "The way of the stars and of runes, of living things and of hidden things. Your father must be a great man, to teach you so much of the world."

"What do you call those fields there?" he asked, quickly changing the subject and pointing off where the Asur forest ran down from the mountains south of Cartegin. Green hills gently rose against the sea, dotted with the flowers of late spring, until disappearing into the forest. Rocky outcroppings jutted above the grass and through the treetops, spotting the landscape like the remains of old mountains.

"Those are the fields of Arron-Ken," Bahira answered. "When I was a young girl, I would hide in the grass there and listen to the great bulls of Asur butting heads in their great strength!! Ah, how they would crack and thunder, splitting the very trees!" Excitement shone from Bahira's eyes.

"Could we go there?" asked Areoch in wonder.

"We would have to leave very early, before the break of dawn... I would like that."

"So would I," agreed Areoch.

The next morning, under the folds of purple clouds promising a glorious dawn, they set out for the high grasses of the Arron-Ken. They brought a satchel for the day, stocked with water, dried fruits, and meats. They did not know how long they would have to wait until the bulls came forth. The grass between the towering rocks of the Arron-Ken rose to their waists and covered them with dew. Areoch laid down his cloak to keep them dry as they lay hidden together. The sun rose slowly, streaking the sky with reds and golds; while white and blue flowers opened among the grass, catching the light as they shone with an unexpected brilliance of color. Areoch could not help but think of how beautiful Bahira seemed, surrounded by such small, grand things of beauty.

"It is... you are... beautiful," he said finally, his heart throbbing as he hoped for a response.

Bahira turned toward him, that small smile playing at the corners of her mouth. At that instant a resounding CRACK! echoed off the stony outcroppings. They turned, peering over the tops of the grass, in the direction of the Asur Forest. A great beast stood there, as thick as it was tall! Horns curled up and around its head. It seemed to recoil, as if from a great blow. Like thunder, another larger beast of the same kind, charged from the foliage of the forest, meeting and knocking down its opponent even as it turned to meet the onslaught. Another crack echoed as they slammed together. Bahira and Areoch were amazed as the bodies and massive horns absorbed the impact.

"The Bulls of the Asur!" exclaimed Bahira, as the creatures slowly retreated into the shadow of the forest. "I do not know if they have another name. Do they walk on the slopes of the mountains in your country?"

"I have seen the Mountain Goats of Ibel and heard tell of the great Sloths of Eridor, but I have never seen these! Rafael, our Warden, would know of them, I have no doubt. I am amazed to see these with my own eyes."

Bahira's eyes shone. "South of the Durgu Mountains is not so different from here after all. Tell me, Areoch, what is it like in Agade, the land of kings and of plenty?"

Areoch started and drew back from her.

"You shy away, as in our first meeting in the garden!" laughed Bahira. "Do you think that was the first time I met you? Do you not know that it was I who found you along the eastern track, not a half-day journey from the Agadian road? I was the one that convinced my father not to pass you by, as all other travelers had done. I am no fool, Areoch, and even before I overheard my father and Meshêk discussing their plans for you, I thought you may be from that far-off country." She paused, then continued, "Well, will you not say anything to me?"

"Do you despise me?" asked Areoch, "If, truly, I am from the land everyone here calls 'enemy'?"

Bahira sidled closer to him. "I do not," she whispered. "How could I? I wonder only how much of you is an act and what is true." She looked as if she would say more, but did not continue.

"I may be under disguise but some things are not false!" cried Areoch in defense. "Bahira, what I feel I must say openly, though it seems you know more of me than I thought possible. You are my one desire. My heart longs for you. When you are not with me, I look for you, and when you leave me, I watch you depart - awaiting your return. I have found that I love you, and I would give all that I am to hear you say the same."

Bahira smiled her small smile and she let herself lean up against him, resting her head on his shoulder.

"You are a fool, Areoch of Sargon household," she said in a kindly tone, as if thinking. "What happens next? You will finish your time of repayment with us and then depart, seeking adventure elsewhere while you finish your Giǵāl, leaving me behind?"

"How much do you know?" shock filled his voice at the mention of Sargon. "You have more knowledge of me than I guessed. But why must I leave? Why should I not stay among your household and then, when the time comes, approach your father with my desire? Is not the son of Sargon a worthy suitor for the household of Birsha?"

Bahira did not answer and Areoch grew distressed.

"Will you at least give me a word of hope that my love may grow?"

"You do not know what you say," Bahira sat up and looked away at the walls of Cartegin. "Let us not think of it for now."

She arose. Grabbing Areoch by the hand, she led him deeper into the Arron-Ken. The rock outcroppings grew closer together and the flowers thicker. Rich, cascading water poured down from the heights, uninterrupted except for the light trilling of larks and the occasional happy chorus of frogs. Bahira led Areoch further, through many ancient standing stones until they turned around a final pillar. Before them was a steep bank, dotted with grass and flowers. At its bottom was a clear pool fed by a rushing waterfall. It seemed an old and ancient place, for the rock walls were time-worn and full of cracks; while the springs of water that flowed from them seemed young and fresh. The flowers along the water's edge dipped their petals into its surface, as if drinking a draught of youth from ancient hands.

"I found this place, long ago" whispered Bahira as she pulled him forward to the edge of the pool. "It was my secret place. Now, it can be *our* secret place." Areoch was stunned. Before he realized it, Bahira was near him and he leaned over her, brushing away her long hair, his rough, scarred hand resting against her soft cheek. She laughed and pushed him away, her eye's beaming, and he laughed with her because his heart was glad.

Chapter Nineteen

A Dark Mystery

Bahira and Areoch spent much time together and the weeks passed swiftly. Areoch taught occasionally, and when he was not teaching he was allowed to wander. Bahira would join him when she could, but she was often preoccupied with the tasks of the household. Some days he walked alone through the city streets and markets, learning something of the ways of the city. He found himself in the low hills and fields of Cartegin more often than naught. There, his heart was free, and he thought of Bahira and what lay ahead for them as he stretched his sore limbs.

It was on the return of one of these long walks that he found himself a little to the northwest of Cartegin. Here, the rushing waters of the Dan-Jor made a sudden sweep, in from the sea, leaving steep and bare banks of rock and mud as the river curved away through distant plains. It was late in the evening. As Areoch walked along the bank, he became aware of a large caravan traveling north some distance ahead. They were traders who had spent several days in Cartegin and now they attempted to ford the river on the way back to their own lands.

What they traded, Areoch could not say, but while the wains had seemed heavy laden on their arrival - they were now less burdened, and scores of people walked with them and sat in the carts. Men from the north guided them across the river with low words and the occasional crack of a whip to encourage the oxen. He noticed that several of the men were armed with staves and spears.

Areoch walked forward, thinking to get a better look, when a shape loomed up alongside him and pulled him down to the earth.

"Meshêk!" Areoch exclaimed with surprise. "What are you doing here?"

"The same thing as you, it seems," answered Meshêk gruffly. "And keep your voice down, I wish to remain unseen."

He turned, vanishing over the bank of the river so that Areoch thought he might have fallen. When he rushed to the edge, he saw that a steep flight of stairs cut into the bank, leading down toward the water's edge. Meshêk looked up at him and beckoned for him to follow. They walked about half-way down the steps, and the river turned enough to allow the caravan and the opposing shore to come into view. They halted, while Meshêk studied the distant group.

"What is it that you look for?" asked Areoch, surveying the matted band. A few men stood in rich contrast to the others: wearing fine silks and linens, belts of gold and other riches; while the rest appeared poor. Several seemed sick and the little ones were carried in the arms of their mothers.

"I do not yet know," answered Meshêk. "These bands have been coming in from the north for months now, even before our return from Magen. They keep their business to themselves and offer nothing but *opportunity* for those that wish to join them. They pay richly for the weak servants, the homeless, and the needy, and Ishshak has no second thoughts about their departure from his city. Those we watch now are the same, people from Cartegin. These northern men have come frequently, and I am troubled about it in my bones."

"I have seen them," Areoch said, gazing at the distant forms, "in the city squares and the markets. They seem to promise wealth and status, power and health to those who have not toiled for such things themselves or have been unable to find it. It is a grand image for those accustomed to little, and the men ask only that they leave everything behind: their households, their city, and their name. Those that agree make a vow in some strange tongue and are given instant riches. There is much happiness."

Meshêk nodded. "It is a tongue I have heard before. It comes from a land called Angfar. I wonder what happens after they cross the river into lands not controlled by Cartegin. Alas, that I am bound here with Birsha! I can do little, regardless. As the mountains separate your land from the rest of the world, so the forest and the river do the same for us. Let us watch what happens!"

They stood and stared, invisible forms hunched under the bank while the far-off group crossed the river. It took time, for the river was wide and deep from spring melts. With the help of the oxen and the tall men, all crossed with little ill effect. Upon reaching the other side, one family seemed to have second thoughts about leaving their home. Their figures were small and far away, but it appeared that a portion of the group began to turn back. There was an exchange of words between them and several men who blocked their way. What happened next could not be made out clearly - something of a struggle broke out! The family seemed to try and push past their keepers, and others joined them as the promise of riches and far-off lands became not worth the journey.

The men acted quickly. For a moment Meshêk and Areoch could only see the running of obscure figures. Dust rose and guttural shouts echoed down the water. It ceased as suddenly as it had begun. Still forms (now bound and gagged), were loaded on the carts by the men, while the rest were driven on, lashed together by rope and thong as whips whirled and cracked above their heads.

"What was that, what just happened?" asked Areoch in dismay.

"I know little, too little," his voice was low and menacing. "But I have now less doubt than I had before, although my heart guessed this purpose when I first heard of such strange things." Meshêk turned aside and continued down the stairs. Areoch followed until the path ended sharply.

They stood in a large recess in the bank, where the river had eaten and deposited pressed mud and rock during a high year of water. The Dan-Jor itself was far below them, and the bank was overhung so that the chasm was invisible from above. The recess was long and wide. While a few small, resilient plants grew on its floor, there was little vegetation. Large mounds, fifteen or more, seemed to grow out of the bank.

"Here is one place in Cartegin you have not yet visited," said Meshêk. "The Barrows of Golgin-shak, who was the first Chief of the ancient tribes that became Cartegin. Here the prestigious families of this city await the final rising of the dawn."

The entrance to the Barrows faced east. Though Areoch could not see inside, he knew their tunnels ran deep under the feet of those who walked above, stacked with the dead of each family household, along with precious items that were deemed fitting for their final journey.

"The abducted and the dead, how alike they are," quoted Meshêk as he gazed among the tombs. He looked back up the river, shaking his head in sorrow. "I fear this is far worse. Let me ask you, Areoch, for here we can speak freely, in Agade, are men and women imprisoned for breaking Agadian law?"

"You mean chained, like a dog who has bitten its master? Nay, no such thing happens. Punishment, fair and equal, is dealt, as the Old Law dictates. For death, death is dealt. For theft, an equal item is taken. Hard is the lesson when the man has not enough to reimburse his debtors! For then it is not uncommon for a fair price to be his hand, if he does not vow to work until his debt has been repaid."

"That does not revolt you, in any way?"

"Of course not," assured Areoch. "It is right and fair for the victim to take what hurt has been raised against him, all know the Old Law. They forfeit their loss from the beginning, for they know the penalty."

"So it is here too, in some regard, though Ishshak's law differs from what was passed down in ancient years. Man has value, Areoch, but it is inherently different than that of a beast of burden. If a man loses a hand, he still may do much in the world - though the loss of a hand is a severe punishment, he is still *himself*.

'Worse than this, indeed even worse than being slain, would be to lose *yourself*: to be chained, until you became nothing more than a beast of burden. If one could remove that freedom from another... What remained would not be...natural. Can you imagine, Areoch, the life of a human without his freedom of will, to be driven like cattle or kicked like the dogs? Is there any debt worth such a steep price? Even in the afterlife some choice remains, and for that death is deemed a fair justice for the worst of actions. Who would take away the *Enlil Imagio*, that which makes us human?"

Areoch pondered the question and the caravan of dark men they saw from afar.

"I have heard whispers of such raiders in recent years, even in Agade. We call them the *Urudu*: marauders, who seek to steal, not treasure or wealth, but men. They are mercifully slain if they are discovered, so the gods may determine their course. Is that what you think we have witnessed?"

"I cannot be sure, but it is my fear. Man has been blinded before in our history. We have only recently come to be so blind as to sell each other unto bondage."

They both stood silent for a while. It seemed to Areoch that the dead in that place could almost speak with a voice, he felt their presence under the earth.

"I can think of only one greater evil than a man forcing such a thing upon another," Meshêk said finally.

"What is that?" Areoch asked, trying not to look at the entrances to the tombs.

"A Power strong enough to blind the average mortal, until they would sell *themselves* into such an arrangement, of their own accord. That, Areoch, speaks of a deeper Evil than of common man's conception. There is something greater and perhaps far older at root here." Meshêk trailed off, as though he guessed something more than he said.

"What you say disturbs me greatly!" cried Areoch. "If man has invented such a thing in this region of the world, I fear that I begin to understand my father's hatred for outsiders too well."

"You see only partially, then," said Meshêk, "if you think Cartegin is the cause of this. We are caught, like an island between two rivers, between the northern and the southern lands. The northern lands of the Jezrial Dynasty and the Kingdom of Agade. What, I wonder, will become of us trapped between two such forces - one that seemingly wishes to suck the very life from our bones and the other who shuns our calls for help. Which is more evil? I do not know."

Areoch did not answer his question, but asked another in retort.

"Does Ishshak know of this plot? Can he not see plainly what is happening to the poor of his city? I would say he does, and yet he either does not care or turns a blind eye, doing nothing. Or even worse, he profits from it knowingly!"

"Does Sargon do any different?" rebuked Meshêk sharply. "Ishshak is blinded by his desire for bronze and strength, it is true. Is that any different from Sargon's own reasoning?"

"My father acts as he does to protect his people from corruption and darkness!"

"Yet he sends his son alone on the Giġāl into the waiting hands of such people!" answered Meshêk dryly. "You must understand, Areoch, Birsha fears you for the same reasons any would. They ask themselves what the purpose was behind such an act. Could it be to start a war, so Agade can take with strength the rest of these lands? Or is there something else at work, that you yourself know of?"

"Birsha has nothing to fear from me, as you well know!" cried Areoch with frustration rising in his voice. "I have done nothing but repaid him for his help since my arrival. Is there nothing I can do to convince him of my loyalty?"

Areoch's thoughts had changed to Bahira, and he felt as if other forces were pulling her far out of his reach. Meshêk looked closely at him from under furrowed brows, as if guessing his mind.

"There is little you could do," he concluded, finally. "You have both much and little to do with Sargon and Agade. Much, for you represent them. Little, for you yourself cannot change them even if you desired."

Areoch turned away, downcast. "Will Birsha not even speak to me? I know he has been at the port and I see that I have been kept away from there."

"I can pass along your desire to speak to him, but I would not allow yourself to hope, Areoch. His mind is convinced. Once you have repaid your debt to him you should move onward in your Giġāl. He will not allow for more, unless his mind is changed by forces stronger than you. Indeed, he has only given you this much kindness to not curse Berran on his own journey into manhood. He holds the danger of being associated with you, too high to do any more."

The river murmured quietly below them and the stillness of that space seemed to fill Areoch's mind with despair.

Chapter Twenty

__Choices and Decisions__

T he sun rose the next day, striking first the tops of the Durgu Mountains and then spreading, like dripping honey, onto the gentle slopes of the Asur. From there the rich low-lands and meadows around Cartegin slowly warmed with the sun's rays. Areoch had spent fourteen weeks in the city. Spring had lifted and the fullness of summer filled the air with a radiating heat.

Cyril, master of Cartegin's southern fields, rose before the sun (as was his custom). His family had long toiled and cultivated the earth east of the Arron-Ken. It had been a good spring, at long last! The barley grew thick and tall, the dates multiplied, and the grapes grew in great clusters upon the vine. It promised to be a winter without hunger.

He walked gradually through his fields, as the golden light began to warm the dirt, checking the western fences to make sure they separated neighboring herds from his growing crops. The fences were firm. He turned at the southern edge, looking across the broad expanse of land he was steward over.

Good it is to be alive, he thought, as he watched the walls of Cartegin glow like fire from the light of morning. He meant it, for he needed little to be happy and he had much.

Even as he stood in pleasant thought, a horrible groan sounded from the plants beside him. Cyril started, for it was a groan that sounded like the last breath of a dying man. He peered into the bushes, brushing them aside with his leathery hands. A leg, an arm, and then a head was revealed. Cyril sighed, for it was a small boy. The child's garb was foreign. Even in the shadows of morning, the boy was noticeably of a paler race than the people north of the Durgu Mountains.

The boy's shoulder and side was caked in dried blood. Cyril gave him a little push with a sandaled foot, but the small figure made no sound. The boy's chest was still. Cyril looked up and around, wondering what calamity might have befallen one so young. He saw nothing to raise alarm. So, he turned, walking with measured evenness back toward the Asur Forest where he dwelt with his family.

He returned, before the sun had risen two reeds lengths above the horizon. With Cyril came Lu'ril, one of his youngest sons, who was pushing a barrow of wood caked with dirt and sod from the morning's work.

"Well, you take the hands Lu'ril my lad and I'll take the feet," instructed Cyril calmly.

Lu'ril nodded. As Cyril pushed back the bushes and grabbed the ankles of the limp figure, Lu'ril trod over the top of the plants until he found the arms.

"One, two, three!" muttered Cyril, but as soon as they raised the still form from the earth, fresh blood poured from the youth's shoulder and the form cried out with pain!

"By Anu! He is yet alive!" cried Lu'ril who quickly let the figure back down to earth.

"Then he is badly wounded and near the pit of Sheol," surmised Cyril, looking closer at the boy's wounds. "You must take him with all speed to Cartegin, to the House of Chief Ishshak, and tell him to call for his healer."

"Yes, father! But what will you do?" They grabbed the boy more gently and loaded him into the wheel-barrow.

"Me? I will wait here, of course, and tend to the rows. Now be off, quickly!"

Lu'ril nodded and heaved the barrow. His legs were young and strong from his labors. The barrow bounced and cracked against the turf as it rolled, causing the boy within to cry out.

"I am sorry!" shouted Lu'ril, not knowing if the youth could understand him, "We must have haste. Stay with me. Stay with me!"

He sped across the hills and into Cartegin, whose gates stood open. The older men gathering under its eaves looked curiously at Lu'ril and his burden as he ran by, kicking up a cloud of dust. Up the center hill of Cartegin he ran, until the pillared abode of Ishshak appeared.

"Chief Ishshak! Chief Ishshak!" Lu'ril called, panting as servants of Ishshak's household ran up to him. Ishshak himself was not far behind, for he heard the cries from where he dined in his hall.

"Ishshak!" Lu'ril cried again as he saw him, "Cyril of the southern fields, my father, found this lad in his vineyard. He is near death! Will you not call your healer to help him?"

"Quickly!" ordered Ishshak to a servant who stood near, "Go and summon Cärmi! Tell him to prepare what art he needs for healing. Go!"

The servant ran away and Ishshak bent over the boy for a closer look.

"Bones in my beard!" Ishshak muttered to himself, seeing the paleness of the lad's complexion. "Does your father know how this boy came into his vineyard, or when?"

"No, my lord, nothing other than he was found this morning. My father believed he was dead until we tried to lift him into this very barrow - which I fear I have cracked and broken in my long run here! My father will have me work all day to repair it."

"Do not worry about the barrow, son of the House of Cyril. You have done well and such things can be mended speedily with help. Go and refresh yourself at my table."

Lu'ril bowed and departed, eager for his reward, leaving Ishshak to examine the boy. He gazed closer upon the blood-caked shoulder.

"Something is afoot," Ishshak muttered to himself. "That cut was made by an axe and not with an edge of flint! I'd stake my life on it."

By noon the boy was stripped and the wound cleaned. He lay resting, wrapped in a dry cloth, where he breathed fitfully. He would have died many hours before if not for the speed of Lu'ril and the healing arts of Cärmi. Cärmi may not have been much of a diviner, but he possessed some skill in healing. He toiled long over the wound muttering incantations and rites. He pressed herbs mixed with honey into the boy's hurts and bound them tightly with cloth.

"The gold of life and the plants of wisdom," he explained to Ishshak, showing off the mixture. Ishshak watched impatiently.

"Can he speak? Have you healed him?"

"He may live yet, though he will need the favor of Tiamat and Enlil," replied Cärmi. "I do not think he will speak today."

Later that evening, Areoch returned to Birsha's courtyard and found a richly dressed man in fervent conversation with Meshêk. Silver arm-bands shone brightly against his skin.

"You must inform your master of my presence!" insisted the man. "I will not be seen at the port, for a reason I cannot fathom! I bring over a thousand head of Ibex - an offer Birsha could not refuse! It must be made known to him. This is the second time I have called!"

"Whether he will refuse or not is yet to be seen," said Meshêk with a frown. "Bahira is his only daughter. I will inform him of your offer and will send messengers regarding his decision in time."

"May it not be too long in coming," the visitor threatened.

"It will come when it will. Good day, master Phintras."

The master Phintras stormed from the courtyard before marching down the road with five servants trailing in his wake.

Meshêk shook his head and muttered some quick words to a servant before seeing Areoch standing in the shadows. Areoch rushed by him and inside of the house, pushing past Maturr before coming out into the great garden. He found Bahira there, sitting on the bench below his balcony.

The blooms of the garden were thick and the buzzing of eager bees filled the air with a steady hum.

"Who was that at the front gate, who spoke with Meshêk?" demanded Areoch.

Bahira did not turn to face him, but remained sitting, her shoulders slumped as if in defeat.

"Phintras? He comes from the largest family of herders in Cartegin. A man of good standing, who looks to add one of Birsha's kin to his own household...to join the many wives he has there."

Areoch took a step back, a look of alarm on his face.

"Is this what you are to do then? Settle for whatever highest price is offered to your father?"

"Did you not say yourself that I should be obedient to him? On this very spot!" she cried. "Am I to throw that away now? I can do little. Many have come to seek my hand, Areoch, and though Meshêk rarely lets them see me, my father is bound to accept one of them. Such is the way of the world: decisions for you are made by others."

"Bahira, please!" cried Areoch. "What must I do to earn your affection? I fear you have grown cold to me for nothing but the will of others. ...I have asked Meshêk to speak to your father."

Bahira looked up, surprised, and a shimmer of hope passed over her features for a moment. The look faded.

"He will not see you," she answered, turning aside again. "It is not possible."

Areoch sat beside her in silence, his mind racing.

"Then come away with me," he said finally, hardly daring to whisper. "Take this decision into your own hands. Leave this place and seek a new adventure with me."

A silence fell. The comment stood between them, like a tangible brink that suddenly needed to be crossed.

Bahira did not answer, but he could see tears running down her face.

"You ask me to do the impossible, Areoch. I cannot."

She would say no more. Areoch felt the blood rushing to his head. He stood and left, leaving her pale and ashen on the bench. He walked with a purposeful stride out the courtyard and up to his room. He paced back and forth. Tears streamed down his face as he fought with himself. Eventually his mind was made up: if Bahira did not love him, there was little reason for him to stay any longer in Cartegin. In fact, it would undoubtedly be his undoing, for he knew in his heart that as long as she was present he would love her.

Areoch was resolute - wiping away his tears, he packed his satchel with what meager supplies could be found. He departed swiftly, without speaking to anyone. As dusk settled about the city, he made his way out of Birsha's great house and strode up the hill, aiming for the gates of Cartegin.

The sky was dark by the time Areoch reached the main gates. The first stars had appeared over-head. The gates were open, though men stood near ready to close them for the night.

"Leaving for a nightly walk?" questioned a familiar voice. Meshêk stepped from the shadows, looking over Areoch and his satchel with a knowing eye. "Or, perhaps you have decided to leave on short notice. You increase your safety by being shrouded in the night, I see."

"I did not mean any disrespect," stammered Areoch hastily, but Meshêk raised his hands.

"There was none taken. You have served your time with us well and you have been free to go as you will since the beginning. But, I wonder if you do not act out of haste? We could supply you better than your meager provision, a token of my gratitude, at least, if you were to leave with the sunrise."

"I will make do," said Areoch stiffly. "Though I am grateful for all you have done."

Meshêk nodded again and his eye's twinkled under his unkempt eyebrows.

"Go then, if you will!" cried Meshêk, clasping Areoch's forearm in a strong grip with his own. "I know all too well how easy it is to run away when things do not go as you will. Harder is the road of patience and endurance...and certainly that of love."

Areoch stiffened at the word.

Meshêk knew he had the youth's attention, and continued softly. "You are young, Areoch, so take the advice of an old man before you depart."

Meshêk turned and faced the city.

"Hearts change with time, not with force. Bahira is young and she is learning - just as you are, to seek and stand for what she believes in. Why, this very evening, just after you left, I believe, that she strode off toward the port with her face set in such a way I thought she was about to make a stand with her father on something rather important. Maybe it was regarding you. Who can tell? I did not stay to discover more and neither, it seems, will you."

Wild hope leapt into Areoch's heart at Meshêk's words and he gazed back over his shoulder where the port was hidden behind the dark rise of Cartegin. The purple and gray of the sun's setting had begun to vanish and the stars were shining brightly in the east.

"I am torn, Meshêk!" Areoch cried suddenly. "You clearly know my heart's desire. What am I to do? I have been saved from disaster by the hands of my father's enemies, but I myself have found here beauty and life that was unlooked for. Is the world so dark, so separated, that love cannot be allowed to cross such a great divide?"

"Areoch," soothed Meshêk, stepping closer and putting a hand on his shoulder, "Men live and die, and cities of men rise and fall, but this truth remains the same: if you run away from your heart now, you will never stop running. Trust that Enlil will make your course clear in the future. For the present... hold your ground."

A determination of will filled Areoch's heart. Meshêk nodded, smiling as he read the change in Areoch's mind. They turned away from the gate back towards Birsha's household, together.

They did not take two strides before yelling burst into the stillness of the night and the call of a horn echoed from somewhere within the city. A great light seemed to jump up from beyond the hillside, as if a large flame was raging. They stopped, watching and listening. Other horns rang out in answer from within the city. Meshêk's grip on Areoch's shoulders tightened and Areoch thought he saw fear flash across the old man's face.

"What is it?" he asked.

"It is the call of the Strong Men: Ishshak is summoning the men of Cartegin to arms! Burning! The city is burning!!" he cried as he raced down the hill. With great speed, Areoch followed and then passed Meshêk as an icy fear gripped his heart.

Ishshak stood over the form of the injured boy.

"You are sure?" he asked again, addressing the servant who stood beside him. "He spoke?"

"Yes, my lord, I am sure. It was common Agadian speech. He said something about 'Joshur'. His name, I think, and then he said something I could not hear. I came to you immediately, as you asked."

"Well done, well done. Leave us now!" Ishshak commanded. The servant bowed low before departing.

The evening light was quickly fading, Ishshak and Ilishu stood around Joshur as the torchlight flickered. Several others of the household stood behind, waiting. Joshur's chest struggled to rise and fall, and his face was deathly pale.

Ishshak leaned close to him. "I am Ishshak, Chief of the city in which you now lay. You have been badly wounded. Who are you? Can you understand me?"

Joshur tried to speak but his throat was dry. Ilishu gently lifted his head and raised a gourd of water to his mouth. He sputtered, choking.

"...am... Joshur," he gasped in a hoarse whisper, barely loud enough to be heard.

"Joshur. Of southern rhyme. It is as I guessed" Ishshak repeated, looking intently at Ilishu and the rest of his house. He turned back to the boy.

"How do you come here, Joshur?"

Joshur struggled to speak, and when he did, all stood riveted, hardly daring to breathe as they listened.

"Father...Kassu of Anshan....dead. Slain... the darkness. Screaming. ...lies. Urudu! ...made for... Cartegin. Ship..... bronze.... Agade missed.... Lies... death. No... No! Father!!"

Joshur heaved and panted, seeming to shrivel before them on the table. Ilishu raised the gourd to his lips one more time and then Joshur fell back, silent but breathing. Cärmi dabbed water over his hot face.

Everyone stood quiet, waiting for Ishshak to speak. He seemed frozen in place. His mind sought out the meaning of Joshur's words.

Ishshak strode swiftly across the room to the great window that looked down on the port of Cartegin. The light had nearly faded and he could see little. He stroked his beard. The Urudu! He knew that name. The tales of their kind were whispered in fear at his gate, though Cartegin had felt little of their bite. The pieces of Joshur's story fit slowly together in his mind, and he realized with anger and rage some part of the truth regarding what had taken place. He turned and faced Ilishu.

"Gather all the men of my household and arm them, quickly and quietly. We make for the port."

"What will we find there?" asked Ilishu, even as he sent others to swiftly gather all the Strong Men who could be found.

"I do not know," said Ishshak, shaking his head. "Something is amiss. We look for a foreign ship. If I am not mistaken, one with a cargo load of bronze has pulled into our port, to refit and supply with stealth, for the Urudu have taken her over."

"We may go to find nothing - if they sailed by, or departed already, or this boy's meaning is incoherent...as is likely," Ilishu muttered the last thought under his breath.

"We will see," Ishshak's eyes were alight with purpose.

So, it came to be that Chief Ishshak and Ilishu, backed by the men of their household, ran stealthily down to the port at evenings close (just as Meshêk stepped out of the darkness with Areoch at the gate). They were armored with short leather jerkins, carrying spears and maces tipped with stone. Their feet rattled the sand of the road and their torches lit up the houses. The men of Cartegin grabbed what weapons they could find and followed in behind their Chieftain as he passed.

Chapter Twenty-one

Joshur of Anshan

The city of Anshan was three full days behind the flurrying waters of the steering oar and the weather continued to move in *The Anchton*'s favor.

The stern of the ship splayed out enough to hold ten men shoulder to shoulder. A small shelter was there, to aid the constant vigilance of the man who held the steering oar. A bronze shrine of Anshan, a Desert Tetari Bird, shone proudly at the prow's highest point. Its outstretched wings caught the sun, reflecting through the spray of the sea as it crashed against the bow. To those who watched on-deck, the water looked like liquid gold as it flew through the air. Wooden shields of the ship's Strong Men were securely tied on either side of the bulwarks. Brightly colored and bearing the outstretched wings of the Tetari, the shields were a warning: the merchant vessel was armed and ready to defend its cargo.

Only a fool would attempt to trade on land or sea without an armed force - especially carrying as much raw tin, copper, and bronze as *The Anchton* had in its hull. Her mission seemed simple enough: to sail through the waters of Agade and trade their precious cargo for unknown riches in the northern lands. But the Kingdom of Agade was vast and strong, and they did not look favorably on any trade passing through their borders. Much less favorably would they treat *The Anchton* for trading bronze...which made weapons...to their enemies in the north.

A strong wind blew steadily north and the sailors raised a tall, fir mast, laying aside their oars in relief. The sound of the wind creaking against the sail was music to the ears and a strong fervor to the heart of the adventurous seamen who manned *The Anchton*. They were passing the city of Marasi. Canoes and fishing boats trailed all around them. The men who weren't manning the ship leaned overboard and shouted greetings, traded items, and exchanged news over the railing.

Kassu of Anshan stood below the steering platform at the stern, peering over a well-tattered, precious piece of papyrus. Maps were a rare commodity, especially those regarding the sea. This one had been pieced together by the Chief of Anshan over several years, specifically for the voyage Kassu was leading.

Kassu was shorter and more well-rounded than most of the seamen present on the voyage, both in girth and in his knowledge about the Great Tanti Sea. Faint shapes on the map showed: the coastal line, the position of rocks and shallows, and even the more dangerous areas of swells and swirling winds.

Cenrill, second in command and leader of the ship's armed Strong Men, stood on Kassu's right. He peered keenly back and forth between the rolling, brown hills passing slowly by and the map, creating a bearing in his mind of their location. Cenrill was taller than most, and even in the heat, his strong build was covered by light, leather armor. He held a tall, ash spear in his right hand that was seldom apart from him. Gold armbands distinguished him as a proven warrior.

Kassu's only surviving son from the famines, Joshur, stood on the opposite side of the table, along with Wabrum and Huando, the chief sailor and head carpenter among the crew. Kassu placed small square pieces of wood, carved with the lines of distance, between their starting point of Anshan and the city of Marasi.

"Quiet down over there!" boomed Cenrill, in response to loud whoops and hollers which broke out after a particularly good trade over the bulwarks of the ship.

The crew's excitement quickly died to a low murmur. Cenrill adjusted one of his arm bands while turning back to the evening meeting. Kassu continued with their voyage update.

"Three days with a favorable northern wind and steady row call, and Anshan is already fifty leagues behind us," Kassu reported to the others.

"That leaves not two days before we must make the pass across Kisad bay," concluded Huando, doggedly tapping the map with a drawn face. The wind blew the sailor's white hair across his weather-worn features. He drew the strands back with his hand, tying them behind his head with a piece of leather.

"We'll be lucky if this wind holds," Huando continued. "It would bear us a little to the west, and we'll need every bit to stay within sight of the shore as we move farther north."

"I would say we'll need more of an easterly course" added Cenrill, gesturing at the map. "The exact location of those Agadian watchtowers has not been confirmed. By my spear, it would be a quick end to our expedition if we were to sail within sight of them. We should pass them in the night, far to the east of Kisad Bay." He drew a line with his finger around Agade, giving it a wide berth.

"We may find too much of an easterly course to be a greater threat than that of the Agadian shoreline, however dangerous our discovery might be," reminded Kassu, tapping a mark on the map farther out to sea which indicated higher swells. "How is our water and supply?"

"No trouble there," chimed in Joshur with a high voice. "We have had fish aplenty as catch and our water will last without ration for another seven days on this light rowing."

"And the hull is holding up well," assured Huando, tapping his foot on the floorboards. "The calk and resin have kept the boards from swelling. I don't expect she will need to be beached and dried for several days!"

"Then we push forward with a sharp eye and good heart," concluded Kassu with a confident tone. "Have the men rack oars near sundown and use the wind throughout the night. That should bring us to the shallow rocks off Cape Kisad before sunrise. Then we will need every hand ready. Huando, keep a close eye on this ship. We need her to stay sound."

The chief carpenter patted the railing of *The Anchton* confidently, nodding his head as the group dispersed.

"Three days," Kassu murmured to himself, looking at the words *Agade* stretched across his map. "Three days of easy sailing and then two of absolute peril. Enki protect us."

Every man aboard was as much an explorer as a merchant, seeking the wealth of other cities and the adventure of unknown lands. Cenrill provided twelve men from his household, tasked with guarding the ship. Though their brightly-colored, wooden shields might serve as a warning to pirates and thieves, they would do little to intimidate the Agadians. It was risky business, but the rewards of smuggling tin and brass through the kingdom of Agade was even higher. It was rumored that in the north cities would pay a hundred times a year's wage for ten pounds of bronze.

Kassu carefully folded up the map and placed it within a leather satchel at his hip. Three days. Three days until they had to leave the safety of the coast, passing the city of Kish and the coastal watchtowers of the E-Kur.

Joshur laughed with gladness as the swells of the sea hit their prow and sprayed over the crew.

"Whoa-ho!!" the boy cried, while the sailors heaved at the ropes, causing the ship to jump from swell to swell. The crew grabbed lines and railing while some of the bold hung over the side, dipping their hands in the passing water.

"Watch out for the Leviathan!!" a sailor cried out. A roar of laughter erupted as those in the water swiftly brought their hands back into the boat's safety, looking around for scales and teeth! The day passed as the green and brown southern hills ran smoothly by.

While the hull of *The Anchton* could hold the hammocks of all resting men during harsh weather and still leave room for cooking meals, the freshness and warmth of the upper deck was preferred during the clear days. As dusk fell, the western sun set ablaze the tops of rolling hills. A light breeze moved the ship steadily northward under the careful guidance of the night watch.

Dangers lay ahead, but they would be the concern of tomorrow. On this night, all felt the companionship and joy, which comes from being in the safest part of a grand adventure! The bulwarks were high enough at the stern of *The Anchton* to provide a windbreak, and torches were lit. The tips of mountains were barely visible, late snow glowing red against the blue sky.

A large table was set in the flickering light and the household servants busied themselves: laying out finely dried meats, freshly grilled fish from the day's catch, and assorted fruits and vegetables from the hull. Kassu and Cenrill, surrounded by their families and important men, sat and stood around the table. Kassu raised his silver cup toward the prow and the sailors raised their gourds.

"First, we put our feet in the boat, then on the dry land!" he recited.

"And as dust we shall return into the sea!" the others replied heartily. Then everyone rolled up their sleeves and dug into the feast.

Meals were a time of stories and recounting old memories. Among the sailors who berthed in the City of Anshan, there was never a shortage of tales. Anshan was one of the greatest port cities in the southern lands, providing a middle ground between the mighty Agade and the wealthy foreign dynasties of the south - keeping sailors and merchants busy with trade. Soon, tales of great sea-monsters and wonders of the land unfolded in crisp detail. The young men opened their eyes wide with disbelief, while the older seafarers roared with laughter.

"Fresh out of the lily pond, these ones, eh?" the older ones jested. Kassu and Cenrill laughed and smiled with the rest. They all had tales of their first adventures. Even Joshur, who had been raised in and around such stories, couldn't hide his awe.

"To be young again, ey?" chuckled Cenrill, nudging Kassu's shoulder.

Huando, perhaps the oldest seafarer among them, pounded his goblet on the table and brushed the wispy white hair from his face.

"You young'uns don't remember the old things of the world anymore. I tell you, *I* remember." He reached over and patted the bulwark of the ship.

"I'm sure you do, you old block of wood!" the crew shouted, "Go on! Tell us of when boats walked on land and camels floated on the water!"

"Some tales are no longer recalled in the far reaches of the world," reprimanded Huando, glaring. "You should have some respect for those that still tell them!" Huando's glare did little to intimidate anyone, all clearly wanted to hear his tale. His voice grew deeper and he began the epic...

176

Ancients in time, men shone like the stars. Gods dwelt among us, Sons of
Enlil.

Words could be spoken: power and life.

Not all were happy. Not all was well.

'Battle!' gods called. 'Fire!' gods raged. 'Against Enlil, the King, let us
remove him from his dwelling!'

Many heard. A fight they stirred. The Sons of High heard. The Sons of
Earth heard.

They set fire to their tools, put aside spades for fire. War they sought:
war in the heavens. Fire in a basket.

Off they went, one and all,

To the gate of the King's abode. There Enlil waited.

'Who accuses me of wrong? Who instigates this battle?

Who is hostile and sows in the darkness?

Who declares war, and brings you to my gates?'

Then Ninĝinĝar, Son of Glory spoke, he spoke for all.

'A reckoning Enlil, a reckoning has come.'

So war was spoken. For six hundred years the thunderbolts raged.

None turned aside. None quenched the flame.

Oh, my Lord, why do you spare your sons? It is against you they have
risen.

Enlil's tears flowed. The basket had burned. He made ready to speak. To
Atrahasis of earth. To a son of earth.

To Atrahasis came a dream. A Tree within a dream. A Life within a
dream.

Yet a torrent came, sweeping with might. All was cast down, a warrior
in a fight.

A branch remained. A root from a stump. Seventy times this root bore fruit. Seven times a new branch grew. One time a new way came.

Atrahasis grew afraid. He knew not what would come.

He called out to Etemmu. He begged her to See.

'Make me know the meaning of the dream. Let me know, that I may look out for its consequence.'

The See'r came.

'Pay attention to all my words!

Flee the house, build a boat,

forsake possessions, and save Life.'

Then instructions came, for the boat to be built.

A roof for her over like the depths,

so that the sun shall not see inside her.

Let her be roofed over fore and aft.

The tackle strong, the pitch should be firm, and so give the boat strength.

Atrahasis worked long. The elders laughed. They continued with war.

Atrahasis would not turn aside.

'I will dwell with my god in the depths of my heart.'

Day came.

The sea vanished, a dry paper left in the sun.

Night came.

Like oxen yoked. The silence came.

Its power came upon the Sons of God and man of earth like a battle.

One person did not see another,

they could not recognize each other in the darkness.

There the Umu stalked. And all the living things ran from it in terror.

Atrahasis fell aside when he saw the Umu come.

Atrahasis knew the Sons of God were there. The fight was at his gates.

All his household fled into the boat. Animals came, running in fear.

Atrahasis could not see. Enlil was not near. The Umu was the night, the *fear in his mind.*

He closed the boat with naught room to stand.

Storm came.

Egal rent the sky with his talons, and broke the sky like a pot.

The flood came forth.

The deluge bellowed like a bull,

The wind like a screaming eagle.

The gale like a roaring lion.

The darkness, thick to taste, the sun gone,

The clamor of the deluge had come.

The table was silent and Huando took a long draft of his goblet.

"That's it?" Ebaz finally asked. "Come, man, tell us the story plainly!"

Huando sat back scornfully, folding his arms. Cenrill spoke before Huando could take more grief.

"The telling was fair! Have none of you heard tell of the epic before?"

"Not like that!" Ebaz complained.

"By my spear," Cenrill retorted with a snort, "if it doesn't smell of fish, you wouldn't dare eat it!"

"I would like to hear it again," Joshur admitted humbly. "Maybe in an easier way, if there is one."

Huando smiled at the youth from across the table.

"There is another version, a tale we tell our children." He winked at Ebaz, and then spoke directly to Joshur.

"Long before the Kingship rested on Agade and long before the Kingship rested on the cursed city of Eridor, the song of the sea, the sky, and the mountains were not as they are now. In these far-off years, lengths of time were like that of stars and men shone with the light of youth for many cycles of the sky." Longing seemed to pass through Huando's voice of these ancient days.

"The Mighty Ones of heaven, gods made by Enlil, still dwelt among men. Yet each man had within his grasp power and life! Each was his own king! But it did not last.

'It was in this time that Kez-Atrahasis, a man born in the ancient world, a Firstborn, the boat-builder, was told by Enlil, King of the Hosts, to build a city which could float - so that he might escape the rebellion which had devoured the land. Many seasons passed and Atrahasis and his household neared completeness in their work. One day, Atrahasis awoke early in the morning with a vivid dream of terror. As he ran out of his house and turned towards the sea, he saw that the ocean was no more.

179

Land stretched away as far as the eye could see, as dry as a leathered hide, and Atrahasis understood the Sons of Evil had discovered his plan and so drank up all the waters of the world."

Huando paused. The only sound that could be heard was the waves gently lapping against the ship.

"Atrahasis was defeated," he said finally. "But before he turned his back to the dried ocean, a black spec upon that forsaken horizon seemed to grow bigger. Even as Atrahasis strained his eyes to see what it was, the earth began to shake as with galloping footfalls. The black speck grew with such speed Atrahasis called for his entire household and all of his herds to flee into the floating city for protection. Atrahasis himself was the last to enter and, as he looked back in fear, a roar shook the foundations of the land.

'It was a mighty Umu! The Great Lion that stands twice as tall as a man, with teeth that can sever an ox clean in two. It was black as night. From it every creature on the earth fled terrified towards Atrahasis until he was overwhelmed and fell back into the hull. The enraged Umu seemed to look among the living things for something to devour, until it stood at the entrance to the floating city's hull. Its shadow stretched out over the fallen form of Atrahasis, even taller than a *Gisigal* of Eridor.

'Even as Atrahasis raised his hands to shield his face, his eyes were mistaken for the shadow shrunk to the form of a small, black kitten, and the Great Umu was nowhere to be seen. Darkness came over the land and Atrahasis saw in the distance a great wall of black water sweeping over the whole earth. Though he was shaking with terror, he pushed closed the outer hatch as the ship was tossed into the darkness.

'So it was that Atrahasis built the first ship and the evil was washed away from the land in what is called the *Great Destruction*. Atrahasis later built the city of Kes, which marked the end of the Old World and the beginning of the new. Upon it the Kingship rested, as in the Ancient days."

Everyone pounded their fists on the table, in recognition of a good tale.

"Though," Ebaz interjected quickly from farther down the table, "We all know Umus don't exist. Lions are bad enough." Several other sailors nodded their heads in agreement. Huando stood up in horror.

"They are as real as you, master Ebaz, and you Enlinda!" he cried. "Though, I may forgive your error, for seldom do you leave the prostitute's lane to see enough of the world to know!"

"That may well be, Huando," Ebaz said tauntingly. "For every time they see me coming, they take up the call: *Umu! The great Umu is upon us!*"

A burst of laughter at the retort went up around the table followed by a fierce debate. Some argued a distant household relative had seen a lion as big as an Umu, with teeth curling back from the jaw as long as a man's arm.

"Well," said Cenrill to Kassu after a short pause in the debate, "Umu or no Umu, hopefully no one drinks up the waters of the world again until we return - it's a long walk home on foot."

Kassu smiled and leaned back in his chair, looking up at the stars. The Chariot, the Ram, and the great Field dotted the sky overhead. Cenrill gazed with him.

"Summer stretches on," Cenrill observed, pointing to the fullness of the Chariot as it hung above the horizon. "Let us hope it lasts long for our voyage home."

Kassu nodded, deep in thought, but gave no reply. After a pause Cenrill sighed deeply.

"It brings me joy, thinking those I love in Anshan may gaze up at the same skies, knowing I do the same. My wife and youngest son are in the care of my household at home. Though travel and trade are my life affairs, perhaps after this venture I'll be able to stay home awhile. How great it is to hold them close and smell my wife's perfume in her hair!"

Kassu smiled, but spoke nothing.

"Come Kassu! Tell me more of your story!" Cenrill cried, slapping Kassu affectionately on the back. "You were not well known in Anshan before volunteering for this risky venture. Even after the Chief chose you to Captain *The Anchton,* not even one of us who sat at his table had heard your name outside of the fishing markets! Surely you must miss something of home?"

Cenrill meant well, of course, and talking of one's family and home when out many days at sea is a typical pastime. Cenrill knew nothing of Kassu's background, for Cenrill came from a household that was both wealthy and well-known. He himself only agreed to enter such a journey as they now embarked because it was his nature to try risky adventures with high rewards. Joshur, overhearing the question at the loud table, looked at his father wondering if he would speak. Kassu's face fell from the stars.

"Everything I have is here," he said simply. Suddenly standing, he excused himself and retired below. Many of the sailors stood and followed him without question.

"A strange man," remarked one of Cenrill's Strong Men, draining his glass and looking around the nearly empty table. "Keeps to himself he does."

"I'm sure we'll know more about each other than we would like, by the end of this voyage." Cenrill reflected, stroking his beard thoughtfully.

Chapter Twenty-two

Veil of Lies

Another day passed, followed by an overcast dawn. Cenrill and Kassu both awoke with an edge in their minds which informed them the perilous part of their journey was beginning. Kassu appeared on deck as dark shadows among the morning fog gave way to rocks, marking their arrival at Cape Kisad. He took the steering oar as sailors ran weighted lines off the prow. They called back to him the measurements of the depths. Cenrill and his men came on deck shortly thereafter, fully armored. They wore thick leather jerkins plated with bronze squares and small yew bows hung, unstrung on their backs. Many held long, ash poles with polished bronze spearheads mounted upon their tops.

"Lower the mast and stow away the sail!" Kassu called. It was lowered carefully, and the sail wrapped and fastened to the side of the ship. The oars were slipped into the water and, as the light grew steadily brighter, *The Anchton* began a smooth pass around the jagged cape. The swish and dip of the oars sounded dull, muffled by the fog. About two hours into the morning, Joshur hollered out to Kassu from his position in the bow.

"Low-laying ship, two reeds off the port!"

The rowers immediately stopped and silence fell across the deck.

"Nothing to fear this far out," Cenrill murmured to Kassu. The men around him fingered their spears nervously.

"We are still two days south. The E-Kur do not keep a watch this far down. It must be a fishing vessel or..."

"It has seen us," interjected Kassu.

The other boat began to move swiftly towards them. It sat higher in the water than *The Anchton*, having only one and a half decks instead of a full two. The hull was long, a vessel made for speed. Ten oarsmen sat on either side of its girth. The rear of the boat was housed in with wood and leather, and undoubtedly provided an access into the hull of the ship for the storage of goods. On top of this cabin was mounted a small ledge where the steering oar was held. Nearly all the oars were manned by strong rowers and the boat made its way rapidly through the wispy fog tendrils for *The Anchton*.

"This is no fishing boat," cried Cenrill. "All hands, man those oars!!"

The incoming ship's speed left turning about or swift flight into deeper waters impossible. Cenrill's Strong Men did not hesitate. In an instant, shields leapt into their hands! Cords were fitted to bows and smooth rocks placed into slings.

A tall man stood at the prow of the strange ship, visible against the bent backs of the rowers. He was dressed in rich garb and stood at ease, casually resting a supple boot against the ship's rail. His brown hair was shoulder-length and blown back in the wind, revealing a serious expression that seemed to study *The Anchton* with as much interest as they themselves did. Kassu and Cenrill both let out sighs of relief. He was clean-shaven and lighter skinned, which made him appear to be of southern origin. He was clearly not the Captain of an Agadian war vessel monitoring the waters.

The oars of the vessel were manned by thick, muscular men. Their caller stood high above them at the steering oar. He was a giant, bald man, as dark as the night and covered in mysterious blue tattoos that seemed to glow through the mist. In a deep and powerful voice, he called the final row stroke. The crew racked oars and allowed the ship to glide smoothly alongside *The Anchton*. Cenrill and his men were an intimidating, defending force as they pressed against the bulwarks and gazed at their opponents, with spear and arrow aimed and ready.

No one on the other ship made a movement. The man at the prow stared unwaveringly at the bright spear-points shining down on him. Cenrill ordered his men back a pace from the rail and stepped forward.

"Who are you and what is your business, to wait in the shelter of the rocks for passing ships? Speak!" he demanded in common Agadian.

The man at the prow did not answer. Cenrill made a motion and his men drew the arrows taunt on their strings. The strange man smiled as he looked back and forth from the hull of *The Anchton* to the bowstrings. He held up his hands, as if to indicate none of them had shown any sign of aggression.

"I am Re'Amu," said the man slowly, "Captain of the *Taradium*. We trade between the southern cities in death balms, oils, and purifying lotions. We deemed you to be pirates and thought forcing you up along the rocks would be a better play than waiting for you to take your leave of us. But I can see by your...clatter..." one of Cenrill's men dropped his spear while trying to string his bow. Cenrill glared at him, swearing under his breath. "...You must be neither pirates nor Agadians trained in sea-warfare.

'As for your insinuation of us hiding near the rocks," Re'Amu continued, "we were putting in at a small outlet there, as it is the last good water until well-past Agade's borders," Re'Amu gestured behind them to where the sharp rocks of Cape Kisad pulled away revealing a small inlet. "And we would not be so foolish as to anchor in the open for, it seems, the same fears as you."

Kassu handed off the steering oar and pushed his way through Cenrill's men until he was looking down on the strange Captain and vessel.

"We too sail between the southern cities," informed Kassu, gesturing with his head at the bronze, Anshan shrine at their prow. "Yet I see no shrine nor mark upon your vessel. What kind of craft would cast down the shrines of their cities?"

Re'Amu smiled knowingly and held up a small, beaten bronze icon, shaped something like a fish, which had lain concealed at his feet.

"The kind of vessel that knows how to sail through the Kingdom of Agade without being boarded," Re'Amu answered with a wry smile.

It was customary for the largest of the vessels to bestow favor on the other, especially of a chance meeting upon the waters. Trade was always safer in groups, and on the water was no exception. Fearsome Urudu pirates were rumored to be wandering throughout the northern waters and Agade was not the only worry of the two Captains.

The Anchton was one of the mightiest trading vessels of the southern seas and Kassu would not have his pride outdone. Re'Amu was invited aboard the ship, while both vessels made their way slowly back toward the small inlet where the *Taradium* had watered. Kassu presented Re'Amu (and his accompanying two guards), gifts of finely beaten bronze hooks and an exceptionally etched copper armband for each. Re'Amu in return presented Kassu and Cenrill fine almond oil in leather casks, light and smooth to the dry skin. Once the formalities had passed, both ships finished taking on fresh water from the bubbling stream which cascaded down the worn rock of the cape.

"You will, please, join my family and crew for an evening meal, before we sail on together?" invited Re'Amu to Kassu, as the crew finished filling their water stores.

"Nay, young master," refused Kassu. "You want none of our dangers." Kassu trailed off and looked to the north. "Our course is set, and we cannot linger. You want none of our fate to be shared with the *Taradium*. You have been successful in your journey south thus far. We travel a different road."

"Perhaps," said Re'Amu, "you would dine with us if our courses were already one? For it is not, as you assume, that we wait here until a change of wind for a southerly course. We also prepare to sail north."

Kassu and Cenrill looked at each other in surprise. They knew they were not the first to try and smuggle goods north, past Agade, but they had never met a crew who was successful! Much less a crew who spoke about such a perilous journey as calmly as if it was simply a canoe ride downstream. Re'Amu was amused by their shocked expressions and stood waiting for their response, a small smile hovering at the corners of his mouth. Kassu bowed low.

"If our courses align, we must beseech you to bring your favored men aboard *The Anchton* this night and allow us to serve you."

"Much of the day is left. Let us sail to the northerly side of the cape where the wind and waves are less. Then it would be our honor to join your table!" Re'Amu bowed lower, as was customary in the southern lands in acceptance, before returning light-footed to his vessel.

"This is a most fated opportunity," whispered Kassu to Cenrill as Re'Amu departed. "Such a meeting! It could only be fate. This is our chance to learn what we must, to be successful in our voyage."

For a moment Cenrill said nothing, but watched Re'Amu's little skiff glide over the water toward the *Taradium*.

"Only a fool talks too much of fate, Kassu," he warned in a foreboding tone. "By my spear! It is like a wet bank: it makes you slip. That Captain is confident and boyish in a reckless manner, or I am a blind man. I do not think good will come of him or the *Taradium*."

Night fell once more on the northern side of Cape Kisad. A table was set, in the finest manner, on *The Anchton's* deck. All the household servants and seafaring men went below as Re'Amu came aboard. With him were his two previous guards, they introduced themselves as Balak and Masahum, seamen of Re'Amu's household and in his favor. Re'Amu laughed and clasped them both on the back fondly.

"We are more like brothers!" he exclaimed as they were introduced.

"Here," Re'Amu continued, holding out two large flasks for Cenrill. "Drinks from our homeland, to add to the finery of Kassu and Cenrill of Anshan!!"

The food was well cooked and the strange drink was like nothing the men of Anshan had ever tasted: fruity on the tongue and strong in the pallet. It was not long before every man was roaring with laughter and each considered another his best and sole friend in that vast expanse of sea. Yet, Cenrill had spoken with the men seated at the table (before Re'Amu, Balak, and Masahum had come aboard), sternly warning them not to speak of their cargo, nor openly discuss their intent to cross Agade's well-patrolled waters.

"And why not?" Kassu had questioned. "Is it not obvious we go the same route?

"We should discover more of them." Cenrill insisted.

The laughter at the table died down and Cenrill leaned forward, emboldened by drink.

"Come, Re'Amu, speak to us plainly of your courage! You sail north and yet you laugh and drink heartily! Is it perhaps because you fear there may be no tomorrow?"

Re'Amu's eyes twinkled.

"Do you not know? We are traders of entombing balms and dead men's wrappings, whom the wealthy pay much silver, gold, and bronze for! I am never sure there will be a tomorrow. At least, if tomorrow does not come, I will sleep in the finest covering a dead man can have!" The men laughed even louder and pounded the table in their mirth.

"But... But" Re'Amu continued, "To answer an honorable man's question: tomorrow often comes with a dense fog or a favorable wind, and an invisible journey through those northern bays is better favored than one which is clearly seen."

"Sharps the word," Cenrill said in reply, unhappy with the response and the looks of admiration Re'Amu received from *The Anchton's* men.

Joshur looked upon Re'Amu and his guests with wonder shining in his eyes. It seemed this strange man was only a few years older than himself, but had conquered the world and made a name for his crew.

"Master," he said from the end of the table, "from where do you come?"

Re'Amu drained his goblet and wiped his mouth. "I come from a land farther south than yours. There lies a great sea of yellow through which no ship can sail, stretching across the surface of the earth. Upon it you can walk and sink, but only to your ankles! Yet, it is hot, and trade across this land is a perilous journey." The men of *The Anchton* looked at each other with wide eyes.

"It is true! I have seen such lands," Huando claimed.

Re'Amu nodded gravely.

"Many a trading caravan has met their death on those high waves of sand! The sea, by comparison, is comforting. It may be still, vast, and without memory - ever changing. It, at least, produces life which can sustain you." He gestured at the finely cooked fish which lay half eaten around them. "More than we can ask for," he continued, "yet we were not always so fortunate." Re'Amu looked at his companions and they nodded as if remembering.

"Long ago we used to trade in those long caravans across the hot deserts. Always thirsty, always tired. Never a journey could we complete without being robbed by thieves among the wind-swept roads. Then we discovered a change: a message reached us, from a ship at sea, that dead men brought a pretty penny. You laugh, I know!" said Re'Amu at several of the smiling faces. "It was a message that changed our fortunes. We took all we had and with it bought the smallest of boats and began trading over the cool and refreshing sea. We have been at it ever since."

"And the Powers that be, have rewarded us for our labors!" Balak chimed in with a smile.

Kassu and several others pounded on the table in agreement, but Cenrill sat back unimpressed.

"You look as one who has seen little of death," Cenrill accused, "to talk about the passing of others into Sheol and your reward for it with less respect than a child." Masahum stood at the insult and all the laughter died in an instant. Re'Amu calmly raised his hand for Masahum to take his seat.

"One who deals in the trade of death as much as we, grow accustomed to its face," he said evenly. "Yet, I meant no harm, nor ill teaching to the younger among us." Re'Amu stood, looked at Joshur, and bowed low before Cenrill and Kassu.

"I raise my glass," said Re'Amu to everyone, "to those whom we can but remember. May they be sweet as honey and linger in our minds."

"Hail!" agreed the others loudly. Kassu nodded, satisfied and raised his glass before draining its contents. Cenrill sat in sullen silence.

Re'Amu, Masahum and Balak departed the vessel well after darkness had fallen, leaving Kassu and Cenrill to discourse about their future. Cenrill paced back and forth on the steering platform of *The Anchton*.

"I don't like it," repeated Cenrill again. "I am the head of the Strong Men aboard this vessel and I tell you we should travel with these strangers no farther! I distrust them. Something doesn't feel right."

"You may be, Cenrill, but *I* am the Captain of this ship, by orders of Chief Rahmsi! They claim to have passed through Agadian waters before. Only a fool would disregard that, even without the clear safety of traveling in numbers."

"I do not wish to risk our lives, and our fortune, protecting a death-ship from marauding pirates! Better to send them on their own way, or let them perish as would be-fit their trade," replied Cenrill coolly.

"I will have no more of this!" cried Kassu. "Your advice has been noted. That will be all." Cenrill did not bow as he swiveled on his heel and left the deck. Angry as he was, he was a man of honor. The orders from the Chief of Anshan to him were clear. He was not in command. He had been overruled.

Meanwhile, Re'Amu sat silently in the prow of his little skiff as it passed between the gap of *The Anchton* and the *Taradium*. It was quiet, in the moonless night, except for the dip and splash of the oars as Masahum and Balak pulled in time across the still waters. Hands soon reached out to help them aboard the *Taradium*. Re'Amu did not heed their questioning glances as he swiftly made his way to the rear of the ship. He pushed aside the leather entrance to the cabin and let it fall shut behind him, sealing out the night. He walked briskly past his own small quarters and into a dimly lit main room, which at first appeared empty. As Re'Amu's eyes adjusted to the deeper darkness, a white face, caked with some painted substance, seemed to appear alone in the shadows of the far corner.

"Well, dearest?" Captain Rais spoke with a hiss.

"It is good," reported Re'Amu, bowing low.

"You seem more... agitated than usual," observed the Captain softly.

"It is nothing," Re'Amu insisted after a pause. "I do not know what came over me. We should make plans for the inlet of Sahhu. The time will be ripe by our arrival there."

The white face studied him in the dark. The gleam of a knife appeared and the Captain proceeded to meticulously slice away the nails on his hand, carving them into points. Re'Amu's skin crawled as he watched the shavings fall to the floor.

"Very well. We shall pass them through Agade safely. Then their fears, and yours perhaps, will be quenched, yes?" the voice hissed.

"Yes, Captain," Re'Amu agreed, giving a small bow.

The white face leaned into the light, revealing dark set eyes.

"Good. Inform Bariquim of his targets and label their Strong Men. And Re'Amu, do not fail me."

"I never do," scoffed Re'Amu. He bowed once more and retreated out of the room. The corners of the white face rose in a small smile as it sat back in the shadows and disappeared.

Re'Amu sealed the entrance to his small quarters before collapsing into his hammock. For most of the night he lay there, swinging back and forth with the waves. The Captain's words echoed in his mind: *you seem more agitated than usual...* Re'Amu tossed and turned as he tried to pinpoint the doubt which had so suddenly manifested inside him after his dinner aboard *The Anchton*. Eventually sleep overtook him and his doubt remained unanswered as he drifted along the shores of weariness.

Chapter Twenty-three

Agadian Plague

The tide was out the next morning, and both ships put farther out to sea, turning their prows northward. *The Anchton* raised her mast and sail while the *Taradium* pulled with men to the oars. Cenrill was sullen on the deck, while Kassu manned the steering oar. Both households could feel the tension between the two leaders. The sky was cloudy, yet the wind continued to carry them out of the south. Both ships moved around the remainder of Cape Kisad at a fair pace. By dusk they had traveled twelve leagues and were beginning to enter Agadian waters.

Much to Cenrill's dislike, Re'Amu had come aboard (in the mid-afternoon), with two burly looking fellows, one of which was the tattooed man. Balak and Masahum from the following evening were not to be seen. Despite Cenrill's distrust, they laughed and joked with the crew and their stories of journeying through these waters several times put the crew's heart at ease.

Later that the evening, Kassu asked Re'Amu directly, "How many times have you passed through Agadian waters? You make it seem so simple." Re'Amu paused from helping Joshur pull in a line that had been set earlier in the day, which now had a large fish attached to it. He turned to Kassu with a small grin and all on deck pried their ears to hear his answer.

"We have passed through Agade more times than I care to count. In this weather we'll simply set a northerly course from there," he gestured toward a small tip of land which jutted off the cape. "The land pulls away west, we'll pass right through the center of Kisad bay, out of site of the mainland, until we are through Agade."

"It is bad fortune to sail out of sight of land... AND you risk the swells of the open sea," countered Cenrill.

Re'Amu nodded, still smiling, despite Cenrill's serious expression.

"It is perilous to smuggle goods through Agade at all, master Cenrill. Yet here we both are."

Joshur yelled with excitement as he pulled on the last bit of line and a large rainbow-colored fish flopped onto the deck with a splash. Its belly was a bright yellow and sparkled with the light.

"A carp of Enki!" he exclaimed.

"A sign of good fortune!" cried Huando, looking over Joshur's shoulder. "It is the largest I have ever seen, unless I'm going blind!"

Re'Amu picked up a cudgel and smashed it forcefully on the head while the crew cheered at the good omen. Cenrill scowled, but everyone else gathered around with broad smiles - they would risk the open sea! No one doubted that this newcomer, and the *Taradium*, had brought them the fortune they needed to meet success on their venture.

They set a course north at the point. The leagues passed quickly during the night and into the next day. Cape Kisad was soon out of sight. The crew quietly went about their work. Every man felt vulnerable as they entered these perilous waters and the land vanished behind them.

One more day of this speed and they would have passed through danger unscathed! But, early in the dark of the second morning, there was a change.

The sky had turned a shade lighter than the black sea when shaking hands woke Kassu with a start. After a few whispered words, he was dressed and arriving on deck, shouting for all hands to be roused, ready to assist at a moment's call.

The wind was changing. *The Anchton* plowed ahead through the depths of night. Not a star in the sky was to be seen. A strong gale hit Kassu as he faced east, causing him to brace himself against the gust. The swells of the ocean rose and fell as high as *The Anchton* itself - and they were growing larger. Kassu gazed intently for the stern-fire of the *Taradium*. As the ship rose upon a mountainous crest his heart fell. The *Taradium's* faint outline could barely be made out. It had turned westward, headed for the shore. A light signaled back for them to do the same.

The wet sail smacked from one side of the ship to the other.

"Get that sail down! Lower that mast!" Cenrill ordered as the crew struggled to regain control.

"The pins! The pins won't pull!" Huando yelled from below deck. Water poured across the ship as a wave smashed into *The Anchton's* side! Kassu heaved at the steering oar, trying to maintain a northerly course.

"We have to turn inland!" Cenrill shouted to Kassu.

"Get ready!" Kassu cried. *The Anchton* struggled to the top of another swell, teetering as the wind and water again crashed into its side, jarring Kassu and several others to their knees.

"The pins will not pull! The tension is too much! The mast is stuck!"

insisted the crew below deck as they heaved against the main mast.

"Pull them, pull with all your might!" demanded Kassu, as water poured down the back hatch. The ship seemed to swing about, wildly. Kassu fell, the steering oar dropping from his wet hands. *The Anchton* was out of control! The ship teetered on its side. Cenrill, seeing the peril of the ship, crawled forward and took control of the steering oar. He plunged it deep into the swirling waters, yelling as his muscles strained with the ship's timbers. They groaned and the prow turned westward! The ship raced inland and the sail slacked, relieved of its burden.

The pins pulled and the mast was lowered. Kassu regained his balance, wiping the rain and spray from his eyes as he did so. He looked about as the crew stood, dripping wet and trembling with fear.

"Inventory! Huando, have everyone check our hull and inventory!" Kassu ordered.

"All is sound, Captain!" Huando called from below.

Kassu walked to Cenrill and relieved him of the steering oar.

"I've got too much at stake in this venture to risk being swallowed alive by the sea," Cenrill murmured as he gave it up. Kassu nodded in agreement. The hull of the *Taradium* rose and fell amongst the waves ahead. The light grew slowly in the east.

"We may not be able to turn out of *this* course," reflected Kassu gravely. "It seems we have little choice."

By mid-morning the swells had not decreased. Through a light drizzle, the sharp line of the mainland was visible. Several times Kassu tried to turn *The Anchton* northward, but even with all hands pulling at the oars and the mast down, it was not possible. The ship lost too much speed in the turn and was nearly swamped by the waves on every attempt.

"No, it is no good. Stow the oars and to every man give a full breakfast," ordered Kassu after their third try.

"We cannot change course, can we?" asked Cenrill.

Kassu shook his head and looked at the line of land grimly. It appeared the *Taradium* was having the same difficulty. In the end, both ships had to allow the wind and waves take them toward their fate.

Kassu had hoped he would never see the mighty towers of the E-Kur. Now they stretched like vast sentinels across the coastline and into the foothills of the Durgu Mountains. They stood tall, built of pressed bricks, evenly spaced; while red standards flew high above them in the wind. The *Taradium* was slightly ahead of *The Anchton*. While Kassu, Cenrill, and their men stood riveted, gazing at the might of Agade, the *Taradium* appeared abandoned - not a figure moved across its deck.

"What are they doing?" whispered Cenrill to Kassu. "Where are they?"

The towers drew nearer and the swells lessened as the ships were sucked deeper into the bay. The great, pale walls of the City of Kish could now be seen. Banners, bright in the gray light, flew from the peaks of tall fortifications. A sprawling port connected the city to the water. The size of the fortress was unparalleled to anything they had seen, and made Anshan seem like a small, trading village.

Kassu raised his hand, ready to give an order to make the turn northward - but it was too late. A dim call from the nearest tower echoed across the water with a brazen blast! Three low-lying dots on the horizon separated from the port and began to approach them at a high rate of speed.

Cenrill looked across the ship at Kassu and their eyes met in agreement. They had decided, long before the venture began, that they would not be taken as captives in Agade. Cenrill's men stood near their shields (which hung defiantly down on the ships sides). They were adorned in their thick strips of leather armor. They strung their bows and removed the protective sheaths from their bronze and copper spearheads. Kassu's men lowered the oars and made ready to bring the ship about for the greatest chase of their lives.

"Ready...." said Kassu. His hand tightened on the steering oar.

Just then a shout echoed out across the water. Kassu and Cenrill ran to the ship's side and looked out. Re'Amu stood at the head of his skiff as Balak and Masahum splashed and dipped their oars, rowing with all their might toward them. He waved his arms violently to halt as if he knew their plan.

"Curse him!" spat Cenrill as he saw the figures approaching. "Look, the *Taradium* is dead in the water! They mean to give us up! Fly! Leave them to their fate!" he cried.

Half of the seamen needed no further encouragement and the nose of *The Anchton* began to come about.

"No!" shouted Kassu sternly. "Wait."

The little skiff was a stone's throw away now. Cenrill stamped his foot and clenched his spear so hard his hand turned white.

"We have no time!" he cried in a high voice.

Kassu was already reaching down and the face of Re'Amu and his companions appeared over the edge of the ship.

"My friends," gasped Re'Amu breathlessly, "quickly, throw down your shields from *The Anchton's* sides! Hide your weapons and send your armored men below!"

Cenrill shoved a seaman aside and stood in front of Re'Amu, brandishing his spear-point in his face.

"I have had enough of your worthless talk," he spat out forcefully. "Return to your boat, or I'll throw your carcass overboard."

Balak and Masahum slowly reached for the knives concealed in their belts, but Re'Amu stepped boldly forward until the spearhead was pressed against his chest.

"Two of my men perished today, in the flight from the sea. We could not go back to save them. The turn was too sharp, and we were nearly capsized. Look! Agade is coming. Do as I say. It is your only hope of surviving this day."

The three dots on the horizon were ships - low and long, rowed by thirty armed men apiece and carrying even more. As they watched, the three dots separated, revealing six ships. Three moved with great speed north up the coast while three rowed straight for them.

"Those are E-Kur troop carriers," insisted Re'Amu quietly, "and you will not be able to outrun them or outfight them. Trusting me is the only way forward."

Cenrill shook with frustration and Re'Amu's blood dripped from the tip of the spear before Kassu spoke.

"Do as he says."

Everyone remained motionless. Kassu spoke again. "Do as he says! Quickly!"

Cenrill hesitated, looking back and forth between the Agadian ships and the sea to the north, like a man trapped in a cage. His men were not with him. The shields were thrown to the deck from the ship's side with the haste of frightened men and Cenrill ruefully commanded his men to withdraw into the hull, though he personally refused.

"I will not sit in the dark like a coward, awaiting my doom," he muttered, though he allowed a cloth to be draped over him to conceal his armor. His spear he placed near the mast, concealed, within his reach.

The Agadian ships were close to the *Taradium* now, and it appeared a small group of Re'Amu's crew had assembled to meet them. Re'Amu, Balak, and Masahum ran about in haste, pulling handfuls of ashes from satchels at their waist, casting the gray dust over the sailors of *The Anchton*.

"Quickly," they whispered, "Rub these all over your face, hair, and arms. Huando, you need more. Joshur, here. Quietly now, everyone do the same!"

The ash melted on the crews wet clothing and skin, caking and cracking to give them a ghastly gray appearance. Re'Amu, Balak, and Masahum briefly checked that all the men were alike before doing the same to themselves.

Onboard the *Taradium*, Captain Rais stood thin and pale at the head of a small group, which awaited the Agadian's arrival. His keen eyes looked ahead to the three ships that approached them, now close enough to see the Agadian's numbers and weapons in detail. Foam sprayed from the lead-ship's prow where a tall commander stood gazing intently at the *Taradium* and *The Anchton*. A spear was clenched firmly in the commander's hand and a sword of bronze hung at his side.

"Yemen. Are they ready?" Rais asked quietly, keeping his gaze straight ahead and barely moving his mouth. Yemen, concealed by the others at the rear of the group, looked back at *The Anchton*.

"Re'Amu has completed his task, Captain. They are ready."

The pale-faced Captain nodded and he raised his empty hands, hailing the commander of the Agadian warships as they drew near. One came along each side of the *Taradium*, fastening bronze hooks to the hull with military precision and speed. The last warship swiftly closed the gap to *The Anchton*. Fifteen men from each warship jumped in unison onto the *Taradium*, clearing the gap over the sea from either side! There was a brief moment of rocking, the pounding of heavy boots, and the clanking of interlocked shields.

"KUR!" they cried together as the E-Kur took control of the vessel in the blink of an eye. Spears were thrust under the chin of each crew member. Rais showed no signs of alarm at the display of weapons and fierce aggression. Instead he calmly turned and bowed to the tall commander (distinguished by his crested helmet of bronze), who was stepping on-board their vessel. The commander parted through the ranks of his men and stood gazing over the motley crew.

"What business takes you into the waters of Agade?" the commander asked in a deep-toned voice. "I have little time for false reports or vague answers. Speak! Your lives depend upon it."

"Master," said Rais in a slimy tone, "I am the one they call Behram Rais, Captain of this small vessel. We trade in the oils of death and balms of entombment from the great southern dynasty of Kemet, Agade's close ally. We yearly pass through your waters for trade, as you well know, per Sargon the Great's mighty decree regarding this matter."

Even as he spoke, several of the E-Kur soldiers stormed the cabin, beginning a sweep of the entire hull of the *Taradium*. Rais pretended he did not notice.

The commander was handed a small tablet that he gazed over briefly.

"Your ship is known to us, Behram Rais. When an inventory of your cargo is complete, you will be allowed to turn upon your way."

"This other craft, however," he said, nodding authoritatively toward *The Anchton*, "I have no record of, nor have I seen its hull in these waters before."

"My lord," said Rais, with an even deeper bow, "If you will allow your servant to explain: King Djeser, Pharaoh of the Southern Kingdoms, received a shipment of artisans and craftsmen, skilled laborers and workers from the northern regions nigh on six months ago. They were the finest the Jezrial Dynasty could supply, and they boasted of mastery in their said crafts - we now know it was a lie, to our great demise..." He trailed off in disgust. "These people were sought to build great towers and palaces of renown for my master, King Djeser. But, they brought upon us nothing but plague and death! Their sickness has destroyed our land, countless have gone down to the grave.

'Our priests and diviners then received a vision - if the artisans and craftsmen, skilled laborers and workers, returned to die on their own land, our curse would be removed and our kingdom cleansed. That ship, that your other craft is fast approaching, is the very ship and it is full of the very same craftsmen. We have been entrusted to see these accursed peoples back to their own lands, for we sail this route often. I beg you my lord, do not set foot upon that ship, lest death be brought to this land as well!" All of the men with Rais, nodded. Their faces were grave and they covered their mouths.

The commander stepped back in disgust and looked over the water at *The Anchton*. The final troop carrier was pulling up along its side and its men preparing to board the vessel. The commander quickly loosed a bronze trumpet at his side and gave three short blasts.

"I will witness this plague myself," he declared. The commander boarded his craft and was quickly rowed toward *The Anchton*. The remainder of the E-Kur brandished their weapons as they continued their inventory of the *Taradium*.

The commander's craft made three, slow laps around *The Anchton*. The sun was still hidden by clouds, and sweat poured down the backs of the crew onboard the *Taradium* as they watched. Finally, both troop carriers pulled away. Another signal was given on the horn and the troops aboard the *Taradium* cast off the bronze hooks and departed with swift oar strokes.

The remaining three Agadian vessels rowed between *The Anchton* and the shore until late afternoon. The Durgu Mountains had replaced the brown and green rolling hills, and scattered evergreens dotted its rocky slopes. When they passed the last E-Kur tower and entered the northern countries, the warships finally turned back for Agade. When they were small dots on the horizon behind them, cheers broke out onboard *The Anchton*.

"Hooray! Hooray for Re'Amu and the *Taradium*!" they cried. Buckets of seawater were raised and splashed upon the crew, washing away the irritating disguise they had born through the length of the day. Re'Amu was hoisted up on Ebaz's shoulders and paraded around the deck again and again. Hands reached up to clasp him as he passed.

"Well done! Bravo!!" they cried. Even Cenrill managed a smile as he bowed low before Re'Amu, when he was finally let down.

"Sometimes being in the wrong is difficult to bear," he said. "By my spear, this time I am grateful for it. I have misjudged you and now we owe you our lives."

That night there was a huge feast aboard *The Anchton* and Kassu insisted that all of Re'Amu's crew join the broad spread which covered the vessel from stem to stern. The ships were fastened together and

Re'Amu introduced his crew as they came aboard.

"My first mate, Behram Rais," introduced Re'Amu, gesturing at a tall, lean man, white-faced and wearing a broad hat.

"And here is Balak and Masahum, who you know, of course. Ah, and this is Bariquim, he oversees guarding our stores and is the caller of our oars." The tall black man, rippling with muscle and covered in dark tattoos smiled and inclined his head, revealing white teeth.

"This is Sapu, Yemen, and Shadeir, our chief embalmers..." Introductions continued, finishing with sixteen brawny sailors who bowed respectfully as Re'Amu named them.

"We are not many," Re'Amu admitted, "for our trade is not the most sought after. We have worked together long and reap both hardship and reward alike."

Cenrill and Kassu greeted each as they came aboard and, for their bravery and cunning, gave them fine gifts from *The Anchton's* stores. More than once, Cenrill stomached the urge to raise his brow at a few of the swarthy fellows. He forced the thoughts from his mind.

"No, you must allow me!" insisted Cenrill as Re'Amu tried to refuse several gifts. "You and your men may have made this journey and faced such dangers before. We have not! Our gratitude and our gifts are well deserved." Kassu nodded, grateful for Cenrill's change.

Extra stores were brought over from the *Taradium,* to supplement the feast, and a finer meal on the sea had never been seen. Bright roasted carp, dried meats boiled with lavender and basil, fresh breads dripping with honeycomb, exotic southern grapes and dates, and rich drink was strewn across the ship. The air was filled with sweet aromas and hard laughter.

Every man's plate was full and his cup filled to the brim. From the Captains seated together at the stern to the lowest servants of the households, the relief of escaping the perils of their journey was shared by all. Soon an assortment of stringed instruments and drums broke out from under the benches and tables, and a lively music floated out across the water. The soft voice of Joshur rose above the rest in light melody:

Onward is the story, which a journey leads us down

Through twists and turns it travels

'for feet can find the ground.

Remember well the rising light, which guides and warms the sand

It's quick to beam and fade away

Leaving nothing but empty land.

Hear my words about this journey, the story of your days
Find, be strong, succeed, my child
For in the end you'll pass away.

Of what I have to give you, I can only answer naught
Lest my song tonight turn from journeying
To the sayings of the bought.

Hear a word from a loving mother
Who gave you life when you were small:

Put aside your fears, lest your heart be bound
For you can live an onward journey,
and by living you'll be found.

The sailors struck up another tune. Kassu gazed off into the still night, lost in memory and a different time, as he heard the words. He remembered the face that he loved, which sang the tune so sweetly long ago. The shadow over his brow passed quickly. He toasted the twinkling stars above and the gentle waves below, before draining his glass and returning to the merriment.

Re'Amu sat as one who had been struck, stunned, though the merriment continued around him. He gazed at the smiling Joshur with a dumb look, his goblet frozen and forgotten half-way to his lips, the questioning doubt previously unpinned in his mind, coming to a sudden horrifying light.

Bariquim, however, had been watching Re'Amu closely from further up the table. He nudged Behram Rais and gestured silently, drawing his attention to Re'Amu's expression. By the time Rais looked, nothing was amiss. Re'Amu had drained his glass and was bellowing forth a chant with all the others.

The evening eventually ended and the crew of the *Taradium* departed for their own vessel. Kassu and Cenrill made Re'Amu promise to sail with them onboard *The Anchton* for much of the next day. His knowledge of the waters that lay ahead was greatly needed, and the crew had not yet tired of praising him for his victory through Agade.

"Of course!" Re'Amu cried, flashing a white smile, much to the delight of Joshur and the sailors. "My first mate could use the practice handling the ship on his own." Rais smiled beside him, but said nothing.

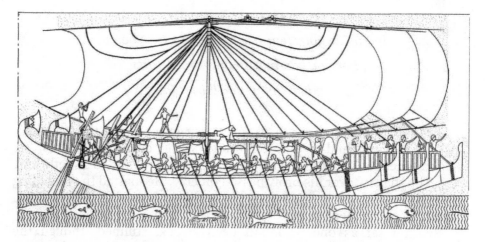

Stone Relief, Merchant Ships bound for Punt. Circa 2000 BC.

Chapter Twenty-four

Piercing Truth

Y ou know," reflected Kassu, the following morning, as Cenrill peered over the well-worn map, "it wasn't always this way." Cenrill paused from scribbling *Rocks* in fine runes in the northern section of their rapidly expanding map.

"I mean, my household ...my family... being like this: exploring, trading, seeking exotic lands, and remembering lingering landscapes. It runs in your blood, Cenrill, there is no doubt. It's just not...not...natural for me to do this."

Kassu paused and leaned against *The Anchton's* railing, watching the northern foothills of the Durgu Mountains roll by - covered with spidery white trunks and bursting pink blooms of the Asur forest, which crept up its hills. Cenrill laid down the piece of fine charcoal that he wrote with and stood by Kassu, gazing with him over the mysterious lands.

"I have been called rash, hot-tempered, even foolish by some," Cenrill said, "and perhaps those things are right at times. But, having success in your fingers, against all the odds... We lose and gain in life, but it's the adventure that makes it worthwhile." Kassu nodded, smiling, and Cenrill clapped him on the back and laughed.

"Ho, Ho! I don't believe my eyes. Kassu the silent and irreproachable has discovered that deep down inside he is an explorer, trader of exotic valuables, and seeker of distant lands!? By my spear, I cannot believe it!"

While Cenrill and Kassu met on the foredeck, Re'Amu worked alongside Huando, pointing out inlets, shallows, and currents as *The Anchton* moved into uncharted waters. Joshur was here and there about the deck, and every time he appeared Re'Amu shot him a sidelong glance, studying the boy quickly before looking away. Finally, Joshur worked alone, pulling up a catch of fish and changing out the lines near the prow of the ship. Re'Amu edged up alongside him and lent a hand to the heaviest lines.

"You are strong for a lad of your age!" complemented Re'Amu as he watched Joshur heave the wet lines, occasionally with a forty-pound catch fighting at its end.

"By the look of you, you've been at home on a ship all your life...?" Re'Amu waited for the boy to take the bait. Joshur shook his head.

"No?" cried Re'Amu, smiling widely with a fake grin. "Well then, tell me, where is your berth? Has your family traded long over the sea?"

Joshur looked up at Re'Amu's tall, chiseled figure and cast a look across the deck to where his father sat, deep in conversation with Cenrill and the master sailors as they peered over the map, occasionally making additions. Re'Amu followed his gaze and raised a questioning eyebrow.

"My father doesn't like it when I speak too much of the past," muttered Joshur as he threw out a new line. "He says one cannot plow a straight furrow by looking backward. But..." he continued hesitantly, "sometimes I don't think he is right. Does that make me a bad son?"

Re'Amu looked at the admiration twinkling in the boy's eyes and swallowed hard before answering.

"No, that does not make you a bad son."

Joshur smiled, grateful for his answer.

"Our household is from Anshan and we trade on the sea for Rahmsi, the chief there." He struggled as he pulled the next line in hand over hand. "My father has worked hard for the Chief's favor. When I was a lad, my father gave all he had in trade for a canoe. He began trading and fishing between the cities of Anshan and Arali. It was not many years before my father knew well those waters and his renown grew as a reliable seafarer. Once he saved his cargo from pirates by flipping his vessel over into the sea amongst drifting logs! He waited to right it until the thieves had passed and rowed it half full of sea water into the Anshan port!" Joshur's eyes sparkled with pride.

"That is quite a story!" exclaimed Re'Amu, humoring the boy with a forced laugh.

"Yes. My father is very brave," explained Joshur. "His fame reached all the way to the Chief's palace, where he was invited to leave fish and poverty behind him and trade the Chief's goods. We sold our boats! We changed our family name! We put everything we had into *The Anchton*, and the Chief filled it with the finest of his stores. He commanded Cenrill to guard our course with his Strong Men and we now sail with you, with rich reward and new days awaiting our return." Johsur's eyes sparkled with excitement.

"The reward must be great, to account for the perils you have faced and the length of your journey! There is much risk for loss. You must be only a lad of eleven or twelve seasons. Why does your father not leave you behind, in the care of his household? Does he not take care, should calamity befall him?"

The harsh tone of Re'Amu's voice startled Joshur, and he stepped back a little from his rebuke.

"I *am* a help aboard this ship," defended Joshur. He seemed to take courage and answered Re'Amu's question with wisdom that went well beyond his years.

"My father is no stranger to loss. During the years of great hardship, when food could not be found, my father traveled far to bring back grain for us. He came back with little, as all did in those times. My mother died from sickness soon after. I was very small and do not remember. But I remember my father. He had no time to mourn. He set out again, leaving me and my elder brothers in the care of his household. When he returned, he found his household scattered, his animals and goods missing, his eldest son dead, and my brother gone. But he found me." Joshur paused and gazed hard at Re'Amu's horror-struck face.

"All that remains to my father and all he has achieved since, is in *this* vessel. I would not be left behind, not even if he had tied me up and left me! I wanted to come. But my father did not ask me to stay. He told me he needed my help. He told me he couldn't do it without me." Tears welled up in the boy's eyes and he turned away from Re'Amu with the finality and certainty of truth that only a small and uncorrupted youth can accomplish.

The impact of Joshur's speech on Re'Amu was astounding. As Joshur spoke, Re'Amu had been gripping the wooden railing so hard his nails dug into its surface. Now he turned and fled the ship as if pursued, sweeping past Balak and Masahum who gave him (and then each other), a startled look as he flew past. He leaped over the side of *The Anchton* in a single bound and into the skiff, picking up the oars and rowing violently away until he sat isolated on the bobbing whitecaps between *The Anchton* and the shore.

There the oars dropped from his trembling hands and the well-kept barriers in his mind were overwhelmed with emotion. Re'Amu gasped breathlessly for air. He pulled out his hair and fell to his knees as memories, so long buried and forgotten, flooded back to him. That unnamed misgiving, the doubt in his mind which had so gnawed on him for the past several days of their journey was now revealed beyond any doubt: Joshur was his younger brother. Kassu was his father. He could barely remember, but it was truth. Faces flashed in his mind. Their mother, the one who had sung the very same song to them during the cold nights. Kassu, then a young man with a different name, whom Re'Amu had long blamed, hated, and then buried as dead in his heart, when he had run away from the biting pain and loss all those long years ago... yet now was the very same father who stood resurrected before him!

Re'Amu struggled for control of himself, walling off the panic, emotions, and memories which threatened to overwhelm him. He quenched the whispered voices which laid claim that he had been a fool, and was now himself a captive on the wrong path. He silenced the small whisper which spoke to him of a second chance, this one chance, that would never come again! He built walls and forced open his eyes to steady himself. It was a fierce battle in his mind, and it seemed he was tossed back and forth.

In the end, repetition and time won. For eleven years he had sailed with the *Taradium*. He was a boy then. Now he was a man. They were his family now. He knew power and could take the life of men whenever he wished. He knew pleasure. He knew wealth. He had all that he had never had at home. Here, he was important. Here he changed the course of the world. There was no going back, the voices whispered.

Slowly, his mind silenced his heart's violent outcry. With a blank face, he once again picked up the oars and made his way back toward *The Anchton*.

Balak and Masahum watched him float farther and farther away from the two ships as they struggled to come up with an explanation to the crew as to why their Captain had so suddenly departed. They gave each other questioning glances, fingering their knives. Finally, the little boat sluggishly returned. Balak and Masahum met Re'Amu at the side. Their eyes asked him if their game was up, as they helped him aboard. Re'Amu's expression was stony and he gave them no sign of what made him flee. Kassu and Cenrill greeted him anxiously, wondering if all was well.

"All is well," assured Re'Amu. "I merely thought the *Taradium* may be in some danger. Did you see her head turn there, all of a sudden? And then my skiff sprung a sudden leak! A bit of tar will hold it for now. The *Taradium* is well, it seems. My first mate, perhaps, dropped the steering oar. It was nothing." They turned away, satisfied with Re'Amu's response, but Balak and Masahum were not so easily contented. When they found themselves alone, returning to the *Taradium*, they questioned him incessantly.

"What was that about?" Masahum hissed as he pulled on the oars. "You jumped overboard as if the very gates of *Sheol* had opened wide upon the deck."

"It was nothing," replied Re'Amu with a blank stare.

"Nothing?" exclaimed Masahum quizzically. "Your face was as white as the sail of *The Anchton*. You have not seemed yourself for the past few days. Everything is going as planned, so what is the cause of your worry? In two weeks we'll be far out of these waters and back where we belong, enjoying the riches and splendor that are promised to us."

"Were those *things* not promised to us the last time, and the time before that?" questioned Re'Amu quietly. "Yet they are all empty ships, floating on a windless sea."

"What is the matter with you?" demanded Balak. He dropped his oar and stood to his feet, rocking the little skiff. "We are kings among men! Desires others can only dream of are in our right hand, and power is in our left! What else is left? There is nothing."

"Power to do what? Take a life? A stone has the same power, falling from a cliff, or a branch loosed by the wind," murmured Re'Amu

Balak looked at Re'Amu like he was a different person and blew a low whistle. He turned away in disbelief.

"We've all got power in our hands," reminded Masahum softly as Balak sat back down and picked up his oar. "Some are afraid to use it. Those of us who aren't, control life itself. Now is not the time to become a philosopher, Re'Amu. You know who we serve. There is no turning back."

Re'Amu forced a smile and nodded. "Do not be concerned. I don't know what came over me. It is nothing."

Even in the twilight, Behram Rais's cabin on the *Taradium* was dark - dimly lit by a few flickering candles. Re'Amu, Masahum, and Balak had not yet returned from their final excursion aboard *The Anchton*, but they were expected to arrive any minute. The whole of the *Taradium's* crew sat still in the dim light, waiting. Rais ran his eyes over a short, torn scroll covered in the black script of Angfar.

Thunk. Thunk. Sapu played with a small knife, tossing it into the wooden table before twisting it out and repeating the process. "What is taking them so long?" he whined.

No one answered him.

Bariquim sat in the corner of the cabin with his huge arms tightly crossed. Four others sat near him, following his example. His black form would have been invisible in the shadows, if it were not for the blue tattoos catching and reflecting the light. He was impatient and finally could bear it no longer.

"We should strike now," he bellowed in a deep voice as he leaned his great bulk forward. "While we still have their trust. Balak and Masahum have well marked the Strong Men among their crew, our task can be easily finished. Tonight!"

Behram Rais stared hard at the intimidating man without saying a word. Even Bariquim could not hold the Captain's gaze.

"We will wait for Re'Amu's return," he hissed softly.

"Re'Amu." Bariquim spat as if the word was bitter on his tongue. He reclined back in his chair. "There is something wrong with him, I tell you. He is not as he used to be."

"His task is deception and in that, it seems, he has fooled even you,

Bariquim. Though I don't think that is an overly grueling task," jeered Sapu with a smile.

Bariquim rose and would have struck him, but Sapu twirled the sharp blade in his hand, quicker than the eye could follow.

"I think not," muttered Bariquim as he thought better of his decision and kicked his chair across the small cabin instead.

He did not have to wait long, for at that moment the shadowy forms of Re'Amu and his two companions appeared at the door and they entered the dark meeting.

"The Urudu welcomes you home, brother," hissed Rais. "You must be weary from your days' work. Come, eat. Refresh yourself." Rais pushed a plate of bread and butter across the table to Re'Amu as he sat. Everyone was still, and the tension in the room seemed almost palpable. Rais's temperament was always unpredictable and though Re'Amu did indeed look tired and drawn, one never knew when he was being tested.

"There will be time for refreshment soon enough, Captain," Re'Amu said as he pushed aside the food. "Balak, give us your full report on *The Anchton*."

Rais nodded in satisfaction and Bariquim muttered something incoherent about finally getting down to business.

Balak stood up, shooting a sidelong glance at Re'Amu. He decided not to mention his strange behavior.

"There are twelve armed men aboard the vessel and twenty-three sailors and craftsmen. Of the first group, at least half will need to be among the dead to tame the rest during our voyage. Of the sailors, we suggest only the household leaders need be slain. The rest will not fight."

Masahum nodded in agreement. "And if they do," he added to Bariquim, "it will be easily put down. We have given fine silver armbands - the ones we have used in the past - to those we will need to kill. They have all worn them proudly and will be easy targets for you and your men to pick out."

Bariquim nodded and the men behind him smiled wickedly.

"And what of the trap, Re'Amu? Are we ready to spring?" asked Rais.

"Unless, of course, you'd rather join their crew," cut in Bariquim, which roused a short chorus of harsh laughter from behind him.

Re'Amu remained silent and looked towards Rais without a change in expression.

Rais leaned delicately over the table.

"Beloved," Rais said softly to Bariquim, "When you speak to one above you in the Urudu order, you do so with respect. One more outburst from you, and I shall strangle you over the ship's side with your own entrails." He spoke so quietly and without emotion that a stranger would have perhaps shivered in disgust and then ignored the comment. But, Behram Rais had done far worse things for nothing more than his own amusement. The crew grew silent, watching and waiting.

Bariquim clenched his teeth and drew back into the shadows.

"The bait is ready," continued Re'Amu after a pause. "The Captain, Kassu, is quick to trust, as is most of his household. All have now bought our act, even the Strong Men. We must act at the right time and without haste.

'We will be upon the inlet of Sahhu by nightfall tomorrow. It will not be hard to convince them to spend one last feast with us in an area suited to our purposes. My original plan holds. We have done our work well in the grove of Sahhu before, and familiar ground makes the task easier."

"It will be as you say," declared Rais without hesitation, scanning again the dark message of Angfar. "Our orders are clear: at least twenty captives for our reward. As you know, alive is double the reward, in any condition. Dead... just good. And the Urudu never fail."

Having decided on their course, the crew stood and left, leaving Rais and Re'Amu sitting across from each other. Though unspoken, Re'Amu knew he had not been given leave. They sat in silence and the candles flickered.

"Perhaps I will kill Bariquim with the others tomorrow," mused Rais, as if he was sharing an afterthought.

Re'Amu ran a hand through his hair, not showing his relief about whom Rais's doubt had been directed toward. He shook his head.

"No, Bariquim is too good at what he does. Let his right hand Shadeir be made an example of at the next outburst, I think even a skull as thick as Bariquim's will understand our meaning. Maybe then he will grow tamer. It will be best to keep a closer eye on him on our next voyage, methinks."

Rais pursed his thin lips and nodded.

"You are not my second in command without reason. You plan far into the future when most look only until tomorrow. You are dismissed."

Re'Amu did not sleep that night, and when he did the same dream played over and over in his mind until his waking. In it, he was a wolf. His pack surrounded a pen of sheep and then slaughtered them like vicious beasts. While he feasted on the hot blood of his prey, he suddenly realized that he was not a wolf at all! He was a sheep, surrounded by wolves himself, and he was covered in the blood of his own kind.

When he woke, Re'Amu simply lay, unable to think and unable to feel. For so long he had run away, run and never looked back. It seems he had not run far enough. The decision of supporting his crew or trying to save his family - both seemed dark. How could he return? He would be shunned for who he had become and what he had done. How could he betray his crew? They were all he had, and to do so would mean death. They served a master that he could not dismiss.

He was afraid. He was the judge, the executioner, and the accused. It was too much for him to bear. In the end, his mind shut down, blank and lifeless. He lay in his hammock, until rising like a dead man in the morning light, habitually preparing for the last day of their long seduction.

Chapter Twenty-five

Captain Behram Rais

The inlet of Sahhu was fed by a bubbling stream, which ran between the sharp northernmost edge of the Durgu mountains and the thick Asur forest. The south edge of the bay was hemmed in by a large, cliff wall of smooth, gray rock. It rose twenty feet into the sky and ran directly west. Between the cliff and the stream, large boulders lay, fallen from high within the Mountains. Beyond the stream, the Asur forest ran away to the north and west, with thick, tall trees standing closely spaced. Outcrops of old rock rose here and there, sometimes higher than the tops of the trees. The locals called that area the Aron-Ken, and said it was an ancient place.

Between the shore, the stream, and the forest there was a large circular grove, empty of trees and bushes. The grass here was soft and tall, and a few smaller trees crowded around its edge seeking an advantage from the dense forest.

It did not take any convincing for Kassu and Cenrill to agree for one more celebratory gathering.

"To feast, take on water, and prepare for Cartegin!" shouted Cenrill, as the crew clapped and hollered. Re'Amu himself, however, left Masahum and Balak to deliver the invitation. He was not seen until the *Taradium* led *The Anchton* into the calm, shallow bay and weighed anchor.

The crew of the *Taradium* unloaded their barrels of drink and fare, and began setting up camp long before the first sailors departed from *The Anchton*. The first arrivals from Kassu's crew saw the finishing touches being made to the evening festivities. Strong smelling, wooden barrels of liquid were opened. Fires roared and crackled happily in the twilight, casting light over a large supply of food for the night's feast. Even the most weathered sailors paused to take in the scene. The two ships floated, their oars racked up in the air like the wings of two shapely birds, resting on quiet water. An orange sky melted into the sea's crystalline clarity, ending in the blue horizon.

Cenrill's men threw lots to determine which two unlucky fellows would remain 'on watch' aboard *The Anchton*, while the rest of the crew disembarked. They waded in knee-high water, which lapped peacefully at a sandy shore. They had not set foot on land since the start of their journey and all breathed a sigh of relief - they had made it! Several of the sailors stooped where the freshwater met the sea and splashed the meeting waters over their heads, a sign of praise to the powers of the sea and earth for keeping them safe on their journey.

Cenrill clasped Kassu as they waded into the protected glade. "Well, who'd ever think we'd make it this far, eh? By my spear!" he shook his head and smiled. "We well deserve a night of rest and merriment after all we've gone through. And then, tomorrow for the prize: Cartegin and riches!"

"Cartegin and Riches!" agreed Kassu, and several of the sailors nearby took up the call.

Bariquim smiled ruefully as the cries floated in from the rejoicing sailors to the grove where he sat, stirring a large brass bowl which hung suspended over a fire. Behind him several large planks had been roughly hewn and were covered with the finest foods and drink left in their store: meats and cheeses, fresh fruits and tubers, soft breads and fine honey.

Re'Amu and Rais greeted the members of *The Anchton* at the edge of the clearing. Flasks and mugs were passed around to every hand, then Rais stepped forward. "Members of *The Anchton*, sailors and explorers: on behalf of my Captain," several cheers rang out as he gestured at Re'Amu, "we welcome you to our table. Fear nothing! Cast off your cares and your worries this night, for you have passed through danger and trial unscathed. You now stand on the shores of safety. We are grateful to call you friends. To Cartegin! To riches! And to your final night before your new lives begin."

He raised his glass and all the men of the *Taradium* and *The Anchton* toasted in one accord, hailing their journey and new-found friends.

Eager hands dug into the fare. Music floated gaily out of the clearing and across the water. The night was warm and it grew dark fast. The fires roared, flickering on the trunks of the forest. The sailors of *The Anchton* drained and re-drained their goblets. They were filled again and again without question - before their bottoms could run dry. No one noticed that no crew member of the *Taradium* swallowed a drop.

Re'Amu found Rais, at one point in the festivities, and pulled him aside, whispering quick words.

"What is wrong?" asked Rais, disconcerted by the drawn expression on Re'Amu's face. "Speak, quickly."

"I fear..." Re'Amu hesitated, looking back towards the flickering firelight, and then beyond to the darkness of the shore and the water beyond. "I fear something may go amiss at the ships. Why did Cenrill leave two men behind? He should have nothing to fear at this point in the journey."

Rais shook his head. "You worry about nothing. It is simply his habit and it makes our work easier. We will handle them in the morning, after our task is finished."

Re'Amu did not seem satisfied. "I do not know. I just do not know," he said, his voice filled with agitation. "Let me watch the *Taradium*, then, until morning. Better to be on watch than to assume the best..." Re'Amu trailed off.

Rais looked at him coolly, studying him closely.

"Very well," he whispered. "Life and death I hold in my hand, but I cannot foresee all things. Do as you wish and perhaps you will be right. If not, you may rest, and dream pleasant dreams for once on this journey. You have been fitful in your sleep Re'Amu. I have heard you these past nights. Go! Your work here is finished and you have done well. We will have what fun is left, do not hesitate to join us, if you have the urge."

Re'Amu bowed briefly before hurrying away, disappearing without notice. He walked softly on the sand of the beach and then waded to the *Taradium*, climbing up its side with trembling hands. Once there, he looked back from the ship's railing. The fires of the grove lit the forest with an ominous glow, standing in sharp contrast to the bright stars above.

'What am I to do?' he thought to himself. Despair filled his heart, chaining him like a captive. He watched in agitation as the fires grew dim.

The laughter and merriment in the grove was loud and boastful, the drink did its work. Old sailing songs were sung and new ones made up in the moment. The night wore on. One by one the crew of *The Anchton* curled up on the soft grass around the warm embers of the fires and passed into peaceful slumber. Even the most resilient stomach of Huando was overwhelmed and he nodded where he sat, propped up against a downed log. His mug slipped from his hand.

The grove was now grossly quiet, compared to the onslaught of merriment which had so suddenly taken over its land. The watchful eyes of the Urudu peered, wide awake, at the still and sleeping forms cast about between the glowing embers. They had waited long, and now they all took their places. Sapu, Yemen, and Shadeir stood evenly spaced amongst the trees on the northern side of the grove, crouched low and waiting to cut off any escape should things go ill. Bariquim and the other Urudu stood silently around the edges of the flickering light, fingering their weapons.

Balak and Masahum had disappeared (without notice), earlier in the night, slipping away behind the trees and out of sight. There they had dug the soft sand, excavating a trench nearly twenty feet long and four feet deep. They had long since dug past the bones of their last victims, which lay piled in a heap behind them.

Behram Rais looked over the sleeping forms and his men in their positions. He waited. He slowly etched and sliced his long nails into sharper points as the time ticked by. The stars wheeled overhead, the only witnesses to what was about to take place. Yet, even the cunning Rais could not foresee everything. Just as he was about to give the word, a tall form stumbled into the low-light of the grove with a loud curse. It was the middle-watchman of *The Anchton*, one of Cenrill's men, who in hopes of catching the last bit of the feast, had abandoned his post.

"Hey, now, where's the..." Bariquim did not hesitate, and like a snake striking from the darkness he wrapped a piece of twine around the guard's throat and pulled his struggling form quietly back out of the firelight. Rais nodded urgently. Like shades, the remainder of the Urudu stalked silently around the sleeping crew. Each target was well-marked by the silver armbands, which sparkled in the firelight. They worked in pairs. Masahum and Balak returned from their gravesite and joined in, unsheathing the small blades concealed at their hips. One sliced the throat while the other controlled any flailing limbs. Bariquim and the rest of the Urudu used woven cords of twine, strangling the life from their hopeless prey.

One by one Cenrill's men perished without a sound and vanished into the dark well of the grave, their silver armbands slipped from their limbs and reclaimed for future use. All the while Rais sat like a hawk perched upon a stump, his eyes darting back and forth among the still sleeping figures while his crew moved from one body to the next.

A shriek and a brief struggle cut through the ominous stillness and Rais leapt to his feet! Balak cursed under his breath. His knife had missed its mark, just enough. Several of the still-sleeping forms rolled over.

On the far side of the encampment Cenrill sat bolt upright, his hand groping instinctively for his spear. But, his spear had been left onboard *The Anchton* and was not to be found! His mind was groggy and slow to focus, as he struggled to his feet. He was still a warrior at heart, and even before he woke he could feel in his bones something was amiss.

"Men, to arms! To arms!" he cried out with a heavy tongue. Before he could say more, Rais was upon him, bringing a quick slash and then brutal thrust fiercely down. Cenrill gasped in pain. It was sharp and pierced through the fog of his mind. He fell over lifeless onto the sand.

It had been enough. The remainder of Cenrill's men and the majority of Kassu's sailors woke up at once in a panic, their adrenaline pumping through their veins, briefly clearing the shadow which hung over their minds.

Rais shouted swift orders. Yemen and Shadeir came running through the trees. Two more of Cenrill's men fell, pierced quickly by daggers and spears, before they could gain their feet. Kassu himself rose with a sharp pain in his head and tried to steady himself as screams of horror filled the grove. He, along with everyone else, did not know what was happening. Death was in the camp!

He instinctively reached down and grabbed Joshur, pulling him to his feet and dragging him back toward the trees with as much nimbleness as he could muster. Several of the more able seamen picked up half-burning sticks and ran for the trees in a large scramble, away from the dark shadows that seemed to lurk over the bodies of the dead.

It was of no avail. Soon the last of the survivors, a group of about twenty sailors, were hemmed in by the Urudu, who howled and screamed in glee at the sailor's terror. Eleven of Cenrill's men lay lifeless. Seeing their peril, Ebaz made a dash into the dark trees about twenty feet ahead. His disappearance was closely followed by a shrill scream and the unmistakable thud of a spear being driven home. Bariquim appeared slowly from the blackness. There was no escape in the shadow. The net had been closed. The trap was sprung shut.

Kassu looked about him and despair filled his heart. He acted swiftly, pushing Joshur down flat against the sand where he disappeared among the high weeds.

"Lay still my son, and be brave," he whispered. He rose and drew back into the group of sailors. They stood shoulder to shoulder in a tight cluster as the Urudu circled with bloodied spears and axes. The sailors stumbled over each other. Some of them were hardly able to stand, due to the drink, and all of them were terrified. Rais walked toward them boldly, laughing as he came.

"So, my dears, your sleep was not so sweet as promised was it?" He chuckled again and the Urudu laughed with him. Kassu and Huando grit their teeth as the betrayal became clear. They gripped their sticks tighter. The other sailors bent to find rocks among the sand.

Rais laughed harder. "Come Kassu, come. Use reason," he said, wiping tears of mirth from his eyes. "You have my word as a Captain: no more of your men will die today if you lay down your flaming brands and little rocks."

Kassu looked about quickly for Re'Amu but could not find him.

"Oh yes," said Rais, reading his mind. "You have been led astray far beyond your wildest imaginations."

Kassu hesitated, unsure of what to do, wishing he had more time.

"Come Kassu, I am losing my patience. Death or life? Choose wisely, for you choose also for your men." The mirth had vanished from his eyes and the cold, hard edge had returned.

Kassu looked at his men. They swayed and stumbled where they stood. A sharp pain pulsated in his head. He staggered, unwillingly. He could still see the bodies of Cenrill and the Strong Men strewn about the faint clearing. He let the stones fall from his hands.

"You are a monster," Kassu whispered. "And for what? Bronze? Gold? You have no sense of the world."

Rais smiled a rueful smile.

"Ah, Kassu, Kassu. You do not know why we are here or who we are, do you?"

"If you don't mean to kill the rest of us and steal our cargo, then what would you have?" asked Kassu boldly, mustering his courage and strength.

Rais gestured for him to come forward and Kassu slowly wobbled out of the group, sneaking a last quick look back at the low plants where he knew Joshur lay, hidden. Kassu stopped an arms-length away from Rais and opened his mouth to speak again. Before he could utter a word Rais's hand struck, grabbing him by the hair and dragging him down until his face was pressed against the biting sand.

Rais struck him again and placed a knee on the nape of his neck. The sailors would have surged forward and given their lives for Kassu, but they were afraid and intoxicated. The Urudu's spears tickled their noses.

"Take them," hissed Rais.

One by one the sailors were grabbed and dragged back into the light, where they were placed into well-used brass shackles and leather thongs. Some of them struggled when they saw the bindings, but they were no match in speed or strength that night. The Urudu mercilessly broke their limbs if they pulled away from them. Joshur was overlooked, and soon the circle of the Urudu collapsed until he was on its outer edge.

"You see?" whispered Rais to Kassu, cruelly twisting the Captain's neck, forcing him to watch his men as they cried out. "I was born with more power than you ever had and now I take what little you have away. Bronze is nothing. But for your blood... I can obtain whatever I desire. Are you afraid?"

Kassu did not have the strength or power to fight back against this man. He gasped in pain as he tried to answer.

"I...I have many regrets and much shame... this is not one of them."

With a great heave Kassu dislodged Rais from his back and rolled, grasping for Rais's neck with his bloodied hands. He was slow and dull. Long before Rais felt in need of air the white-faced Captain sunk a short blade deep into Kassu's side. Rais pushed the man off of him into the dirt with something of a struggle, flustered that the fat Captain had mustered the determination of will to fight back.

Joshur lay motionless in the bushes, terrified enough to remain silent as he watched the events unfold around him. On seeing his father slain, Joshur could not help but let out a wrenching sob. Shadeir started at the sound and then jumped in shock as Joshur's form leapt up from the shrubs and sprinted for the cover of the dark trees. Shadeir let out a yell and took off in hot pursuit with Yemen close on his heels, motivated by the yells of Rais: "After him! Do not let him escape!"

Kassu struggled to speak as he lay on his side and Rais bent over him to listen.

"I now die," Kassu whispered, "but you... you have never lived. I... I..." Kassu never finished his thought, and faded into the clutches of Sheol.

The gap closed rapidly as Shadeir and Yemen jumped through the high shrubbery after the fleeing form of Joshur. Joshur had barely slipped between their reaching hands and into the dark cover of the trees, dodging the shades of trunks as they appeared in front of him. Branches whipped by. The crashing and cursing of his pursuers dwindled, until it seemed only one remained on his tail. That one was gaining.

Joshur changed angles at the last moment, running parallel to the edge of the forest and the sea. A loud curse and the whoosh of an ax echoed over his shoulder. He had gained a lead, but his chest and lungs burned with exhaustion. Without warning the spidery fingers of a great root reached up and caught his foot in the darkness. He stumbled and fell hard. His wrist crumpled beneath him and he let out a shrill cry as pain shot up his arm and side. He scrambled, trying to get back to his feet. A dark shadow loomed up behind him, and a heavy boot struck him venomously in the side.

"Where do you think you're going boy?" Yemen gasped. He wiped the sweat from his brow with one hand and held a second hatchet loosely in the other. Yemen stepped on Joshur's limp wrist as he tried to scramble away, causing Joshur to nearly faint with pain.

"No, no, no," Yemen whispered in Joshur's ear. He grabbed a handful of hair and pulled the boy's head back. "It's time for you to join the rest of your miserable crew."

Joshur, like his father, was full of surprises and hidden strength. With his left hand, he reached out until he grasped a large stone and brought it smashing against the sneer on Yemen's face.

"You little devil!" howled Yemen. He brought his hand away from his face and found it covered with blood. He swung his ax blindly, but his hold on Joshur's head had loosened. Joshur pulled away with all of his might! The ax swung wide, its edge striking deeply into Joshur's shoulder. Joshur could feel its bite severing bone and sinew and he fell back, lying motionless at the feet of his attacker. The dark shadows of the trees loomed overhead, and high above Joshur could see a twinkling star, which found its way through the knit branches. He heard the waves of the sea crash softly in the distance.

"It looks like there won't be any survivors in your family after all," Yemen spat and he held his ax high for the final blow.

It never fell. A light whistling seemed to cut through the air, followed by a loud thud! Yemen gasped and fell where he stood, his ax still raised! The point of a spear appeared out of his chest. Joshur tried to push himself farther into the roots of the trees as another form detached itself from the darkness and slowly walked closer. Joshur shied away, expecting another axe to fall. Instead Joshur found strong hands lifting him to his feet and he cried out with pain as something was bound tightly around his shoulder.

"Fly!" a voice commanded him. He stared dumbly at the face. The voice spoke again, loud and paired with a furious shake that rattled him to his senses: "Fly!! Be brave. Flee from this place. Go!"

So Joshur fled through the trees, leaving the stricken face of Re'Amu in the shadows far behind.

Chapter Twenty-six

A Traitor Among Thieves

An uprooted tree, grotesquely planted in reverse above the grave, was the only sign of the Urudu's work the night before. Sand had been sprinkled over the fresh blood and the bodies that could not fit inside the *Taradium* had been concealed within the deep grave. It was the Urudu way, as they waylaid travelers and traders, to escape detection and move on to their next victims.

They were ruthless and skilled in every aspect of their work, and the transportation of their priceless cargo wasn't any different. The strongest of *The Anchton's* crew were strapped by leather thongs, to oars on the *Taradium's* main deck. The weak and injured were stacked below, where the bile, blood, and filth ran over all, and the air was sour.

By mid-evening after the night of the attack, the walls and port of Cartegin had come into view. Behram Rais, Bariquim, and Sapu stood on the main deck, watching the city draw nearer.

"We should waste no time," growled Bariquim, eyeing the city walls. "Let us grab what we need and depart quickly. If they should catch wind of our cargo, the city might rise against us."

"It would only take one to cry out," whined Sapu. "We should send them all below at once and gag them. No risks - that's the way to do it."

"Then you would be rowing yourself to the port, you rat," spat Bariquim. "The city is far off, we have much we can still use them for today." He raised the whip over his head, making it whine and crack. Those bound to the oars ducked their heads, their eyes wide with fear as they pulled harder.

Rais eyed the walls and the distance between them.

"Sapu is right in this matter. Send them all below and bind them so no sound can be made. We will row the final length to the city ourselves. Sapu, come with me, my dear."

Sapu jeered over his shoulder at Bariquim, as he walked with Rais to the fore of the ship. Bariquim released his anger upon the slaves, dragging the captives mercilessly below deck.

Re'Amu caught snippets of Rais's conversation with Sapu as the wind blew up the leather flap of the cabin. They spoke earnestly, looking toward the city. Rais rubbed his hands together impatiently. Sapu smiled an evil smile and nodded. Rais sensed an observer. Looking back, he saw Re'Amu watching them. He sent Sapu away and strode casually nearer.

"Re'Amu, Re'Amu. What is to be done with you? Some more air, perhaps?" Rais pondered, folding up the leather sides of the cabin, stepping aside every time Bariquim tossed a slave into the ship's rear hatch. Rais examined Re'Amu closely. His limp body hung upside down off the ground, moving with the sway of the ship. His eyebrow bled from a fresh cut and Re'Amu grimaced as Rais's hand drew near to wipe away the blood from his face. Rais felt the tension in the leather cords that held Re'Amu fast.

The Captain shook his head and drew a sharp fingernail across Re'Amu's cheek.

"Re'Amu. My dearest, my most trusted lieutenant. What is this sickness that ails you so? You have acted so strangely on this trip, though we have made it a dozen times. Then Bariquim finds you in the forest, standing over Yemen lying dead upon the ground. And that boy, the sweet little boy, vanished without a trace. Still will you say nothing about it? Nothing to defend yourself?"

"Bariquim is so dull he cannot see beyond the tip of his own nose! Had he not stopped me we would have never lost the child." Re'Amu answered without batting an eye. Rais said nothing and walked around Re'Amu like a vulture circling its prey.

"Are you disappointed," asked Re'Amu lowly, "that you must now take the time to find another little boy to prey upon within the city? I know you well, Captain. Clearly you do not know me."

Rais paused and looked at Re'Amu with surprise.

"Oh, I do," Rais said, pacing around him. "I think I know you all too well, Re'Amu. You are disgusted by me. I see it in your eyes. How can that be? How can you turn away from me? I saved you. I gave you a life when you had none! I taught you how to be powerful, how to be free of your weakness and shame!!" Rais kicked and struck Re'Amu as spittle flew from his lips.

"You should have killed him when I first caught him," reminded Bariquim as he passed by. "I knew he was going soft, but you paid me no heed."

Rais ran a hand through his hair and steadied himself. He leaned forward next to Re'Amu's ear suddenly, like a snake.

"What is it that has so abruptly changed you, my love?" he whispered. "Where is the Urudu warrior who takes as he pleases, the one who is more powerful than any ordinary man? Where is my lieutenant who desired to never feel pain or abandonment again? Now you are... sick. Yes. You are ill."

Re'Amu looked away from Rais and did not answer. Even as Rais turned away to leave, Re'Amu's voice rang out clearly.

"Rais! I have followed you without question ever since you took me in. It is true, this trip has been a trial for me. I have been uneasy. I have not slept. I have been filled with unexplainable sorrow. I have questioned many things in my mind. But did I not deliver for you as I always have? Free me! Bariquim deceives you with lies, you have always known that. He does so again now."

Bariquim laughed harshly. "Should I free you from your nightmares and unexplainable sorrow?" he asked mockingly. He drew forth a sharp dagger and tickled Re'Amu's neck with it.

"Bariquim!" commanded Rais. "Do not harm him."

"Do you still treat this white-belly with kindness?" Bariquim spat. "You have seen it yourself, he is a traitor."

Re'Amu said nothing as blood trickled from his bleeding mouth down his cheek. He stared defiantly at Bariquim. Rais came nearer and wiped away the blood with a soft cloth. Re'Amu struggled to maintain composure as those hands and sharp fingernails came so near his face.

"I don't know," said Rais, shaking his head. "Re'Amu, of all of us, I would not doubt. Yet, I cannot help but question. Perhaps when we get to Angfar I shall know the truth behind your actions. There is one there that cannot be deceived. Until then..." Rais swiftly cut the cord that held Re'Amu airborne and he fell to the deck. "Until then you will be bound but treated as an Urudu. Sapu! Make sure we pick up oil of the Carn'ee from Cartegin. I want Re'Amu to be healthy when we arrive in Angfar if he is to stand before the Dominant."

"The Dominant?" Sapu's face twisted with horror at the thought.

Bariquim tied together a leather flap at the stern, closing off the rear as the final slaves were lashed firmly together below. "I see no reason why you still protect him, if that is to be his fate!" he added gruffly.

"Do not question me Bariquim!" cried Rais turning on him. "You too are doubtful in my eyes. Feel lucky that *you* are not bound! I do not know which of you to believe. Re'Amu will be confined to his chambers. Tie him hand and foot! But do no more to him. Those are my orders."

Re'Amu was dragged to his small quarters. His hands were tied behind him and his feet securely fastened to the floor with thongs. Finally, he was left alone. Loneliness and despair seemed to fill his little room. The leather door of the cabin flapped mournfully in the wind as he gazed back, catching brief glimpses of the flurrying waters behind the steering oar.

The glade where his father lay, cruelly buried, had long since disappeared - along with the smoke from *The Anchton's* burning hull. Tears welled in his eyes, but he was too ashamed to let them spill.

"Who am I?" he whispered to himself. "What have I done?"

The Urudu pulled slowly at the oars with dip and splash. Cartegin grew closer.

"We should arrive by late evening," informed Rais to Sapu. "Remember what I have asked of you. Bariquim, make sure all stay aboard. Keep those slaves gagged and quiet." Rais turned and addressed the rest of the crew. "Sapu, Balak, Masahum - you will come ashore with me to fill our empty jars of grain. Once we resupply we shall leave immediately. Remember: move quietly and we should pass through, undetected." Evening came as the *Taradium* pulled slowly into the port of Cartegin.

The port was set in a small bay, carved out by human hands. Its wide mouth fronted the sea and then curled back, forming a semi-circular shape that was both a docking port and drying shore for water-logged fishing and trading vessels. As soon as the *Taradium* passed inside, the water grew calm and the surf was left behind. A wooden dock ran around the port, surrounding a small island of wharf and mooring posts that stood in the center of the water.

Farther south an isolated beach had several ships drying on the sand. Fishing and trading craft were moored, and wooden buildings and shacks crowded around the edge of the water. Many people walked to and fro over the dock. The fishing vessels had returned from the sea with their day's catch; busy hands moved nets, sacks, and rope. Orders were shouted and bells rang out across the expanse of water.

Beyond the waterfront ran a busy road, winding up the hill of Cartegin and fading into red-clay houses. Here craftsmen and merchants set up booths along one side of the road to appease the busy ship-commerce, while the other side of the road was a stock-yard of supplies. Wood lay stacked, drying in heaps, and large clay pots bubbled with the smell of pitch and tar over large fires. Rope and cured beams, cut and lacquered, were visible along with piles of mud and straw.

"We are here," whispered Rais. "Make fast the ship and unload those empty grain stores, we will return in no less than an hour."

Re'Amu tried to see from under the leather of the cabin, as the *Taradium* made fast to the dock. Rais, Sapu, Balak, and Masahum leaped over the side and the empty grain jars were handed down to them. Soon, the small party disappeared up the hill and into the busy street.

Balak and Masahum each heaved an empty jar on their shoulders as they walked. Balak nodded toward the shipyard as they passed, several huge skeletons of ships lay partially visible behind a tall wooden fence.

"It seems the Chief of Cartegin is having some ideas of his own," he muttered, shifting the weight of the jar.

"Ideas about what?" wondered Masahum in reply. "Of trade? Or of strength?"

"Ask no questions! Keep moving!" hissed Rais impatiently.

They did not travel far before reaching their destination. A quarter mile up the hill was a shack stacked high with sacks of grain. Laborers came and went to claim their daily wages. The merchant looked up and took a quick step back, knocking over a sack of beans, when he saw the white-powdered face of Rais staring down at him.

"Foreigners! You're not from the ship-yard. Or from the fisheries. Ah," he said, looking at Balak and Masahum and then closer at Rais, scrambling to push the rolling beans back into the sack. "Northern types you folk are. I thought to myself, for a moment, you were from *down there,* if you take my meaning. Chief Ishshak would have been mighty pleased to see a southern ship in his waters..."

Rais laid out roughly cast gold and silver bands on the table, one at a time, until the Merchant ceased his jabbering.

"We come from Angfar, merchant, and we are in haste. Grain, to the brim of both these jars, and quickly. Or we will deal with a more suitable trader."

"Angfar?" the merchant asked with a slight shudder, eyeing the gold hungrily. "I have heard few good things about that place and all of them old tales. The Jezrialites trade with us often and they speak well enough of the northern parts. To the top it is, then."

The merchant whistled over his shoulder and pocketed the gold, while servants busied themselves. Balak shuffled his feet impatiently. It was dark and torch-light made the shadows waiver along the road. One jar was finally filled.

"Sapu, give me a hand with this. Sapu? Sheol-Mak! Where is he? We are in haste!" cried Balak looking around. Sapu was nowhere to be seen.

"He is on my business," declared Rais sternly. "Masahum will help you, quickly. To the *Taradium.*"

They carried the heavy grain between them and arrived back on the dock a few moments later. The dark, intimidating face of Bariquim stared at them from the shadows as they approached.

"What is taking so long?" he hissed. "We should have departed by now."

"We are going as quickly as we may," answered Balak, hoisting up the heavy jar. "Has there been any trouble here?"

"One or two inquisitive faces, they were easily taken care of."

"What does *taken care of* mean, Bariquim?" demanded Masahum, looking around as if expecting to see concealed bodies. "We don't have time for your devilry!"

Bariquim looked down into the water. Still forms could barely be seen floating under the weight of a heavy net. Before he could explain, several things seemed to happen at once.

A sharp shriek broke out from behind them, coming from between the shipyard and the port. Sapu appeared suddenly, dragging two squirming sacks as he ran for the *Taradium*. Behind him came a greater commotion of voices yelling. And then, as if in swift reply, a glare of many torches appeared coming down from the hill, approaching the port at a fast rate of speed. There were at least a hundred men stacked behind a Chieftain of large stature and their numbers were growing.

Re'Amu bit at his bonds inside the cabin. They were loose, but still held him fast. He did not have much time! "What is this foolishness!?" he heard Masahum cry in alarm from the dock. Re'Amu pulled at the leather thongs until his wrists bled, feeling their fibers grow weak. They snapped. He quickly untied his legs and stood, peering out from the side of the ship, as Sapu threw two wriggling bags on-board with a thud.

Re'Amu speedily rubbed his wrists and ankles before carefully sliding through the leather covering, over the ship's side, and onto the dock. He waited, concealed in the shadow of his vessel. Many torches flickered farther inland.

"Did you not hear Rais's orders?" demanded the voice of Masahum with alarm. "Where is the Captain?? What have you done, Sapu?"

"This *is* on Rais' orders, filth!" yelled Sapu in reply. "Do you not know what the Captain desires on the long voyages?! This other urchin got in the way and..."

A great shout ceased the quarrel. The Urudu turned and Re'Amu peered into the port's shadow. There, about midway down the dock, was the Captain. He struggled forward, his lithe form heaving a half-filled jar of grain. Behind him the crowd of torches seemed to recognize the source of the commotion and flooded upon the dock in quick pursuit. Yelling voices and pointing hands singled out the *Taradium*. Heavy boots ran closer. Rais threw aside the jar and sprinted for the ship as the Cartegin's closed in behind him.

"We have no time! We are discovered!" Sapu cried. "Shadier, cast off from the moorings! Out with the oars! We must fly!"

"No!" cried Masahum. "We will wait for the Captain."

Grain flew everywhere as the jar shattered and Rais leapt forward down the dock. Suddenly there was a sharp crack, the docking under Rais's boot splintered and gave way! He fell heavily, crying out with pain as his leg sank into the water. He struggled, clawing at the wet planking, trying to pull himself free. He could not.

"Bariquim! Balak! Masahum! Help me!" he cried.

"Come! Quickly!" resolved Masahum, beckoning to Balak as he turned toward Rais. He paused when Bariquim and the others did not follow.

Bariquim looked between the forms of the city's Strong Men (fast approaching), and where the Captain lay.

"No," he said firmly. "Go after him if you will. *We* are leaving."

Re'Amu watched from the darkness of the ship's side. The torches grew nearer, filling the dock like water flowing down a hillside, as they approached. There was no escape through them. He cursed under his breath. The fear of being caught and killed as an Urudu was a chill that filled his mind with dread.

Is this how I shall die? Will I perish as one surrounded by no good choice? I have no ally. Truly I am alone, he thought to himself. *Even here, at the end, I have no honor. If I flee from the Taradium I will be killed. If I stay, I will face worse. Every option is black before me.*

He was afraid. The will to survive rose within him and he looked frantically for another way. Rais was a small and dull form, scrambling to no avail in the shadows. Though Re'Amu's face twisted in disgust at the thought, he saw a way to survive. Like a desperate man drowning in the sea, he clenched the only rope he knew.

"No!" Bariquim cried suddenly. "It is Re'Amu! The traitor is escaping!!" Re'Amu fled past him even as Bariquim drew a sharp axe from his belt. Re'Amu's shadow disappeared farther down the dock and Bariquim's eyes grew wide as he saw hundreds of angry Cartegin's cutting off his escape. Their footfalls made the dock echo and the planks shake.

"Go after them if you will," Bariquim challenged Masahum again, sheathing his axe and gritting his teeth. "They can both meet their own end. *I* am in command now."

Hands ran about the *Taradium* as Bariquim climbed aboard, lowering the oars and cutting loose ropes from the dock.

Masahum cursed, looking back and forth between the Captain and the *Taradium*. Balak jumped on-board the departing ship and finally Masahum did the same.

Re'Amu sprinted down the dock, towards the fast-approaching torches, as fast as his sore legs could carry him. He came to a sliding stop. Rais squirmed while twangs and sharp thuds rang out. Arrows and stones were being loosed at the slowly departing *Taradium*. Volleys in reply whined over his head and fell among the mass of Cartegin men who rapidly advanced in their direction

"Get me out of here!" Rais begged hoarsely.

"Can I prove my loyalty to you any other way?" asked Re'Amu. "You question me, but here - when all others have left you, I alone remain."

With a heave, Re'Amu dislodged Rais and they dove into the water as several spears lodged into the jetty where they had just been.

The *Taradium* slowly pulled away. Bariquim ducked his head as stones and arrows clattered off the side of the ship.

"They have seen us!" Sapu cried. Shouts filled the air as the numbers of angry Cartegins grew.

"Row!" shouted Bariquim. The Urudu heaved at the oars. He and Masahum stood at the fore edge of the ship, pushing it away from the dock as it circled around the port and back toward open water. He ducked as the occasional arrow flew near him.

"We'll never make it around the turn! Look!" Masahum pointed ahead to where several men had run around the dock, laying a net and many planks across the ship's path. "They try to cut off our escape! Row, row!"

"We'll make it. Weapons, weapons to every man's hand!" ordered Bariquim. "Shadier, bring out the *Akukati*! And bring me a torch."

Ilishu and Ishshak paused on the jetty as the *Taradium* broke free from the dock.

"They make for the sea!" cried Ilishu.

"They'll never make it," insisted Ishshak sternly. "Cut off their escape! Bring those nets and those beams! Quickly, to the other side of the dock!"

"You men, with me!" demanded Ilishu as he bounded away. They ran around to the mouth of the jetty, cutting off the *Taradium*'s escape. Strong hands grasped spars, rope, and netting and they began to lay the barrier across the water.

"Chief Ishshak!" cried a voice, "The ship has taken captives from the wharf on-board their ship! We do not know how many."

"Urudu," growled Ishshak to himself. "They won't get away from me!"

Arrows fell among them as the Urudu returned the Cartegin's fire. Ishshak plucked one from the ground at his feet and stared at its bronze head.

"Stop them! Nets! Arrows! Stones! You men there, go assist Ilishu!" he ordered.

A heavy net was thrown across the starboard side of the ship, tangling the rower's oars. Still the ship moved slowly on, pushed by the dark men who stood in the rear. More Cartegins hoisted beams and rope, laying them across the ship's path; while others threw spears and shot arrows back at the shadowy forms aboard the mysterious ship.

Ishshak measured their progress. The dark ship had made it three quarters of the way around the harbor's bend, but nearly fifty of his men stood before the bay's exit, led by Ilishu. They were preparing to lose the main blockade of spars and beams.

"That's it!" he cried triumphantly. "Stop them! We have them!"

Ishshak's eyes were drawn to the deck of the *Taradium*. No arrows were being fired back. A single torch appeared within their shadowy midst. It seemed that two or three men heaved at a heavy object, bringing it near the fore of the ship. He saw the glint of bronze in the torchlight and then what appeared to be the yawning mouth of some great creature.

"What on earth..." muttered Ishshak.

Suddenly the net that had entrapped the *Taradium,* exploded in a wreath of flame! All on board the ship came into focus. Several dark forms stood around the flickering maw of a strange, bronze figure. What it was exactly, Ishshak could not tell. He saw sharp, curling horns and great, bronze teeth dripping with liquid fire. The Urudu were barely visible now, a barrel of their foul grog was half-empty as they poured its contents into the bronze idol. A sudden motion, the fire spewed forth again, farther this time.

All the northern dock exploded into bright flame and leapt from building to building! Raging fire abruptly towered over them! Ishshak fumbled with the ram's horn at his side and blew upon it a great blast. Answers came quickly from farther within the city as all able-men ran to the Chief's call.

Again, the Thing loosed its fiery bite. The barrier that held the *Taradium* captive from the sea, was now aflame, along with most of the surrounding dock. The sea itself flickered, as if burning. Ilishu and his men were trapped on the northern side of the quay.

"Ilishu!" he cried, seeing their peril. Grabbing a clay jar he began dousing the flames with water from the sea. Ilishu and his men did similarly, dropping their ropes and nets to quench the growing fire - but water only made the fire spread!

"It is a cursed fire! Ilishu! Ilishu!" cried Ishshak.

Ilishu and his men were forced back to the last pier as the flames grew. With a deafening crack, the mooring on which they stood gave way, collapsing into the sea. The men were lost into the flaming water.

"Pull back everything from the port to the shipyard! Create a distance between the fuel and the fire and wet everything that is not already burning!" ordered Ishshak. Hundreds of hands joined to aid! The city was roused!

"Chief, what of the ship! They are getting away!" pointed out one of the men.

The *Taradium* had reached the entrance to the harbor, its oars digging deeply as it met the swells of the sea. A dark figure, tattooed with mysterious blue lines, was looking back on them. To Ishshak it looked like the figure threw back its head and laughed before turning away.

"See to the port!" commanded Ishshak. "We can do nothing more."

Chapter Twenty-seven

Flight of the _Taradium_

Bariquim laughed with mirth as the _Taradium_ turned away from the blazing dock of Cartegin and headed into the open sea. He leaned carelessly against the curling shoulder of the Akukati, its bronze mouth and head still warm from the spewing fire and destruction it had wrought.

"Good job my lads!" he boasted. "I'd say that went just about as well as it could have." The dock of Cartegin splintered in several places and fell away, hissing as it collapsed into the sea. The fires that consumed the city lit up the night with a warm glow, but quickly grew dim behind the ships dipping oars.

"As well as it could have?" asked Masahum quizzically. He dropped his oar and rose to his feet, turning sharply on Bariquim. "What of the Captain? And Re'Amu?" Masahum's question hung heavy in the air. The rest of the crew paused. The rowing of oars ceased and the barrels of foul grog being rolled away rumbled to a halt. Everyone fell silent, looking back and forth between Masahum and Bariquim, wondering what was going to happen next.

"What of them?" Bariquim demanded. He slowly drew forth his wide axe and let it hang loosely at his side. Masahum swallowed as Sapu, Shadier, and the crew said nothing. Only Balak rose and stood behind him.

"Sit down," advised Balak into his ear. "Unless you want to get us both killed."

Bariquim smiled and spun the axe carelessly in his hand.

"I am the Captain now," he crowed, looking fiercely into the faces of the rest of the Urudu. "You will do as I command."

"Is that so, my love?" a thin voiced hissed from the dark of the cabin behind him. Bariquim spun around as if he had been bit, and stared into the darkness with wide eyes. A white face seemed to float there, ghostly

224

and terrifying. The Urudu gasped with fear.

"It is Rais!! He cannot be killed!! He is among us!" they shouted as they scrambled over each other in a panic.

Rais took a step forward into the light and Bariquim's axe lowered, a look of confusion written over his features.

"Re'Amu?" gasped Bariquim in shock as another face appeared beside Rais. Re'Amu smiled woefully at Bariquim.

"Disarm him!" ordered Re'Amu loudly to the crew, pointing at Bariquim. They hesitated, unsure of who was real and who was in command.

"NOW!" Re'Amu insisted.

There was no question who was in charge now, as the fear of Rais filled the hearts of the crew. They drew spear and dagger, surrounding Bariquim. He stumbled backward, until feeling the ship's railing. Re'Amu stood prominently beside the Captain and the crew looked toward them, awaiting instruction. Awe and shock still shone on their faces.

Bariquim held his axe high and looked back and forth between the stony eyes of the Urudu, licking his lips nervously.

"Are you going to kill him?" asked Re'Amu. Rais stepped down from the railing, somewhat limping. Cracks ran through the fresh pigment on his face, as it dried.

"No," Rais said loudly. "He would kill me, I have no doubt, given the chance. No, he is ready for something else."

"Ready for what?" Sapu whined.

"Ready for promotion," Rais said with a smile. "He can do no more with me. He is ready for a ship of his own. Drop your axe, Bariquim! Do it now and you will sail with us as far as Angfar. Then, you will choose some to come with you and can depart from me forever."

Bariquim chuckled, a slow smile revealing itself on his features. He flipped his axe and sank it forcefully into the timbers of the *Taradium*.

"Very well, Rais. You win this time." He folded his large arms tightly across his chest.

"Bring up the slaves and lash them tightly to the oars! We go north!" ordered Rais.

The Akukati was covered with a lightly oiled cloth and placed back within the cabin of the *Taradium*. One by one, the former members of *The Anchton* were dragged up from below and lashed together. Bariquim watched over them relentlessly. His axe remained buried in the deck. He brandished a whip in its place. He showed his pleasure by flaying the skin from the slaves' backs. They pulled on the oars and the *Taradium* ran away northward through the dark waters of the night.

Chapter Twenty-eight

<u>The Breaking of the Altar</u>

Bahira was silent, as were the remainder of the captives. The night grew late, but no one seemed to notice. The hissing mist of the Oodan crags filled the silence.

"So much has happened," Eli'ssa wondered aloud. "So many people, interwoven like the thread on the loom. Oh, the final cloth! What shape will it take? What choices will each make?"

"There is much we do not know. Why did this man Re'Amu show you such kindness? Who is he? Why does he sail with the Urudu?" Guzzier pondered. He sat riveted, the events of Bahira's journey coming together in his mind.

Bahira shook her head. She did not know Re'Amu's story. She did not have the answers.

"Surely this man, and many others, have choices before them. Only the powers of heaven know where they will lead," Shukiera said softly.

"Perhaps here," whispered one of the captives.

"It is by looking back and coming to terms with the journey of our past, that allows us to move confidently into the future," Guzzier reflected solemnly. He looked at the faces around him. "Let us learn here from our precious Bahira, one of our own, to have strength, even when no strength remains. So she has done, and so will we."

When the sudden light of morning finally came, the few that remained on the high crags of Oodan stood obediently before Guzzier and Shukiera.

"Well, now what is left for us?" Bahira asked.

"We stay here, paralyzed by fear, until we are weak from hunger and thirst and we die," Shukiera answered bluntly. "Or we die trying to claim from the pools that which we came for."

"There must be a way," Eli'ssa wondered. "A diversion, a gathering at night..."

Guzzier shook his head at each suggestion.

"We have tried everything, over the years," Shukiera murmured. "The S'acar are many, and clever. They will not let us near their pools any longer."

"I am tired of taking what is theirs!" Guzzier cried. "If I am to die upon these crags, I will not do so as a slave of Angfar, hunting for what they seek."

The mist above his head cleared as he spoke, revealing blue sky.

"Then let us escape this place," Bahira resolved.

"There is no way," Shukiera replied. "Back is the only path, and Z'gelsh is true to his word. They will kill us if we return empty handed. We have seen it."

"What of the north?" Eli'ssa asked. "The gaps between each high ledge is small, you and Kah-Mel jumped them yesterday. How far do these mountains stretch on?"

"I do not know if there is an end," answered Guzzier, hesitantly. "Some of them are not passable, but we have journeyed less than a day north."

"Oh, then let us go as far as we may!" Eli'ssa cried. "If there is no return for us, what is the harm?"

"We will be in the open, the S'acar will not let us pass," reminded Shukiera.

"We do not have what they want," Guzzier whispered. "They may let us, if we stay far from them."

"It is worth a try," Bahira suggested. The others nodded. Their faces were set. Guzzier stood to his feet and his face changed from sadness to wild determination.

"Then let us take all that we can carry. As much rope as we have! Cut it free from the rocks and coil it - we will need it! We go where no one has ever walked, and we will most likely meet our end!"

They went about the tasks quickly, using shards of rock to cut free as many of the ropes as they could. By mid-morning they regathered.

"Everyone, follow my lead," Guzzier requested. "Make no quick motions or loud noises. The S'acar must not see us as a threat."

Slowly they departed from the boulder field. Guzzier led them a different way, instead of coming out upon the edge of the mysterious pool they appeared some distance to its side. The edge of the cliff face was near them. The drop made Bahira's stomach turn. Far, far below, boulders the size of cities could be seen resting in the shadows of the cliffs.

The S'acar had not left the pool. Many crowded around it. Others came up from its surface, shaking shining droplets from their plumage.

When the S'acar saw them, their feathers rose and many ran to the side of the pool, crying out in shrill voices. Guzzier made no motion toward them, and they stopped, not willing to leave their guarded treasure. They hissed, revealing long, forked tongues.

"Everyone stay here," Guzzier whispered. He picked up a long coil of rope and continued alone, slowly stepping around the outer edge of the plateau until he came to a spot where the gap lessoned. The S'acar were less than a stone's throw away. He bent and secured one end of the rope around a large boulder. He rose carefully, the other end still in his hand. Then he turned and ran for the edge as fast as he could, jumping over its great gap with a mighty spring! He landed hard, clawing at the rock on the other side as he struggled to pull himself to safety.

The S'acar screamed and several took to the air by diving off the cliff's edge. They circled around, cutting him off from the pool that lay upon the plateau he had stormed. Guzzier lay unmoving as if dead, waiting. The S'acar drew back to their ceaseless perimeter. Guzzier slowly rose, tying off the rope and beckoning to Shukiera. She led the rest toward the edge.

One by one they scaled the heart-pounding gap. Hand over hand they pulled themselves across to Guzzier. Shukiera came last. Guzzier pulled her up from the edge and they all huddled together.

"Well. No eggs for breakfast... but perhaps we won't get eaten ourselves," Guzzier joked with a small smile. "Let's see how far we can get today. Our biggest enemy will be our thirst. We will not be allowed near any water up here."

They were out of water by the afternoon. Still they pressed on. They crossed eighteen gaps that day, before coming upon a lone mountain amid the plateau. Its top was not as level and a S'acar pool did not fill its contours.

"We will not find a better place to rest tonight," Guzzier said. "The S'acar will not disturb us here. The winds will be cold, summer wains in the flatlands. As hot as it is during the day here, it will be twice as cold at night. We will need to huddle together for warmth."

An alcove provided small shelter from the unceasing wind of the night. The dark was cold, biting at their faces like a ghoul, snatching away all the heat it touched to fill its emptiness. By the time the warm sun of morning cascaded over Bahira and Eli'ssa, freeing them from the war of the night, they could not feel their toes or fingers. The sun was a hand's width above the horizon before the group thawed and could begin to travel. By that time over again, they were hot and covered in sweat. The Red Mountains seemed unending.

The pools of the S'acar appeared intermittently, but lessened as they crossed increasingly more gaps. The plateau surfaces became smaller, and the gaps between the islands - though more frequent, were easier to cross. Large crystals appeared, hidden in the shadows of rocky slopes, their hexagonal shapes growing out of the ground. They grew, each larger than the last. Finally, the group halted at a single crystal that rose higher than Guzzier could stand.

He examined it closely, walking the crystal's perimeter. The gem appeared red near its root, where it grew from the rock, and became clear near its top. Heat and steam poured out from small fissures at its base.

"What is it?" Eli'ssa asked.

"It is a moon crystal," Guzzier replied in awe. "I have never before seen a gem this size! They are sacred to my people." He tapped it lightly with his finger. It rang clear, like a bell, humming as the vibration ran through it. He looked at the other ones, growing from the slopes around them in clusters. It was hard and cold under his hand, despite the heat of the sun.

"It is beautiful," Bahira breathed.

"Perhaps it will melt and turn into water," Eli'ssa said longingly.

Guzzier licked his dry lips and began whistling his all-to-common tune, dragging his hand over the crystal's smooth surface.

"High above the fortress' reach, above the mountains and the keep

There the altar of El'Perran, risen high of stone and crystal sands.

Egal-Mah, the Lord of Old, touched the floor of red and gold

S'acar came forth, bound no more, to the dust which was his home..."

His whistle rose and fell and the crystal vibrated softly. Guzzier smiled as his tune died, placing his hand flat upon the clear stone. But, the sound of his tune reverberated, growing more and more amplified. The crystal vibrated under his hand, echoing his notes across the land! Suddenly, the gem shattered!

Guzzier and the others jumped back as the steam and heat around the crystal's base, rocketed into the sky. A deep rumbling came from within the earth and the platform on which they stood shook.

"Guzzier!" Shukiera yelled, "What did you do? What is happening?"

Guzzier did not move but looked quickly at the earth around them. The stones began shaking as the rumble increased. Then, with terrifying slowness, the mountain on which they stood began to fall.

The captives tumbled to their knees.

"Guzzier!!" Shukiera cried.

Stones rolled past them as the incline they traversed suddenly shifted directions. Boulders rumbled off the edge and tumbled into the abyss, deathly quiet until they dimly crashed far below.

"Ahead! Ahead!" Guzzier yelled. There, across a small gap, was another plateau of red stone that their massif of rock was sinking towards. They ran for it, jumping even as the stone fell away under their feet. They rolled to a halt and small, red stones bounced around them. Dust rose from the gorges on either side. Suddenly the massive finger of stone across from them trembled and began falling. On the other side, the mesas quivered and began tumbling downward.

Like a giant ripple, the high hills about them all began tilting, crashing into those nearest and sending them plummeting as well. It was like being caught in an avalanche of stone! The mountains roared. The sound of cracking rent the air and the earth quaked.

Guzzier pulled Shukiera to her feet with a wild look in his eyes! He ran, half dragging, half carrying her, and he laughed in absurd desperation.

"Ha-Ha! Run!" he cried in a booming voice. "We will fly like the S'acar across the mountains and then death will take us! What stories they would tell if only they knew - this was how Guzzier would meet his end!!"

In a frenzy, they leapt across the colossal stones even as the mesas fell away, careening along their tops in an endless race. Their breath was ragged in their lungs and their eyes full of rising dust. Eli'ssa and Bahira struggled to stay behind Guzzier. Others disappeared, the stones crumbling under their feet, and they were lost.

A final highland of stone appeared, separated from them by a long fissure. Its base was wide, unlike the mountains which fell on every side. Guzzier grabbed Shukiera, and with a mighty leap, cleared the gap. Eli'ssa and Bahira followed! For a heartbeat, there was nothing except the freedom of the air whistling through their hair as the highlands crashed away behind them. Then they hit hard earth and tumbled to a stop.

Like water flowing against a stone, the final mesa crashed against the mountain and fell aside with a roar to the earth far below. Eli'ssa struggled to sit up and looked around. They were at the edge of a steep shelf, still high above the rest of the land. Far away, some of the distant mountains trembled and rocks fell from them, but the earth under their feet was solid. Where the vast expanse of tall mesas and precarious stone-tops had been, there was now emptiness and heaps of rubble far below. Dust clouded the sky as far as she could see.

Bahira lay nearby. Large stones lay about her unmoving form. A pile of rocks shook as Guzzier pushed them off, appearing out of the rubble. Underneath him was the unconscious form of Shukiera. Blood ran down her eyebrow, but she was breathing. Guzzier pulled her free, laying her gently on the stone before crawling over to Bahira. He examined her closely and his face looked grave. He looked around. They were alone.

Eli'ssa slid towards them, both of her legs throbbing in pain.

Guzzier stood and hobbled over, pulling Eli'ssa up until he carried her.

He laid her down near to Shukiera. Bahira lay just out of reach.

"Oh, Bahira! Are you alright? Talk to me!" Eli'ssa cried. Bahira did not answer. Guzzier held Eli'ssa, wrapping her in his strong embrace as she groped in the direction of Bahira's limp form.

"Peace, Eli'ssa," he whispered. "Her hurt is deep. Touching her will only make it worse. I cannot mend her."

"I will not leave her," Eli'ssa sobbed. "We have been through so much together. We can make it through this. We must!"

Guzzier held her close and looked around. The rock on which they lay was a lighter color than they had seen before. It looked older, somehow, than the rest of the mountains. Sharp crystals grew in thick clusters all around, rooted deeply into the stone. Jagged slabs of granite appeared out of the surface here and there.

"This is far deeper into the mountains than I have ever heard of someone traveling," he mused. "*Slabs of crystal sand...*" he murmured. Guzzier stood and limped nearer to a granite slab, running his hand across it. Several of the tall, flat stones hemmed in where they stood, like pieces of an enormous wall. A small path led through them and Guzzier approached the gap slowly.

As he drew near, a piece of granite trembled, as if alive. The earth shook and Guzzier fell back. The slab unfolded, revealing a creature that towered above Guzzier, four times larger than the height of a man. A thick body of stone appeared, along with a head of few facial features. Its arms were crossed and strange symbols covered it from head to toe, engraved upon its rocky skin. The blue flowers of the mountains dotted it, swaying gently as their peaceful rest was disturbed. Granite crystals sparkled as the creature looked over them with blank eyes. It slowed as it drew to its full height and came to a halt.

Guzzier scrambled away until he stood in front of Eli'ssa and Shukiera. They held their breath. The clattering stones, disturbed by the giant's appearance, rolled to a halt. Soon it appeared the creature was not moving any farther.

"Guzzier, what is that? Is it alive?" Eli'ssa whispered.

Guzzier shook his head and swallowed.

"I do not know, Eli'ssa," he murmured. "There is no other way out of here but forward."

He slowly approached again. The thing did not move. Guzzier walked between its legs and around it, looking up at the granite giant in awe.

"It is as if a statue rose to life and just as quickly fell back into slumber," he remarked in amazement.

Even as he spoke the head of the creature straightened. With pounding footfalls, it stepped over Guzzier. Reaching out it grasped Bahira who lay unmoving. Her still form disappeared in the enormous hand of stone. It turned, approaching Eli'ssa and Shukiera.

"Guzzier!! Guzzier!!" Eli'ssa cried out in fear as the hand scooped up her and Shukiera, carving away the slab on which they sat. The whole of the rock's surface rose into the air as easily as one might lift a grain of wheat.

Guzzier darted underneath the giant, striking its legs with all his strength. It was like attacking a wall of stone. He cried out in pain as his hands bounced off the impenetrable surface. The creature paid Guzzier no heed. It turned and stepped over the stone slabs of granite and disappeared.

Guzzier turned and ran in pursuit, through the narrow opening. On the other side, many crystals grew, higher and thicker than before, casting a marvelous pattern of light across the ground from the evening sky.

The creature of granite was waiting for him. As Guzzier ran near, several other giants stood, rumbling as they appeared. Guzzier's heart beat violently as five and then six of the rock creatures towered around him - where he had seen only a granite slab before. They stood still, unmoving for a breath of time before turning and walking slowly away.

Guzzier ran after them, sprinting to keep up with their massive strides. Yet, every time he fell behind, the creatures paused, waiting for him. He cried out to them in the common tongue and in the native tongue of El-Loz, but the granite giants were silent. They continued into the night. Still he pursued them until the crystal and red rock around him became so dense he could not pass, though the giants continued with ease.

Darkness had overtaken the sky and the crystals gave off a strange white light, as though they captured the light of the stars and magnified their glow. Guzzier panted, his mouth parched and dry. He looked about. He could not go any farther through the gemstones. The granite giants stepped over the barrier that refrained Guzzier and disappeared.

With a rumble, the last giant came to a stop above him. Its eyes were of cold stone and did not look as if they could see. Yet, the being reached down for him. Guzzier grit his teeth and let himself be taken. The hand of stone around him was firm, and spaces enough for him to see (but not fall through), appeared between the giant's fingers. The ground fell away beneath him and he saw fields of crystals, stretching up and over the rocky terrain in the distance.

The night passed, the stars wheeled overhead and the wind swirled about them. The stone of the giant's hand was strangely warm, like a rock in the early morning sun. Guzzier fought as sleep began to overtake him, straining to keep his eyes fixed on the two stone beings who held Bahira, Shukiera and Eli'ssa. Gradually, he yielded to the relentless assault of fatigue and drifted into slumber.

Chapter Twenty-nine

Servants and Sages of Cartegin

arly morning found the city of Cartegin in a thick layer of smog. Smoke still rose from the port and weary hands continued to beat at small pockets of flame. Ishshak and Ilishu rested on the hill near the shipyard, surveying the blackened harbor below them. Ilishu, though damp, was alive. Only a few burns, the black soot over his face, and his shorter, singed beard showed his narrow escape with the fire.

"Well, it is over," sighed Ishshak wearily.

"There has been much loss," remarked Ilishu. "We need a final count, but I know at least six of my men are missing."

"It has been an ill-fated night!! What law have I broken to deserve such a curse?"

Ilishu was silent for a time.

"I wonder if we cannot change some of this into our gain."

Ishshak raised a tired eyebrow. "I am too weary to think of what you mean, Ilishu. Speak plainly!"

Ilishu nodded toward the shipyard. "Birsha's son Berran and his daughter Bahira are among the missing. Some say they were seen being taken aboard the Urudu ship."

"He will take it grievously when we tell him!" cried Ishshak. "Could the morning light bring with it worse tidings? Curse the Urudu and their ways."

"The Urudu are a fleeting enemy," reflected Ilishu slowly. "Here today, gone for ten years. We can do nothing about them. Agade, however, is our continual trouble. And Birsha will not openly work with us against them."

Ishshak pursed his lips, thinking. "Perhaps if Agade were behind this attack..."

"Perhaps Agade really is behind this attack," murmured Ilishu. "Did not the youth speak of Agade and the Urudu in the same breath last

233

night, when this threat was first discovered? It seems reasonable for me to believe. Should Birsha believe it also, we would find him united to our cause with fresh fervor. Cartegin as a whole would be ready to rise and strike at Agade. He would make the rest of the fleet ready for war."

Ishshak's eyes hardened with determination. He gazed around him at the destruction of his city and grief was evident upon his face.

"I will do anything to be free of the shadow of that forbearing land. Curse the Urudu and curse Agade. Our people have once again died without cause. We are weak. It is time we made a purpose for ourselves."

Areoch and Meshêk were among the workers at the port, singed and covered with soot and grime as they struggled to salvage what they could from the charred timbers. Many others worked with them. Wails broke out as the people uncovered a still form here, or came across the ruins of a structure there.

Chaos had reigned when they first arrived, and as the morning dawned, the full amount of damage could be seen. The port was destroyed.

"The shipyard is safe, it seems" Meshêk reflected, startling Birsha as he rested against a blackened mooring post. A light wind blew from above, clearing a path through the mist so that the mighty fence of the shipyard was visible. The sea was left shrouded in morning fog.

"Yes, by some miracle" mused Birsha. "I wonder if that was not the original intent of the attack, which failed? Rumors fly this morning and it seems everyone has a different story. What now? The port is ruined. I felt overwhelmed by the task in front of me before this happened. Now we are far behind."

"You overwhelm only yourself," Meshêk reprimanded softly. "There is no law stating you must stay away from your home from early morning to dusk to finish a task in months, that should take years to complete! Ishshak pushes you too far."

"Ishshak does not push me any more than I allow. We have spent years on this mission already," reminded Birsha. "Our people must be able to trade on the open sea. It is our hope. My sacrifice is one that must continue."

Meshêk shook his head, refusing to go further into an argument they had many times. "You may realize, too late, what is worth sacrificing and what is not, Birsha," said Meshêk.

"I am too weary for our usual debate this morning, Meshêk," Birsha sighed, rising. "Ishshak will have a meeting in the shipyard an hour from now, and he will tell all the truth of what has happened."

"The truth? That is hard to see after so short a time."

Birsha waved his hand as if warding off Meshêk's comment and departed without another word.

Areoch picked his way through the charred rubble, until he worked alongside Meshêk.

"Of all the faces I have seen working here, I have yet to see that of Bahira's," Areoch said hoarsely, looking around him.

"Nor that of Berran's," agreed Meshêk with a frown. "I too have been looking for them. Do not worry yet, they are likely at their home. Birsha just informed me that Ishshak holds a council in the shipyard. We will go, find out more, and learn what will follow."

Less than an hour later, Meshêk and Areoch left the port, traveling up the hill, until they met the tall, wooden fence. Areoch stood with his mouth agape as he passed by the wooden structure for the first time.

Behind it, suspended between platforms of pressed brick and wooden tiers, were the skeletons of immense ships. Two decks tall, they stood amidships nearly twenty feet deep from rail to floor. A single beam of wood, curved to give the ship more depth, stretched across their bottom. Areoch thought he saw the glint of bronze or gold shining out from below the water line on the nearest ship's prow, but a rough covering of fabric was draped over it, preventing him from seeing clearly.

At least six of the great ships could be seen in the shipyard, though there appeared to be more. The farthest one from him had little more than a skeleton of boards, while the nearest ship looked to be water-tight. All around him men would have been hewing at the remains of great, massive logs, shaping and bending planks, pouring and raising bitumen tar, pitch, and bees-wax in buckets. But, the ships were not the concern of the morning. Men continually streamed between the port and the shipyard, carrying fresh mooring posts and docking planks, as the small army of workers directed their attention to the damaged port.

Ishshak, Ilishu, and Birsha stood near the shipyard's center and several others crowded around them in a tight circle. At least thirty prominent households of the city were represented before Ishshak began speaking.

"There has been much loss this night and much death," he began solemnly. Ilishu nodded beside him, looking every bit like the city's champion. His armbands shone under the soot, catching the morning light.

"We still do not know the full extent of the damage nor all those who are missing, so I will be brief. Most of you do not know how this has come about, so I must tell at least some of the story:

'Yesterday morning a strange occurrence happened in the household of Cyril, master of Cartegin's southern fields. Most of you know him well. He discovered a boy, a foreigner, who appeared of southern origin, near death in his field. This boy was brought to me and during much of the day my healers struggled to keep him alive."

"You should have called upon my house! My healer is the best in

Cartegin!" interrupted Birsha.

"Many things could have been different. It was all sudden and nothing can be changed now," said Ishshak. "We did what we could for the boy and near nightfall I discerned from him there was some danger in the port. He mentioned the name *Urudu* and with it the name *Agade* before he passed beyond the skill of any healer. He is now dead."

Several there yelled out exclamations of surprise.

"Urudu!" cried Nansi, the mistress of the port. "How did such a boy come to be in Cyril's field?"

"Was he a captive or an Urudu himself?"

"What do they have to do with Agade?"

"Surely the Urudu are the enemies of everyone!"

"Listen, listen!" Ishshak cried as the circle erupted into a sudden chatter. "What is sure anymore, these days?" He looked slowly in Birsha's direction. "With the bones in my beard, at least this is clear: we were attacked last night by a dark ship that harbored briefly here. This ship had no name, and it sailed from Agade. We challenged it and fire was set to our port. And, it was by no accident.

'I will tell you all what I fear: I fear that the Urudu and Agade have some dark alliance. Some of you know what I have discussed with Birsha regarding these ships here." He gestured around the port as his words settled in. "Of using them directly against Agade. What if instead of being designed for the speed of trade they were made for the strength of war? There is nothing I can be sure of. My guess is that Agade discovered my thoughts by some devilry and they have struck us in an attempt to destroy what could be their demise."

"This is black news. I expected it was no more than some ill misfortune which caused the flame," Birsha exclaimed with furrowed brows. His gaze fell to the ground. Then suddenly his eyes rose and settled on Areoch. His face darkened.

"To say we were directly attacked by Agade... That is to go too far," interjected Meshêk from the back of the group.

"Agade's reach has grown, Meshêk, servant of Birsha," said Ilishu. "They have discovered our plans and partnered with the Urudu to destroy us! They have burned our city! Birsha you must reconsider your initial course of action: trading through Agade will not last, if it works at all. It will come to war. It *has* come to war! We *must* be ready for it."

Ishshak stared hard at Birsha who remained silent, his face downcast.

"The fire was a planned attack," Ilishu continued. "We made for the port as soon as we learned of the Urudu and there was indeed a strange ship here. It pulled off at our arrival and attacked us as we tried to stop its departure."

"This is true," agreed Ishshak. "I myself saw the fire spew forth from the ship. It was as if some terrible beast was aboard that released chaos and wreckage."

"A beast?" asked Meshêk. "That is most interesting. It does not sound to me like a planned attack. They were in port before you arrived, and yet no damage had been done? Why would they wait for all the Strong Men to arrive before initiating a planned attack?"

Darts flew from Ishshak's eyes as he looked at Meshêk.

"You were not there, servant of Birsha. It would be wise to hold your tongue," he snapped. Looking at Birsha, he spoke earnestly. "Nine from my household were lost last night in the flames, Birsha. One more from the Yegesh household drowned in the waters during the dock's collapse. And, two are missing. They are of your kin: Berran and Bahira. They are not to be found. Agade, it seems, has struck you personally."

Birsha's face flushed as white as a shell. His knees buckled where he stood and it looked for a moment that he might fall. Birsha clutched desperately at Meshêk, shaking his head in a blinded disbelief.

"No. No," he begged.

"Steady, friend. Easy, breathe," Meshêk whispered.

Birsha finally sobbed, his voice choking in a hoarse whisper. "Why has this happened to me? Where are they? Have they been killed?"

"We do not know, Birsha," said Ilishu. "Some at the port say they saw one of the Urudu take Berran upon the dark ship by force. Bahira was with him, and they took her as well. How they knew of your family, I cannot guess. Agade's reach is truly further than we imagined. I fear they are lost. What now will you do?"

Birsha held himself on Meshêk's shoulder, stunned by the news. His eyes, red with exhaustion and tears, scanned the faces in the crowd, as if searching for an answer. Suddenly, Birsha saw Areoch! His mouth was open in unspoken distress at the back of the crowd. Birsha's grip on Meshêk tightened. In an instant, Birsha's face changed, setting like a stone in rage and accusation. Meshêk opened his mouth to speak, but Birsha silenced him with a gesture.

"Some things, at least, have become suddenly clear to me," Birsha's voice quivered, barely containing the emotion he felt.

"I have been a fool, Ishshak, and it seems I have brought this disaster upon myself." Birsha composed himself and turned to Ishshak, speaking forcefully. "How, you ask, could Agade have known about our plan? How could they have known about my family?? I have an answer for you. Seize that man there!" Birsha cried, pointing at Areoch. "Bind him and bring him forward!"

"Birsha, no! You do not see clearly," cried Meshêk jumping forward. Birsha ignored him. Ilishu pushed Meshêk aside as several men fetched rope, binding Areoch's hands tightly. They knocked him down and dragged him through the mud by his wrists to the fore of the group.

"What does this man from Magen have to do in this matter?" inquired

Ishshak, looking in surprise at Areoch.

"He is not from Magen!" shouted Birsha. "I have deceived you, to my own ruin! We found him wounded upon our road home and we took him in. He is from *Agade*!" Birsha choked out the words. A gasp erupted from the crowd. "I see now it was his plan all along: to join our caravan, deceive us, and plot our destruction. I did not tell you at first," Birsha admitted, "for fear of what you might do to him, but now I care little. Question him as you will! I will be here." There was finality in his voice, "At least in my ruin, I will strike hard back at Agade. You will have your way, Ishshak! I will not cease until these boats are equipped for battle. Then you will have your war."

"No, my lord Birsha!" cried Areoch. "Please! You do not understand. I would die before I caused hurt to your family! Agade has nothing to do with the Urudu! You must believe me!"

Birsha gave Areoch a long, cold stare before turning aside to his own grief.

"Take him away!" commanded Ishshak.

"Meshêk! Help me! Help me!" Meshêk did nothing. Areoch was hauled violently up the road, towards Ishshak's palace, by Ilishu and several others.

"I am sorry," consoled Ishshak, pausing in front of Birsha as he prepared to follow the group up the hill, "for the loss of your family. It appears we had a snake in our midst. You did right in telling me. Together we will rebuild and avenge your kin." Ishshak's words brought a strange sense of comfort and clarity of purpose for Birsha.

Meshêk thought swiftly. "Chief Ishshak," he said, stopping the chief as he began to depart, "did you not say Berran and Bahira were *taken* and not killed? Perhaps then there is still some small hope." He turned and faced Birsha.

"Birsha, should we give up so quickly? Allow me to take *The Alalia* and give swift pursuit!" he gestured to the single completed ship in the yard. "My bond to you and your family lies with Berran. Is it not right that I should follow him? Let Ishshak stock her with supplies, and let me gather a crew."

"It is hopeless to pursue," interrupted Ishshak. "The dark ship turned north, it could head anywhere. The waters north of here are not charted and there are none among us who know them. They are a maze of islands and currents! We would be wasting the only completed ship we have!"

"Strange, for an Agadian ship to continue north," remarked Meshêk pointedly. "Regardless, would this not be a small sacrifice for the chance to save Birsha's family? And you are wrong in your assumption, Ishshak. I know those waters, for it is from there Birsha and I originally came many years ago. With me there is hope. Send me," he requested, looking earnestly at Birsha.

"You?" asked Ishshak with a sharp laugh. "How is it that you would lead such an expedition? Such a thing would be for trained warriors, not old household servants."

Meshêk paid Ishshak's question no heed and waited for Birsha.

Birsha did not raise his eyes. His head was downcast.

"Hope? What is hope, Meshêk? I have none." Grief overwhelmed his heart, "You have failed me. All is lost, despite my toils. Go! Find my children, if you can, or strike vengeance upon those who have caused me such pain. You are free from the burden of service to me. I do not know why you stayed anyway."

Ishshak opened his mouth and then closed it again. He grew red in the face.

"So be it," he said with effort. "You should depart quickly. Every hour lessens your success."

Meshêk nodded. Ishshak turned away and stomped up the hill. Birsha remained, standing limp, lacking hope. Meshêk put his arm around him.

"I stayed, not because of my promise to you, all those years ago, but because I cared for a good friend," Meshêk explained softly. "I gave my word, which I will not break. We are accountable for each syllable we utter, for they have power."

Birsha sighed.

"I feel like I am drowning, Meshêk. Leave me to my anger and spare me no more words. Go and do as you will. Come back with my children or come back not at all."

The rest of the day passed for Areoch like a thick fog. He was dragged up the hill and thrown into a small, dark room somewhere in Ishshak's complex.

"Ishshak will entertain you tonight, *Agadian*," spat Ilishu. "He takes his time. You will wish you had never heard the name Cartegin."

Ilishu slammed the door, leaving Areoch sitting on a rough, cold stone floor. He sat there and wept, the tears stinging his tired eyes. He wept for Bahira and for himself. He could not save her.

"Who is there?" asked a weak voice through the darkness.

Areoch started and looked about him. All was imperceptible. The bounds around his feet had loosened and he was able to stand. Peering into the shadows, his eyes adjusted. He saw a small, square room. There were no windows and the rock from which the cell was hewn was rough cut and uncomfortable for him to stand on. A small bench of smoother stone lay near the far wall and Areoch dimly saw straw strewn across it and the floor. A small figure propped itself up on one elbow and stared toward Areoch.

"Who are you? Where am I?" the scared voice asked again, and Areoch realized the voice belonged to a young boy.

"I am not here to hurt you," assured Areoch, raising his bound hands so the boy might see them. Areoch approached him slowly and knelt beside the shelf. The boy had a thick bandage wrapped around his right arm and chest. The arm hung useless beside him.

"I am Areoch of... Magen," he hesitated. "Do not be afraid. I do not mean to hurt you. You are in the city of Cartegin."

"Cartegin," whispered the boy with a sigh of relief, falling back. "Father! Father, if only you could be here! We made it."

"Who...who are you?" stammered Areoch.

"My name is Joshur of Anshan," explained the boy, as tears welled up in his eyes, "and for the past many days my family has desperately sought this city. They were... They were taken."

Areoch's eyes opened wide. "You were the boy they found in the southern fields!" he cried. "Why... How are you alive? Ishshak told us you were dead!" He stood to his feet and paced the small room, his mind racing. "You must tell me your story," said Areoch, coming back to the boy's side. "For I fear we are both held wrongly as captives. How did you come here?"

For the next several hours, Joshur told Areoch all that happened aboard *The Anchton* and the long seduction of the Urudu and the *Taradium*. He told, with many tears, the tale of his father's last moments and his long flight through the dark Asur forest; until his memory failed in the early morning, when he collapsed as Cartegin came into view.

Areoch sat back, astounded as the youth finished his tale.

"Surely, you deserve these armbands more than I do, Joshur of Kassu's household! I am familiar with the Sahhu Inlet. You do your father honor, for you were injured and ran more than twenty miles in the few hours of morning. It is no wonder you were near death!

'Alas, though, for you were too late. The Urudu ship you speak of was the one which set fire to the city last night. Agade had little to do with the matter, as Ishshak no doubt knew! He desired only to turn Birsha against me." His fists clenched as he spoke.

"Ishshak?" asked Joshur.

"He is the chief of this city, and he is not in his right mind. He befriends the strong to his own cause, and slays those he has no use for. He told the city leaders you were dead - even as I stood among them! What that means regarding his intentions for you, I can only guess. You and I are in danger, Joshur. We must get out of here."

Areoch stood and pushed at the stones around him. They did not budge, there were no weak points. After searching briefly through the cell, he came back and sat, exasperated.

"Is there no way out of here?"

At that moment there was a great rending of wood! The blast sent the straw smoldering into the corners! Light streamed in from a gaping hole where the door had stood moments earlier. Shards of wood landed around Areoch and he cast himself down by Joshur, covering his eyes with his hands. A shadow in the door blocked the light.

"Meshêk!" The recognition surprised him, "What are you doing here?"

Meshêk stepped in through what remained of the door and several other figures entered behind him.

"A better question, young Areoch, is *where are we going.*" Several hands lifted him to his feet and Areoch found his bonds being cut. He was helped through the door.

"Joshur, we cannot leave Joshur," said Areoch breathlessly. Meshêk had already given orders, several men gently lifted Joshur and carried him out of the cell. Areoch looked in shock at the familiar faces of Birsha's household, unfamiliarly armed with flint and stone weapons. On either side of the doorway, lay the guards, unconscious. Upon arriving outside, Areoch took a deep breath of freedom. The sun was shadowed by dark clouds, it was late in the evening.

"How..." began Areoch, but Meshêk cut him off.

"The full story must wait," he chided. "We must make it down to the port undetected. Tor'i, Shil'de, quickly," he ordered the two men next to him, "put them in the sacks. Both of you, be quiet and still."

The last thing Areoch saw was Meshêk, shouldering a heavy sack of grain, before he was stuffed into a coarse sack and hoisted up in a similar way behind the back of Tor'i. Joshur cried out briefly in pain and then was silent.

Suddenly, voices seemed to grow louder from above them, as though many people had entered a room to continue an earnest conversation.

"Did you not feel that sudden shaking?"

"Do not try and change the subject when I speak to you, or you will feel my hand! You are sure, he will be asleep for several days?" the clear voice of Ilishu floated down to them.

"I gave him a strong mixture. He will not wake for many days, and we placed him out of sight in the lower cellar," mumbled the unmistakable voice of Cärmi.

"The lower cellar?! You fool! That is where we placed the Agadian. Why did you not speak about this earlier? You were told to place him in the lower chambers!"

Cärmi cried out as the sound of a cuffing drifted out of the window. "We will need to check on him. Quickly, send some men before the Agadian can do any more damage. Who knows what he has done to the boy since we put him there... maybe it will save us the need to kill him..." The voices trailed off.

Meshêk looked around. They stood under the rear wall of Ishshak's palace. The broad window over their heads led into Ishshak's main hall.

The port was below them. The hill ahead fell away steeply and the descent looked to be impassible. Meshêk gestured the men with him to be quick and silent, as he led them near the brink. A small path appeared, zigzagging its way down the hillside.

Chapter Thirty

The Pursuit

Laborers cleared a path through the port's wreckage, and now *The Alalia* floated like a gem among burnt chaff; its double-decked hull glistened off the smooth water. Oars stood stiff from its middle deck, the first ship of its kind to hold rowers within the hull. Birsha's key design glinted subtly in the evening light. A bronze ram, nearly four feet long and two feet wide, attached to the prow of the ship under the surface of the water. The smiths had toiled long to forge a solid piece from nearly every scrap of bronze Cartegin possessed! Thunder-bolts were engraved upon its surface.

Even with its weight and a full stock of supplies, the ship rested easy in the water. Meshêk and his men hurried aboard, carrying their sacks of supplies below deck.

Birsha met Meshêk, standing on a temporarily repaired section of dock, as they boarded. His face was calmer than it had been earlier.

"Are you sure of this, Meshêk? Even with the men from my household and those that have volunteered, there are not enough to pull even half the oars."

"We will try anyway, Birsha. Trust me, as you always have," Meshêk said with a small chuckle.

"You were right, you know. I have been blind to what is most valuable and so it has been taken from me. How cruel is the bite of fate! We should never have taken that Agadian in."

"Do not give up hope yet!" cried Meshêk, even as he hurried to untie *The Alalia's* final ropes. "We see a moment in time. It is easy to look back in regret when you cannot see the future. Understanding comes with wisdom, and wisdom comes with patience. Do not give up hope!"

Meshêk jumped on-board as several oars pushed the ship farther out into the bay. Birsha raised a hand in farewell. Even as he did so a sharp-horn call rang out from Ishshak's palace and many shouts echoed down the hill.

"It seems something is amiss, should you wait to depart?" shouted Birsha over the water.

Meshêk smiled back at him. "We cannot wait, my old friend. We have had many adventures together! Farewell, should we meet again. Hang onto hope!"

His call drifted back across the calm sea as the ship's large sail was raised and *The Alalia* caught the wind. She cut through the waves, with her prow pointed into the north.

Areoch rolled out of his sack as he was tossed onto several other bags and jars of grain. He did not see Joshur. Areoch realized that he had somehow fallen asleep in his bag, and he must have been left in peace to stem his weariness. He stood, rubbing his stiff and sore limbs. His head cracked forcefully on a solid, low ceiling and he toppled over. It took him another try to find his balance. It was dark, and the sound of gurgling waves seemed to echo through to his toes. A wooden hatch suddenly opened above him, and a pair of strong, rough hands reached down to help him scramble up.

He found himself on a low deck, which was both long and wide. Hammocks swung at the stern and prow, while the backs of twenty rowers pulled at oars between. The rowers sat a hair above the water line, and the deck looked as if it could be fitted to have at least ten more men rowing. Thin planks ran above his head. Below those ran three thick cords of woven raw-hide, stretched taut from stem to stern, relieving some pressure from the ever-rolling sea.

Areoch was surprised to find the strong hands belonged to another youth, who appeared to be about the same age as Areoch himself. He smiled as Areoch took in his surroundings and then extended his forearm.

"The names Lu'ril, Lu'ril of the southern fields," the youth introduced himself happily. "Meshêk said you'd be hungry, there is food above on the steering platform. He is tending to your friend." He nodded to a leather sheet separating the farthest section of the lower deck. "Meshêk didn't seem mighty pleased when he found how badly the boy was injured."

Areoch nodded quizzically. "Where exactly are we?"

Lu'ril nodded, smiling. "Meshêk said you'd be a bit dazed. He'll be up himself shortly and said he 'ought to do the explaining'. I need to tend to my oar!" Lu'ril pointed to a short ladder on Areoch's right before ducking back down the hull and grabbing an empty oar as happily as if it was a new-found friend.

The sound of the row call and waves dissipated as Areoch climbed the ladder and found himself upon the main deck of *The Alalia*.

Areoch walked toward the stern, passing more platforms for rowers that stood empty on either side. *The Alalia* was a ship designed for many men, more than three-fold the crew than it had now. Yet, it showed no lack of speed. A large-bladed oar was handled by a keen-faced man on a slightly raised platform at the stern. He dug it into the water and Areoch saw another steering oar beside him that was unmanned.

"You are Areoch of Magen!" declared the man.

"I do not believe I know you," replied Areoch, coming closer. He stopped when he recognized him as one of the men who accompanied Meshêk in his rescue, and a familiar face from Birsha's house.

The man laughed at Areoch's expression. "Yes, but I know of you! My name is Tor'i, previously a carpenter in Birsha's household - both in Cartegin and before, in the city of Bulha-Mit. We have met before in Cartegin, all but briefly. I don't expect you to remember it! You must be tired and hungry. Please, eat some of this refreshment here!"

Baskets full of fresh fruits hung from the railings near the steering oar and Areoch realized how hungry he was! He ate without question, glancing occasionally at Tor'i and how he handled the steering oar.

"Sometimes it is as easy as it looks," Tor'i commented, patting the long oar in his hand. "Other times the sea makes bad decisions, and you must remind her that not all of life is rolling hills and pleasant valleys!"

Areoch nodded absentmindedly. His eyes scanned over the passing lands, wondering where Meshêk was.

He did not have to wonder long as the man soon appeared, walking spryly across the deck.

"Thank you, Tor'i," Meshêk said, relieving him of the steering oar. "It is good to have someone else aboard this ship who knows something about navigation! Go and rest. I will need your strength and energy here soon enough."

Tor'i nodded and departed, leaving the upper deck empty and quiet, save for the billowing sail and occasional call of the rowers echoing up from below. Meshêk calmly surveyed the waters ahead, while holding the steering oar casually in one hand - as though he had been a Captain on a ship his entire life. He sipped from a mug of his usual brew of tea in the other hand. Rolling, green hills met a wide, sandy beach on their left and the sea faded into the cloudy sky on their right.

"We make good time, considering our numbers," he reported to Areoch in an unconcerned tone. "Birsha should be proud of his design. If only we had fifty more men! We might even come upon the Urudu and take them by surprise. But alas! I fear we are still more than a full day behind."

Areoch sat back against the stern's railing, looking at Meshêk in wonder. He seemed younger than he remembered.

Areoch struggled to ask the question he found most pressing. "How... Who... Why are we on a *ship?*"

"How else are we to give chase?" Meshêk casually remarked. "We pursue the cursed Urudu ship, the *Taradium*, in hopes we may take back what we have lost, or avenge them trying." Meshêk grit his teeth.

"You know of the *Taradium*?" asked Areoch in shock. "You have spoken to Joshur, then. How much do you know? How did you get us out? How did you *get a ship?!*"

"You ask many questions, as usual!" sighed Meshêk with a smile. "Let it be known, Areoch, that I am no fool. When Ishshak spoke to us in the shipyard this morning I knew he lied, or was at least, twisting some version of the truth about the attack last night. His story made little sense. It was an absurd claim to say Agade and the Urudu were connected. Only a man in shock would believe it. Ishshak hates Agade and desperately needs Birsha's help to make Cartegin strong.

'The tricky part was determining what part of what he said was true. I guessed the ship that attacked us was truly an Urudu ship, and that Birsha's children had indeed been taken by them. Ishshak is not yet so cruel as to knowingly slay the children of his friends for his cause, though it was easy to stir up Birsha, as he clearly intended; and he did have some knowledge of the attack before it happened. At the very least, I knew you were not involved."

"How did you know that?" asked Areoch, relieved.

"I have watched you closely since your arrival, Areoch. I will not deny that at first, I might have suspected you. But, after these many months, even a blind man could see your love for Bahira. You would do nothing to put her in harm's way."

Areoch did not say anything for a moment and the sound of the sea passing by filled his ears.

"Do you think she is still alive?" he asked finally.

Meshêk pursed his lips. "They both may be, Areoch. We must hold to hope."

He took a sip of his tea and studied the drawn face of the young man. Areoch's eyes were wet, full of tears.

"Areoch," he said, "This is not your fault."

"Can you be so sure?" cried Areoch in frustration. "It seems wherever I go, death and disaster follow close behind. If I had not left, Bahira would be safe."

"Safety was never Bahira's desire, Areoch, nor yours if I am not mistaken. Do not give yourself too much credit. There are other things at work here that have been in motion since long before you were born.

'I spoke with Joshur, as I tended him, and he told me much of what he told you. It was easy for me to fill in the rest: chance, it seems, led him to Ishshak's waiting arms at just the right time to confound the Urudu's plan of resupplying their journey northward. And, it was chance again, that led Bahira and Berran to the port last night, at just the wrong time."

"The odds of so many unlikely things happening at once are impossible. There must have been some *will* behind it," thought Areoch aloud.

"Yes," agreed Meshêk with furrowed brows. "But for good or for ill? It was not the will of Ishshak, as you think. It was something else. Something greater."

"Something greater?" repeated Areoch.

"Yes," said Meshêk. "Something older. Do you remember the men we saw at the crossing of the Dan-Jor? I think they and the Urudu are on some related purpose."

"Related purpose? What *purpose* is there behind capturing people you have not even identified?"

"I do not know," admitted Meshêk, shaking his head. "I have only guesses and dim memories. Whatever it is, it is rooted in the north. There lay the Black Mountains and the ancient realm of Ninĝinĝar. Angfar it was called, in the days of the Old World, when I walked there last. Long has it been since I have heard that name, and I had hoped I would never hear it again."

Areoch looked at Meshêk in shock.

"I do not know what stuns me more: that the one whom I love has been taken toward such a dark place or that you know of it so well! How is it that a servant of Birsha can say he has walked there in the days of the Old World? That was before the Great Destruction. It has been over twelve hundred years of man since those days, or so Marqu has told me in my schooling."

Meshêk looked at Areoch closely. "Marqu? This was the name of your teacher, in Agade?"

Areoch nodded and Meshêk stroked his beard. "Hmmm. Well, then, I guess there are at least two of us left," he said, as to himself, with a far-away look in his eye. Then he spoke louder and addressed Areoch.

"Well, Areoch of Ur? It seems we have both made mistakes and both have secrets about our identity. I could not stand by and watch Ishshak torture you and hold you at ransom, so I have freed you. The Urudu have taken Birsha's children, as you know, and I have no doubt that I am meant to go after them, for their sake and for this greater purpose. Will you join me, or shall I set you ashore to find your own path?" he paused, "What will you decide?"

Areoch looked Meshêk up and down as if expecting to see some display of hidden power.

"These are black tidings if what you say is true!" exclaimed Areoch slowly. "It makes me wonder what else is connected and what else I have not clearly seen. I do not yet know what to think. I am afraid. Why is this happening now, at this time? And what can I do against it?"

Meshêk looked kindly upon Areoch and sipped on his tea.

"We do not know our part to play in the Great Story until the tale has been told in full. Come with me, Areoch, and pursue Bahira. It is good and noble to do so. And from it, perhaps, another course will appear to you. That, truly, is that path I walk upon myself - to keep an old promise. It is not shameful to start with a small, but good intention, only to find yourself upon a greater purpose."

Determination filled Areoch's eyes. He nodded.

"I will," he agreed.

Areoch slept most of the night, though every four hours the rowers and steersman changed their watch, driving forward hastily in the darkness. When Areoch awoke in the morning, sharp cliffs had taken the place of sandy shores; stretching high above the ship as they continued into the north. A sharp wind blew out of the east and Meshêk ordered the sail to be furled.

"Every hand to the oars now!" he cried, as the caller doubled the pace. "Pull, pull for the *Taradium*!"

Healed enough to participate, Areoch took up an oar. As he rowed, he discovered that about twenty men manned the ship. Everyone was of Birsha's household, except for Lu'ril. He was of Cartegin's southern fields, and had volunteered to join the adventure. The others of Birsha's house seemed to know and respect Meshêk.

The day passed quickly. The cliffs on their left stretched out of sight, blocking all view of the country they passed. Night fell again, without sign of the *Taradium* or any other ship.

"We should find a landing soon," suggested Tor'i to Meshêk. "This is a new ship, she cannot take being in the water for so long. We need to beach her for several hours and let the air dry her."

"There is no spot," pointed out Meshêk, looking at the impenetrable wall of rock. "And we do not have several hours to spare. Have everyone row in shifts throughout the night and make sure the forward watch is vigilant! We are passing out of charted waters. We will see what the shores look like with the morning."

Tor'i did not seem convinced, though there was little else to be done. The ship sped onward. Every time Areoch awoke to take his turn on the oars, he saw Meshêk tending to Joshur. His wounds did not appear to be healing well. When Areoch slept, he dreamed unsettling dreams that he could not remember. Each time, he woke in a cold sweat, the sound of different shores echoing in his ears and unknown faces fading from his memory.

The third day out from Cartegin dawned with bright summer sunlight, chasing away the northerly clouds. Areoch arrived on-deck to find

Meshêk at the prow, looking at the land around them. The sharp cliffs had turned westward, a quarter mile behind them, running inland. Ahead were many islands of varying width, all covered with trees, standing just off the cliffs of the mainland. On their right, far off in the distance, another jetty of land or low cloud could be made out. Meshêk stared long at its vague shape before putting aside whatever thought filled his mind.

"The current runs strong here," commented Tor'i, looking at the swirling waters. "It pulls us north, away from the mainland. Do we let it take us, or turn aside to scour the shore and the islands there?"

"We do not know where the Urudu make berth," added Areoch, "or how low they were on supplies. It is likely they could be among the islands, or making their landing upon the shore beyond. They will not expect to be pursued, they may have stopped."

Meshêk shook his head, looking again at the far-off shape to the east.

"This place has changed since I was here last. I fear both choices are as likely as the other. We risk passing the *Taradium* completely if we continue north, and we risk losing valuable time if we search among the islands and find nothing."

"I deem it worse to pass them by completely. Then they could return to Cartegin, or another place if they wished, and wreak more havoc! Let us explore this place as quickly as we may and leave no hidden inlet unsearched!" advised Tor'i.

"That may be difficult, if the land here is as it was when I last passed through."

They were divided, but finally decided on searching out the islands. Though Areoch feared for time, it seemed the best option. Meshêk and Tor'i both grasped a steering oar and *The Alalia* swiftly turned aside, following the channel west between the cliffs.

They discovered that many small islands encircled one large one. A search of the perimeter took longer than they had expected. It was both wide and long, and they discovered many small inlets as they passed. Tall, needle-bearing trees (like those in the Asur Forest), filled the bulk of the island; while broad-leafed maples hid the interior from observation. Joshur stood occasionally on the deck, with the help of Lu'ril. He leaned heavily on Lu'ril and the rail.

It was nearing dark when the shore of the largest island began to curve northward. No sign of the enemy ship had been seen.

"An entire day wasted," complained Areoch mournfully, as Joshur came beside him. "We are too far behind to catch up now, unless we were to sprout wings like birds and fly across the sea after them!" Gulls cawed and circled above their head, diving in and out of the wind.

"I find it strange that not a single vessel has been seen," remarked Joshur. "In my land, boats for fishing and trade are ever travelling between the cities. One could not journey on the open sea for an entire hour without meeting another boat, yet these lands appear to be uninhabited."

"These lands are not uninhabited," corrected Lu'ril. "We must be close to the Jezrial Dynasty. We deal often with them in Cartegin. They trade primarily over land, though it is said their trade over the sea used to be great. Where are you from, to be in so prosperous waters?" he asked, looking curiously at Joshur.

Joshur was about to answer when Areoch suddenly gripped Lu'ril's shoulder. "Look there!" he cried, pointing ahead. "I see a ship, dark and low in that far bay! There, behind that stack of rock!"

A final, smaller island slowly revealed itself as *The Alalia* turned north. The spit of land looked as if it was a broken-off piece from the larger, separated by rising waters. Its coast was rocky and inaccessible, except for a single bay that lay concealed from all other angles. Its mouth opened into the channel they had entered. The dark hull of a ship could be seen mooring there, resting behind a sharp sea-stack towering in the center of the bay. There was no sign of other civilization.

"I see it too!" Lu'ril gazed excitedly, squinting to make out the ship in the dim light. "Quickly, we must bring *The Alalia* around and get out of sight - we still have the element of surprise!"

He jumped down to the second deck while Areoch ran to the steering oar. He hesitated briefly, and then dug it into the water, turning the ship's nose around. The baskets swayed, and crashing noises indicated much of their store had fallen over. Tor'i quickly appeared on-deck with Meshêk in tow. Areoch was promptly relieved of the oar and the rowers heaved, pushing *The Alalia* back into concealment. The moored ship was barely visible beyond a sharp point of shadowed rock.

Meshêk leaned over the bulwarks, gazing at the bay and the ship moored within.

"You know the *Taradium* better than any of us," said Meshêk to Joshur. "Is that the vessel?"

Tor'i and Areoch looked at Joshur intently.

"It can be no other!" exclaimed Tor'i. "I saw its black hull set fire to Cartegin. That is the one!"

Joshur's face was pale and ashen. He nodded in agreement.

"I think so," he said meekly, his lip quivering.

Meshêk nodded and his eyes narrowed. "Lu'ril, take Joshur below." Then, addressing Joshur, "You need to rest more than you have, my boy. That wound is still not closed." Turning again to Lu'ril, he ordered: "Then bring up the rest of the crew."

Meshêk waited until everyone had gathered and then spoke.

"It looks, against all odds, that we have come upon our quarry," he said calmly, as the twenty sailors of Cartegin stood in silent anticipation.

"And, even better, it seems we have caught them unaware. We must now plan our attack and carry it out swiftly."

"We are outnumbered," remarked Tor'i. "We should use the ram. It is our greatest weapon and will spare us what could be a bloody fight." Several others nodded in agreement.

"It would be our only hope of not being taken ourselves," agreed a few others.

"We cannot use it," answered Meshêk firmly. "There may still be captives alive in the Urudu's hull. We cannot use it until we know otherwise."

"What shall we do then?" asked Lu'ril.

Meshêk paused. As he stood looking over the waters a small smile grew on his face.

"I have a plan," continued Meshêk wryly. "It will take all of us, with steady heads and steady hands."

Tor'i grinned. "If I have any guess as to what is coming next, it will be good most of us know Meshêk well," he whispered to Areoch, nudging him with his elbow.

Chapter Thirty-one

The Tribes of Tel-Brak

The moon was thin and a deep darkness covered the strait between the two isles. It did not help Areoch and Lu'ril, as they struggled to climb up the western cliff-face of the small island. *The Alalia* had long since disappeared back into the channel, which separated the larger and smaller islands; leaving them groping blindly up a rock.

Areoch looked down, he could barely see the surf, flecked white and far below. He gripped the cracked rock-face in front of him harder and forced himself to continue ascending. They had to climb to the top of the bluff in order to complete the first step in Meshêk's plan.

"Meshêk is blind if he thinks *this* cliff wall was the shortest on the island," complained Lu'ril with a grim chuckle. "The one around the next point was twice as short, if anyone was going to ask me." A leather bag clunked at his back as he reached for another hand-hold.

Lu'ril slipped as one of the rocks he gripped came loose from the wall. It fell for several seconds before splashing below.

"*And* he gives me the heaviest thing onboard the entire ship to carry up," Lu'ril muttered under his breath. Areoch couldn't suppress a smile.

After what seemed like an age, they made it to the top. Lu'ril reached down and pulled Areoch up the final lip. Sharp rocks rose on their right and left. The far side of the island and the cliffs, which surrounded the hidden bay, could not be discerned through the trunks of a small forest.

Areoch steadied himself and they both crouched together.

"Alright," whispered Areoch, "first step complete."

"Oh, yes," said Lu'ril, mockingly "and the hardest part too, I shouldn't wonder. Now all we have to do is run blindly through the forest, avoiding any pitfalls or sunken grades on this infertile rock, until we come to the opposite side. Then we'll sneak *back* down the cliffs, as close to a murderous ship-full of Urudu as we possibly can, break into its hull, without waking any of the said killers, and free any captives within that may not actually exist. Then we sneak back onto the island, without anyone knowing...brilliant plan!"

Areoch smiled grimly and Lu'ril winked at him in the darkness.

"You forget the diversion," reminded Areoch.

"Ah, the diversion! I'm sure that will help us plenty," he answered dryly, but with a glint in his eye, "though Meshêk was rather short on the details...other than we need to be out of the ship before it happens! I'm beginning to wonder: exactly what kind of work did Birsha have Meshêk do on a regular basis? He doesn't seem like the kind of servant that makes tea."

"We should not waste time. I will say, Meshêk *does* have a strong taste for tea."

They bounded off into the darkness, leaping over rocks and logs, as they made for the bay.

It did not take long to cover the distance. The island seemed to be shaped like a shallow bowl, with a high rim of rock that smoothly faded into a wooded center. They slowed as they approached the opposing cliffs, flitting within the shadows until they peered over its edge.

At the bottom of a sheer drop, a sea-stack rose in the middle of a small bay, obscuring much of their view. On its other side floated the Urudu ship, moored far enough away from the sharp rocks along the shore to keep from splintering. The inlet was enclosed by the cliffs similar to the one they had scaled. A small beach, not more than twenty feet wide, stretched along the shore near the middle of the bay. A path from the beach led into a crack within the cliff-face, leading into the heart of the island. *The Alalia* was nowhere to be seen in the dark channel beyond.

Areoch motioned to Lu'ril: they would need to go around to the opposite side of the bay. They groped their way back into the trees and began a steady trek around the cliff's edge, moving quietly and keeping to the shadows.

They came to an abrupt stop mid-way around the island. A deep gully opened in the rock at their feet, over thirty feet wide, and scattered with a straggle of trees - which seemed to cling for survival on the steep bank. The echo of the sea resonated up the cleft and a flicker of firelight could be seen farther down the ravine.

Areoch and Lu'ril backed away from the edge.

"This ravine must connect to the beach we saw from the cliff face," whispered Areoch. "We need to get around it. It seems this is where the Urudu have made their camp."

"It could stretch across the whole of the island, as far as we know," whispered Lu'ril in reply. "I fear we don't have much time left."

Areoch nodded. "So, we jump."

Lu'ril looked at the gully and then back to Areoch. "You're as crazy as Meshêk!"

Areoch pointed toward a sharp boulder, which stuck out from the ravine's lip above them.

"The distance lessens over there," he explained, "and we will have the favor of height."

"We'll need more favor than that!" Lu'ril insisted, but Areoch was already scrambling up to the giant rock.

They clambered to its top as silently as possible. The boulder did jut out over the edge of the ravine and its top was relatively flat. Lu'ril crawled to the edge and peeked over before returning and shaking his head.

"The firelight seems to be directly below us now, and the far side is only slightly closer. What our landing area would be, I cannot say, it is too dark. We could land in a tree for all I can tell."

Areoch sat up. "We cannot delay! Are we to jump, or try going around? We must decide."

Even as Areoch sat up, the sound of small rocks falling away into the gorge on either side of the great rock could be heard, and the surface of the stone quivered.

Lu'ril looked at Areoch with wide eyes and they both stood, running toward the dark tip of stone as fast as they could, leaping with all their might as the rock gave way and fell with a sickening crash down the slope behind them.

Areoch landed heavily on small, loose stones covered by thick tufts of grass. Lu'ril rolled to a stop beside him, the bag around his waist clanking hard against the gravel.

Whatever noise they made was lost in the turmoil of the ravine: the flickering firelight had been extinguished, many shrill cries, and hoarse cursing rose from the gorge. They did not tarry to find out the extent of the damage, but disappeared quickly into the darkness, hoping they had not been discovered.

Another ravine, smaller and less steep, appeared shortly after. It also seemed to lead toward the water. They followed it, making for the shore as swiftly as they could scramble.

The sound of the surf crashed louder and louder in their ears, until foam rose around their ankles and the ravine ended in the bay.

"We are in luck," whispered Lu'ril to Areoch. The hull of the Urudu ship floated ahead. The dark cliff walls rose on either side. They set down the leather bag and opened it, each picking up a stone chisel that had been carefully wrapped in leather. These they bound to their belts before plunging into the water. The wet rocks were slippery, cutting through leather breeches and skin alike as the water rose about their waists. Soon they were swimming, in broad strokes, toward the floating ship; fighting against the waves that pushed them back into the rocks.

Lu'ril reached the ship first, floating (as still as possible), and straining his ears for any sound of activity. Shouts echoed across the water from the beach, but the ship was quiet. He scanned the ship's hull. Picking a crack that ran through the wood, above the water-line, he drove his chisel into it. Areoch did likewise, farther down the hull in the same crack. Then they both took a deep breath and dove under the surface of the water.

They came back up, each bearing a fist sized rock. The waves beat against the side of the ship and with the waves they tapped their chisels deeper into the soft wood: *clink, clink, clink.*

The crack grew wider, and then split in two. With a mighty heave, they grasped the sides of the plank and ripped it from the side of the Urudu ship. A dark hole gaped at them, even darker than the surrounding night. They could not see or hear anything inside.

They listened, their hearts racing.

"Ready?" asked Lu'ril. Areoch nodded. Lu'ril grasped him firmly by his jerkin and forcefully pushed him under the water before pulling with all his might. Areoch exploded out, landing half in and half out of the ship's hull. He scrambled up and wiped his eyes, peering into the darkness.

A smell like decaying flesh filled the air, causing Areoch to cover his face. A shuffling noise seemed to come from further within the darkness, and then suddenly a ghastly white face appeared. Its eyes were as dark as the night that surrounded them. It came at Areoch, like a white phantom gliding in the blackness.

Areoch fell back, terrified. Then another face appeared, followed by another. As they drew closer, Areoch realized that they were not apparitions at all! They were men's faces, painted white down the middle with strange designs. It made them appear frightening in the night. Over twenty faces were looking at him with wide eyes. They were bound with leather thongs about their hands and feet. Some were tied to the ship's boards above and to the floor below.

Lu'ril leapt through the hole beside him and gasped, startled by the white faces. Areoch made a quick motion to their hands and feet, Lu'ril understood: they were not the Urudu. They were captives.

They went to work quickly, using their sharp stone chisels to cut the thongs. Some of the prisoners were bloodied and shied away as Areoch and Lu'ril drew near, speaking shrilly in a guttural tongue they could not understand.

The noise of running footsteps echoed from the boards above their heads and many cries suddenly rang out from above. Areoch looked nervously at Lu'ril. Something was happening.

"We must hurry!" urged Lu'ril in a hushed tone.

Areoch cut the tallest stranger's bonds. He was, without any doubt, a leader among them. He seemed to understand their purpose and went to and fro, speaking in a low voice to the rest. They quieted, letting Areoch and Lu'ril do their work, before slipping out of the ship's cracked hull, one at a time, into the water.

"Do you think they are ready?" Tor'i whispered to Meshêk. "It has been nearly three hours and we have seen no change."

Meshêk nodded. "We have given them enough time. If we wait longer they could be dashed up against the rocks, or captured themselves."

"If we go too soon there could still be captives on-board, if there are captives at all."

"We will see," answered Meshêk. He made a motion to a sailor who ran below, whispering quick orders to the rest of the crew.

The oars were stealthy lowered and *The Alalia* floated forward. Like a whisper in the night, they entered the channel. The cliffs of the small island rose on their left side, a tall shadow against the starry sky. The main island was an ominous, distant shape to their right. Both Tor'i and Meshêk held a steering oar, guiding the ship slowly toward the bay through the dark water.

They had not gone far when a commotion in the bay broke out. Torches bobbed as small figures ran between the rock wall and the sea. Signals seemed to be sent to the dark ship at anchor and voices echoed out dully across the water.

Meshêk whistled and the rowers dipped and splashed with more fervor. *The Alalia* picked up speed. The sea-stack was off their starboard bow as the full inlet came into view.

"Light it," ordered Meshêk.

Tor'i let go of his oar and set light to the stern fire behind them. Its bright gleam reflected off the water.

More shouts echoed out from the beach, followed by hoarse calls from the ship. They had been seen.

"Here we go!" cried Meshêk. The sudden, rhythmic pounding of their row call rang out loud over the water, and the rowers dug in their oars with all their strength.

The blackened ship freed its moorings. Dark figures swarmed over its deck as oars were lowered and the ship began to come about.

"They will try and cut off our escape!" cried Tor'i, glancing between the cliff wall and the sharp edge of the sea stack rising out of the waves on their right.

"Come on, come at us. Come at us," Meshêk murmured the challenge.

The Urudu ship came about until it faced them, its oars digging into the water as it picked up speed. It did not have far to travel before it sat between the sea stack and the shore, blocking what was now the only exit to the little bay *The Alalia* had. They would have to come to a complete stop and turn around.

The Alalia did not stop. She picked up even more speed.

Boom, boom, boom, boom. The drum throbbed even faster, echoing back from the cliffs at a triple pace.

"Just to its port now Tor'i, just to its port! Steady!" cried Meshêk.

The Urudu pirates could be seen manning rope, hook, and weapon as they prepared to take the oncoming vessel. Surely now it would realize its err and attempt to turn and flee! One or two of the Urudu nearest to the prow began to back away as they looked at the oncoming ship. The weapons fell from their hands - for *The Alalia* showed no sign of slowing. Soon all the Urudu realized their peril and they cried out to turn. The black ship had no speed and the single steering oar did little to move the boat in the water.

"Rack those port oars. Brace yourselves!!" cried Meshêk.

The bronze ram of *The Alalia* seemed for a moment to reflect the light of the stars as it cut through the water like an arrow from a bow. Meshêk twisted his oar slightly and the two ships met. A rending shriek echoed out between the cliffs like the sound of a thousand battering rams. The Urudu ship keeled to one side as *The Alalia's* ram shattered its center beam, skidding along its length as it passed through like a hurricane.

Several unlucky Urudu were caught in the ram's path and smashed into the wreckage. Others fell or jumped overboard and the rest soon followed - paying no heed to those trapped onboard as the ship rapidly filled with water and sunk down to the depths. The survivors swam for the sandy beach. Some found themselves dashed against sharp rocks, while others drowned in their panic.

The impact had thrown Meshêk and Tor'i onto the deck. They quickly picked themselves up, dug in the steering oars, and brought *The Alalia* around. The crew ran up to the main deck to witness the aftermath of their charge and gaped at what they saw. Curses and screams filled the night. Wreckage was strewn throughout the water along with the bodies of the dead. *The Alalia* was undamaged.

"That... that was unbelievable! If only Ishshak and Birsha had seen..." Tor'i began, but Meshêk was not listening. He scanned the water, looking for the forms of Areoch and Lu'ril. He could not see them.

The boys had finished their work as the sound above deck became louder. They speedily searched the lower hull, there were no more prisoners. The strange leader had remained with them, unspeaking, but now he flung himself through the crack, leaving Areoch and Lu'ril alone in the darkness. The ship began to turn, pulling away from the shore.

"We must away, Areoch! Quickly!" cried Lu'ril as he ran for the crack.

"No, wait! Bahira and Berran, they are not to be found! They must be here!"

"They are not Areoch! To stay is death!"

"They could be above! I will not leave them!" insisted Areoch, as he made for the closed hatch at the rear of the ship. Lu'ril grabbed him forcefully by the arm, dragged him out of the ship, and leapt into the water.

Areoch surfaced, wiping the stinging saltwater from his eyes. He reached out to climb back aboard, but the hull of the ship was already too far away. He could not catch it.

"Lu'ril, you fool! You condemn them to death!" he cried, turning around. Lu'ril was gone, already making his way toward shore with broad strokes. Areoch set off in pursuit, his anger and frustration growing with every stroke. They made shore, clambering up the sharp rocks.

"Lu'ril!" Areoch's voice was shrill. He would have struck him, had it not been for the expression that appeared on Lu'ril's face.

"Look," he said in awe, pointing, and Areoch turned around.

There, far out in the middle of the bay, *The Alalia,* as if in slow motion, closed the gap and destroyed the Urudu ship. The sheer explosion of sound at the impact made boulders fall loose from the cliffs above. They stood still in wonder.

The swimming forms of the Urudu making for the shore stirred them from their reprieve. They turned and froze. Twenty faces looked at them expectantly. The faces of the freed captives were no longer white or horrifying. The sea had washed away the paint, leaving behind a dark-skinned people with fair features. The tall leader walked forward and made a swift motion with his arm at the incoming Urudu and the shores behind them.

"Manake de'la muna le lan'i. Ushas-brak h'au noamon," the man said. Lu'ril looked at Areoch and raised his eyebrows.

"My name... Ushas," the leader said haltingly in the common tongue. "We go, this path. Quickly." Then he turned and led his people swiftly over the rocks into the small gully.

"I guess he means for us to follow him," suggested Lu'ril.

"And we must. I will not forget my anger, Lu'ril" Areoch spat, hoarsely.

"And I will not forget that I saved your life," he countered back.

Ushas traversed quickly up the narrow gorge, nimbly dodging between rock and stone. His feet were bare, as were the others, but it did little to hamper their speed. He turned aside, down a small watercourse, which Areoch and Lu'ril had passed in the darkness unnoticed. They followed it for about fifty strides before it joined with the main ravine the two had leapt across.

At this intersection they halted, and their mysterious leader leaned forward as if listening. To their right Areoch could see the edge of the stone which had fallen from their earlier jump - its girth blocked the whole of the ravine. Ushas looked at it with a long, confused look.

Scattered embers of a fresh fire were spread about the floor of the gorge, still smoldering. Here and there an exposed hand and bloodied boot lay limp, jutting out from under the massive stone's base.

Ushas spoke words in a strange tongue and his people began to move rapidly up and over the stone's side into the interior of the island. He and two others, along with Areoch and Lu'ril, waited, facing the shore, listening to the sounds of fierce, angry cries.

"They will come," Ushas informed, nodding toward the shore.

"There will be no other option left to the Urudu that survived. We need to hurry!" cried Lu'ril. He bent and picked up a thick shaft of wood.

Ushas nodded his head, whispering words of swiftness behind him.

"My people... weak. We guard now," he said, pointing at himself and two of his people that stayed behind.

They all picked up weapons as they could find. Areoch gave a low whistle as he picked up a spear from among the camp's wreckage and showed it to Lu'ril. Its point was solid bronze.

Thump. Thump. They waited. Quick footsteps from the beach grabbed their attention. A large figure ran up. He was powerfully built, and blue tattoos seemed to glow from his face in a mysterious pattern. He was dripping with water and came to an abrupt halt as the five figures blocked his way. His eyes grew wide and his mouth opened in a silent gawk.

"Gah!!" Ushas cried, waving his arms in the air and taking a few bold steps closer.

The figure turned and fled back as he came, as if running from a ghost.

"Shalg tunaz de'brak! Tunaz de'brak!!" the tattooed man cried as his footsteps faded out of hearing.

"Doesn't anyone speak the common tongue in these parts?" asked Lu'ril quizzically, but Ushas did not show any sign of understanding. They turned, quickly scrambling over the rock until they joined the rest of the captives.

"This way!" cried Ushas. They ran. With all possible speed, they followed the twisting course of the ravine as it gradually turned back toward the center of the island. The ravine's sides became less steep and the thick shrubs boarding its edge thinned. Soon the plants disappeared and the group scaled its lip to the south. Free of the gully, they hurried up the island's gentle slope. Thin trees appeared in the darkness. All were exhausted; several of the captives were injured, weak, and needed to be supported by the others. Sounds of pursuit grew behind them. Areoch and Lu'ril were heaving for breath as they crashed through the underbrush, coming out upon the edge of the island. The southernmost tip was ahead, and it was for this point that Ushas ran.

"What is he doing?" cried Areoch to Lu'ril. "This is the highest point of the whole island! There is no way down! We will be trapped!"

It was too late to change course. All that remained of the Urudu broke from the trees behind, cursing in a foul language as they scrambled after their quarry. The Urudu were many - too many for them to hold off.

Ushas reached the edge of the cliff, and to Areoch's amazement, he walked off the edge.

"Hoy!!" exclaimed Areoch, leaping forward. But Ushas reappeared as quickly as he had vanished, walking as if floating on air.

"By Anu of ancient days..." whispered Lu'ril.

The strangers followed him in a line, walking over the crashing waves with their hands held high above their heads. Areoch and Lu'ril hurried to the cliff edge and the riddle was discerned: two great ropes of woven fiber stretched taut from the edge of the cliff into the darkness, one as high as their face and the other at the height of their feet.

The sounds of the Urudu were close and they did not waste any more time. Grasping the high rope, they began to walk forward. The wind swept them back and forth, in an erratic rocking motion, as great gusts blew against the cliff face. The ropes quivered in their hands. Areoch did his best to focus on the form of the freed captive in front of him, but even the injured seemed quicker and more adept at the task than they. Soon all the captives had vanished from sight. Areoch and Lu'ril pressed on, hand over hand. Shouts echoed behind them and the rope sagged, the Urudu had found their escape route.

How long they walked in that high place, Areoch never knew. Hand over hand, foot sliding after foot. The cliff faded behind and still the ropes stretched onward into the blackness. Soon, only the stars above and the faint shifting of the sea below reminded Areoch of where he was. He felt as if he was a spirit, walking high among the cathedrals of the heavens, wandering shapeless among their swirling wonders.

Lu'ril's voice stirred him, yelling to be heard above the gusting winds.

"Do you see anything ahead?"

Areoch peered into the shadows until his eyes hurt. His hands were cold, despite the warm night, and they felt clumsy from the ceaseless clenching.

"Yes, I think I see something!" Areoch cried back. A large wall of thicker darkness slowly appeared as they neared it.

"We must hurry!" insisted Lu'ril in a trembling voice. "I can no longer hear the Urudu behind us, but I fear they may be closer than I think. I dare not turn my head!" He added with emphasis, "There is no pleasure in this for me!"

Soon the shape of a cliff wall, rising out of the sea ahead, became clear.

"We are almost there!" encouraged Areoch. They gripped the ropes with determination, as their strength waned.

Lu'ril peered around Areoch, full of hope and relief, but his eyes became wide with fear. A group of people were gathered around the cliff-top. Areoch could see white faces with the same barbaric design that had frightened him within the ship. The one nearest was making swift motions. With horror Areoch realized the figure held a long knife and was cutting the ropes he and Lu'ril walked on!

Areoch cried out and they both scrambled ahead with renewed vigor. They were close now, just feet away from safety, and with a final gasp they made it to the edge. Areoch gripped the solid rock with frozen hands, struggling to pull himself up; his body hanging over the brink for a terrifying moment. He slipped, and with a rolling stomach began to slide backward! A figure from the cliff's edge darted out and strong, warm hands gripped him, pulling him to the crest. He faintly saw Lu'ril being drawn up behind him. They collapsed on the loose rock, kissing its cold surface. Ushas stood over them.

Sounds of shouting echoed from the edge and the painted forms quickly went back to the ropes. Sharp flint knives reappeared and they resumed cutting, with deft strokes, what remained of the bridge. Areoch sat up and their pursuers appeared over the brim. The Urudu had been right behind them, and they were about to gain the island! They scrambled forward as quickly as they could, crying out as their peril became clear. With a snap the upper rope broke, flying free. A moment more and the bottom one severed. The Urudu screamed, clinging hopelessly to the ropes. They disappeared into the darkness.

Areoch did not hear a splash from over the cliff's edge; only the wind, whispering of those it had claimed as it continued its journey. White faced figures stood around them now. Their bodies were covered in paint, other than a wide loincloth bound around their waists. They shouldered long, thin spears. Some grasped intricately carved knives of stone. The freed captives stood somewhat behind this new group, their olive skin making them nearly invisible in the dark. Ushas conversed in their strange tongue with another painted man. The two gestured toward Areoch and Lu'ril as they spoke earnestly.

Finally, something was decided, and Ushas helped Areoch and Lu'ril to their feet.

"You come homeward with us." He gestured into the darkness, then to himself and the group, and then back to them as if doubting his words were correct. The white figures around them walked ahead, helping the injured who were unable to keep pace.

The blackness of the night was so thick they did not know where they were headed. Areoch often felt the unfathomable heights fall away on either side of the path they walked. Ushas reached out a hand to correct Areoch and Lu'ril when they strayed too near the edge. They crossed two more rope bridges, shorter, but of similar design as the first. Areoch could hear the sea crashing loud below them on each occasion.

"I'm not excited to see where *home* is for these people," muttered Lu'ril on the last bridge. "Their houses are probably made of nothing but woven cords strung over sharp rocks."

On the far side of the last bridge, tall shadows of trees appeared on their right. The emptiness of the rocky cliff edge could still be felt on their left. Areoch had learned to watch his feet carefully, for large cracks and precipices occasionally opened unseen as they walked. He looked up, realizing that their numbers had swelled. At least forty painted faces now surrounded them, before and behind, appearing from the silent trees as they joined the group.

Their path sloped downward and wooden beams, lashed securely together at their feet, formed a clear path for the first time. The group picked up speed. The trees grew denser and then abruptly pulled aside. Areoch could see a distant cliff face. Countless lights flickered, mounted on the wall of the cliff itself. Wooden buildings and the sharp tilt of many connecting walkways could be made out. The path they followed dropped over the edge, suspended by large ropes and beams as it wound around the rock, making a path for the lit city.

"Crah-si ge'g Tel-Brak!" Ushas gestured at the light. They were close.

Lu'ril stopped, stared at the city, and then at the path as it stretched over unforeseen depths.

"See, what did I tell you?!" he cried in distress. "They roost on the rocks like birds! I need good, dark earth under my feet. I think I'll stay up here and camp among the trees."

Areoch laughed despite his weariness. "After all our peril, you shy away from our refuge? I don't care if my bed is suspended over a lair of sharks, as long as I can sleep!"

Lu'ril reluctantly followed the group, though he muttered something about collapsing into the sea in the middle of the night.

Despite Lu'ril's fears, the path was sturdy and solid, neither creaking nor giving way, as they walked over the cliff's edge and down its face. Beams of wood jutted out from the sheer rock, and taunt ropes angled above their heads. Lu'ril marched as near the solid rock as possible looking nervously toward the outer edge, much to the amusement of Ushas and their guides.

The city itself was structured the same way. The cliff face tilted back, offering a less-steep face. Thick, woven ropes and rough beams appeared all over the rock, holding up the foundations of many buildings. Curving roofs of a dark-colored wood, adorned with draping eves, covered high walls. Some of the largest structures sat perched on irregular outcroppings of rock, which acted like footings.

Word of their arrival had preceded them. Torches lit up every corner of the city. Dozens of white, painted faces ran toward the group, embracing some of the free captives. Others looked curiously at the new-comers, and Areoch realized that he stood among male and females. The white paint had distracted him. Every man, woman, and child's head was as smooth as a sea-worn rock. The shapely form of the women, the angular curves of their faces, and their slimmer shoulders made Lu'ril blush.

The number of the group diminished, as the people moved into various buildings. Ushas led Areoch and Lu'ril into a medium-sized, wooden structure in the center of the city. It had many rooms. Two soft beds of bracken protruded out of the cliff-side, layered upon boughs of springy wood. Ushas gestured at these before laying out a soft bread-like fare on a small table. He bowed and left without a word, shutting the door behind him. Even as he shut the door, Areoch and Lu'ril felt their limbs grow heavy with exhaustion.

"Well, this isn't so bad of a place," remarked Areoch, cautiously feeling the bed.

"I am too tired to disagree with you," Lu'ril muttered wearily, casting aside his wet garments and then himself on the soft bracken. "I do hope everyone on *The Alalia* is alright. I wonder, how they will find us? I don't even know where we are."

Areoch yawned. "We can do nothing about it now," he said sleepily. "We will have to wait until morning, Ushas will help us."

Chapter Thirty-two

Kez-Matura

Though the sun rose early on the cliff-dweller's city, Areoch and Lu'ril did not stir. Suddenly, their door was thrown open with a loud CRASH! Their dwelling seemed to sway softly as if the foundation of the structure had given way and naught but ropes held it aloft!

"AHHH!!" cried Lu'ril. He rolled out of his cot and onto the floor, scrambling to grab something solid. Areoch sat bolt upright, gripping the edge of his bed.

A soft and familiar laugh filled the air.

"Ah, well met again, my friends! The sun is already awake, but you still slumber! Rise up! Wash yourselves! We are in haste!"

"Meshêk!" exclaimed Areoch, loosening his hold on his bedside.

Lu'ril opened his eyes, peering around the post he clutched tightly with both hand and foot.

"I should have known!" he said with a groan as he collapsed back onto his bed.

"When did you get here?" Areoch asked in amazement. "How did you find us? We only just arrived... we don't even know where we are!"

"*I* have only just arrived, *you* have been here all night! And *we* are already late," he answered curtly. "Breakfast will have to wait. Come, quickly now!"

A small spring ran down the cliff-side. Areoch and Lu'ril dressed, and washed their arms and faces in the cool water, before following Meshêk outside onto the platform. The air was chill in the shadows of the cliffs, but the blue sky above was bright. The sun streamed over their heads from the east.

It took a moment for Areoch's eyes to adjust to the sudden change of morning. When they did, he saw the intricate detail of the structures around him. Perfect and precariously mounted (they seemed), held up by white, wooden beams. Rope, larger than Areoch's arm, was wrapped everywhere. Interlaced tiles of clay covered the rooftops, curling up at the edges. Windows, covered with thick flaps, dotted each structure.

To Areoch's left, sea-stacks rose from what appeared to be a maze of channels. Some towered above where he stood and others seemed wide enough to be small islands, covered with trees and the greenery of moss and lichens. Birds cawed and dove from rocky nests upon their sides. Through them the currents of the sea crashed and swirled in intricate forms. Directly below, the water churned calmly in a large, circular eddy. Moored near the cliffs was a ship.

"*The Alalia!*" exclaimed Lu'ril, pointing downward.

"Yes," said Meshêk, walking briskly ahead, "and the bay of *Ka'bier*, as it was called of old. In those days, no people lived on these walls and this place was... sacred," he trailed off and the smile vanished from his face. "We must hurry," he insisted, shaking his head.

"Meshêk, what of *The Taradium*?" cried Areoch, stopping in his tracks. "We did not find Bahira or Berran in the hold. And then... You destroyed the ship."

"Do not be distressed, Areoch," assured Meshêk. "I have already guessed that you did not find them by what I have heard since last night - you found something else. Your questions will be answered soon enough. Now we must hurry! The whole city will be waiting for us. Don't speak, you two, without my leave. You are about to meet one whom none of the outside world has ever seen: the Chieftain of Tel-Brak."

Other planked paths ran above and below them. The city continued everywhere, covering the span of the cliff face. The sloping eaves of buildings could be seen through cracks under their feet. The path they followed turned sharply with the rock face and ran underneath a broad arch of stone. The arch seemed natural, though it was smooth, and it stretched over their head before connecting to a sea-stack footing in the sea. Mosses and ferns draped down, covering the path like a trailing veil. Meshêk pushed aside the tendrils and the city vanished from view.

Before them, a small spring cascaded from the side of the cliff, splashing around their feet. Above the spring, appeared the largest building they had seen in Tel-Brak. It was nestled between two sharp fingers of rock, and many rooms extended back into the stone from its main hall. A wide, flat expanse opened before them, and it was filled with the painted faces of several hundred people. Some standing were not painted. They recognized Tor'i and a few others of Birsha's house, all displaying shocked expressions as they gazed around.

Broad steps ran down from the building to the clearing, and coming down these steps with grace and dignity were three, tall figures.

Foremost strode a man, lofty in gaze. His head was smooth and his jawline pronounced. Tendrils of what looked like a growing lichen, gold and shimmering in color, extended from his back and ran down his front, leaving Areoch's eyes wondering if he was clothed or not. The same plant encircled the contours and wrinkles of his face and forearms with thin, golden lines, giving him an appearance that was both intimidating and beautiful, young and ancient. It was hard to determine his age, for the same white paint, which the others of Tel-Brak wore, covered his skin. His shoulders and arms were bare and exposed, revealing aged cords of muscle. In his right hand he held a tall shaft of bleached bone. Upon its top the golden lichen wound around a single pearl, as large as a fist.

Somewhat behind him stood two similar figures. On his right was a woman, striking in appearance. The golden lines encircling her head flowed down her back like thick lengths of hair. On his left another man walked, a younger image of the older.

The three came to a halt at the bottom of the steps and Meshêk stepped forward to meet them. All present kneeled and Areoch and Lu'ril did likewise as the leaders halted. When Areoch looked up again he was shocked to find the Chieftain and his companions were also bowing, stretching forward until their hands were laid out on the ground. Meshêk alone, stood tall. For an instant Areoch caught an image in his mind of Meshêk as some ancient figure, robed in a power even greater than those who were before them.

All rose. The chief placed his palms together and approached, averting his eyes from Meshêk.

"Mahakay, Kez-Matura," he said. "De'fa tela h'au noamon a Bazi." Areoch and Lu'ril recognized with shock that the youngest of the three mighty leaders was none other than Ushas, painted in finery. He smiled at them, as the Chieftain backed away from Meshêk, and began to speak to the crowd.

He spoke, in the Brakian tongue, the story of those who had been held captive. His voice rolled up and down like the waves, and those in the clearing stood attentive, listening. Ushas nodded his head and sometimes stood, acting out part of what had happened. Lu'ril could hardly take his gaze away from the graceful woman who stood next to the Chieftain Brak. She smiled in his direction as Ushas and the Chieftain told the tale.

Finally, the story ceased. The chief approached Areoch and Lu'ril. He raised his hand until it was level with the staff he carried. With a sharp prick, he pierced his palm until a drop of blood swelled. Then he placed his hand on Areoch and then Lu'ril's head.

"Chieftain Brak is honored to meet you. He gives some of what is most precious of himself, to you, for returning what is most precious to him," Meshêk explained. Chieftain Brak nodded, as if understanding, and stepped back, speaking slowly (and with difficulty), in the common tongue.

"Welcome again Kez-Matura and you new-comers, to our dwellings. We have seen few faces outside of our own kin since the days of Asurla, and none of us now venture onto the mainland. I am one of the few among us who remembers the common speech. This is my son, Ushas-Brak who you know, and my daughter Eshas-Brak. You are safe here within our city. Tel-Brak it is called, or City of the Highlands in your language. I have many thanks to give you. Please, come with us into our hall."

Meshêk, Areoch, and Lu'ril followed the three up the wide steps. Chieftain Brak pushed aside two broad double doors, designed of a rich-colored wood, flowing with a bright grain. The floor inside was of the same rock as the cliff, but was as smooth and level as glass. Natural veins of silver, gold, and granite ran sparkling under their feet as the building broke into several, long rooms. As they walked, the walls were sometimes the rock of the cliff-face and other times paneled wood decorated with many symbols and barbaric masks. Veins of precious metals continued along the floors and walls, growing thicker and wider, like small streams and brooks running together as they progressed deeper into the hall.

Finally, they entered the widest and longest of the chambers. Lu'ril nudged Areoch, pointing to its far side. Majestically flowing across the floor, wall, and ceiling of the passage, all of the golden veins converged. The lode stretched like a flowing river, at least twenty feet across; gigantic, dazzling, and bright. Yet, the splendor was not from the ore, but by the shape it took. For by some ancient hand or more powerful will, the end of the lode had been carved to form a tree, rooting into the rock. It spanned across the wall and from floor to ceiling, as if a tree from the ancient days had been petrified in a pool of gold. Areoch imagined the bark could peel off in strips if he tried to pick at it. However, the grander of the tree filled Areoch with fear, and he dared not approach the towering branches.

The bole of the tree was made of six pillars, interwoven together to form one trunk. In each pillar was formed a terrifying, beautiful creature. Areoch could not distinguish them all. Each figure was large, even larger than a man. They seemed to have the face of a man, yet the features of different beasts: the horns of the Asur Bull rose from one, the tail of a lion from another, and the wings of a bird could be distinguished. Areoch felt that he had seen this marvelous image before, but he could not say where.

A raised circular platform in the middle of the hall was covered with soft fabric and cushions. The Brak's motioned Areoch and Lu'ril to rest upon it. They struggled to avert their eyes from the tree and its splendor. Meshêk continued toward the tree alone, leaving the others on the raised dais. Soon, the boughs of the great tree were high above his head. His hand stretched forward until it rested gently on the tree's base! It seemed to Areoch that the high golden leaves and the shapes within them quivered lightly. The sound of a whispering wind drifted through the hall, as though they stood upon the edge of a forest in the midst of a mighty gale. For a moment Areoch was filled with terror that something within that tree had come alive and he closed his eyes!

"It has passed my friends," Ushas assured softly.

Meshêk walked back from across the hall. He cast himself down, as though exhausted.

The Chieftain Brak did not seem to be shaken. He saw the tears that fell from Meshêk's eyes.

"You have long run from your past, Kez-Matura. You have been hiding who you are."

A silence stretched throughout the room.

"It is time you return and become the man you were born to be."

Meshêk sighed. "Part of me fears the world has seen enough of me and my kin," he paused before continuing. "And the other part of me fears I have not done enough. I am guilty of both. Perhaps it would be better if I too perished, along with all that is left of the Ancient World." He looked at the tree from underneath a furrowed brow.

The Chieftain Brak shook his head. "You believe that what you and the Seven did in the days of Asurla, defines who you are now. You are haunted by their blindness, for it was your blindness. Even with all your study and all your wisdom you would rather run from these memories, burying them under an average life than face them."

Meshêk's face grew tense. "You do not know of what you speak!" he cried. "You will never know the shame of what I did."

"I know the shame of why you hesitate now," Brak replied evenly. "Did you know, Kez-Matura, that it was Kez-Bazi who brought us here at the beginning, when Asurla first claimed the Kingship in Eridor? Our people have remembered and passed down, through the generations, what the world was like then. We remember that mankind was afraid. They were afraid of the Great Destruction, of how they had been blind in the past. Asurla used those fears to lure even you, Kez-Matura. Kez-Bazi and his house convinced our forefathers that it was better to run away from Asurla's obsession rather than take part of it."

"Kez-Bazi and Kez-Maldek were the best of us," declared Meshêk solemnly. "They were the wisest. It is for that reason they had no part with Asurla! He searched relentlessly, but he never found them nor their kin."

"Thirteen of my fathers have lived and died on this island since then, Kez-Matura. And I will tell you that Kez-Bazi was wrong." He nodded toward the great golden tree. "We escaped the darkness that haunts you. For that we are a pure people. But I wish we had not left. I wish we had stayed and fought."

"Asurla could not be defeated. You and your kin would never have been born."

"That may be true," consented the Brak. "Though you are older than me Kez-Matura, I give you this counsel, for it is wisdom our people have learned: it is better to act and later regret, than not to act at all."

Meshêk ran a hand through his long hair.

"You are right, Tel-Brak. You are right. It is for this reason that I am here. I must act, I have waited too long. My shame has not lessened through the years, as I once thought it would. It has only increased. Now, I hope I may reclaim some of what I have lost."

While he and Meshêk were conversing, Brakians had brought large platters full of thin, wheat cakes, lentils, and a soft, rich meat from some crustacean. Lu'ril tried not to stare at Eshas-Brak as she gracefully supped, her lithe form rippling with shimmering gold as she moved.

Areoch swallowed. "Chieftain Brak, you speak to Meshêk as if you have known him for many years. Is today not the first day you have met? I feel as if I still do not know him, though I have known him for many days longer than you."

The Brak studied Areoch closely, his eyes resting on the fiery grain of his wooden armbands.

"I have not heard of armbands like that in my time," he mused.

"They are from Magen," Areoch quickly explained.

"The city of Kes? That is the most ancient of all cities on this side of the Shinar. Old, old bloodlines flow through that people." He paused again and studied Areoch more thoughtfully before continuing.

"I apologize for my rudeness, we do not often have visitors. You ask of Meshêk? Kez-Matura, it seems, has many names now," reflected the Brak. "Still your question does not make sense to me. We are different in Tel-Brak than the men who dwell on the mainland. I have never met Kez-Matura face to face, but when you stand in the presence of a *Kez del Ugn*, there is no doubt. They are set apart from creation as it is now. Mankind has a dim shadow of the power we were once entrusted with, in the days when we were untainted."

"You keep saying *Kez*," interrupted Lu'ril, "though I have never heard that term before. What does it mean?"

Chieftain Brak looked even more surprised. "Ur-taz! *Kez del Ugn* h'au de mafalu," he said.

"Chieftain Brak does not know how to answer you," said Ushas, leaning forward and looking at his father. "Though in the modern tongue you might translate *Kez del Ugn* to mean 'First-Born'. They are the undying race, the first sons and daughters of earth, whom Enlil walked with in the Ancient Days."

Lu'ril looked at Meshêk with a newfound curiosity and Areoch was about to ask another question when Meshêk raised his hand.

"Your many questions must be answered later," he determined. "For now, time is pressing and we have much more to discuss. Have you forgotten in the moment the task we have at hand? Bahira and Berran are not among you, and though I have heard Ushas-Brak's account of what happened last night I guessed they were not re-captured or slain during your mission. They were not there at all, were they?"

"We did not search the whole of the ship," said Areoch spitefully, shooting a dark glance at Lu'ril. "They were not below with the other captives."

"Do not fear, Areoch," assured Meshêk. "We searched the water and did not see any trace of them. I do not think they were there. I do not think the ship last night was the *Taradium*."

"You ought to at least explain how you found us," piped in Lu'ril around a mouthful of sweet meat, "since you seem to know everything that happened to us already."

"That is not a pressing question," scolded Meshêk dryly. "To curb your curiosity, Ushas found *The Alalia* in the channel early this morning. The peoples of Tel-Brak have long watched the maze of waterways which leads to this dwelling, both by cliff-top and by boat. They knew you were with us and guided us in... while you were still asleep!

'The more pressing matter is that of the Urudu." He turned, facing Ushas and the Chieftain Brak. "You already know some of why we are here: we pursue a dark ship of the Urudu which captured two of our kin. We hoped we had come upon them last night and would take them by surprise, but instead Areoch and Lu'ril found Ushas and the Brakians. Clearly the tribes of Tel-Brak have felt the Urudu's bite. What else do you know of them?"

The Chieftain Brak shook his head sadly and Ushas looked at the ground with down-cast eyes.

"The Urudu," Ushas spat. "We know of them all too well. We have been kept safe in the past, hidden and forgotten by the world here. But the Urudu have no borders. You pursue one dark ship. As you have guessed, they have many. They are not a disorganized group, they seem to share a common port and pursue a common aim. They have grown bolder in the last many months."

"Then this could have been a different ship?!" Areoch cried. "I do not know if that makes me glad, that they may yet be alive, or afraid that now there is no hope at all."

"The vessel you attacked could not have been the same vessel you seek," determined Ushas slowly. "Our story of how we came by this ship has not yet been told in full, even to my father, so I will tell it now.

'This ship waylaid us on the island you rescued us from. There are many good spots for fish in that place, and I led a large group of my people over for the final days of the mid-summer run. This was not three days ago. The Urudu came upon the other side of the island by night and burned our canoes - for we do not travel by air-bridge unless we must. They cut off our escape, trapping us for two days among the sea caves on the northern side of the island. There the weather is harshest. The caves are a treasure to us, where our dead can rest facing the east, and their exact location is a secret. The very night you broke us free was the night we were taken. They found the secret paths into the caves. Two of us perished in the fight, but we were surrounded and I surrendered to spare the rest of our people."

"What you say troubles me deeply," said Chieftain Brak, shifting on his seat. "We expected you to be gone many days and we saw no sign from the island that you were in distress."

"They knew our ways and our secret paths. They knew how to take us alive."

"That was their goal then?" asked Meshêk eagerly. "To take as many of you alive as they could?"

"It is the way of the Urudu," clarified Ushas. "They kill only when needed, those they take north are never seen again. I was afraid, father, in the bowls of that ship! I did not think there would be any return."

"North? Where in the north?" pushed Meshêk.

"Yes," answered the Chieftain. "Always north they sail heavy in the water, and have done so for many years. Even here on this island we have heard strange tidings. The land of Angfar is whispered. You, Kez-Matura, would know more of their landing than we."

Meshêk sat back, stirring a cup of tea the Brakians had brought him. Areoch sat facing the far wall of the hall. The heads of the strange figures embedded within the golden tree seemed to grow. He shook his head to clear his vision.

"There have been others," Meshêk said finally, "on the mainland who seem to be after the souls of men, alive at any cost. The Urudu appear to be after the same thing. Such a thing is not a coincidence. It has troubled me, and is part of why I am here. I cannot seem to grasp what it reminds me of, but it feels old, like a new tree springing up from a rotted stump. Something stirs in my mind... I cannot place it." Meshêk trailed off tapping the edge of his foot as he thought.

For the first time Eshas-Brak spoke. Had it not been for the grief in her voice, it would have been the most beautiful sound Lu'ril had ever heard.

"It seems the Urudu know our ways well, father. Too well." Her eyes spoke more than she said. The Brak sighed.

"You think it is him, then?" he said with a sad shake of his head.

"Is any other possibility more likely?"

"Who? What?" asked Lu'ril quizzically looking between the two of them. "What are we talking about?"

"Many years ago, we lost one of our own to the Urudu," said the Chieftain Brak.

"He was captured?" asked Meshêk.

"No," admitted Ushas. "He was driven away."

"Driven away? I have never heard of such a thing happening in the history of Tel-Brak!"

"Never has there been, Kez-Matura. This man was the first. He did things... horrible things. We found his family, washed up on the shore days after he walked into his adulthood. He could not, it seemed, feel joy; but only the need to inflict pain upon others. We have learned from Asurla that killing our own does nothing, yet he deserved death. So we sent him away."

"We should have slain him," said Ushas bitterly.

"My son," the Brak encouraged softly, "You acted bravely. Do not question the past to try and make right the present. That road leads to no good end."

"He must have joined the Urudu and helped with your capture! It seems he found a people like himself," said Lu'ril knowingly.

"What was his name?" asked Areoch.

"Behram," said Ushas. "Behram Rais."

Everyone was silent for a time. The food and dishes were removed and Areoch shifted on his cushion.

"So all is lost," Areoch mourned. "Bahira and Berran, we have pursued them in vain. The *Taradium* is gone beyond our reach."

"Not in vain. Not at *all* in vain" assured Meshêk. "Had we not come, Ushas and two dozen of his people would now have little hope from escaping the Urudu's hands. The Urudu seem to prefer their prisoners alive. Why do so, if they are to be killed upon arrival in the north? No, there is still hope, Areoch. The north is not some forbidden place, though it has been forgotten."

"It has not been forgotten in Tel-Brak," assured the Chieftain Brak. "We still remember our dealings with the Amorites of the peninsula. Kez-Bazi warned us before leaving that the north was changing, and our trade with them stopped. We have heard the Amorites have grown evil, I would avoid them."

"Time, time," Meshêk murmured to himself. "If only I had more time! I would seek out Bazi, perhaps he would know if Kez-Meldek still lives. I feared they both had perished. Perhaps together we might be able to change something of the past. But to turn aside would be to abandon what we have started and I cannot do so."

He paused and spoke a little louder.

"We must depart, and quickly, if we are to have any hope of catching the *Taradium*. I feel that we should first re-visit the island where we battled last night, maybe there is something left of the ship, or even an

Urudu alive that we could gain more knowledge from."

"If there is a chance Bahira is alive, we must go after her!" cried Areoch, leaping to his feet.

"If you are to have hope, then you should depart. You will need all haste," agreed the Chieftain Brak, also rising. "We watch the sea and what goes here and there upon the waters. Our watchers saw two days ago a second ship, similar to the dark one you have described, sailing around our island from the south. This may have been the vessel you seek. Go with all speed and find your people."

"And find what is precious to you," added Ushas, looking knowingly at Areoch.

Meshêk bowed to the Brak and took one last look at the golden image stretching high above them.

"Where are the Shedu now, when we need them most?" he murmured. "Though I am your elder by many, many generations Chieftain Brak, you are wise. I am grateful for your counsel this day. Let all the world know that wisdom and strength still live on the islands of Tel-Brak!"

The Brak smiled and the gold, ingrained within his features, shimmered.

"Wisdom has a way of coming in its own time, Kez-Matura. I do not think we will meet again. Bring what was good and strong of ancient times into today, and find what power is behind this madness!"

Chapter Thirty-three

Rise of the Uttuki

Meshêk, Areoch, and Lu'ril were joined by Tor'i and the rest of *The Alalia's* crew and with haste, made ready to leave. Ushas guided them back down the broad steps and to another small stair. They zig-zagged sharply down the cliff-side, descending swiftly, until the sea was loud in their ears. Suddenly the bay of Ka'bier was at their feet. The water here was still, and several long canoes were tied at stem and stern along the walkway. *The Aralia* floated calmly offshore.

The people of Tel-Brak seemed slow to speak, but had a strange understanding with one another. As Meshêk, Areoch, and Lu'ril boarded their ship, nearly twenty white-faced Brakians joined them.

"You have a great need for haste and these men desire to help you regain what you have lost," Ushas offered solemnly. "If you accept their service, they will help you in your journey in whatever capacity you may need."

"As long as they understand the risk," pointed out Meshêk. "We go into many known perils ...and unknown danger."

"This, they understand," Ushas replied.

Meshêk nodded and the Brakians boarded *The Alalia*.

"I will lead you through our islands to Tintar, the island on which we were attacked," Ushas offered. "Stay close to us and do not stray down another channel. The current here is swift and the rocks are sharp."

Ushas jumped into one of the long canoes and pushed out into the bay. Several other Brakians followed him in canoes of their own. On *The Alalia,* the Brakians manned the upper oar-bank with the ease of a sea-faring people, while the crew from Cartegin manned the second deck. The ship let out after the canoes, nearly skimming the face of sharp sea-stacks on more than one occasion. The double steering oars effectively maneuvered the ship through the tight corners.

"This is a maze of water I would not like to navigate again," Tor'i complained, more than once under his breath, as the wood of *The Alalia* came within inches of scraping rock. Ushas guided them well and Meshêk deftly manned his oar.

Finally, the open sea stretched before them. The mainland was barely visible in the clear daylight to the northwest, and Tintar's rocky shore was little more than a small, black mound in the sea topped with green. Ushas and the small fleet of canoes made their way across the channel while *The Alalia,* given the freedom of the open waters, rowed with quarter oars so as not to overtake them.

Areoch and Lu'ril ate and refreshed themselves before meeting on the upper deck. Tor'i was there with most of the crew. They shared briefly their tale of adventure and how the Brakian's help had been offered.

"Well bless my sails," said Tor'i as he heard the story. He gazed with new respect at the painted figures who pulled on the oars. "Perhaps now we do have a chance, however slim, of making up for the lost time."

"And destroying the *Taradium* when we find it!" cried Lu'ril. "When you and Meshêk smashed into the Urudu ship last night... I have never seen anything like it in all of my days."

Tor'i shook his head. "Nor have I, or the rest of us here. How *The Alalia* suffered so little damage from such force I will never know. Birsha always was a keen architect of watercraft!"

"Make ready those ropes there!" called out Meshêk from the stern. "Tintar is close, prepare to push off the rocks!"

They looked up, surprised to see how quickly the time had passed. They picked up long poles to fend off the shallows, while Tor'i and the crew moved to their stations.

"I always knew Meshêk was more than he seemed," murmured Lu'ril to Areoch as they stood at the fore, fending off the rocks as they landed. "All those years in Cartegin he seemed to stay to himself, but I thought there was something more about him. Then he and Birsha vanished to Magen during the hard years and I knew something was happening. Then, just when everything strange begins, he shows back up with you. Do you think he is some sort of enchanter?"

Areoch chuckled.

"No, he is not that at all. In my land, we call men like Meshêk *sages*. They advise kings and kingdoms. I guess some small number of sages are more than they seem, these *Kez*. I have met three, I think: my teacher, Marqu, a man named Melkezadek, and now Meshêk.

"Are they all as secretive and annoying as Meshêk?" Lu'ril wondered aloud.

Areoch laughed again.

"Yes," he replied, stilling his mirth. "Though each has shown it differently, it's as if they know something none of *us* do, and they are either afraid to try and explain it or they know we won't understand."

Areoch continued to muse, "Birsha, I guess, was able to bind Meshêk to his service. I wonder how that happened..."

Lu'ril shrugged his shoulders. "I don't know. They came to Cartegin from the sea when I was but a small lad. He was ever and always Birsha's servant, I assumed his entire family had been." He looked back over his shoulder at the Isle of Brak, now shadowed in the distance. "I would like to come back here someday," he murmured longingly.

The Alalia was made fast just off the sandy shore where the Urudu ship had been destroyed. The carnage of the wreckage still floated here and there. Meshêk and Tor'i met Ushas on the beach with a group of about twenty armed men. The rest stayed with the ship and the boats.

"Most of the wreckage has been dashed to bits upon the rock, the current takes no prisoners. There is nothing useful from the ship. What do you hope to find?" Tor'i asked, looking around at the debris from the previous night's battle.

Meshêk kicked at a shattered plank and looked into the heart of the island. The ravine through the cliff stretched away. The boulder that fell the previous night could not be seen. There were no signs of life.

"At best, I hope we may take an Urudu alive. If not, maybe there is something else that may be of use to us, or something that will give us more knowledge about our enemies. Keep your weapons near at hand. Judging by your tale, most of the Urudu perished last night in your pursuit. I find it likely that at least a few survived."

They began working their way inland, picking slowly across rubble and rock, careful not to make any sound. Their eyes and ears twitched at every quivering bush and singing bird. But no signs of the enemy were found; neither a dead body, nor the remains of a recent camp.

They paused at the site of the great boulder. Here at last some of the Urudu remained: those who perished under the giant stone were partially visible. An arm and several legs, stiff and crooked, protruded from underneath the massive rock. Tor'i whistled and shifted his grip on his spear.

"That is one large stone!" he exclaimed. "I doubted at first the truth of your tale, but I see, if anything, you did not give it enough justice!"

"I am more impressed by the jump," remarked Meshêk, surveying the canyon's top. "It must have been a twenty-foot leap, even with the stone in its initial place. There is nothing here that will tell us much, everything is smashed or charred. Ushas, where were you and your kin taken captive?"

"Not more than a mile from here, on the north side of the island," he answered, gesturing beyond the boulder.

"Let us go there and see what we find."

The sun climbed high in the sky as the troop moved farther inland. The canyon ended and the forest grew thicker. They spread out as they moved north, combing the forest in a loose line as they searched for any sign of the Urudu.

Soon the sound of the sea grew louder and the trees began to fade. Suddenly, they stopped altogether. Black rocks stuck out of the sea and waves crashed up the island's sides. Ushas came to a halt.

"This is as far as your men may come, Kez-Matura. Even though it seems our hidden sanctuary here has been betrayed, only the Brak's may continue. It is a place our kin hold dear."

Meshêk turned and addressed Tor'i. "Have everyone take a meal here and be refreshed - do not let down your guard! I will go forward with the Brakians. If we do not return in an hour, go to the ship and come back to search us out in force."

Tor'i nodded and the men gratefully cast themselves down, peeling off their leather jerkins. It was getting hot.

Meshêk carefully followed Ushas as they neared the cliff's edge. The charred remains of campfires marked the Urudu's vigilance of their previous attack. Ushas ducked behind two small trees which grew from the rocks and then vanished. Steep stairs made their way down a dark maw, invisible from any side, except the sky. The sea roared from its gaping jaws. The stone was pitted from years of sea tide and sand.

Slowly, they made their way down, taking care not to make any noise. Water dripped from the ceiling, the slow, steady trickle echoed in various, small pools. The tunnel narrowed and then turned, widening as it approached the cliff's edge. Several cracks opened to the sea, letting in thin rays of afternoon light. Meshêk walked with Ushas, while the Brakians behind tightened the grips on their spears. Their painted white faces shone like ghosts in the darkness.

Ushas bent over and a sudden light flared, adding to the sparse sunlight. He raised a sputtering torch above his head and the darkness fled. The ground had softened and opened into a wide, circular space. Almost a hundred low mounds of thick, wet sand spiraled around in an ever-closing circle. Each mound was topped with a sharp circlet of large rocks. The largest of the mounds seemed far away, barely visible but for the sparkling, white granite stones which caught the light.

"This is the house of Sheol, Kez-Matura," whispered Ushas. "It was here my kin and I fended off the Urudu for three days until we were captured. I thought we might end up here forever, buried among our dead."

"Something is amiss," Meshêk whispered, bending over the nearest mound. "More light!" he insisted, "Bring over more light!"

Twe other Brakians lit torches, holding them high.

"What is it?" Ushas asked.

Meshêk gestured to the mound. Its crown of stones was pushed aside and the earth was moved and scoured, leaving a low, dark hole where the grave should have been. "Did you prepare for the death of your comrades while you waited here? Or for yourself?" Meshêk demanded.

Ushas brought the light nearer and his face darkened.

"No. We did not," he replied with repulsion. "What devilry is this? Did the Urudu prepare to bury their own in our sacred place?"

"No," assured Meshêk, his voice quivering. He raised his hand and pointed farther in the chamber. "That is not what has happened here."

Ushas looked up and several of the other Brakians gasped in horror and fear. Many ran back towards the stairs and the light above.

"The graves. They are empty! They are all empty!" Ushas panicked, running from tomb to tomb. He came back to Meshêk, panting, the torch in his hand, shaking. "Kez-Matura, what has happened here? Who would desecrate our dead? What would seek to capture them as if they were the living?"

Meshêk did not answer. His face was ashen and he drew his hand through the scarred earth slowly. He rose, taking the torch from Ushas.

"Get your people out of here," he whispered.

Ushas trembled with fear but planted his feet firmly.

"I will not abandon you Kez-Matura."

Meshêk grabbed him violently and threw him back toward the entrance with tremendous strength.

"Go!" he demanded. "There is nothing you can do here. Wait for me in the passage if you must."

Ushas nodded. Fear laced his voice as he commanded the Brakians to retreat to the entrance.

Alone, Meshêk turned back to the empty graves, holding the torch in his hand. He walked deeper into the cavern, slowly dipping his torch in each grave as he passed. All were empty. He continued across the expanse of the chamber. He travelled past the granite mounds of the Brak's ancient Kings. Here, too, the earth was scarred. Still Meshêk walked. As he drew near the far side, a sudden gust of chill wind blew through a low crack and his torch went out.

The rays of light that snuck through the rock above seemed thin, wavering in the air. Still Meshêk went on, stepping over each dark hole as they appeared in front of him. Sweat beaded on his forehead. Finally, he halted. The air was tight. He raised his hand and spoke a Word of Power.

" 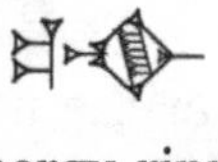 !"

Energy ripped through the expanse of the chamber, like a strike of lighting! The remainder of the cavern lit up with a flash! There, towering in the shadow, rose a dark, inverted tree. Its twisted roots stretched like claws, vainly grasping for earth as they snaked into the air. What was left of its branches remained buried beneath the dirt in the final grave.

Though the chamber was filled with light, it remained dark and rotting, resisting the Power of the word Meshêk has spoken.

Meshêk's eyes grew wide.

"No. No! NO!!" he cried as he raised his hands. "It cannot be!"

Even as he spoke the light went out as suddenly as it had come. The rocks above shattered with a thunderous crack and the ceiling trembled.

Meshêk turned and fled. Rocks flew about his head as he leapt across the empty graves. The tunnel flicked in and out of his vision as the ceiling shifted like waves. His foot caught a stone and he fell hard, landing in one of the empty graves. A boulder the size of a house sent dirt flying as it landed upon his left. Suddenly, Meshêk found strong hands pulling him up. Ushas was beside him and they were both fleeing behind the Brakians, up the stairs, and back into the sunlight. Dust flew up from the maw as the group collapsed among the small trees. Thundering rocks closed the entrance forever.

Tor'i, Areoch, and Lu'ril came running, weapons held high and eyes wide. They stopped short when they found Meshêk and the Brakians, all accounted for and heaving for breath. Meshêk looked up from under dusty eyebrows at Ushas.

Ushas was trembling. "Is death no more, Kez-Matura? Are the legends true? I feel in my bones, some dread, that turns my heart to water."

Meshêk struggled to his feet, leaning heavily on Ushas. He did not answer, though his eyes were dark.

Tor'i interjected, "What happened? Did you find what you were looking for?" he gazed with a questioning look at the collapsed entrance and rising dust.

"No," answered Meshêk wearily. "We found something worse. Something much worse."

"Go," Meshêk whispered hoarsely to Ushas. "Tell your father what you have seen here. Tell him it is time to take up the spear and the shield! Tell him it is time that the Brak's rejoin the fight. Tell him that the Kez hide no more in the land of the living..." Ushas' eyes were wide and steady, Meshêk finished his message "for the *Uttuki* have risen."

The prow of *The Alalia* cut through the waters with vigor as she bounced from swell to swell. The sun was a finger breadth above the western horizon as they raced northward, the tribes of Tel-Brak and the islands were a distant shadow in the south. Tor'i manned the steering oar as Meshêk leaned against the forward rail by himself. He had stood there alone, gazing with narrowed eyes across the northern waters since they had made sail. Areoch eased in next to him, pushing a steaming cup of tea and a warm loaf of bread into his hand.

"Ah, thank you my lad," Meshêk said gratefully, stirred from his thoughts.

Areoch stayed next to him. Low mountains were visible in the northwest, bathed with golden light as the sun sank behind them.

"Meshêk," asked Areoch finally, "what was it that you found in that cave? I have never seen you so, you haven't said a word to anyone since. The men are worried about you. They whisper something about the dead rising."

Meshêk took a long drought of his tea.

"There was a sign, Areoch. A sign from the ancient world. One that I have not seen since long, long before you or any of your forefathers walked upon the earth. It was the sign of the Uttuki."

"The Uttuki..." Areoch began and then stopped. He paused and then continued slowly. "My whole life I believed these *things* were no more than legend. It seemed like a thing of story alone. Yet, I have heard more about them, and the Shedu, in the last few months than I ever have! The more I think, the more I see, the more I find myself believing what most men call *myth* to be *true*. Everything that has happened so far... it cannot simply be chance. You, I think, know more of this than most."

Areoch let his words hang in the wind-swept air.

"What is it that you mean?" Meshêk persisted.

"I mean that you are no household servant born under the care of Birsha's family. You found me upon the road from Agade as if by *chance*. Protected me when you had little cause to do so. Convinced me to turn back when I was to leave. Broke me free from the binds of Ishshak! At every turn, you have guided me to where we stand. Even the Brak's know you and respect you." Areoch studied him closely, "Well? Will you not tell me what you know? Will you not tell me plainly who you really are?"

Meshêk smiled a wry smile.

"It seems, Areoch of Ur, that I owe you an explanation. So I will reveal to you what few men know: I am called Meshêk by you, but I have been known throughout the generations of your forefathers as Kez-Matura, the son of Šuruppag the Wise of the household of Atrahasis, a Firstborn of Man. I was born in the Ancient World, into the raw power of Life when it was new, in times long forgotten. And I remember it, Areoch! I remember that ancient power, which all mankind once possessed. I was there, at the time of the Great Destruction." Meshêk lamented, "Oh, that deadly consequence of our abused Words! That unending conflict, where the Lords of Light battled against the Uttuki, the Powers of Darkness! That utter end of those ancient days, where all but a remnant of the Firstborns perished. I survived the torrents in Atrahasis's household. And I, to my everlasting shame, was one of the Seven, the greatest and last of my kin, who helped Asurla the Slayer become king over all men. As is the way of the Firstborn, I have endured through the years of time since."

Even as he spoke, the wind blew the frayed hair aside from Meshêk's face and the sea crashed like thunder against the ship. Areoch saw Meshêk in a new light, as if a veil had been removed. The wisdom of many years seemed etched into his features, but Areoch could not see a wrinkle of age. Meshêk stood tall, revealing a broad chest and a commanding stature. He gazed keenly at Areoch and it seemed as if an old fire was kindled deep in his eyes, as both a young and an old man stood in the same body.

"Listen to me, Areoch: the Shedu and the Uttuki are not legends! They are *real*, though I myself have long doubted any remained among us. Above all my fears it seems the Powers of Darkness have risen again from the sludge of the earth, or are rising even as we sail, and are once again twisting and corrupting the hearts of men. I will not stand by again and do nothing!" Meshêk resolved. "I must not, though I fear I will fall into darkness, as I did in the days of old.

'I guessed at first it was only some remnant of Uttuki thought, but now I am sure there must be at least one Power that has survived. By Enlil, I hope it is not the Ninĝinĝar. No, I will not even speak of it. It could not be so."

"The dead," Areoch began, "do the Uttuki claim the dead? Is that what the men speak of with such fear?" Areoch asked breathlessly.

Meshêk shook his head. "I have never seen anything like this, Areoch. I do not... I do not know."

The sun sank behind the mountains, streaking the summer sky with red and purple against the high clouds. Meshêk's power became veiled and it seemed only a tired, old man stood before him.

"Can you kill one of... them? asked Areoch, "Can you kill an Uttuki?"

"You do not know what you ask!" Meshêk replied, his voice tight. "I will not speak of such things ever again."

Meshêk looked out across the waters. Eventually, he sighed, and continued in a softer tone. "It should not be spoken of, Areoch. Our words have power." Meshêk gave him a grave look. "Asurla sought out this question too far, in the elder days. It was for this reason that he is known in tales as 'The Slayer'. But, it was not just the Uttuki that he hated. It was anything that was from the Ancient World. Including my own kin. And the Shedu."

"Is that what you did? Slew the Shedu ...and your own family? Is that what Chieftain Brak spoke to you of?"

Meshêk clenched the railing and his eyes fell.

"Yes, Areoch. To my great shame." He faltered. In a whisper, he continued. "I have been a fool, Areoch," he admitted sorrowfully. "All of their faces, the faces of Atrahasis house... I still remember. He slaughtered them, Areoch. Asurla slaughtered all of them. Oh!" Meshêk threw back his head as though injured, and continued, "Oh, the beauty of Etemmu and Jemdet! The depth of light within them! Their daughters of today are *shades* of who *they* were. We watched, Areoch! We did nothing. We *helped* him!"

Meshêk's voice lowered.

"It was not enough. Even *that* was not enough to quench his hate. It grew as if alive, until we could barely recognize him. Asurla began to hunt for the Uttuki and the Shedu. Though it is not for the Uttuki that I grieve. The battle against their lies has raged since the beginning of my memory. It is for the fall of the Shedu... I fear I may never be forgiven... The Shedu... Oh, my heart fails me.' He turned aside, his face ashen. The water mirrored the purple sky above.

'I do not think any remain, though if my guess is true, now is when we will need them most."

Areoch stood in stunned silence, watching the northern mountains grow darker.

"The Urudu are not our main threat," muttered Meshêk in a low voice. "Alas, many things are finally clear and too much... I still do not understand." he trailed off. "The Urudu's speed, their craftiness, their knowledge and unity - all can be explained now. The Uttuki are guiding and empowering them. The Uttuki always favored the north, they must be drawing the Urudu there.

'But, the abducted and now the dead vanishing... that mystery still puzzles me. I fear in my heart what it could mean. Alas, for the wisdom of my father when he says, *The abducted and the dead: how alike they are!* I am frightened by this prophecy. I fear for Berran and Bahira. I fear for them, Areoch, and for what we will find as we move farther north. As for me, my heart is set: I will see this through."

He turned and laid a hand on Areoch.

"Kez-Matura walks among you now, uncloaked, though still ashamed. Go and rest. The past few days have been long. All of us will need strength for what we find ahead."

Chapter Thirty-four

The Lord Egal-Mah

Guzzier awoke with a start and lost his balance. The stone giant's hand was open upon the ground and Guzzier rolled out, landing softly. It was still night. The silent beauty of that wild land, deep within the heart of the Oodan Mountains, was almost more than he could bear. Shukiera and Eli'ssa were next to him. Shukiera was standing and she smiled when she saw Guzzier.

"Shukiera," Guzzier whispered, "are you alright? Can you walk?"

She nodded. Eli'ssa appeared well, though her legs would not bear her weight. Bahira was not with them. The giant who released Guzzier stood again to its full height and then fell silent, unmoving.

All around them grew mighty crystals. Their boles were thicker than tree-trunks and their height was taller than trees. Across the red, rocky floor (and clustered near each base of crystal), grew the blue flowers of the high crags, glowing in the night. A path through the enchanted gem forest could be seen, leading back the way they had come.

Some distance ahead, as a row of trees marks the edge of a forest, the crystals stopped. A wide, oval clearing was laid bare. In its center was a low structure. Like the fortress of Par'adam, it was built of ancient red stone that rose sharply out of the ground. No markings marred its surface, but the blue flowers grew everywhere, hiding most of the cracking rock's exterior. Granite giants stood tranquil around it - between each of the strange, silent creatures there was no difference one could tell.

The women looked at each other with wide eyes.

Guzzier gently picked up Eli'ssa and the three turned toward the low structure, walking underneath the glowing crystals. Their calloused, bare feet were quiet over the smooth stone.

A faint sound resonated in the crystal forest, an ancestral noise, enchanting and beautiful, as if the gems faintly echoed an ancient song sung by the stars. As they passed from the crystal trees and stepped into the clearing, the noise faded. The silence was absolute, and their breathing seemed loud and dissonant.

They drew to an unspoken halt. Half-hidden by a veil of blue flowers, a small entrance in the red structure faced them. Guzzier led them slowly toward it. The veil of flowers quivered as if moved by a light breeze and then suddenly, they were moved aside.

It seemed for a moment that the wings of a bird filled the space, bright and glistening like the many colors of the S'acar! In a flash of plumage, it disappeared, and a human-like figure stood before them. From the waist-up he glistened as if sculpted from a precious stone, and from the waist down he shone like a blazing fire. Brightness streamed from him like the morning dawn - a radiance of terrifying splendor. They fell, their faces to the ground. They felt a voice shaking the ground with power.

"Mortals, stand. I am the Red Stone, The Windswept Canyon, the Lord Egal-Mah, and you have been brought to me."

At the sound of his voice, blackness overtook their vision and their breathing stopped. The Lord Egal-Mah reached forward and touched them. His splendor seemed to lessen, and they found they could look up and see him. They rose, shaking, to their knees.

"Do not be afraid," the Lord Egal-Mah commanded. "I have been waylaid long by the kingdom of Ninĝinĝar. The Lord Núnimar, chief of the Shedu, has intervened to aid me. Now I am here to help you understand what will happen to your people."

While the Lord Egal-Mah spoke, Eli'ssa looked at the ground and said nothing. Then something, like a human hand, reached out and touched her lips and she spoke.

"My Lord, my heart is like water poured out upon the ground. How can I speak to you? I can hardly breathe."

"Peace, dear one," the Lord Egal-Mah assured, looking at them each in turn. "Take courage. Be strong."

Courage and strength seemed to surge within them as if alive, and Guzzier rose to his feet, his eyes alight!

"Soon I must leave to fight against the Lord of Darkness," the Lord Egal-Mah continued. "I have waited, so that I may tell you what has been written in the Book of Ancient Days. When it was opened, I was there."

"Why do we not know of you, Lord?" Guzzier gasped. "My people dwell not far from here and I have lived among them my whole life. Yet, no tale or word of this place has ever been spoken."

"The song you sang upon the mountain top is such a tale," the Lord Egal-Mah answered. "Though its meaning has passed from human memory, its words have power. Long ago, I was given dominion over this realm. But, I have been held a captive, besieged by the Dark Power. Few remain to fight them except the Lord Núnimar. It was he that broke through the Uttuki ranks to reach me. The Dominion of the north is coming. Many who have been long dead and buried will wake up, until the Prince of the holy mountain comes."

"What you say makes no sense to me, Lord," Shukiera whispered. "I cannot understand it."

"The message is sealed until the proper time," the Lord Egal-Mah explained.

"Bahira, my friend, is dying," Eli'ssa choked. "When we raced over the mountains, she fell... You must know where she is, will you not save her?"

"Mortal, you speak of death as though it is the end," rumbled the Lord Egal-Mah. "You know that this is not what you should be afraid of. Bahira has found the path, the Truth of high esteem! She has found *Life*."

All were smitten with the word like a billowing roll of distant thunder, traveling from their toes up, up through their beating hearts and into their noses. It left the fragrance of a warm spring rain, fading into a soft sense of fullness.

"She is within." The Lord Egal-Mah gestured behind him to where the blue veil of flowers gently swayed.

Eli'ssa did not hesitate. She pushed herself up to her knees, and then to her feet, gazing with determination at the structure ahead!

"You cannot pass forward," the Lord Egal-Mah instructed, "or you will surely die."

"Oh, but Bahira is there!" Eli'ssa cried in dismay.

"Yes," the Egal-Mah said. "And many are with her, but they are not among the living. Though you love her, and your love remains within you, Bahira was never *yours* to treasure, past the allotted time. Grow, dear one! Grow into the depth of understanding your love. You will meet again. It is written that today is not that time."

Eli'ssa nodded and fell silent, drawing back.

"What is next, Lord Egal-Mah?" Guzzier asked. "We have lost so much, escaped from danger, yet left many behind. My people have been enslaved and slaughtered! Those I have cared about have been taken from me. Where now shall I go?"

"You, too, are highly esteemed," the Lord Egal-Mah replied, turning his infinite gaze upon him. "Safety is never your aim. The easiest path never chosen. Love given when retribution due! Unlike my servants, who move by my will alone, your path is your own to walk. You must choose Guzzier, where your next step will take you - though you may not know yourself where it will truly lead. My servants will carry you, after you have rested, and lay you upon a road to the west. From there, you must decide your course."

The Lord Egal-Mah grew silent and the three in front of him did as well.

"It is time," he said. "I leave you now. Know that upon your enemies I will fall and my glory upon them will be terrible. In the end, all will be made new." He turned away. As he began to push aside the soft curtain of flowers, Shukiera's heart filled with memories of sadness.

"My Lord, why do you not leave this place?" she blurted. Her voice trembled. "All the faces of those I have lost, I remember. Their names fill my heart with grief. Their loss, I cannot bear. Here with you, in this place, that line of grief - which has strangled me for so long, has thinned. I feel it still, like a cold night that has vanished, leaving a memory of its chill in the warm rays of sun. I fear, Lord, that when I leave your presence it will again overwhelm me. Why do you choose to dwell among us? Why? Why do you not leave us alone in our brokenness?"

The Lord Egal-Mah turned back and came near to her.

"Beloved," he said softly, "Here, for a moment, you see clearly - like your ancient mothers. But you do not understand. Let me show you, Eternity."

Gently, slowly, he reached forward and touched her eyes with his fingertips. After only a moment, he pulled back. He smiled on her, and then vanished back into the holy edifice of stone.

"What did you see?" Eli'ssa asked her later.

Shukiera looked up at the sky and smiled, her eyes beaming. What she had seen played across her mind: an unexplainable wholeness bridging across an infinite divide, healing and making new all that had been and all that was left to be. Exactly what she saw, she could not remember. She could not find the words to say.

How long they stayed among the trees of crystal, they never knew. They had no need for food or water. It seemed that it was always evening there, with the starlight dancing among the glowing branches of the gemstone trees.

After a time, a single granite giant came and carried them far away from that place. As they left, they could see hundreds more of the creatures marching to the south. In their midst was a chariot of crystal. From it a great light shone and they knew upon it was the Lord Egal-Mah, riding forward unto battle against the lands of Angfar.

Chapter Thirty-five

A Torrent of Justice

The night passed without a sign of the *Taradium* and *The Alalia* continued to sail swiftly through the waters north of Tel-Brak. Areoch slept fitfully. When he closed his eyes, dreams of darkness and hoarse cries filled his mind, stirring him from sleep. When he awoke, the haunting, white faces of the Brakians surrounded him, pulling ceaselessly on the oars in their endless vigilance. Finally, Areoch could stand it no longer and sat up from his hammock. Low moans of pain came from behind the sheet at the far end of *The Alalia* and Meshêk appeared. His face was drawn. Areoch arose and walked with him to the upper deck.

"Joshur is not well, is he?" Areoch asked.

Meshêk shook his head. "No. He has been feverish since we left Tel-Brak and it will not break."

"He was hurt badly before he made it to Cartegin," Areoch observed.

"That is not why his wounds are refusing to heal," Meshêk replied. "We are near Angfar. The Power of the Uttuki is strong here, even to the very core of the earth. Their will is not to mending but to destroying."

The night air blew on their faces as they walked on the main deck. A faint light shone far off in the east and stars swirled brightly overhead. The dark edges of canted mountains could barely be made out on their left. Tor'i murmured a greeting from the steering oar as they passed and then let them walk in silence.

"Is this Angfar?" Areoch asked, gesturing at the outlines of the distant mountains.

"No," answered Meshêk. "This is the land of the Amorites. They used to be part of the Jezrial Dynasty, a city state of the northern lands controlled by Zoar - the most powerful city state of them all. They were outcast and shunned by the northern Kings for their *Alshnazbad.*"

"*Alshnazbad?*" Areoch asked quizzically.

"In the common tongue, you may say the 'eating of man'. Ushas warned me of stopping or pulling ashore here. The Brakians think more than they say, but have little doubt the Amorites and Angfar are in league. Zoar as well, I would guess, at least to some degree of trade. It is only a guess. The King of Zoar has been powerful in these parts ever since the Great Destruction. Amri, its current King, and his Queen Izével, may not know the level of Power they trifle with in Angfar. Then again, they may."

"Meshêk, how is it possible to defeat such evil that has been around for so long? I feel as if we sail to no good end."

The light grew slowly brighter in the east and the first shades of red and purple filled the sky. The dark of the Tanti Sea gave way to its pale reflection.

"Have no fear, Areoch, for we are all immortal, until Enlil calls us to Himself. You hold more power within you than you dare to guess. Power for much good or power for much darkness. How you use that influence is a decision *you* will make, whether you do it intentionally or not. Your actions and thoughts are rooted with the same power that is in the Spoken Words of Old, though to a lesser degree. Stand firm in what you know to be True, regardless of the cost to yourself or the response of other men. That is the way of the Shedu. Believe, Areoch, that no matter who you are, the Ancient Powers run through your blood. Turn your will toward them, and the Power you discover within yourself may surprise you."

Three light calls echoed over the air from the stern.

"That is the rotation," Meshêk concluded, turning away. "I must go relieve Tor'i before he falls asleep leaning upon that oar!" Areoch did not return to his hammock as the crew of *The Alalia* switched. Lu'ril suddenly appeared beside him, stretching and yawning.

"Ahhh!" he growled. "I could sleep for a week on end if only I could stop swaying back and forth. Every time I close my eyes, I imagine the ship is rolling completely over and I wake up in a panic."

Areoch laughed, grateful for his honest complaints after their long journey.

"I cannot sleep either. We are close to our goal and it weighs heavy upon me what will come about when we reach that end. Meshêk says we are less than a day away from the lands of Angfar."

"Then we battle against the Urudu!" Lu'ril cried, rubbing his hands together eagerly. "I have never been in a battle, but I feel the same as when the bears come down from the Durgu Mountains in bad winters and I go to defend the herds of Cartegin with my father. Have you ever been in a battle?"

"No," admitted Areoch. "Though I saw one, long ago. I do not remember much of it. The parts I do remember, do not make me wish to be in one. Zakkaria, the commander of our Strong Men, would tell us about them during our training. He would say that you never really win in a battle - other men, like kings and diplomats, they may win. But, for the man on the field behind the great shield wall, the only point is to survive, and help your brother do the same."

Lu'ril looked at Areoch with curiosity.

"That sounds silly to me, but I have only heard stories of battles. I have never trained to kill a man or stand in a shield wall. How is it that the Lands of Magen have such training and commanders of Strong Men?"

Areoch was not listening to Lu'ril's question. He peered over the front of the ship as the sun broke the horizon, sending bright rays of sunlight leaping over the water.

"Lu'ril! Look, there, quickly! Do you see that?" Areoch cried, pointing off the port side of the bow. Lu'ril leaned over the railing, shading his eyes.

"What? What are you talking about?"

The land nearest to them was several hundred yards away. Bare hills stood tall with low-lying shrubs and coarse bushes running up the sides of steep ravines etched within their faces. Sharp boulders dotted the land here and there, and dark mountains rose intimidating behind them.

"There it is again! Onshore, before that low-lying hill!"

Lu'ril sucked in his breath. "What on earth..." he wondered.

Clear in the rising daylight, a great lion attempted to scale a steep ravine and crest the hilltop beyond. Its fur was black as the night, and even from their great distance the beast seemed larger than it should. Flicking from boulder to shrub, the lion stealthily moved through the morning, quiet and invisible were it not for the rays of sun catching on its glossy fur. It advanced into the hills, then abruptly stopped and its ears perked forward. Suddenly it leapt backward, hissing and spitting as several large, scaly forms rose from the rock, striking as they advanced.

"What are those?" Areoch asked in shock. "Snakes?"

"If they are, they are the biggest I have ever seen. And that, bless my father Cyril who taught me, must be an Umu! If only he were here to see it!! At the city gate in Cartegin he tells, on occasion, of seeing one on the slopes of the Durgu Mountains. Often, he is laughed at for being an old, blind farmer!"

The Umu retreated, batting with its huge paws as two, then three, and then ten of the slithery creatures appeared from the brush, driving back the great beast. A large outcropping of rock rose up and the scene vanished from view.

Areoch craned his neck, trying to see more, but he could not. He reached up and touched the scars that ran across his face, that he had received upon the road in the Valley of Dry Bones.

Lu'ril made a low whistle. "We are in strange country, sure enough. I hope we don't have to land for some time, we'd get eaten alive by Umu's or snakes - or both!"

Areoch did not reply, but stood up higher on the foredeck, looking ahead. The dark mountains seemed closer now and the bright sky was growing overcast. He peered closer at the water ahead of them.

"Do you see anything ahead of us, Lu'ril?"

"Aye, it looks like we're headed into a fog bank," Lu'ril replied. "and those black mountains seem to run clear down to the water's edge, they are sharp and sheer. The current of the waves beats against them, sharpening their sides!"

"Do you see that black spec, directly in the middle of where we are headed?" Areoch asked, pointing ahead.

"It could be no more than a stack of rock in the water," answered Lu'ril cautiously.

They both stared forward and the spec grew larger.

"Go tell Meshêk and raise the alarm," Areoch instructed. "Go!" he insisted louder.

Meshêk joined Areoch and Lu'ril at the prow.

"It is difficult to say in this light," Meshêk mused, examining the fog bank and the black shape before it. "It seems to be growing closer to us, faster than we are moving towards it."

"It may be nothing more than the fog," reminded Lu'ril.

"Is it a ship?" Areoch asked.

"We will find out soon," said Meshêk. "All hands to the oars, wake the off-watch and prepare for engagement."

Soon shouts were yelled out and every hammock was emptied. The white-faced Brakians laid their long, wooden spears and large shields beside them. The crew from Cartegin felt the edges of their stone axes. Areoch stood beside Meshêk on the steering platform, fidgeting with the bronze spear he had taken from the Urudu upon Tel-Brak.

All was silent beside the dipping of the oars. The dark spec on the northern horizon advanced swiftly towards them. As the sun rose higher, the hull of a ship could be seen.

"It must be from Angfar, or a ship of the Amorites," Meshêk surmised. "Is it an Urudu ship? Or one of another purpose? Lu'ril, go below and help Joshur up to the deck. He knows the design of the Urudu ships better than any of us."

Lu'ril hurried below and then reappeared, supporting Joshur (who leaned on him heavily). Joshur's face was pale and sweat soaked his brow and jerkin. Tendrils of fog darkened the day, but the oncoming vessel did not waiver or turn aside.

"Slow!" commanded Meshêk loudly. The dipping of the oars stopped. They stood out straight from *The Alalia* as the ship glided smoothly forward. The oncoming vessel did likewise and seemed to nearly stop, fighting against the northern currents.

The timbers of the foreign ship were black, either by the nature of the wood or the treating of the planks, one could not tell. It sat sleek and low in the water. A makeshift covering was over the rear quarter of its stern. Upon the covering stood a steersman, manning his long oar with a commanding view. Several other figures, at least five to either bank of oars, were visible on its main deck. At their head, standing tall on the prow of the ship, was a young man. His hair blew back in the wind revealing strong features, but he was not smiling.

His face was drawn and downcast, as if belonging to a man continually haunted by unseen tormentors. He gazed on *The Alalia* with a look of question on his face. It seemed that he was about to hail them, when suddenly his face grew tighter and his jaw set, as if making a decision. He turned and fled from his position into the hull of the black ship and out of sight.

Tor'i looked at Meshêk with wide eyes, "What do you suppose that was about?"

As quickly as the strange man fled, Joshur fell to his knees, trembling and shaking despite Lu'ril supporting him.

"What is it?" Lu'ril asked softly, lowering Joshur down to the deck. Meshêk leapt down from the steering platform next to them.

"It is he," answered Joshur weakly. "The man who deceived us. The man who killed my father. His na... His name... is Re'Amu."

Joshur's breath came in gasps and then all at once they ceased.

"Joshur. Joshur!" cried Lu'ril. He wept as he held the dead boy in his arms. Meshêk rose slowly. His eyes narrowed, and he turned his gaze back upon the dark ship.

"So, at last we come upon our quarry: the *Taradium*." Meshêk's words were sharp, laced with anger. The Brakians on the upper deck stood in unison, grasping spear and shield firmly in their hand.

The *Taradium* and *The Alalia* drew slowly alongside each other and another man appeared from the dark of the cabin. For a moment, uncontrolled, violent anger lashed out from Rais' eyes in response to Re'Amu's sudden abandonment, which was quickly replaced with an absurd look of welcome. The look rapidly changed to that of horror as he saw the Brakians. Twenty white faces, painted like his own, gazed down on him. Rais fell backward in terror.

"Flee!" he cried in a high voice. "Turn, inland! NOW!"

The Urudu froze in shock at Rais's panic.

"NOW!" Rais screamed.

All at once they scrambled to their oars and pushed off *The Alalia*, turning the *Taradium* toward land.

Meshêk was too fast. He leapt back upon the stern's platform and, grabbing *The Alalia's* steering oars, he careened the ship until it slammed into the *Taradium's* side! There was a shuddering rumble and the groaning of timbers as the bronze ram gouged deep into the *Taradium's* stern, knocking everyone to their knees as the two ships were united together.

"For Joshur! For Cartegin! For Bahira!!" cried Areoch and Lu'ril. They charged, leaping across the prow of *The Alalia* toward the fractured stern of the *Taradium*. The men of Cartegin followed, and the Brakians rained spears down on the Urudu from above.

Suddenly, ten more Urudu jumped out from the cabin interior armed with spears and bows. *Twang!* rang the song of their strings as they returned the attack. Several of the Cartegin's fell, pierced deeply with bronze tips. Areoch, Lu'ril, and two Brakians made a mighty leap and landed atop the cabin of the *Taradium*. Sapu fumbled with the steering oar, trying to not let it drop while pulling forth a thin axe from his belt. With a loud cry Areoch sprang forward, smashing the shaft of his spear across Sapu's head and neck. He crumpled to the deck.

"Row! Fight!" cried Rais. The Urudu hastily pulled on the oars while others fended off the attack. The water-soaked hull of *The Alalia* splintered, cracking as the weight of the *Taradium* strained against the ram. There was a sharp snap, and *The Alalia* recoiled, freed of the *Taradium's* weight. The ram remained buried within the hull of the Urudu ship, where it had split in two.

"The Urudu have broken free!" Tor'i cried to Meshêk. "Areoch and Lu'ril! They are onboard the *Taradium*!"

Four of the crew members following Areoch lost balance and fell screaming into the sea. Caught in the current without steering, the *Taradium* was dragged slowly northward as its stern filled with water. *The Alalia* floated adrift, the swells drawing the two ships farther away from one another.

Areoch grabbed Sapu's axe and stood firmly to his feet. Spears fell among the Urudu, some finding their mark, and jagged arrows whined in sharp return. With a shout, Areoch leapt from the cabin's top among his enemies, knocking them flat as he rained down blows upon them. Lu'ril and the Brakians were behind him as they clashed spear and shield with the Urudu. The battle raged across the *Taradium*. The boarding party was surrounded on every side, ducking, bobbing, and weaving as the Urudu focused their attack. Blood covered the wooden planks. Lu'ril slipped and fell hard, the stone farmer's axe in his hand clattered across the deck. Masahum stood above him, gloating as he twirled a long bronze dagger in his hand.

"Lu'ril!" cried Areoch, seeing his peril. He spun, striking at the nearest Urudu with his axe and spear, but as one opponent fell two more rose up in their place. As Masahum reveled over his fallen opponent a long-thrown spear from *The Alalia* sailed through the air and struck him in the shoulder, throwing him off balance. Areoch threw his axe! It spun once and buried itself deeply into Masahum. He fell unmoving. Lu'ril scrambled to his feet and winked at Areoch, managing a light-hearted smile even in the midst of the battle, then his smile wavered.

The pale face of Rais stood menacingly before him. In his hand Rais held a long shaft of dense wood, upon which double rows of shark's teeth lay firmly buried, their tips red with blood. The bodies of the two Brakians lay at his feet, along with many fallen Urudu. A merciless smile appeared on his face as he stepped over the motionless forms.

Like a serpent striking, Rais flew upon Lu'ril, twirling his vicious weapon in a careening attack. Again, and again Lu'ril parried and dodged, as chips flew from his axe handle. Finally, he stumbled, falling on the deck, overwhelmed. He raised his hands, dazed, and Rais struck downward. Once! Twice! The blows were heavy, and Lu'ril's hands fell limp.

"No!!" cried Areoch. Many Urudu still blocked his path, fending him backward. The soaring spears from *The Alalia* had ceased. The *Taradium* was out of range. Only six Urudu remained standing and they drew back from Areoch's renewed attacks, breathing heavily. They smiled ruefully at each other as they surrounded him.

"Where is Bariquim when we need him?" remarked Shadeir grimly, tightly holding his arm where Areoch's axe had cut him. "He could dispatch this cur without a second thought!"

"He's mine," insisted Balak, looking to where Masahum lay on the deck, spear and axe still protruding from his motionless form.

"No," ordered Rais firmly. "I have seen enough of men to know this one is from the southern reaches. Is that not so, my love?"

Rais walked forward, slowly. The tip of his shark-tooth sword dragged behind him over the deck, gouging the wood as it passed. "You hold your spear like the Agadians do. Move like they do. I wonder if you die like they do."

Areoch tightened his grip on his spear and faced Rais.

"You are the one the Brakians call *Behram Rais*." He spat out the name. "I have heard of you. You are an outcast, even from your homeland. A murderer. You burned Cartegin. You stole Bahira and Berran. For what?! For the worth of your soul? For your own pleasure?" Rais licked his lips hungrily, but Areoch continued. "You killed Joshur and Lu'ril, my friends. And you have slain many more. You smile, because having power over the lives of others is the only thing that brings you joy. Know that you have no power over me!"

Rais lashed out at Areoch in a sudden rage, the toothy edge coming within inches of Areoch's neck.

"Is that so?" hissed Rais. "We will see. Where are your friends, my dearest?" Rais taunted. "They are too far to save you. You are alone."

Areoch dove under the toothy sword as it cut near again, striking at the legs of Rais before thrusting for his head. They both slipped on the blood-covered deck as they circled, clashing spear and razor-toothed sword.

Areoch panted heavily, wiping the sweat from his eyes. He had no respite. Rais came, pushing his attack tirelessly, again and again, each swipe closer than the last. Suddenly Areoch slipped and fell hard near the prow. His spear fell from his grasp and rolled to the railing. Rais stood over him, pinning him to the deck with a blood-soaked boot. The black jet bracelet that was once Berran's caught in the light, shining from his hand as Rais leveled his weapon.

"You see?" Rais cried. "I kill and I take as I please. No man has the power to stop me!"

His toothy blade cut through the air towards Areoch's neck and he braced for the final blow.

"AHHH!!!" came a fierce cry, and within an inch of Areoch's throat the blade came to a crashing halt! A long bronze dagger stopped its path as a new body careened into the fray. Rais was thrown to the ground and he looked about to find his new attacker.

Re'Amu stood tall between Areoch and the rest of the Urudu, his blade unsheathed between them.

"No more Rais! I say, no more! You have slain enough! Lied enough! Stolen enough! And I have buried enough! Stood by enough! I have died every day since you slew my father. My brother! You have slain me, in every way a man can, other than death. No more. There will be no more."

"Re'Amu," hissed Rais, standing slowly. His eyes narrowed. "Do you wish death? Know that there is no escape where the dead go. I have seen it and will take you there!"

Rais leapt headlong into Re'Amu, clashing with him in a new fervor. As they struggled, the eyes of the Urudu grew wide with fear and their mouths fell open in terror.

The wind seemed to shift, and dark clouds enveloped the face of the sun. An electric rawness filled the air, tingling in their mouths. *The Alalia* no longer floundered in the water outside of their reach. She turned toward the *Taradium* like a bear awaking from its slumber. White-crested water rolled back from her sides as she charged forward at a startling pace. The broken stump of the bronze ram flashed through the air as the ship seemed to take flight, high upon a tidal wave of water. Ship, spray and cresting sea threw itself inland on a gust of air and power. Through the sweat and blood on his face, Areoch saw Meshêk, the wind whipping through his long hair as he stood on the steering platform of *The Alalia*. His mouth was open with a word of Power still fresh on his lips and his gaze transfixed upon the *Taradium*.

The Urudu screamed and fell as they slipped backward, scrambling over themselves. *The Alalia* crashed broad-side into the *Taradium*. With a rending shriek of wood and bronze, the nose of *The Alalia* was torn asunder. For a fleeting moment, everything was floating as both ships were shorn in two with a sickening jolt. Slivers and planks of wood flew in the air. Waves crashed over ship and man as everything was thrown high, and with a breathless plunge, all was sucked into the depths of the sea.

The last thing Areoch saw was Re'Amu, grabbing Rais by the neck and pulling him firmly onto his dagger, and they both vanished into the darkness of the churning torrent.

Deep inland, Eli'ssa looked toward the ocean, back over the path they had traveled. The Laḥmu circled them, a full day away from reaching the encampment of the Gray Watchers and the crags of Oodan beyond. Bahira lay weak from thirst upon her lap. The clouds gathered, promising an oncoming storm. Eli'ssa didn't know what lay ahead, but she felt as though a familiar voice called her name from far away. She heard it, clearly. Resonating, she could feel it. She wasn't afraid.

No hope could be seen.

The Journey Continues in *Bloodline of Kings* Volume II, *An Ancient Prince*

The water was cold, the current fierce. It seemed to chill Areoch's very soul as it swept him down into the depths, swallowing him with the vigor of a hungry beast. The light grew dim. He felt himself being drawn inland and northward at a great rate of speed. Salt stung his eyes. He fought, pushing upward, in need of air, but there was none. He panicked, choking on water as he gasped. But, whether it was real or imagined, he felt strong hands grasp him firmly and pull him upward into the light, even as he lost consciousness.

Areoch opened his eyes as a wave splashed over him. He sputtered and pulled himself away from the icy water, his hands shaking and sinking into smooth shards of rock and sand. A fine gravel bar stretched around him. The surf continually pounded, crushing the stones into a finer silt.

An impenetrable wall of black rock rose sharply above his head, disappearing into a deep fog that enclosed him on all sides. On his right and left the cliffs came straight down into the water. The surf perpetually crashed, booming and foaming upward with the full force of the sea. Immediately ahead, the cliff face drew back into a low-lying cavern. Rows of rock, honed by the sea into sharp points, formed a maw that encircled the cave. Areoch peered into the mist and dark fissure as he slowly stood, surprised. The worst effect he bore from the fight was developing bruises and a choking taste of salt water.

A sharp sob startled Areoch out of his reprieve and he realized he was not alone. An Urudu knelt on the beach some distance away. Areoch looked about quickly for some weapon and then halted. The Urudu was none other than the man who had saved his life...

Appendix One

A Brief History

The *Bloodline of Kings* entwines our oldest surviving history with what many believe to be myth. Set in a similar world as our own circa 3000-2300 BC[1], the setting varies little from historical records.

This saga is based around the time of Sargon the Great and the invasion of the Gutium, as recorded on the Sumerian Kings List (University of Oxford, 1923). The term "Gutium" has no agreed-upon translation. Though the Gutium are described - even to the degree of eating raw flesh - some believe the term refers to "northern barbarians", while others record the translation more literally as "shadows of men". Due to the nature of these historic documents we can only speculate on the reality of this ancient world and its effect on the inhabitants at that time.

The Kingdom of Agade could be translated as "Akkad" and was the first multi-people kingdom established under the rule of Sargon, sometime around 2800-2300 BC. This story reflects both the early oral tradition and the earliest forms of cuneiform and proto-writing. Akkadian Cuneiform writing has been discovered as the "common language" between the ancient kingdoms dwelling in the old world.

Similarly, little is known about the earliest form of sea-travel except for many of the circumstances listed in this novel. Boats were woven from reeds & rope, riding upon animals was a modern design, and flint was commonly used in the building of tools and weapons. One of the earliest forms of naval warfare was through the ramming of vessels. The origin of this practice is unknown. Evidence of sailing has been discovered as early as the Ubaid III period, circa 4000 BC (Auguste, 1894).

---

[1] *See Rohl, 2001, regarding why proposed absolute calendar dates after the Santorini synchronism should be considered hypothesis, at best.*

Bronze was a highly sought-after commodity. How the smelting, refining, and casting of copper (and later bronze) began, is unknown. Bronze daggers grew lengthier as the quality of crafting progressed, until the sword first evolved into being.

Though little is known about this time period, techniques of farming, house-building, beard waxing, and many other elements of this story, are viable reflections based on historical documentation.

Images and Transcriptions Cited

Dalley, Stephanie. "Myths from Mesopotamia: The Epic of Atrahasis." Oxford University Press, 1989.

Gaba, Eric. "Stele of the Vultures in the Louvre Museum." Louvre Museum, 2020, www.louvre.fr/en. Circa 2600–2350 BC.

Jacobsen, Thorkild. "Eridu Genesis: Composite English Translation" 1981. Circa 2300 BC.

Kovacs, Maureen. "The Epic of Gilgamesh Tablet XI." 1989. www.ancienttests.org/library/mesopotamian/gilgamesh/tab11.htm. Circa 2000 BC

Layard, Austen. "Discoveries in the ruins of Nineveh and Babylon" (pp. 348-349). Nabu Press: Egypt, 1853.

Layard, Austen. "Monuments of Nineveh, Second Series' plate 5." British Museum, London, 1853.

Mariette, Auguste. "Stone relief of Deir-el-Bahari, "Mariette's Deir-el-Bahari", Merchant Ships bound for Punt, plate 12." 1894. Circa 2000-1400 BC.

Millard, Alan. "The Atrahasis Epic and Its Place in Babylonian Literature" University of London, 1966.

Nigro, Lorenzo. "The Two Steles of Sargon: Iconology and Visual Propaganda at the Beginning of Royal Akkadian Relief." *Iraq*, vol. 60, 1998, pp. 85–102.

"Relief of a Lamassu as a Lion-headed Eagle." Louvre Museum, www.louvre.fr/en. Early Dynastic III Period, circa 2550–2500 BC.

Rohl, David. "A Test of Time: The Bible from Myth to History." Arrow: England, 2001.

Thureau-Dangin, François. "Utu-Hengal Victory Stele." Louvre

Museum, 1944, www.louvre.fr/en. Circa 2100 BC.

"Unknown Victory Stele Fragment of Akkadian soldiers slaying enemies, possibly from a Victory Stele of Rimush." Louvre Museum, www.louvre.fr/en.

"Weld-Blundell Prism inscribed with Sumerian Kings List." Ashmolean Museum, University of Oxford, 1923.

Stele of the Vultures

Stele of the Vultures & Sargon's Victory Stele

Sumerian Kings List

UTU-HENGAL VICTORY STELE
AO 6018

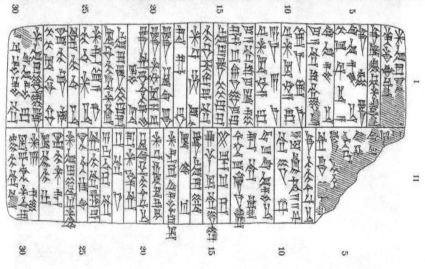

Relief of a Lamassu & Unknown Victory Stele Fragment

"About thirty feet to the right, or north, of the lion gateway was a second entrance, at each side of which were two singular figures. One was that of a monster, whose head, of fanciful and hideous form, had long pointed ears and extended jaws, armed with huge teeth. Its body was covered with feathers, its fore-feet were those of a lion, its hind legs ended in the talons of an eagle, and it had spreading wings and the tail of a bird. Behind this strange image was a winged man, whose dress consisted of an upper garment with a skirt of skin or fur, an under robe fringed with tassels, and the sacred horned hat. A long sword was suspended from his shoulders by an embossed belt; sandals, armlets, and bracelets, completed his attire. He grasped in each hand an object in the form of a double trident, resembling the thunderbolt of the Greek Jove, which he was in the attitude of hurling against the monster, who turned furiously towards him. ...The singular combination of forms by which the Assyrian sculptor portrayed the evil principle, so prominent an element in the Chaldæan, and afterwards in the Magian, religions system, cannot fail to strike the reader."

Stone Relief in the Temple of Ninurta. Layard, 1853

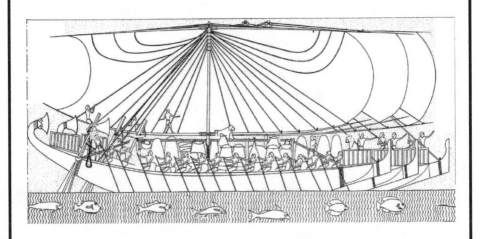

Merchant Ships Bound for Punt

CPSIA information can be obtained
at www.ICGtesting.com
Printed in the USA
LVHW091938140921
697832LV00013B/521/J